A NOVEL OF VERSAILLES

COURTING THE SUN

PEGGY JOQUE WILLIAMS

Black Rose Writing | Texas

ISBN: 978-1-68513-412-9
LIBRARY OF CONGRESS CONTROL NUMBER: 2023950308
PUBLISHED BY BLACK ROSE WRITING
www.blackrosewriting.com

Printed in the United States of America
Suggested Retail Price (SRP) $24.95

Courting the Sun is printed in Book Antiqua

*As a planet-friendly publisher, Black Rose Writing does its best to eliminate unnecessary waste to reduce paper usage and energy costs, while never compromising the reading experience. As a result, the final word count vs. page count may not meet common expectations.

In memory of all my many-times-great-grandmothers
who lived and dreamed in France.

EARLY PRAISE FOR
COURTING THE SUN

"Williams' delicious debut immerses us in court life of France's Louis XIV as we follow a wide-eyed teenager with village values into the sumptuous intrigue of the Sun King's world. With smart writing, brilliant dialogue, and sensuous settings, Williams takes us behind the scenes of salons, games, and galas in Paris and Versailles where Sylvienne must find her place among both loving and scheming nobility."
–Lucy Sanna, author of *The Cherry Harvest*

"A bright young woman from a French village receives the chance of a lifetime when she is summoned to the court of the Sun King, Louis XIV. Sylvienne is swept up in the life of nobility at Versailles, the heady salons and arts of the day, but is wholly unprepared for the intrigue and brutality lurking beneath the surface of courtly glamour. From village to Versailles, this well-researched and fast-paced story immerses the reader in 17th century France all the way through the final startling pages."
–Anne Davidson Keller, author of *Empty Chairs*

"Young Sylvienne's journey from rural France to Louis XIV's glittering and scandalous Versailles presents harsh challenges and difficult choices, as she joins the multitude of courtiers vying for power and privilege. Her transition from innocent country girl to worldly, wary courtier is effectively depicted, as is her frequently onerous connection to the monarch. Historical fiction fans will welcome this well-written debut."
–Margaret Porter, bestselling author of *The Myrtle Wand*

"Peggy Joque Williams plants her flag in the realm of historical fiction with this tale of a village girl plunged without preparation into the glittering life at Versailles under Louis XIV, the Sun King. The reader is swiftly engaged in Sylvienne's life as she steers her course from hope to sorrow and back again. The prose is unerring and fast-moving. Williams's sharp dialog, realistic characters, and rich descriptions of

Bourbon court life keep you enthralled in ever-changing developments. The end of the story is more a beginning than an end, and one is left impatient to read the next chapter. Thumbs up for this pointed evocation of seventeenth-century court life."
–Larry F. Sommers, author *Price of Passage*

"Peggy Joque Williams' historical novel "Courting the Sun" is an absolute page turner that I finished in just two days. Set in the time of the French Sun King, Louis XIV, we follow the adventures of Sylvienne, a country girl who follows the tabloids (of that time) and dreams of living a fairy tale life. One day, she returns home to find the King sitting in her salon and having a deep conversation with her widowed mother. How was that possible? Her mother had never shown the slightest interest in anything to do with the royalty. But after that meeting, Sylvienne is summoned to court, and her fairy tale life begins. Or does it? Despite the luxury of the palace and the non-stop entertainment all the nobility enjoys, most people she meets are insincere and seek only to gain power for themselves. After the secret that Sylvienne's mother had been keeping all these years is revealed, Sylvienne begins to discover what is really important in life.

Williams has crafted a world that was so believable, I almost felt like I was seeing 17th century France with my own eyes — the countryside, the fashion, and the food. Oh, the food! I do hope that a sequel is in the works because I'm dying to see what Sylvienne will do next."
–Diane Nagatomo, author *The Butterfly Café*

"*Courting the Sun* takes us on a vivid canter into 17th century French court life and the perils of upward mobility. With deftly drawn descriptions, and expertly developed characters, this debut author immerses us in the world of a young, naïve country girl as she reaches for her dreams. A true delight!"
–Jane Loeb Rubin, author of the Gilded City Series: *In the Hands of Women* **and** *Threadbare*

COURTING
THE SUN

CHAPTER ONE

Amiens, France, Spring, 1665

I knew if I were caught, I would feel the heat of Maman's seldom-used switch against my backside; but Madame du Barré always kept her windows open on mild, breezy days, and the view from my perch in the maple tree was too enticing to ignore, even for a ten-year-old. The black and red coach parked out front, its driver stiff in his red livery, signaled a reason to keep watch.

There was something about the elegant stone manor on the other side of the hedge, with its rows of shuttered windows and its gabled dormers, that I found endlessly fascinating, if foreboding. I closed my eyes against an unsettled memory, a dream perhaps, no more than an impression of black curtains and weeping. To ward off the gloom, I imagined I was in a palace. Nay! The tower of an ancient castle, the captive of an evil potentate — a word I had just the other day encountered in one of my beloved novels — and my prince on his way to rescue me.

"Mademoiselle! What are you doing up there?"

Startled, I clutched at a bough to keep my balance and looked down to see a boy not much older than myself shading his eyes with his hand.

Against my protest, he scrambled upward, sending clumps of maple seeds hurtling to the ground. After throwing his leg over the same limb on which I sat, he pushed a lock of his fair hair out of his eyes, their blue more so than the sky. "What are you so intent about?" He wore a clean linen tunic and a vest that hung low over his breeches, and he smelled of leather and lanolin.

"Go away. This is *my* tree." I swatted at him as if he were one of Blondeau's bees.

"You don't own this tree. I can sit here if I want. What are you — ?"

"Shhh!" I hissed.

His eyes shifted to follow my gaze. "*Mon Dieu!*"

Across the hedgerow, we stared at Madame du Barré, lying naked on her bed. A man hovered over her, wearing only his linen shirt. As he kissed his way down her stomach to her *nombril*, Madame du Barré moaned. Or was that the wind? With a deep sigh, she spread her legs, and her visitor pushed his face into —

"Oh!" I gasped.

The boy grabbed my arm in time to keep me from falling. I held my breath and scanned the window lest we be exposed for the spies we were. I needn't have worried. By now Madame du Barré was beyond hearing as she writhed and gasped and pulled at the man's hair.

My mouth went dry. I glanced sideways at my tree companion. His mouth hung open. One hand still grasped my arm, the other tucked, unheeding, between his legs.

"Oaf!" I pushed him. Almost out of the tree.

"Sylvienne!" he shouted, grabbing at a branch.

"How do you know my name?"

"I know the names of all the girls at the convent." He glanced at the window. "And your shoe sizes."

My gaze followed his back to the house. "You know my shoe size?" Madame du Barré was nowhere to be seen. Her lover lay sprawled on the bed.

"You wear a shoe not much smaller than your mother's. Bigger than most girls your age, but narrow." He straightened his vest. "You are a student at the convent school."

I glared at him. "Have you been spying on me?"

"I deliver shoes to the nuns. They say you are the brightest of all the girls under their tutelage. But you cause them much consternation as well."

"They said this to *you*?" I let my doubt soak through my words.

He shrugged. "They talk as if I am not in the room. To them, I am nothing more than a spider hugging the corner. Is it true you filled the cistern with frogs?"

"Toads." I scanned the window again. "It was no more than a bucketful." The bedchamber was empty. "What's your name?"

"Etienne Girard." He pointed to a parcel down on the grass. "Those are shoes for Madame du Barré. I am on my way to deliver them to her."

I frowned. "You won't tell her we were spying, will you?"

"And go under the horse whip?" He scoffed. "How stupid do you think I am?"

Breathing a sigh of relief, I turned to gaze at the house again. "Someday I will live in a house bigger than that one."

"Look!" He pointed to the coach. Madame du Barré's lover was climbing in. "Is it true he is your uncle?"

"Yes, but we do not speak to him."

The coach rattled down the lane, splaying dust behind it.

Etienne gave me a sidewise glance. "Why does his mistress live in the château, and you and your mother in the groundskeeper's cottage?"

I shrugged. "Maman says she is happy where we are. There is plenty of room for us. And for Tatie and Blondeau."

"Lucky for you. You don't have to share a bed with four little brothers and fight over food with a passel of hungry sisters."

"Food!" I slid down the tree trunk, mindless of my skirt catching on the rough bark. Snatching the basket of morels from where I'd left it in the grass, I ran across the yard to the stone cottage that was my house.

Maman sat near the front window with Marie-Barbe Lesage, who lived farther down the lane and whose belly was swollen with child. A sleeping baby lay swaddled on the floor next to her chair. Eager to hear what Maman was discussing with our neighbor, I rushed my basket into the kitchen.

Tatie eyed my offerings. "You were gone an awfully long time."

"The morels are scant this year." I reached for a slice of fresh-baked bread, but she slapped my hand away.

"I doubt that." She set the basket aside. Tatie did our cooking, laundry, and scrubbing. She wasn't really my aunt, but she had been with our family since before Papa and Maman married, and I had always called her that.

Back in the sitting room, I nestled at Maman's feet, watching as she loosened the drawstrings of a small, embroidered silk pouch. A deep magenta, the silk shimmered with silver and gold stitching curved into delicate swirls. She dumped thirteen pebbles no bigger than chestnuts into her lap.

"Close your eyes. Choose six," she said.

Marie-Barbe's fingers blindly probed the stones before picking six. She opened her eyes and gazed at them. But Maman focused on the ones left in her lap.

She pointed to a translucent bit of amber. "You will have many healthy children." And then to a milky crystal Blondeau called quartz. "Your garden will have several lean years, but you will get through them without hunger."

The baby awoke as if reminded of her own hunger. She bawled so loud Marie-Barbe reached down and brought her to her swollen, leaking breast. "You've given me much comfort, Madame d'Aubert. *Merci*." She fished a coin out of the folds of her skirt and handed it to my mother. Once the baby had suckled herself back to sleep, Marie-Barbe stood, settled the infant into the crook of her arm and, with a curtsy to my mother, took her leave.

Maman put the coin into a small, lacquered casket she kept on the side table. "Were you climbing trees again, Sylvienne?"

"Maman, ladies do not climb trees." I pictured the view through Madame du Barré's window and Etienne's hand on my arm to keep me from falling. "You've said so many times."

"Then how did you get that tear in your skirt?"

"I had a wrestling match with a bramble bush while searching for morels."

She eyed me for a long moment. "You would do well to fetch your needle and thread before spinning any more tales."

"*Oui*, Maman." I curtsied the way I imagined noblewomen did.

She scoffed, then went into the kitchen.

Maman was raised in a convent from the age of seven until she was rescued by Papa when she was fifteen. That's how Maman told the story. After Papa died, Maman took to helping Tatie with cleaning the vegetables, hanging the wet clothes and bedsheets, and sometimes even scrubbing the floor. Tatie, who was older than Maman, said she was grateful for the help, for her knees had begun to ache in cold weather and her fingers, too. Maman insisted that working about the house offered opportunities for prayer and self-reflection. I was fond of neither work nor prayer and busied myself as much as possible outdoors.

Reaching for the silk pouch Maman had left next to the lacquered casket, I sank to the floor and dumped the stones into a pile. I marveled at the textures and colors, the agates with their swirls of orange, green, and blue, a sea-green bloodstone splattered with red. I palmed a smooth black stone with thin white stripes, the warmth of my hand heating it.

"Sylvienne?"

Startled at Maman's sudden reappearance, I dropped the stone.

"Why did you arrange them that way?" She frowned.

I shrugged. They lay where they lay. Maman sank to the floor opposite me, examining the stones.

"What do they tell you?" I asked.

She scooped them up and dumped the entire lot into my cupped hands. "Drop them again."

I let the stones tumble onto the floor, then looked up at her. "Maman?" The way her eyes darkened frightened me. "What do you see?"

"A man." She stared at the stones, her voice seeming far away. "He holds the sun in his hands. So bright it blinds."

I held my breath.

"And…a storm…"

"What does it all mean?" I asked.

She scooped up the stones, slipped them back into the pouch. "The future will be what it will be." She stroked my cheek with her fingers. "Go find that needle and thread. You have a tear to mend."

CHAPTER TWO

Five years later - June 1670

Sœur Magdalene hovered, wringing her hands, making nervous clucking sounds, garlic on her breath as she leaned over me. Her black veil framed her plump face. Splotches of bouillon from lunch stained the bib of her wimple. With her help, I had moved from the hard floor onto which I'd collapsed to a narrow pallet in a corner of the schoolroom.

The other girls stood in a gaggle near the small leaded window, peering at us like anxious geese. At fifteen, I was now among the older girls at *le Couvent des Ursulines*. Only Marie-Catherine and Claudette were older, Marie-Catherine besting me by half a year, and Claudette by just a few weeks.

"What happened?" Claudette's voice sounded more skeptical than worried.

Sœur Magdalene leaned in close to hear me.

"Sister, I believe it may be my time of the month."

"Oh, dear. Perhaps you should go home."

With a dramatic sigh, I held out my hand for Marie-Catherine to help me off the pallet. Obliging, she put her other hand over her mouth to hide her grin. Claudette scowled.

"Should I send for your mother?" Sœur Magdalene asked.

"Non! No. I can walk home on my own. It isn't far."

Marie-Catherine walked me to the door. Heads close together, I whispered to her, "I left a book for you in the wall crevice behind the rose bush."

"Merci." Marie-Catherine squeezed my hand.

"Thank you, Sœur Magdalene, for your kind attention," I said before hurrying across the convent courtyard.

The moment I approached the heavy wooden front gate, a voice called out. "Mademoiselle Sylvienne!"

I spun around. Sœur Simone, the Mother Abbess, stood with her arms crossed over her chest, her white wimple hugging her cheeks, a mole to the left of her mouth her most prominent feature. I groaned inwardly. Was my ruse exposed?

"Where is your coif?"

I touched my hair, expressing surprise to find it loose. The stiff white cap dangled from ribbons around my neck.

Mère Abbesse sighed. "Put it on. Your hair is as wild as a squirrel's nest."

I bowed my head and complied. Once the gate closed behind me, I bolted, running without stopping—my coif sliding off again and my dark brown locks bouncing in the breeze—all the way to the guildhall where Etienne and I had made plans to meet.

Nearing the boxy stone building with its towering windows and massive wood doors, I slowed to what I hoped was a seemly pace and, still breathing heavily, tucked my hair back into my coif. The heady aroma of grilled fish and skewered lamb mixed with pungent cheeses and fruit compote from the food merchants made my stomach growl. Vendors hawking their wares lined the avenue leading up to the guildhall.

"You! Gorgeous!" a man shouted. "Try one of my mirrors. See how lovely you look."

Another tried to sell me wired spectacles. "To see the performance better," he claimed.

"I can see just fine," I said over my shoulder.

One vendor caught my attention, a gazette seller. I handed over a coin and eagerly paged through the pamphlet looking for sketches of the latest fashions and stories about life in King Louis's palaces. Princess Henriette Anne of England, who had married Philippe, Louis's foppish brother, was with child again, according to one scandalmonger. Some wondered if the babe would have the Prince's aquiline nose or that of an unmentioned courtier.

Inside the guildhall, Etienne waved to me from the crowded *parterre*. He had saved a spot for me on a long wooden bench in the fourth row of the makeshift theatre.

The Paradis Theatre Troupe was staging the new Molière musical, a farce called *"L'Amour médecin."* Jean-Baptiste Lully had composed the musical score. Everyone in France with any taste for the arts adored the music of Lully. Placards and handbills announced that an actor named Georges Delestre would play Molière's role. Men of Molière's rank seldom performed in small towns like Amiens.

I slid in next to Etienne. "Did you deliver the shoes?"

"I did. Monsieur Delestre gave me an extra *livre* for my timeliness."

"Can we make room?" I wriggled over a bit. "I invited Perrette." The chatter among the crowd was at fever pitch. Glancing around, I asked, "What is all this excitement?"

"Haven't you heard? His Majesty will be travelling through Amiens in a few days' time."

"King Louis? But why?"

"He is on an expedition to inspect his holdings in the northeast provinces. I suspect he will have several regiments and his own musketeers with him."

I was impatient now for Perrette to arrive. Privy to news provided by customers who came into her father's bakery, she would have the latest gossip.

"Sylvienne! Etienne!" Perrette waved from the end of the row. She edged past a burly fellow, whose grumbles changed to a sly smirk. Already drunk in the middle of the day, he reached for her breast. She slapped him away with a curse and settled in next to me.

"I'm glad you could come." We kissed each other's cheeks.

"I'll have to work late tonight to make up for being gone, but it will be worth it." She spied the gazette on my lap. "May I look?" She couldn't read, but she loved to study the illustrations. Running her fingers over an emblem, a crown bordered on either side with a *fleur-de-lys*, she said, "The shopkeepers are all abuzz, saying King Louis and his court will be coming through."

Etienne pointed to a headline below the emblem. "This confirms it."

"Queen Marie-Thérèse will come with him." She raised her eyebrows suggestively. "And the Marquise de Montespan."

"His *maîtresse-en-titre*?" I couldn't believe it.

"His mistress and the Queen! In the same carriage!" Perrette slapped her leg with glee.

Like everyone else in provincial France, we lived on stories of King Louis's love life. Tales swirled in delicious whispers amongst the townspeople, in the shops, and throughout the assembly halls. The stories even made their way into the convent school, the nuns pretending to be too busy to listen.

"Perhaps he will bring both mistresses," Perrette said.

"He has more than one?" Etienne looked skeptical.

"Yes. Mademoiselle de La Vallière is still at court." My friend's eyes crinkled with delight as she launched into the scandalous details of Louis's overlapping love affairs, summarizing with: "Louise de La Vallière's favor is waning. Athénaïs de Montespan's star rising."

"When I marry, I will show respect for my wife by being faithful to her." Etienne gave me an oddly pointed look.

"We'll see if you say the same when you've been married more than a fortnight." Perrette arched her eyebrows, a challenge. Watching him blush, she laughed.

"They say that in Paris, Molière is the star in all his plays." I sought to change the subject, feeling awkward about Etienne's outburst.

"Too bad we are not in Paris." Perrette scanned the assemblage.

"I would give an eyetooth to see Molière up on the stage." I sighed. "Everyone says he is so handsome."

"Mmm...as handsome as that one?"

Up in the *loges*, the box seats, sat a young nobleman dressed in high fashion—a plum-colored doublet with black trim and a lace collar that hung low over his chest. He noticed us ogling and pursed his lips in a kissing motion.

Perrette and I giggled.

Etienne scoffed. "You're acting like a couple of mooncalves."

"Don't be a sour apple," I said. "We're only having a bit of fun."

"He doesn't mean anything by it anyway." Perrette twirled a lock of hair that had escaped her coif. "Although maybe I wouldn't mind if he did."

I glanced up, but the young nobleman was jabbing his friends and laughing. Then he looked down and winked — at Perrette, I assumed, since she was so much prettier than me. But she was looking at Etienne. Had the man winked at me? Heat rose into my cheeks.

The Master of Ceremonies stepped out from behind the great crimson curtain to introduce the theatre troupe. The audience erupted into applause. Etienne put his fingers to his mouth and whistled. When it quieted again, I settled back to enjoy the play.

Even without Molière, today's performance in our small theatre was delightful. I leaned over to comment to Perrette, but she was peering over her shoulder, smiling at the young rake. I nudged her elbow. She gave me a dagger of a look but straightened her shoulders and feigned interest in the play.

My concentration broken, I glanced up into the *loges* again. The young man's eyes met mine, his lips broadening into a lascivious smile. I pivoted back toward the stage.

"Wouldn't it be grand to be up on stage one day?" I said, following my friends out onto the cobblestones that fronted the guildhall.

"You'd make a fine actress," Perrette said, her gaze sweeping the crowd.

I suspected she was looking for the flirty nobleman. "Not an actress. A dancer."

"Do you even know how to dance?" Etienne asked, his voice peevish, likely still irritated by our giggling over the nobleman.

"I could learn."

Perrette touched my arm. "Sylvienne, I forgot to tell you. I have a letter from my cousin Annette!"

"Wonderful! How is she faring?"

Annette had been orphaned when she was but thirteen and taken in by Perrette's family. Annette's prospects for marriage were non-existent, and so she had accepted a recruiter's offer to sail to the colony in New France where men were supposedly lining up to take a wife. She had been gone almost a year now.

"I have it here with me. Would you be willing…?" She fished the folded page from her skirt pocket.

"I would love to read it."

The plain wax seal had already been broken. A quick glance at the script told me a scribe had penned it. "*À mes chers oncle, tante et cousins,*" I read out loud. "I am writing so you will know I have arrived safely."

Perrette nodded her relief.

"The voyage was long and difficult. When we arrived at Quebec, men crowded the dock to observe the new women. What a sight! The nuns took us to their convent to care for us until we could wed. I chose a very nice man to marry. His name is André Besset. He is not much to look at, but he has already built a house. He is a fur trader and gone much of the time. I am with child, so I won't be alone for long." I glanced up at Perrette. "A fur trader. Poor Annette."

Etienne rocked back on his heels. "They say there's wealth to be had in beaver furs."

"Mother will be pleased to hear that she is having a baby. I suppose she will have had it already by now."

I read the rest of the letter to her, refolded the page, and handed it back.

"Merci, Sylvienne." She gave me a hug before hurrying off.

Etienne shuffled his feet. "I can take you home if you like. I have Jolie with me."

"Yes, please. If I'm too late, Maman will suspect I've been up to something."

He seemed pleased as we walked to the chestnut mare tied to a hitching post. I reached up to pet the blaze of white across Jolie's forehead. She nuzzled my hand.

Etienne mounted first, then to my surprise hoisted me up to sit in front of him, my legs dangling to one side, rather than riding astride behind him as we usually did. I hadn't noticed until this moment how strong he had become. His familiar leather and lanolin scent mixed with the raw essence of the mare's hide, his thigh now pressing against my leg.

As we started out, I spied several young men loitering in front of a nearby tavern. "There's that roué Perrette was flirting with."

"Only Perrette?" Etienne teased. "Guillaume Boivin. His father owns a château an hour's ride upriver."

"You know him?"

"I know his shoe size."

I laughed. "And…?"

"He has nothing to brag about. He is a small man with a big opinion of himself."

Jolie's hooves beat a rhythm as we trotted over the Pont Becquet, the languid Somme flowing beneath. I grew increasingly aware of Etienne's arm around my waist, the warmth of his breath on my neck.

Once we had passed through the arched city gate, he shook the reins with a "Hyrrah!" and Jolie flew into a rollicking gallop that caused me to fall back against Etienne's broad chest. His chuckle rumbled against me.

We turned down the lane toward my cottage where Blondeau stood painting the shutters. A deep humming, much like the sound of the hives he kept beyond the garden, floated on the breeze.

"Bonjour, Monsieur Blondeau!" Etienne called out. "How are your bees today?" He slid off Jolie then reached for me.

Blondeau paused in his painting. "Shoeless, young master cordonnier, every single one of them."

Etienne laughed. "Well, it's a good thing God thought to give them wings."

"That it is." Blondeau winked at me.

Before he married Tatie, Blondeau had been a menuisier, a carpenter, in a village a half-day's ride away. But he had accidentally sawed off his right thumb while cutting wood for a door. He could no longer hold a hammer in his right hand, thus losing his ability to drive a nail straight and true. Apparently, Papa had not concerned himself with whether the nails in our house were straight and true, for he hired the former carpenter and even encouraged his aspiration to raise bees. Blondeau, with only nine fingers, built row upon row of skeps, small domed hives made of coiled straw. When I was younger, I was hard-pressed not to stare at his stump of a digit. Still, he never seemed to mind my toddling after him, and often wiggled his fingers to make me giggle.

Etienne scooped water from the well for Jolie. Then, picking up an apple that had fallen from the tree, he used the knife he kept tucked in his belt to cut it into quarters. He offered a slice to me, but I shook my head. With an impish look, he popped the slice into his own mouth then held the rest out for Jolie, who eagerly downed the lot.

"Thank you for bringing me home, Etienne." Why did I suddenly feel like I could drown in those liquid blue eyes?

"My pleasure, *ma chère amie.*" He leaned in close, as if there were more he wanted to say. Or do.

Blondeau cleared his throat.

Embarrassed, we backed away from each other. "I must go." Etienne climbed back onto Jolie. "Perhaps we'll see each other tomorrow."

Shading my eyes, I watched him urge the mare into a gallop. "I would like that," I said into the wind.

CHAPTER THREE

"Maman!" I ran past Blondeau and into the house, breathless. "Maman!" I found her out back, taking laundry from the clothesline strung between two trees. "Everyone is talking about it. The King!"

"Did I hear a horse out front?" She shook out a pillow covering.

"Etienne brought me home. That was Jolie you heard. Maman, King Louis! He will be passing through Amiens any day."

Was that a cloud passing over Maman's face? "The entire village must be agog with excitement." She tugged on the last bedsheet. "Take that basket. Will the Queen be with him?"

Nodding, I picked up the clothes basket. "And, they say, his mistress—"

"Those need folding." She strode back into the house. Maman did not tolerate gossip, and she especially refused to listen to the scandalous stories of King Louis's illicit love life.

With more than a little consternation, I hefted the basket and followed her. I would share my news with Tatie. She loved a good story about royalty, the more salacious the better.

The chance to catch Tatie alone didn't come until the next day. Packing a basket of carrots, cabbages, and medicinal herbs, Maman had gone off to visit a sick neighbor. Once my chores were done, I sought out my gossip compatriot.

"Tatie! I have the latest copy of *La Gazette*."

Kneeling in the garden, she was taking advantage of the cool morning air to pull weeds. She had pushed her sleeves up her plump arms. A single grey tendril poked out from under her linen coif.

"You had best not let your mother see you with that." Tatie raised an eyebrow at the pamphlet I held out, but she pushed herself up from her knees and made her way to a small wooden stool she kept at the garden's edge. "What news of the King and Queen?"

"They will be stopping in Amiens on their progress through Picardy."

"So, the gossip is true." She mopped her brow with a cloth.

I sank onto the ground next to her and spread open the gazette. "King Louis has begun construction on the château at Versailles."

"He needs another palace?" She scoffed.

"There is a sketch of the proposed building."

"Hmph!" She squinted at the intricate drawing.

"He is ordering orange trees for the gardens," I said.

"And how will he possibly keep orange trees alive this far north?"

I shrugged. "Did you hear about his mistresses? They say La Vallière has been shunted aside by Montespan."

"As well she deserves."

"But Montespan is married!"

"And you think La Vallière, because she is a maiden with knees chapped from praying, has just cause for thumbing her nose at the King's wife?"

La Vallière was renowned for her penitence and religious devotion. Tatie had little patience for either when they were so flagrantly abused; but she enjoyed the gossip, nonetheless.

I sat back and gazed over the hedgerow at the gabled roofline of the château visible beyond. "Tatie, have you never wanted to live in a big house? Maybe a palace?"

"Big houses are more work. And a palace? Phfft!"

"Someday I will marry a wealthy nobleman with a château. And I will have beautiful gowns and lots of servants. And you can live with me and be waited on."

"Now that would be grand, wouldn't it? But what about that shoemaker of yours?"

"Etienne? What about him?"

"He's got his eye set on marrying you, I swear."

"Etienne? No, I..." I had never thought about our friendship that way. We played in trees until Maman said I was too big, roamed the banks of the Somme, explored the hills on Jolie. But marriage?

"Sylvienne," a voice called from the window. Maman had returned.

"Coming!" I jumped to my feet and ran toward the house. When I looked back over my shoulder, Tatie had scooped up the gazette and was peering at it, humming and harrumphing to herself.

"Do you have schoolwork to do?" Maman pulled out her sewing basket and began work on a sash she was embroidering.

"Some reading." I grabbed my book—a history of Greece—and curled up on the red and gold Turkish carpet Maman kept just far enough from the hearth to ensure hot flying embers would never spoil it. A wedding gift from her father, the rug was one of the few items I remember Maman bringing when we moved into this house. Papa hadn't lived long enough to see me grow up and marry. It saddened me that I would have nothing from him to take with me when I had my own house, wherever that might be.

I opened the history book and read a few paragraphs. When Maman got up to go outside and consult with Tatie, I pulled my favorite novel—Volume One of the forbidden *Artamène ou le Grand Cyrus*—from its hiding place in my sewing notions box. My schoolbook forgotten, I was soon immersed in the world created by Mademoiselle de Scudéry and the desperate travails of her romantic hero, Cyrus, who searched far and wide for his lover, Mandane.

"I have an appointment with Monsieur Barthelme," Maman said awhile later, reaching for her shawl.

I snapped my book shut, startled to be yanked without warning from Cyrus and Mandane's romance and back into everyday life.

"Come with me. We can stop at the dressmaker's shop afterward."

The dressmaker! "Oui, Maman." When she turned her back, I thrust Mademoiselle de Scudéry's book into my notions box.

Twice a year—always after her visit with Monsieur Barthelme, one of Amiens's elite *banquiers*—Maman and I visited Madame Trouillet's shop to get fitted for new dresses. Silk and linen for the hot months of summer and garments of wool to keep us warm when the weather turned blustery.

Grabbing my own wrap—a silk scarf meant to keep the sun off my shoulders and the dust out of my hair—I hoped we could stop by Perrette's bakery. And the shoe shop. Tatie's earlier comment about Etienne still on my mind.

My eye caught a movement out the window. "Why must Blondeau go with us to the bank?" He stood near the lane, waiting for us.

"He has always done so. Hurry. We do not want to be late." She coughed into a linen handkerchief.

Tatie hustled out from the kitchen, her wool cloak wrapped around her shoulders, a basket hanging from her arm. "I will walk with you as far as *le marché*. We'll have fish for dinner, and I need some spices for the pantry."

Maman nodded and ushered us out the door.

The morning was beginning to warm, the faint aroma of wood smoke lingering in the air. Under a canopy of leaves, we walked briskly along the rutted, sun-dappled road. The town center where the banks, shops, and open-air market were located wasn't more than a half hour away. Blondeau whistled a tune, ending each refrain in a sort of buzzing hum, ignoring the bees that seemed to follow him everywhere. I held my breath when one came too close to me. Blondeau had taught me never to swat at them. They were tiny creatures with an important job to do. If you left them alone, he said, they would do you no harm. Still, it took all my willpower not to slap at the annoying little beasts.

Tatie had no such compunctions about letting insects know their place in her world. She carried a swatter made of woven reeds, and woe to any creature—a hard-working bumble bee or any other—who got too close to her.

Before long, we passed through the city gate. As we approached *the marché du centre-ville,* the cries of the fishmongers filled the air.

"Mackerel here! Fresh herring!" Barrels with cod, eels, and lampreys lined their stalls.

Tatie squared her shoulders, her footsteps quickening. Her demeanor bespoke a woman on a mission. She loved scrutinizing the market stalls, eager to unearth treasures for her kitchen and battle with the hawkers and peddlers over price.

We strode past the noisy, stinky makeshift pens housing goats, sheep, pigs, and cows. The dust in the air captured the stench of dung, sweaty hides, and urine-filled straw. Wagons bearing crates filled with every kind of flustered and squawking fowl bumped past us, bits of down floating in their wake. My nose quivered with delight when we passed the oriental spice stalls with their exotic offerings: cinnamon, cloves, nutmeg, and peppercorns. Tatie spotted her favorite cheesemaker and hustled away, her basket swinging with great purpose on her arm.

A block past the market, we approached the business district, dominated by an imposing stone building with tall arched windows and ornately carved doors—*la Banque d'Amiens.*

Blondeau reached for the brass handle just as the door pushed open. A tall man with a walking stick emerged. He wore a scarlet doublet, matching breeches, and a black wide-brimmed hat with a single scarlet feather. I cringed. *Oncle* Claude. Papa's brother. He did not acknowledge us, nor we him. Since shortly after Papa's funeral, when Oncle and Maman had had a falling out, we avoided each other. I hardly knew his four children, all younger than me. The only time Maman ever allowed us to visit my cousins or *Tante* Judith was when Oncle was out of town. Which, sadly, wasn't very often.

Blondeau emitted a barely perceptible grunt, letting Oncle pass, then he held the door for Maman and me to enter the bank.

Blondeau and I sat together on a bench outside the private office of Monsieur Barthelme. He stared straight ahead while I studied the tapestries that adorned the oak-paneled walls, my foot tapping the whole while. The intricate woven images depicted scenes of bloody battles. After a while, I turned my gaze to the half dozen scribes and calculators in somber waistcoats standing at tall tables along one side of the vaulted lobby. Quills in hand, they scribbled in silence. Across the room several expensively dressed men occupied ornate desks — moneylenders, I presumed — deep in discussions with merchants and noblemen, all of whom smiled and fawned as if their lives and their livelihoods depended upon the outcomes of their conversations. As they likely did.

At last, the door to Barthelme's office opened. Blondeau and I stood.

Barthelme, a portly man with a neatly trimmed beard but whose face always wore a cloud, ushered Maman out. "Madame d'Aubert, you would be well-advised to reconsider my offer," he said. "It is unseemly for a woman to live without a husband to look after her affairs." He scowled in Blondeau's direction.

"Merci, Monsieur Barthelme." Maman offered an indulgent smile. "I appreciate your kind gesture. But I assure you my situation is nowhere near as dire as you suggest. Au revoir."

Barthelme bowed his head in dismissal, cast a disapproving eye at me, then turned on his heel and marched back into his office.

"Did he propose to you again?" I asked once we were outside.

Maman sighed. "Let's go to the shoemaker next."

She handed Blondeau a sizeable leather pouch, which he slid into an inner pocket Tatie had sewn into his jerkin. The pouch, I knew, contained Maman's pension for the season. She received a small sum from Papa's trust and a much larger sum from the Crown on behalf of her father, a duke by the name of Gaston who had died a year or so after Papa. Le banquier Barthelme delivered both payments.

The duke's *ecrus*, nestled safely against Blondeau's hearty chest, reminded me that I knew nothing of my grandparents. Maman said she had never met Papa's parents, Laurent and Marie-Françoise. And she refused to speak of her own, Gaston and Marie-Jeannette, or her upbringing, other than the fairy tales she would spin when I was little. I had once asked her what lands constituted *grand-père's* dukedom. Maman replied it was an inconsequential bit of property, too far away to concern myself with. It seemed odd to know so little of my lineage, especially living in a country that prized ancestry and heritage beyond worldly goods.

We stayed only long enough at the shoemaker's shop to put in our order—a pair of practical brown leather shoes for Maman, a pretty indigo pair for me. I hid my disappointment at not seeing Etienne, for of course he was at school. I envied the enlightened education he received—mathematics, history, natural philosophy, and even astronomy. Sometimes, I snuck down to the bookseller and perused books by Descartes, Galileo, and others, wishing I could buy one. I loved reading romantic novels, but I craved to learn the new ideas I imagined men argued about in coffee houses, even those that were frowned upon by the Church.

The cowbell jangled when we pushed open the door to the bakery. Madame Raveau greeted us. While she and Maman chatted, I sought Perrette who was busy washing bread pans in a large tub.

"Have you seen him?" I asked as she set the last pan on the rack to dry.

"Seen who?" Perrette wiped her hands on her apron.

"Don't act coy. That handsome nobleman from the theatre. I learned his name is Guillaume Boivin."

She paused for a dramatic moment then grabbed my arms and squeezed. "Sylvienne, he spoke to me!"

"He did? When?"

She crossed her hands over her heart. "He said I have delicious eyes."

"Where did you see him?"

"Right here in the shop. It was near closing, and he asked for a loaf of bread for his dinner." She looked around to be sure no one could overhear. "He asked if I would care to walk with him along the canal one evening."

I put my hand to my mouth in astonishment. "You did not accept, did you?"

"Of course not. I am not a trollop. But he is quite charming."

"He is quite bold, if you ask me."

"Maybe you're jealous."

Maybe I was. To be told you have delicious eyes. I couldn't help wondering what it would feel like to be kissed by such a charmer. "I'm thrilled for you."

Maman called from the front of the shop. She had paid her monthly bill and was ready to finish our errands. "Au revoir, Perrette." I hugged her. "Be careful, please."

We crossed the cobblestone street to the dressmaker's shop. Two expensively dressed young men approached on the boardwalk. I thrilled to realize one of them was Perrette's charming nobleman, Guillaume Boivin. As we came closer, though, something about his smile made me uncomfortable. He winked at me, then turned his attention to my mother, his eyes bright with lust.

"*Mesdemoiselles*," Boivin said. Was that wine that colored his lips despite the early hour? "What a lovely set of sisters."

Only recently had I come to realize how young Maman looked. Whereas the mothers of my schoolmates showed hints of grey, Maman's hair was honey-colored and lustrous, even now when all that could be seen were tendrils that had escaped her perfectly starched coif. While the other mothers' teeth had become dull and cracked, Maman's were white and even. My friends' mothers had all lost their shapeliness, their breasts sagging due, they complained, to multiple childbirths. Of course, my mother had borne only me, which is why, I supposed, her figure was still intact and her breasts shapely. Only once had I the temerity to ask her age. "Old enough to tan your hide for rudeness," was her reply.

"Could we entice such beauties as yourselves to share a bite to eat?" Boivin asked. "A glass of wine? Perhaps accompany us..." He nodded toward his friend. "On a walk along the canal?"

Blondeau stepped up and positioned himself between us and the men. Maman pretended she had not heard and walked on. My step faltered, and I could feel the burn in my cheeks, but I took my cue from her and refused to look in their direction. Blondeau emitted a low growl, elbowing the men out of the way as we passed. Boivin and his friend broke into raucous laughter, lurching away.

Pushing through the door of the dressmaker's shop, confusion washed over me. Boivin's flirtation had beguiled me when we'd first encountered him in the theatre. I'd even felt thrilled for Perrette and, yes, jealous that he had complimented her and invited her to walk with him. But now? What was I to think about him accosting me while drunk? And my mother.

"Bonjour, Madame et Mademoiselle!" Madame Trouillet, the dressmaker, greeted us.

She guided Maman toward the interior of her shop. Tarrying near the front window and peering out, I realized I was shaking. Blondeau had taken up position next to the shop door. In the past he had always gone off to enjoy a bite to eat at a nearby tavern while Maman and I looked at fabric, got measured, and placed our order. However, today he hovered. I found his fealty to be both comforting and disconcerting.

"Sylvienne!" Maman held up a swatch of lilac fabric. "Come see what Madame Trouillet has in mind for you."

"Oui, Maman." A movement caught my eye. I watched Boivin and his friend enter the bakery. Perrette's bakery. A sudden foreboding knotted my stomach.

CHAPTER FOUR

"You've grown," Madame Trouillet chirped, flinging her tape measure around her neck. "We'll have to alter the pattern of your bodices to accommodate your bosom."

I crossed my arms over my chest and shivered in my chemise. Maman handed me my skirt and my apparently outdated bodice and, as I dressed, I wondered if I should say something to Perrette? But what? That the handsome young man had tried to flirt with us? That his invitation to walk along the canal was...what? Perhaps I was making too much of the scene. Was he just being friendly? When we left the dressmaker's shop and hurried past the bakery I glanced in, but Perrette was nowhere to be seen.

The next day at school there was no time to brood over rakish noblemen. Marie-Catherine and I spent the first hour of the morning on our hands and knees, scouring the floor of the chapel of Our Lady of Sorrows with bristle brushes. The other girls were tasked with cleaning the dining room, the courtyard, all the public areas of the convent. The Sisters of Ursula adhered to a belief in obedience, chastity, poverty, and above all cleanliness. Their educational curriculum paired instruction in literacy, music, and manners with scalding hot water and elbow grease. Today, however, we scrubbed for a special occasion. A visit from the Queen. And we recited the *Beatitudes* while we worked.

King Louis, Queen Marie-Thérèse, and their retinue would pass through Amiens any day now as they convoyed north from Paris.

Most likely, Etienne had told me, the normal two-day journey would take a week or more with the hundreds of carriages and wagons needed to carry all the accompanying courtiers, soldiers, servants, and their supplies.

Queen Marie-Thérèse had specifically requested to visit le Couvent des Ursulines d'Amiens to inspect the chapel and receive the holy Eucharist. According to Sœur Magdalene, King Louis had insisted upon attending daily Mass at the Cathedral in Amiens, but the Queen refused to take public Communion in the presence of his maîtresse-en-titre, Madame de Montespan. So, in the interest of diplomacy, a quick stop to visit the Ursulines would allow her to receive the Eucharist in private before the entourage moved on to its next stop. The convent was abuzz, gossip weaving its way among the *Beatitudes* and the psalms as we washed, scoured, polished, and buffed. My heart raced just thinking of it. Would Queen Marie-Thérèse look like her portraits? Would I catch a glimpse of King Louis? Or his mistress?

Dirty, soapy water splashed onto the spot I'd just cleaned and against my cheek. I looked up to see Claudette pirouetting away, her wash bucket swinging to and fro. Wiping my face with the back of my hand, I grumbled, "Why does she hate me so?"

Marie-Catherine reached over with a rag to help me mop up the mess on the floor. "You get better scores on your tests."

"She could improve hers if she worked harder. I've offered to help her study, but she snubs me. I don't understand her."

Marie-Catherine sighed. "She's jealous."

I snorted. "What is there to be jealous of? Her family is among the wealthiest in Amiens with their textile factories. Her father is the major donor to the convent, assuring her a seat in the school for as long she wants it."

Marie-Catherine sat back on her haunches and regarded me. "Sylvienne, have you picked up a looking glass lately?"

"Maman has one. But why would I? I know what I'll see. My eyes are too dark. My mouth too wide. I can barely get a comb through my hair most days for this mass of curls."

Marie-Catherine glanced around before reaching into her skirt pocket. She pulled out an oval case no bigger than her palm. The silver filigree etching was simple but elegant. She pried the lid open. A hinged looking glass. I glanced over my shoulder. If the nuns caught us with such a thing, they would lecture us on the evils of vanity and send us home.

"Look." She held the small mirror close to my eyes, then slowly pulled it away until I could see my whole face. I had changed since the last time I'd gazed into a looking glass. In the mid-morning light, the skin over my cheeks glowed. Tendrils of dark hair poked out from under my white linen coif. I still wasn't sure that what I saw was worthy of anyone's envy, but the face looking back at me wasn't unpleasant.

"Do you understand now why Claudette is jealous? Even the sisters have taken notice." She lowered her voice. "Enough that they worry about your virtue."

I snorted again. Before I could say more, the clacking of Sœur Adélaïse's wood-bottom shoes hurrying toward the chapel caused me to stiffen. Marie-Catherine thrust the mirror back into her pocket. We swiveled together to greet the old nun.

"Bonjour, Sœur Adélaïse!"

She gave us a suspicious look. "That spot near the altar needs to be redone."

We bobbed our heads in assent and grabbed our wash buckets.

As Sœur Adélaïse headed out into the courtyard, I turned to Marie-Catherine. "Do you think she saw it? The glass?"

Marie-Catherine wrung out her washrag then dropped to her knees. "If she had seen it, we would be on our way to Mère Abbesse already."

"We will use this opportunity to practice our handwriting skills," Sœur Magdalene announced that afternoon during our study of Latin.

I groaned. Handwriting was not one of my talents.

"We will copy each of the *Béatitudes* five times, and I expect each will be an improvement over the one prior."

Rubbing the small lump that had developed on the side of my forefinger from gripping the quill so tightly, I angled the paper on the table in front of me.

"*Commencez.*" Sœur Magdalene walked among us inspecting our penmanship. "*Bien,*" she said to Claudette. "*Très bien!*" This to Marie-Catherine. When she moved to my table, she rapped my knuckles with her own quill. "Slow down, Sylvienne. This is not a race."

I gripped my quill tighter. *Beati misericordes quia ipsi misericordiam consequentur.* "Blessed are the merciful, for they will be shown mercy." My lips moved as I translated from the Latin.

Sœur Magdalene left the schoolroom for a moment. As soon as her black habit disappeared through the doorway, Claudette turned in her seat.

"I know about the book," she hissed at me.

"And what book would that be?" I did not look up but kept writing. *Beati mites...* Blessed are the meek, for they will inherit the earth.

"The one you hid in the courtyard wall."

Marie-Catherine went rigid.

Claudette leaned in even closer. "It's one of the forbidden novels, isn't it?"

I glanced around to see if any of the other girls were watching. They all were. All except Marie-Catherine who kept her eyes downcast.

"Are you wishing to borrow it?" I asked loud enough for the others to hear.

Claudette's cheeks reddened.

"Because if you dare mention it to Sœur Magdalene or anyone else, I will tell them I got it from you!"

Claudette gasped and turned back to her table. Several of the other girls giggled. I glowered at them, and they quickly leaned back into their writing.

I dipped my quill into the inkpot again. *Beati qui esuriunt et sitiunt iustitiam...* "Blessed are those who hunger and thirst for justice," I muttered, teeth gritted, "for they will be filled."

Later, during our midday recess, Marie-Catherine and I sat on a bench in the courtyard. Claudette sidled up, two of the younger girls following her like puppies.

"I know what you are up to with those books," she said. "But it doesn't matter. Mother says you are nothing but a foundling." She turned up her nose and walked away, the younger girls scurrying after her.

"That little—" I jumped up intending to thrash her, but Marie-Catherine laid a hand on my arm.

"Ignore her. She is nothing."

Fists clenched, I sat again. "What did she mean by that, anyway? A foundling? Everyone knows who my parents are."

Marie-Catherine shrugged. "She is mean-spirited. Don't pay any attention. Let it go."

But I couldn't let it go. I vowed the next time I found myself alone with that little ferret I would give her a thumping she would not forget.

The late afternoon sun, warm on my face, helped soothe my muddled thoughts as I walked home from school. Claudette's words still rankled. What did she mean by calling me a foundling? I walked this very road with Maman and Papa, my hands in theirs.

Papa. Everyone said he was the noblest of men. Maman often declared, when she was most frustrated with me, that I possessed his quick temper, his exacting sense of righteousness. Tatie would then remind her I also enjoyed his sense of curiosity, his thirst for knowledge. What neither of them knew was the secret guilt I harbored, a guilt that haunted my dreams.

CHAPTER FIVE

We lived in the manor house once. The one on the other side of the hedge. For the longest time I thought I had dreamed it, but Tatie reminded me that the nursery had been on the second floor in a wing directly under the eaves, the turret dominating the opposite corner. She had worked as Papa's cook even before he married Maman. She disapproved of the new shutters Oncle had recently installed, claiming the red paint made them look garish. I thought they looked elegant.

It was my fault Papa had climbed onto the roof that day. I had complained of rain leaking through the ceiling into my bedchamber. Papa announced he would fix the roof and went to fetch the tall ladder. When Maman complained it was too dangerous, that he should hire a man to do the repair work, Papa said he was happy to do it himself. But the rain had made the shingles slippery. Papa's shout rent the air when he slid. Maman found him sprawled on the ground near the rosebush. He was already dead.

Instantly the house became dark. Heavy black curtains hung across the windows. Maman and the staff dressed in black. Tatie put me in a black dress, too. The dark sky threatened rain as we walked behind his coffin to the small cemetery on the hill behind the church, a black horse pulling the funeral cart. I thought my life would never again be filled with light or color. And it had all been my fault.

Maybe that's why Claudette's words bothered me so much, why they stuck in my head. A foundling, indeed! Foundlings don't attend their father's funeral.

The aroma of peppercorns and fennel seeds competed with the pungency of malt vinegar as I walked into the kitchen. Tatie was preparing beets, cabbages, and onions for pickling. I hovered over her shoulder for a moment; then, still disquieted, I went back into the sitting room. There I gazed out the front window past the riot of flowers Blondeau had planted to bring color back into our lives the summer after Papa's funeral. I could see the corner of the manor house across the hedgerow. I skulked back to where Tatie was lopping a cabbage.

"Why are you haunting my kitchen?" she asked. "If you must be here, make yourself useful. Get a knife and start chopping." She thrust a clump of beets at me.

I grabbed a knife and sliced off the roots and then the bright red stems. ...*nothing but a foundling.* I chopped furiously, leaves flying across the table. *A foundling.* My knife swung up and down.

"*Arrête!*" Tatie stopped my hand with hers. "You'll chop your fingers off!" She took the knife from me. "I'll finish the beets." She handed me a small cloth-lined basket. "Go find some blueberries so I can make a compote."

Basket in arm, I rushed outside. Despite the rising heat, I welcomed the bright sunshine, But when I looked up, there was the manor house on the other side of the hedge, taunting me with its dark windows. I fled in the opposite direction, bounding down the lane until I found the well-worn path that would take me to the berry patch.

The sweet, musty scent of the blueberries lured me. My mind somewhat eased, I set to work filling my basket and my stomach with the tangy fruit. The basket was nearly full when I heard a sound. It came from the pond on the other side of the rise. A splash?

My blueberry basket held tight against my hip, I crept over the berm. There it was again. *Splash!*

Sheltered by a cluster of birch trees, I scanned the length of the pond. The only sound now the chattering of birds in the trees. Suddenly, a body rose out of the water, a young man drawing in deep breaths of air before diving back down again. A whinny from the pond's edge caused me to pivot. Jolie! I turned as Etienne rose out of the water once more, his back to me.

Oh, that I could plunge in and join him, I did so love swimming. But he was naked. A heat beyond that of the afternoon sun rose into my cheeks. I glanced along the shore to where his shirt, breeches, and leggings lay in a pile. An impishness overwhelmed me. When he dove under the water again, I crept out from behind the trees and scurried to a large boulder just the right size for sitting. I waited until he rose again, shaking a spray of water from his hair.

"Have you turned into a fish?" I called out.

He spun around, then sank again until the water lapped at his chin. "What are you doing here?"

"Tatie sent me to pick blueberries." I plucked one from my basket and tossed it at him. It landed with a tiny plop in the water directly in front of him.

"I'd like to come out and get dressed."

"Would you now?" I threw another berry. *Plop!*

"If you insist on staying, would you at least turn around?"

The next berry hit him on the head. "I think I'll sit right here for a while."

He glared at me. I smirked, taking delight in my torment of him.

"Sylvienne, I—"

Plop!

"I'm coming out whether you turn away or not." He began sloshing through the water. A moment more and I would see everything that made him a man.

I shrieked and spun around on my rock, but I could not help laughing all the while he sloshed nearer. After a moment, I heard him grunt as he pulled on his clothes. Then, without warning he was behind me, putting his wet hands on my shoulders. I shrieked again, and in my effort to push him away we tangled and fell, Etienne on top of me.

He put his hand over my mouth. "Quiet down, you crazy goose."

I looked into his blue eyes. He removed his hand from my mouth, both of us breathing heavily.

"You're wet," I said, my voice low and husky.

"I am." He gazed at me, then leaned down and brushed my lips with his. They were soft and warm, and I could taste the pond water. Then I felt something grow hard against me. At once he pushed away and jumped up, turning his back. "I am late for home."

He grabbed his hose and strode over to Jolie. His back to me, he asked, "Would you like me to take you home?"

Damp hair clung to my face. My heart yearned to say, yes. I shook my head, no. "I need to pick more blueberries." My basket had tipped and spilled its contents.

With a smile of regret, he mounted Jolie and urged her onto the trail.

Exhaling all at once, I closed my eyes, Claudette's earlier taunts banished by the lingering taste of Etienne's lips and a confusing, new yearning between my legs.

CHAPTER SIX

We were told to be at the convent at sunrise, bathed and wearing our best dresses. Today was the day Queen Marie-Thérèse was to visit. Maman complained that I was fussing too much — about my hair, my nails, my skirt and bodice. But Mère Abbesse had chosen me to serve at Her Majesty's luncheon table after Mass. Everything had to be perfect.

The night before, Blondeau had rolled the oversized oaken cask into the kitchen. After helping Tatie carry bucket-loads of water from the cistern as well as several pots of hot water from the fireplace, I stepped into the warm bath and melted into a puddle of contentment. Tatie scrubbed my body and hair with lye soap mixed with lavender. When my bath was done, she took a comb to my impossibly snarled hair and tugged it back into compliance, wrapping the curly strands with rags to keep them smooth overnight.

In the morning, before rushing out the door, I affixed the tight-fitting coif over my hair. I did not want to look windblown on this of all days.

"Are you sure you won't come?" I asked Maman.

"I'm feeling feverish. It is best if I stay home today." She tied the ribbon on the back of my coif into a neat bow, then sent me off with a hug.

At the convent the chapel, reception area, and courtyard were spotless, to which the blisters on my hands and knees from a week of scrubbing could attest. The butterflies in my stomach, however, bade the blisters to stop grousing. This was to be an unforgettable day!

Mère Abbesse presented her usual serene demeanor. "Remember to smile when you sing," she admonished as we practiced our hymns. "Round up the chickens and lock them in their coops while the Queen is here," she told Sœur Adélaïse, who dashed off in a fluster of clucking and clacking. "Those roses look lovely," she said to Sœur Josephte. "Perhaps a few in a vase on the Queen's table would serve to showcase God's glory."

Unlike Mère Abbesse, the sisters of the convent were as agitated as bees at the arrival of a badger. Sœur Clotilde fretted over whether the baguettes would arrive on time, whether she had ordered enough, and whether they'd be fresh. Sœur Josephte insisted that Sœur Marie-Marthe interrupt the choral practice and send us girls out into the garden to pull weeds she was sure had sprouted in the hour since the last weeding. And Sœur Magdalene insisted on rewashing spotless windows and polishing candlesticks until the moment the convent's benefactors, parents, and other invited guests began arriving. I wished Maman were here to see how wonderful everything looked. I had hoped Etienne might come as well, but he planned to be among the crowd in front of the cathedral awaiting the arrival of the King.

At long last, the call of trumpets sounded in the distance.

"I see them! I see them!" shouted one of the younger girls assigned lookout duty high on the convent's outer wall.

Everyone — students, novitiates, nuns, and guests — ran to the gate vying for position to view the arriving convoy. The clatter of wagon wheels over cobblestones grew louder, and soon came the creak of carriages and harnesses, the snorting of horses. A volley of men's voices shouted for the cavalcade to halt. My pulse quickening, I stood on tiptoe straining to catch a glimpse of the Queen and King. And perhaps the King's mistress, the Marquise de Montespan.

Mère Abbesse clapped for us to form rows for the reception. Marie-Catherine and I scurried to find our places. I glanced across the courtyard in time to see an odd smirk on Claudette's face. She turned to Françoise next to her and whispered behind her hand.

Sœur Marie-Marthe hummed a note, our cue to begin the welcome song. Members of the Queen's guard marched in first, followed by officious-looking men dressed in black.

A moment later, Queen Marie-Thérèse stepped through the convent portal resplendent in a red and black gown stitched with gold thread that glistened in the morning sun. Gasps of elation flittered through the trills of our anthem. Trailing her were ladies-in-waiting all in variations of red and black.

There was no sign of the King—we knew he hadn't planned to come to the convent, but we'd hoped—and of course no sign of his *maîtresse*. The disappointment must have shown in my face, because Sœur Marie-Marthe frowned at me then made her lips curve up in a smile to remind me to do the same.

As the Queen approached, Mère Abbesse dipped into a deep curtsy. A hush came over the courtyard as we all followed her lead. Queen Marie-Thérèse tilted her head in acknowledgement and Mère Abbesse rose, the throng in the courtyard rising at the same time.

"Thank you for welcoming me to your convent." Queen Marie-Thérèse spoke in simple French tinged with a Spanish accent. Considering her Spanish roots, I thought she would have dark eyes and dark hair, but I'd forgotten she had both French and Austrian forebears. Her hair was blond, and her eyes shone blue as she surveyed the garden and the crowd of eager subjects. The welcoming convocation seemed to please her. Her shoulders visibly relaxed as if she suddenly felt at home.

Sœur Marie-Marthe hummed another note and our voices again lifted in song. Mère Abbesse led Queen Marie-Thérèse and her entourage into our small but spotless chapel, followed by the benefactors and other guests. When it was our turn to file in, I became aware that Claudette was behind me.

My voice raised in song, I followed the other girls into the chapel. That's when I felt the tug from behind. I stopped singing. Marie-Catherine's eyes darted in my direction. She gasped. My coif had slid sideways and now perched cock-eyed on my head, a mass of curls escaping from under it. A snort from behind told me Claudette was the culprit. I ducked my head, attempting to straighten my headpiece, but to no avail. As the girls ahead of me slid into the pew, Sœur Magdalene thrust out an arm to pull me out of line. The coif now in my hands, I stood in the aisle with my hair exposed.

Snickers and giggles ended our processional song. Shame and anger burning my cheeks, I hurried out to the vestibule where I struggled to push my belligerent hair back into the coif. When I had succeeded, after a fashion, I re-entered the chapel and slid into the last pew. Right behind Claudette.

I sang the words "*Kyrie Eleison*" as sweetly as I could while inwardly fuming. It wasn't until we had filed up to the Communion rail and past the Queen—who, I realized in dismay, had taken note of me with a questioning look—and were back in the pews kneeling, eyes closed in deep and reverential prayer, that an opportunity to retaliate presented itself.

Opening one eye, I noticed a lanky daddy-long-legs ambling its way along the back of the wooden pew in front of me. I glanced around. All heads were bowed, all eyes still closed. I positioned my prayerful hands to let the graceful spider crawl onto my finger.

Marie-Catherine must have sensed my movement, for her eyes opened. She covered her mouth with steepled fingers, and her eyes widened as she watched me lean over and shake the harmless creature onto Claudette's coif. A moment later it crept onto her cheek. Claudette slapped it. Then screamed.

I offered a quick prayer for the unsuspecting spider and watched in astonishment as Claudette fainted dead away. The novitiates scurried to her aid.

Lest there be something foul in the air causing the poor girl to keel over, the Queen's ladies and guards hustled Her Majesty out of the chapel. Just before disappearing through the door, amid the flurry of rustling skirts, clanking swords, and querulous voices, her royal gaze fell upon me for the briefest of moments.

CHAPTER SEVEN

Kneeling on the cold stone floor of the chapel—my penance for causing the commotion during Mass—I was relieved to see Marie-Catherine slip in through a side door.

"Mère Abbesse says Sylvienne can go home now," Marie-Catherine said.

Sœur Magdalene nodded curtly, giving me permission to rise. Her look let me know she was glad to be rid of me.

My legs ached and my knees burned. The walls began to spin; I must have tottered because Sœur Magdalene thrust out her arm, this time to keep me from falling. Marie-Catharine took my hand and guided me out of the chapel.

"Is my coif on properly?" I asked through parched lips.

By the time I got home, word had reached Maman about the incident in the chapel. I told her I believed Claudette to be the culprit concerning my coif, but I did not mention the spider.

She gazed at me for a long moment before saying, "I wonder what caused Claudette to scream and faint?"

I shrugged my shoulders, unable to look her in the eye.

"I've no doubt your punishment covered a multitude of sins." When I still did not answer, she said, "Sins that will not be repeated?"

"Oui, Maman."

She nodded, satisfied. "I'm sorry you had to miss the luncheon." She knew how much I had been looking forward to serving the Queen. "Go help Tatie with supper."

The next day I kept a wide berth from Claudette, and she from me. In the classroom, Sœur Gillette put us to work doing sums. I enjoyed solving problems with numbers and often helped the others when they got stuck. Claudette groused over a frustrating calculation, but I turned my back and focused on helping Jacquette, one of the younger girls.

So intent was I on her problem, I didn't sense the old nun hovering over us. Sœur Adélaïse cleared her throat. "Mère Abbesse wishes to speak with you."

All chatter stopped, the room suddenly silent. My eyes shifted to Marie-Catherine, who gave only the slightest shrug of her shoulders. Jacquette's eyes were wide as saucers as I stood to go. Claudette snickered. How could she possibly have gotten me into any more trouble than I'd already experienced?

Standing outside the door to the Mother Abbess's office, I took a deep breath, then knocked.

Her voice sounded muffled through the thick wood. "*Entrez.*"

The small room held only a desk, a bookshelf, and a wooden guest chair. To my relief Mère Abbesse didn't mention Claudette or anyone else.

"I have an errand for you." She handed me a small leather purse filled with coins. "We are in need of more bread. Please ask Madame Raveau at the *boulangerie* to have a dozen baguettes delivered tomorrow morning."

The boulangerie was a good distance away, and I suspected Mère Abbesse thought sending me would be an addition to my already served punishment. In fact, I relished the opportunity to be away from the convent and to visit Perrette, for it was her family's bakery to which I was being sent. There was so much I wanted to talk with her about, the Queen's visit, of course, but also my confusion about the handsome Boivin. And maybe I would see Etienne along the way. With the pouch of coins nestled in my skirt pocket I hastened to the town square.

The first time I had set eyes on Perrette, I was about eight. A girl only slightly taller than me and with red hair stood on our doorstep next to her mother.

"I understand you have the gift," Madame Raveau said when Maman greeted her, "for seeing the paths in one's life."

Maman invited them in, handing me the basket of fresh bread they had brought. "I make no promises, but I am happy to listen." This was how Maman always started her advice-giving sessions. And, like all the others who came to her, within moments Perrette's mother was pouring her heart out.

After delivering the bread to the kitchen, I hovered near Maman, staring openly at the girl who stared back at me. Madame Raveau twisted her hands together and looked on the verge of tears.

"Sylvienne," Maman said, reaching for her pouch of stones. "Take Perrette outside and show her the garden. Perhaps the two of you can pull seeds from the sunflower head to save for roasting."

Perrette followed me out into the garden. "Can she truly read the stones?" Perrette asked once we found the sunflower Maman had set aside.

I placed the enormous flower head between us on the ground. "As easily as you and I can read a book."

Perrette glowered. "I can't read."

"Oh." I didn't know what to say. I ran my thumb under a row of seeds, feeling their resistance as I forced them out. "Anybody can learn to read."

She bit her lip, and I realized I had hurt her feelings. Before I could apologize, Maman and Madame Raveau came out into the garden. Madame Raveau seemed comforted.

"It's time to go," she said. Perrette jumped up and ran to her.

Watching as they set off down the rutted lane, Maman put her arm around me. We walked back to the garden to finish working on the sunflower head.

"Save some for planting," she said as I popped one of the grey and white kernels into my mouth. "Every seed holds a promise."

"What do you mean?" I asked.

"Never take the future for granted," was her answer.

The aroma of fresh-baked bread welcomed me into the boulangerie. Madame Raveau doled out the loaves and baguettes from behind an enormous oaken counter.

"Bonjour, Madame!" I said. "The sisters need bread. I've come to place an order." I glanced around. "Where is Perrette?"

Madame Raveau frowned. "She went upstairs to have a *tête-à-tête* with the chamber pot." She wiped flour dust from the counter with a rag. "I can't imagine what's keeping her. She should have been back long before now."

"Is she not feeling well?"

"Well enough. It's not like her to be gone so long."

"Would you like me to go and check on her?"

Madame Raveau looked relieved. "Would you? You can go up the back stairs."

Before I could say more, a tall man edged me aside. "Three loaves!" He threw his money down.

"Tell her to hurry," Madame Raveau said.

I nodded and ran past the hot ovens and out into the cool alley behind the shop. Hiking my skirts, I climbed the creaky wooden steps to the family's living quarters. There was no sign of Perrette. From the top step, I peered out along the alley. Where could she have gone? I was almost to the bottom again when a noise stopped me short. A frightened squeal.

"Stop! I beg you!" a familiar voice cried.

I raced to the carriage house across from the stairs. It was dark inside. The sweet-sour tang of straw mixed with horse dung assailed my nose. It took a moment for my eyes to adjust.

She cried out again, "No!" And then a muffled scream.

I flung open a stall door and drew in a sharp breath. "Perrette!"

Guillaume Boivin had her bent over a wooden crate, her skirts pushed above her waist, one of his hands over her mouth. The other hand clutched at her breast as he thrust against her, grunting, Perrette's horrified face smeared with tears and dirt.

"What are *you* doing here?" Annoyance colored the sheen on Boivin's face. "You want some, too?"

"Get away from her!" The sight of his wet, swollen manhood caused bile to rise within me. I grabbed his arm. "Let her go!"

He shoved me away. I stumbled backward slamming into a rough bale of hay, the breath knocked out of me. Scrambling to my feet, I grabbed the nearest thing I could find, a pitchfork, the stench of manure on its tines. I thrust it at him.

He tried to push me again, but ran his arm into the tines, ripping his sleeve. "*Merde!*" he cried out, letting go of Perrette. A trickle of blood darkened his blouse.

He stepped toward me but backed off quickly when, with a deep growl, I thrust the pitchfork again. "Stay away. If you touch this girl again, I will ensure all of Amiens learns what kind of man you are."

He laughed. "What will they care what a crazy bitch like you says?"

"They won't care that it was me. But they won't stop laughing when I tell what a pitiable shrinking appendage you possess." I jabbed the pitchfork lower this time, and he stumbled back once more. "If you want to preserve your manhood, you'll stay far away from us."

He yanked up his breeches and fumbled with the buttons. "You'll regret this, I swear." He spat into the hay before squaring his shoulders and shoving past me.

Once he was through the door, I dropped the pitchfork. Perrette crumpled, sobbing, into my arms.

"I didn't invite him, Sylvienne. I would never." Her whole body shook.

"Hush. He won't hurt you anymore."

"He followed me from the shop. I tried to get away, truly I did. But he...he..." She started to keen.

"We'd best get you upstairs." I led her out of the barn.

She leaned on me as we climbed the wooden steps. The stench of his spent manhood clung to her, mixed with the odor of musty hay. When we reached the apartment, she staggered to her pallet before collapsing.

"What will Mother and Father say?" She groaned. "I swear, I never meant to lead him on."

"I know you didn't."

"*Mon Dieu*, I feel so…so…"

"Let's get you cleaned up." I fetched a washbasin and a rag.

She flinched when I lifted her skirt and gently wiped her. Tears coursed down her cheeks. "Am I bleeding?"

"A little."

She moaned.

I glanced out the window and realized the sun had shifted considerably since I had left the convent. "You should try to sleep."

"No." She sat up abruptly. "I am needed in the bakery."

"I'll tell them you've had a dizzy spell. Or that you're ill."

She shook her head vehemently, struggled to her feet. "Mother and Father must not know anything happened. I'll tell them I had a moment of nausea, but that it is over. No one will question me."

It amazed me she could hold her chin high as she moved toward the door. But when she stopped at the top of the stairs, her hand trembled on the banister, her knees sagged. I rushed to her and wrapped my arm around her again.

"Sylvienne, what if I…what if he…?" She put a hand on her stomach.

"There are herbs you can take. A drink. In case there is…" I hesitated.

"Where do I get such herbs?" Her eyes clung to hope.

"Come to my house tomorrow or the day after." I dared not tell her about the witch I'd heard whispers about. "But don't delay too long."

Inside the bakery, her mother greeted her with a quizzical look. "You've been gone a long time."

"Sorry, Mother." Perrette grabbed the broom and moved to the back of the shop.

My own hands shaking now, I slipped one of the coins out of the leather purse, palmed it, then thrust the pouch at Madame Raveau. "Mère Abbesse wishes to have a dozen baguettes delivered first thing in the morning."

Madame Raveau nodded and emptied the pouch into a small wooden box without bothering to count the coins. She gave the purse back to me then turned to another customer. With one last glance at

Perrette, already busy sweeping despite looking pale and exhausted, I pushed through the door and back out into the late afternoon sun.

My stomach in knots, I checked to make sure Boivin was nowhere around. I hurried along the avenue, darting to avoid holes, puddles of waste, and horse droppings. Was I to blame for what had happened in the barn? I had flirted with him at the theatre along with Perrette. Did we, in fact, lead him on? And I had never warned her about our encounter with him — Maman and me — when he tried to entice us to join him and his friend. The lust in his eyes when he looked at Maman.

"You there!" a man's voice shouted.

Jumping out of the way of a pair of draft horses, I looked up in shock at the loaded dray they were pulling.

"Watch where you're going!" The driver scowled down at me. "Are you crazy?" He pulled the dray to a stop on the other side of the street, in front of Etienne's shoe shop.

The familiar voice rang out before I saw him. "*Salut*, Henri, *ça va?*" Etienne greeted the driver with his usual cheer. "What do you have for us today?"

I turned away quickly as if to peer into the window of the nearest shop, hoping the wagon between us would keep Etienne from noticing me. My heart pounded, and my chest tightened. I could barely breathe.

"I've got a shipment of leather for you," the driver called out. "But first, look at my boots! The holes are big enough to scrub my toes through."

Etienne laughed.

I flinched, wanting desperately to run to him, to feel his protective arms around me. But confusion and shame burned inside me. To keep from wringing my hands, I stuck one inside my skirt pocket only to find the coin I had stolen from Mère Abbesse's money pouch.

"I have a new pair I've been saving for you, Henri. Come inside." The warmth in Etienne's voice was too much to bear.

As soon as the shop door slammed behind them, I turned and ran.

CHAPTER EIGHT

Instead of returning to the convent, I ran toward the city gate, wanting nothing more than to be home, in my own room, in my own bed. But at the last moment, just before going under the stone arch, I spotted the lane that would take me to the herbalist. Her stone cottage, set back among a stand of oak trees, was barely visible from the lane.

Now, fingering the coin in my pocket, I slowed my steps until the lone carriage on the road disappeared around a bend leaving only a trail of dust. With a quick glance over my shoulder to make sure no one was in sight, I hurried to the cottage door and rapped, tentatively at first then with vigor. From the road, the ivy that covered the facade had a certain charm to it. Up close however, I could see the tendrils grabbing possessively at the stones, encasing the entire house in a living sheath. The door opened, startling me, and a hand reached out to snatch me in. The door slammed shut behind me.

Trembling, I scanned the chamber that served as a hearth, greenhouse, and laboratory all in one. The fragrance of freshly picked flowers and herbs mingled with an acrid scent I couldn't identify. Burnt hair?

"Madame Paillot?" I steadied my voice.

Surprisingly young, perhaps not much older than Maman, she wore a simple housedress, her apron stained and frayed. A coif hugged her neat braids. Based on her reputation, I had expected a crone with a shock of white hair sticking out in all directions.

"You are Isabelle's child." She surveyed me with the intensity of a hawk, even as one eye drifted off to the left, unnerving me. "Why are you on my doorstep?"

"I have a friend who is in need of…" I looked about not sure how to explain it.

"A love potion?" Her lips curled into a lascivious grin.

"Oh! No. Nothing like that. She's…she's beyond that." I wrapped my arms across my chest, as if hugging myself could ward off evil.

"This friend of yours, has she already been with a boy?" She peered into my eyes.

I took a step back. "Not…not in the way you're thinking. Not by choice. He…" It pained me to have to say the words. "He forced himself on her." I exhaled all at once, as if to dispel the horror of it.

"Ah." Her eyes shifted to my stomach. "And this friend…does she wish to keep his seed from sprouting?" My face grew hot realizing she thought my friend imaginary, that it was I who needed her elixirs. "I don't dispense my remedies for free."

"I have money!" Digging in my pocket, I produced the coin.

She grabbed it from my hand, perhaps afraid I would change my mind and tuck it back into my pocket. "Come."

She led me to a rough-hewn table strewn with plants, mixing bowls, and clay vials. There she laid out a square of bright red fabric. With a wooden scoop, she poured a mixture of herbs from a cannister onto the cloth. She added a sprinkling of some sort of musty white powder and several drops of a liquid so pungent it stung my nose when she unplugged the bottle. Gathering up the ends of the fabric, she tied it into a sachet with a yellow ribbon and thrust the packet into my hands. "Mix it with a full cup of chicory water. Drink it before the full moon wanes."

"Merci." Holding the sachet at a distance from my nose, I doubted the wisdom of coming here.

Madame Paillot sidled to the window, pulled back the muslin curtain. "Go now. Tell no one you were here."

Glad to leave the unfamiliar smells behind, I bolted out of the house, head down, taking deep breaths to clear my lungs. I didn't see Claudette until it was too late. She stopped in the middle of the lane and stared at me with astonishment. She didn't say a word, just turned and walked on. Heart pounding, I nestled the small parcel of herbs deeper into my skirt pocket where the coin had previously resided, a new knot forming in my stomach.

Two days passed before Perrette stood on our doorstep, a basket of bread in hand. Two days during which I fretted and paced, unable to concentrate on my studies. I pulled her inside much as Madame Paillot had pulled me into her house, anxious to assess with my own eyes how she was faring. A deep purple bruise had developed on her neck, though she took pains to cover it with her collar. Her lower lip was still a bit swollen. And her eyes seemed distant and somber. When I asked, she admitted she hadn't slept since the incident in the barn. I hugged her then bade her sit on the damask-covered stool near the window.

"I have something to tell you." She hesitated. "I've met with a recruiter."

"A recruiter? I don't understand."

"An agent of the Crown. I'm to go to Quebec under the King's sponsorship."

"What?" I was stunned. "Perrette, why?"

"Annette has found a good life there. Papa doesn't have enough money for a dowry for me. And now…" Her shoulders shook as she fought back tears.

I knelt in front of her and covered her hands with my own. "Perrette, are you sure this is what you want? What about the bakery?"

"It is done. Papa signed the papers for me." She squeezed my hand now. "I leave in a month's time."

I drew in a breath and rocked back on my heels. How could this be? She was my best friend in the world, and before long I would never see her again. *Before the full moon wanes.* I surreptitiously glanced at her belly, then chided myself. Even if his seed had taken hold, it was far too early for any changes to have taken place.

"Are you sure this is your only recourse? It's such a drastic decision."

Perrette offered a wan smiled. "I will have a proper dowry. It is my only chance to gain a husband." She hesitated. "Were you able to…?"

I nodded, pulling the small bundle of herbs from my pocket. "You must drink the mixture today. It won't be pleasant."

Grim but determined, she took the packet.

"Perrette! Bonjour. What are you girls up to?"

We both startled at the sound of my mother's voice. She wore her gardening apron and carried a spray of flowers. Before I could speak, she spotted the sachet tied with its bright yellow ribbon. "What is that?"

Perrette began to cry again. "I am so sorry, Madame. It's all my fault."

"No, Perrette, no." I squeezed her hand.

"What is your fault?" Maman took the packet from Perrette. "Is this from Madame Paillot?"

Perrette stood as if to bolt for the door. "I shouldn't be here. I should go."

Maman stopped her with a hand on her arm. "Perrette, are you in trouble?"

The anguish on my friend's face told Maman all she needed to know. "Come. Sit over here." She directed my now wildly weeping friend to a chair and pulled up another to sit next to her. She put an arm around Perrette but directed her words to me. "You'd better explain."

Standing before her, wringing my hands, I told the whole ugly story, haltingly at first, but soon the words tumbled out. When I finished, I waited for her rebuke.

All she said was, "Did he hurt you as well?"

"He didn't have a chance." The memory of his engorged manhood, how he shoved me against the hay bale before turning back to Perrette, caused me to ball my fists. "I left a pitchfork gash on his arm. I don't expect he will bother me anytime soon."

"Don't assume anything with men such as that." She frowned. "What did Madame Paillot give you?"

"I don't know. She said it should be mixed and drunk before the full moon wanes."

Maman nodded. She disappeared into the kitchen, returning a few moments later with a mug of steaming liquid. "It has a bitter taste. This is chicory water. I put some honey in to make it palatable." She handed the cup to Perrette. "Drink it now. Eat a bit of bread if it helps. You might feel nauseous, but it won't hurt you."

"What will it do?" I asked.

"In a few days there will be bleeding." She touched Perrette's arm. "It could be a bit heavier than you are used to."

How did Maman know about the herbs Madame Paillot sold to keep a man's seed from growing? There seemed to be much about my mother I didn't know, but I was grateful for the way she so calmly took charge of the situation.

Perrette drank the disgusting mixture. My stomach churned at the smell of it.

CHAPTER NINE

A week passed by before I had any word of Perrette. The way she had been violated shook me to my core. At odd moments Guillaume Boivin's lusting face entered my thoughts. The danger that men presented to innocent girls, to women caught unaware, was not unknown to me. But to encounter such violence, to have it thrust upon my dear friend—I didn't know what to make of it. And I worried whether the herb mixture could truly keep her safe from his seed.

It was Charlotte, Perrette's younger sister, who came to the house with the breadbasket late on a Sunday morning after Mass.

"How fares Perrette?" I asked, attempting a casual tone.

"She must have eaten something left too long in the sun," Charlotte said. "She vomited for three days. And her courses started early."

I must have paled at the news, for Charlotte was quick to re-assure me. "She is better now. She's back at work in the bakery."

Overcome with relief, I took the breadbasket with a shaking hand.

The sun had not yet crested the horizon when I awoke to the smell of Tatie's stew pot set to boil for the day. I lay on my mattress loath to get out of bed, for despite it being the last week in July, the morning was unusually cold. My mind drifted to the book I'd been reading by candlelight the night before.

A sharp rapping on the door downstairs stirred me from my reverie.

Tatie's voice called out to Maman. "Someone from the convent is here to see you."

I drew on a house dress and hurried down the stairs, my hair unbrushed. Maman was already at the door.

"Mère Abbesse sent me to fetch you, Madame d'Aubert." Agathe, one of the novitiates, stood in the doorway shivering from the early morning dampness, only a light shawl drawn over her shoulders. The sky behind her was a dull grey.

"Did she say why?" Maman asked.

Agathe shook her head then turned and walked away. Maman and I exchanged puzzled looks.

"Go put on your best school dress," she said. "We'll go together." She seemed to struggle for breath, but she was already reaching for her cloak. "And comb your hair. There is a clean coif in the chest."

While I dressed and pulled my hair tight, I wondered if perhaps Sœur Simone had noticed that I'd made a genuine effort since the Queen's visit to apply myself more diligently to my studies. Had she decided to confer with Maman about my progress reading French literature? Perhaps she wanted to accelerate my studies. I knew I had a bad habit of asking too many questions in class, but my teachers seemed to enjoy my curiosity.

Of course, there was the incident of the unfortunate spider during Mass with the Queen. To make up for that, I had asked for and was granted permission to study mathematics, something beyond basic sums. I'd overheard Mère Abbesse talking with Sœur Gillette about the need to have someone who could help balance the convent's account books. Maybe she was going to tell Maman she was grooming me for a job within the convent to assist with my tuition.

The sun hovered large and red when Maman and I stepped out of the house and began the long walk to the convent school. The dampness had begun to dissipate, and I warmed quickly as the sun rose higher. It occurred to me that perhaps Mère Abbesse had learned of my work with the younger girls. Had Sœur Magdalene or Sœur Gillette recommended I train to be a teacher?

When we walked through the convent courtyard, the sisters and novitiates were hurrying into the chapel for morning prayers. Except for Mère Abbesse. She waited in her office, where the scent of melted candle wax and crushed cloves hid the faint odor of mustiness the nuns were always trying to scrub away. A large wooden crucifix, Jesus bleeding in his final agony, loomed on the wall behind her. I glanced at his bloodied face, a sudden pang of apprehension hovering over me.

At Mère Abbesse's invitation, Maman sat down on the lone guest chair. I stood quietly behind her.

The nun folded her hands in front of her on the desk. "Thank you for coming. I am afraid I have some difficult news."

"Did I not do well on the examinations?" I blurted out. It was unimaginable, but disappointing if true.

"You did very well, as always." Mère Abbesse maintained a rigid bearing, her face implacable, her thin eyebrows never moving. Her clenched hands were the only sign she was unhappy about something. "Extraordinarily well, as a matter of fact."

"Is that why you called us in?" Maman asked.

"No." Mère Abbesse took a moment to compose her thoughts. "I called you here to inform you that we have taken Sylvienne as far as we can in her education. We have nothing more to offer her."

Maman and I exchanged confused looks. Outside the open window, a faint murmur of voices chanted in Latin. A tawny kestrel swooped into the courtyard.

"I don't understand," Maman said.

The kestrel flew back up, a breakfast of fresh mouse clutched in its talons.

"We are dismissing your daughter. As of today, she is no longer a student at Sainte Ursula."

Did I hear her right? "No. You can't." I tried to argue, but nothing more would come out of my suddenly parched lips.

"Why would you dismiss someone who earns high marks?" By the tone of Maman's voice, I knew she was as angry as she was bewildered. Yet she kept her voice calm. She coughed and pulled a square of embroidered linen cloth from her sleeve to cover her mouth.

"As I said, we have taken her as far as—"

"I know what you said." Maman's voice was sterner now, if not louder. "But it makes no sense. You are dismissing my daughter with no prior notice."

Mère Abbesse raised her chin, her eyes taking on a hard glint. "It has come to our attention she has engaged in activities which are...inappropriate."

"Activities?"

"She solicited the services of..."

Maman waited, unblinking.

Mère Abbesse let out a rasp of air. "A witch."

I blanched. The herbalist. Claudette had seen me at her doorstep.

"A witch?" Maman let loose with a short, disbelieving laugh.

There was nothing comical about the Mother Abbess's countenance.

Maman straightened her shoulders. "This is preposterous." She glanced at me. I only shrugged.

"She was observed coming out of the domicile of..." The nun hesitated.

"You are speaking of Madame Paillot?" There. She dared utter the name.

Mère Abbesse inclined her head.

"She is not a witch," Maman said.

"She has a reputation," the nun countered.

"Madame Paillot is a good woman. She provides cures and relief for ailments. Nothing more."

"She dabbles in the black arts."

"I hardly think so. Her sole purpose is to help people."

"It is God's responsibility to help people." Mère Abbesse's lips curled into an unfriendly smile. "And the decision regarding your daughter stands."

Maman put a hand on the desk. "She has been a good student. An outstanding student. We've paid her tuition on time every quarter."

Mère Abbesse clenched her jaw. "I am sorry. The decision cannot be reversed." She rose. "I wish you both the best. God go with you."

Maman stood without another word. Stunned, I fought the tears threatening to fill my eyes. How could this be? I was the convent's most advanced student. Of course, I knew the real reason. Claudette. Now my eyes burned from anger.

"I have never liked this wicked school anyway!" I hissed at Mère Abbesse.

"Sylvienne. Hush," Maman said. "I won't have you speak this way. We'll discuss the matter when we get home."

Maman strode at a furious pace down the road, ominously silent. I had to race to keep up with her. How could that nun dismiss me from school so summarily, without any warning or opportunity to redeem myself? Why could Claudette do this to me? I knew she had never liked me, but to say something so egregious it caused me to be expelled—who could hold that much hate in her heart? Now I hated her.

Fortunately, I knew Maman, unlike most parents, would never thrash me in public where curious neighbors could observe. The few times in my life she decided my behavior warranted the switch, she had marched me up to my room where even Tatie's disapproving eyes couldn't take satisfaction in my punishment. I doubted she would march me up to my room even today. At fifteen, I was as tall as she. Still, I didn't look forward to the dressing down she would give me once we were home.

In the yard, Maman stormed past Blondeau, who was on his knees repairing a wheelbarrow, and straight through the front door. I followed meekly. She yanked at the ties on her cloak. "That wicked, wicked woman!" She jerked her cloak off her shoulders and tossed it onto a chair.

"I am sorry, Maman. I discounted the rumors of her being a witch." Tears threatened anew. "I only wanted to help Perrette."

"Oh, ma chérie, I am not speaking of Madame Paillot. It is Mère Abbesse who should be horsewhipped."

By now Tatie had poked her head through the kitchen doorway to see what all the fuss was about.

"How dare that woman accuse Madame Paillot of being a witch! And how dare she tell you that you cannot go back to that school."

"Cannot go back to school?" Tatie asked. "What do you mean?"

"There has been ridiculous nonsense bandied about."

"Madame Paillot," I said.

"The witch?"

"She is not a witch!" Maman slammed her hand down on the table, causing both Tatie and I to jump. "I will not tolerate that word spoken in this house. Do you understand?"

Tatie bobbed her head and disappeared back into the kitchen. I stood in front of Maman, blinking.

She took a deep ragged breath. "There are no witches," she said, her voice calmer, her breath raspy. "That is an ugly accusation made against women whom others want to see...disposed of."

I nodded, not daring to move.

"As for your schooling, Mère Abbesse is correct. The sisters have taught you as much as they can. You have no future at that school."

"But Maman, I am not ready to end my education. There is so much more to learn." Tears welled again.

"We will hire a tutor. You need not stop on account of some senseless nuns."

"But tutors are expensive."

She pulled me to her, hugged me. After a moment, she held me at arms' length, studying my face with her own penetrating eyes. "You are an intelligent girl. And strong. I know you won't let this defeat you."

"Oui, Maman." But in truth, I wasn't so sure.

"Good." Her countenance relaxed for the first time since we'd left the convent. "Now go out into the garden and find weeds that need pulling."

I groaned. But Maman's reassuring smile hid a firmness I knew not to challenge. With a heavy heart I changed back into my house dress, then rummaged through Blondeau's garden chest and found the leather kneeling pad he'd sewn with his own thumbless hand.

Stepping into the garden, I dropped the pad between rows of carrots and parsnips and fell to my knees. The words of Mère Abbesse ran through my head. *We are dismissing your daughter...* I grabbed a fistful of weeds. *It has come to my attention...* I yanked. *She is no longer a student...* I tossed the weeds aside. *The decision stands...* I grabbed another fistful. *We are dismissing your daughter…* I hurled the weeds over my shoulder.

"Are you purging your garden of carrots?"

Startled, I jerked my head up. Etienne! I had to shade my eyes to see his face against the bright sky.

"Are they blighted?" He furrowed his eyebrows. "I'd prefer they were blueberries."

I looked at the pile of weeds I'd created. At least half of them were carrot stalks. One dangled from his shoulder. "I didn't…I mean, I don't…" I had an incredible urge to throw myself into his arms, the comforting arms of a good, strong friend. Something prevented me, however. Pride? Foolishness? "Bloody blazes!" I ran out of the garden before he could see my new round of tears.

"Sylvienne! What are you doing up in that tree?"

Etienne stood below my branch, shading his eyes from the sun as he had all those years ago when life seemed so much simpler than today. He was taller, of course, his shoulders broader. The maple tree had hardly changed since the day we first met, but he'd grown into a handsome young man. Me? At this moment, I felt I'd never reach womanhood.

I sucked in a ragged breath.

It took him only a moment to climb the tree and find his spot next to me on the thick branch. His thigh muscles bulged through his breeches, and today he wore a sleeveless jerkin. I resisted the impulse to touch his brawny arms, brush my fingers through his long, thick hair.

"Are you spying again?" He guided a bee away from my head with a gentle hand. "I thought you gave that up a long time ago."

"Madame du Barré left for the South of France last week. There is nothing to see." I wiped the back of my hand across my wet cheek, avoiding his eyes.

"What's going on? Marie-Catherine said you were not in school today."

Shame overwhelmed me. I sniffled and pulled a square of linen from my sleeve to wipe my nose. After composing myself I asked, if for no other reason than to divert the conversation, "Etienne, do you enjoy being a shoemaker?"

He looked at me as if I were crazy. "It's not a matter of enjoyment."

I frowned, perplexed.

"It's about pride." He pointed to my foot. "When I make a shoe, a good shoe—no, a great shoe, one that fits well and makes the wearer look like he's stepping out with confidence—I know I've accomplished something worthwhile."

My gaze drifted off over the hedgerow. "It must be grand to know your work, your life is worthwhile."

"Do you think yours isn't?"

"What do I contribute?"

"I thought your dream was to marry a nobleman. Have you given up on that?" He smiled, teasing.

I shrugged. "It was a foolish dream."

"What about your purpose as a woman?" At my questioning look, he continued. "To bring forth children. I'd say that is a worthwhile purpose."

"I suppose that's something." Snapping a leaf from the tree, I ran my fingers over its veins. "Do you think about marriage?"

He blushed at that. And then I did, too, flustered that I would utter such a question aloud.

"Right now, I must focus on learning my family's business. Someday I will be the one to take it over from my father."

"Your goal in life is to be a shoemaker, yet you devote so much time to school."

"A businessman must excel at reading, writing, and computation. A craftsman must understand the mind of man."

"Philosophy?"

"And understand how the various elements of creation interact."

"Alchemy."

"Natural philosophy," he said. "But there is a modern name for the study of the elements. It is called chemistry." This was something new, something intriguing. Before I could ask about it, though, he said,

"But what about you? Despite all the vexations you confer upon the sisters, you are their star pupil."

I held the leaf close to my face, pretending to sniff at it so he wouldn't see the shame burning in my cheeks.

"Marie-Catherine tells me you are reading Madame de La Fayette."

"*La Princess de Cleves.*"

He laughed. "I take it Sœur Magdelene doesn't know." He'd heard me complain about the nun often enough. "And what are you reading for school?"

"The poets this year, de Malherbe, Milton, Shakespeare." Was it a lie? I *had* been reading those. But no more. I burst into tears.

"Sylvienne?" He touched my arm.

Barely able to speak between the sobs, I managed to say, "I…I've been…been turned out. The nuns. Mère Abbesse. They…I…"

He wrapped his arm around me. "Hush. Tell me what happened. It can't be as bad as that."

Relishing the feel of him so close, comforting me, I willed the heaving in my chest to subside. "It's true," I said between breaths. "I have been expelled from the school."

"Merde! But why?"

"There is a girl. Claudette. A couple of weeks ago she saw me going into the house of Madame Paillot."

"The witch? What were you doing there? Everyone knows she's evil!"

"She's nothing of the sort. She has a knowledge of herbs and medicines. And I…I needed something." I dared not tell him about Perrette or what I had gone to Madame Paillot's cottage to purchase. "I think Claudette has been spreading lies about me. She has hated me for a long time. And her family is a benefactor to the convent, so they will listen to her regardless of the truth."

Etienne let out a long breath. His arm tightened around me. "What does your mother say?"

I ripped the leaf. "That she will find a tutor. But who could she employ?" I let the pieces drop. "I fear this is the end of my studies."

"Don't say that. Your Maman is clever." He moved his arm from my shoulder—much to my dismay—but then took my hand in his gentle, strong, callused one. "And she is of the same mind as you when it comes to learning. She will figure something out."

"And now Perrette is going away." The warmth of his hand kept me from sobbing again.

"Why? What do you mean?"

"She has signed on with a recruiter to go to Quebec."

"Quebec?"

"In New France."

"I know where Quebec is. But why?"

How much could I tell him? The truth was between women. "Her father can't afford a dowry for her. And she's not of a mind to enter a convent."

"Then I suppose it's a wise decision."

"But to go so far away!"

"Doesn't she have a cousin there?"

"Annette. Even so, it's...it's dangerous, and cold much of the year, and...and..."

He filled in the words for me, his voice soft, sympathetic. "And you'll never see her again."

My shoulders shook. He pulled my head against his chest and wrapped his arm around me again.

"So much is changing, Etienne. I don't know how I will bear it."

"I'm not changing." He grazed my face with his finger, brushed the hair off my wet cheek. "I'm here." He leaned closer, so our foreheads touched. Before I knew it, I was savoring the salty sweetness of his lips, welcoming the strange intimacy of his tongue.

CHAPTER TEN

Perrette stood on our doorstep one morning in early August, a parcel in her hand. It had been nearly three weeks since she drank the herb mixture. She looked thinner, gaunt, and there were shadows under her eyes.

"How are you?" I asked, ushering her in. "I've been so worried about you."

"I'm healing. Because of you." She held out the parcel.

"What is this?" I examined the burlap-covered package, secured with twine.

"A farewell gift." She settled onto the chair I offered near the window.

"Perrette, you shouldn't have." Perching next to her on my embroidered stool, I tugged at the string. "A book!"

"The peddler said it was a collection of romantic poems. I know how you love poetry."

I glanced at the title. Biting my lip to keep my amusement from showing, I leafed through the pages. *A Compendium of Manners, Social Graces and Obligations for the Proper Wife,* dated 1601. Not a poem anywhere among its pages. "It's a wonderful gift." I would not think of betraying my dear friend's kindness. My lower lip trembled. "Oh, Perrette, I can't bear the thought of you going away."

"It's for the best." She took my hand. "Sylvienne, I am sorry they released you from the school because of me."

"It wasn't because of you. Please don't think so." I squeezed her hand. "And, like you, I will have other opportunities."

"I always wished to go to school. To learn to read like you. And write." She offered a wry smile. "How will I sign my marriage contract after I've chosen which of the colony's many *galantes* I will take as a husband?"

"Galantes?" A snicker escaped, despite my best effort to suppress it. "Perhaps a bear hunter."

"Heavens no. A fur trapper! I wish to be draped in furs!" She mimed wrapping a robe around herself, causing me to giggle. An idea occurred to me. "Perrette, I have the perfect going away gift for you. Wait here."

In the kitchen, I fetched a tray, a cup full of milled flour, and a wooden stylus. I set them out on the dining table then sprinkled a layer of flour over the tray. "I am going to teach you to write your name."

"Sylvienne, truly?"

She watched intently as, using the stylus, I traced the letter *P* in the flour. I wrote each of the other letters in turn, naming them. Then I shook the tray causing the letters to fade away. Handing Perrette the stylus, I formed each letter again with my finger so she could copy it. After several trials, she traced her entire name.

"*Très bon!* Let's try it for real." A sheet of writing paper before us, I dipped Maman's quill into the small pot of ink she kept at the ready. I handed the quill to Perrette. "Write your name here."

Perrette carefully drew the letters of her name onto the linen paper. When she was done, I sprinkled it with blotting powder and shook it into a small bin. "Now you will be able to sign your name on the marriage register. Take this with you so you'll never forget."

Perrette clutched the paper, her eyes filling with tears. "Merci, ma chère amie. Merci." She embraced me in a fierce hug. When we pulled apart, she said, "The thing I am saddest about is that I won't be here to celebrate with you and Etienne when your time comes."

"Etienne and me? What do you mean?"

"When you marry, silly. Surely you must be making plans."

"Why do you think Etienne and I plan to marry?" I asked, looking at her askance.

"Of course you will marry. Promise me you will have a grand wedding!"

I shook my head. "Perrette, you are wrong about us." But then I remembered the kiss in the tree. Heat rose to my cheeks.

She held my gaze for a long moment. "Sylvienne, believe me, Etienne thinks of *you* that way."

"It is friendship. Nothing more." Except for that kiss. I couldn't meet her eyes.

Maman came in from the garden. "Perrette, how nice to see you again." She kissed her on her cheeks. "You are soon off on a big adventure."

"They say I will have my pick of husbands in New France." Perrette held up the paper with her name on it. "And look, Sylvienne has taught me to write my name. So I can sign the marriage register."

"Ah, bien." Maman glanced at me, her eyes reflecting her approval.

"Maman, will you read the stones for Perrette?" I asked.

Maman nodded, and I reached for the silk pouch. When the stones tumbled onto the floor in front of her, Perrette gazed at them with hope and yearning.

"I see many healthy babies in your future," Maman said.

Perrette's eyes lit up.

"And perhaps a few unruly bears."

Now Perrette's eyes widened.

"But only a few." Maman winked at me. Then she grew solemn as she fingered the stones. "It won't be an easy life, Perrette. Not every baby will survive, but most will. The husband you choose will be a faithful provider, and you will share a long life together, watching your children grow."

"Merci, Madame d'Aubert! Merci!" Perrette hugged Maman and then me. "I must go. They will miss me in the bakery. Sylvienne, will you come to see me off next week?"

"Of course I will." Nothing could keep me away. I thanked her again for the book and, my heart heavy with grief, I watched as she walked out our door for the last time.

"Will she truly have a faithful husband?" I asked Maman.

She put her arm around my waist. "Her marriage will not always be easy, but it will be a far better life than what she would have had here."

I leaned my head against her shoulder. "I don't know how I will bear never to see her again."

"Never is a fickle word," Maman said. "It's best not to set too much stock by it."

CHAPTER ELEVEN

The early morning heat dragged at me as I wrapped my arms around Etienne's waist. He urged Jolie into a gallop, not stopping until we reached the city gate. This was the day Perrette would sail out of my life. Not far inside the walls we ran into a blockade, a throng of people milling about.

"What's the problem?" Etienne shouted at a guard posted next to the barricade.

"No problem," the man called back. "King Louis and his court will be passing through on their way back from the northern provinces. We're to keep the street clear until they've come and gone."

"Merde." Etienne turned Jolie around.

I glanced over my shoulder with a flicker of regret. To see the King! But today there was no time. Etienne steered Jolie down an alley and several side streets until we arrived at the river's edge. We slid off Jolie and rushed to the wharf where Perrette and her family huddled among others waiting for the call to board.

Perrette threw her arms around me, the wool dress she wore for the long ocean voyage scratchy against my skin. Etienne gave her a warm hug. Perrette's sisters sniffled and wiped tears from their cheeks, while Monsieur and Madame Raveau waited with impassive expressions.

Two brawny dockhands carried the travel chests across a wooden plank and onto a barge bobbing sluggishly alongside the pier. A limp sail hung from the single mast. At the stern was a makeshift shelter of rough-hewn boards with benches along the outside walls.

Grasping Perrette's hand, I thought to imbue her with strength and the courage to go off on her grand adventure. But perhaps it was she giving me the courage to let her go.

"They assure us the ship that awaits in Dieppe will be a modern, ocean-worthy vessel," she said.

"I'm sure it will be." I gazed out over the river that would take her away from me.

"*En voiture!*" The captain called.

Perrette held me tight for the longest moment. Then she hugged her family before boarding the vessel with the other girls.

A deckhand untied the dock line and tossed it to another before jumping onto the barge. As his mate coiled the rope, the deckhand hefted a long pole and pushed away from the dock. Perrette waved. Her sisters wept openly now, but she, like her mother, maintained a stoic expression. A heaviness settled in the pit of my stomach.

"*Bon voyage!*" the small crowd shouted as the barge floated downriver.

When it disappeared around the bend, Monsieur Raveau put his arm around his wife's heaving shoulders. She buried her face in his broad chest and wept.

"Godspeed, my friend," I whispered. "*Bonne chance!*" I could no longer prevent my own tears. Etienne's hand clasped mine. I turned to him and wept against his shoulder, grateful for the arm he wrapped around me.

The Raveau family left the quay and climbed onto a flatbed wagon. Monsieur Raveau whipped the horse to get it started. The wagon edged onto the cobblestones then bumped past a jauntily dressed man standing in the doorway of *Le Poulet Rouge*, a quayside tavern. I gasped.

"What is it?" Etienne asked.

Guillaume Boivin's eyes were fixed on the bend in the river where Perrette's barge had vanished. I was glad she was gone, beyond his reach. But how many Boivins would she encounter where she was going? I hoped she would find a husband quickly, someone who would protect her, take care of her. Hair rose on the back of my neck when his gaze shifted and he regarded me, his lips curling into a crooked smile.

I grasped Etienne's arm. "Let's go." As we strode toward Jolie, I glanced back over my shoulder. Boivin was nowhere to be seen. He must have gone into the tavern. I let out a breath.

Etienne untied the horse. Noticing a hint of color in the dirt, I stooped to pick up a smooth grey stone with sparkling pink speckles.

"What's that?"

"A page from my future," I said without thinking.

"What does that mean?"

I shrugged then laughed, embarrassed. "Just words. It's nothing more than a river rock." I slipped it into my skirt pocket. "To remind me of the day the river carried our friend away." I looked into Etienne's blue eyes. Why had I never noticed how they reflected the sky?

"Maybe we can still see the King," he said.

"Yes! If we hurry."

We mounted Jolie and raced back toward the barricade. To our disappointment, it had already been taken down, the guard and the crowd long gone.

Etienne let Jolie set the pace on the ride home. She was in no hurry. I sat in front of him now. Though neither of us said much, my grief at saying *adieu* to Perrette gave way to a sort of bliss at the feel of Etienne's body against mine. A breeze tickled my face now, easing the heat that rose within me.

When we turned onto the lane leading toward the manor house and my cottage, Etienne muttered under his breath, "What the hell?" He reined Jolie to a sudden stop, causing her to prance nervously. A long line of buckboard wagons and baggage carts had stopped all along the road and up around the bend.

I gaped in bewilderment. "What's going on?" Something must be wrong.

Etienne kneed Jolie into a trot past the caravan, at the front of which were several dozen carriages accompanied by blue-coated officers of the *Gardes du Corps* on horseback. In front of those was a majestic coach with six white horses. A driver in blue and red livery sat stiff-backed up front, and two liveried footmen stood at attention on the coach's back perch.

Clumps of people, neighbors and some whose faces I didn't recognize, crowded the lane, craning their necks to get a glimpse into the carriages, gesturing toward the house. Two boys stood on tiptoes peering into my front window. Foot soldiers and musketeers in their distinctive blue capes and plumed hats stood at attention in my yard. Had they come to arrest us for consorting with the witch?

In a panic, I slid off Jolie and, gathering my skirts, ran toward the house. "Maman!"

A trio of mastiffs lolling under the maple tree jumped up and lunged, barking. At my front door guards crossed long-shafted halberds to stop me from entering. Another grabbed me from behind.

"Let me go! My mother's in there!" I struggled against him.

"Sylvienne!" Etienne, close on my heels, tried to free me, but a pair of soldiers thrust him to the ground, pinning him there.

From inside the house came an unfamiliar male voice. "Let the girl pass."

The man who held me let me go. The guards at the door withdrew their weapons. Heart pounding, wary of what might await me, I stepped inside. It took a moment for my eyes to adjust to the dimness of the sitting room. My mother, in her simple cinnamon-colored housedress, sat perched on our brocade-covered stool, her hands folded in her lap. Across from her in her favorite armchair sat the King of France.

CHAPTER TWELVE

King Louis XIV, wearing a crimson traveling cloak edged in ermine, crimson leggings, and black leather shoes with three-inch heels painted gold, scrutinized me with overt curiosity. I blinked to make sure the light wasn't playing tricks with my vision.

Quite sure I had stopped breathing, I feared I might swoon. Coming to my senses, I dropped into a deep curtsy.

"Rise," he said, his voice surprisingly gentle.

As I rose, Maman kept her eyes downcast, her cheeks flushed. Tatie and Blondeau stood gawking in the kitchen doorway.

"Who might this be?" King Louis asked Maman.

He was as handsome as everyone said, with his square jaw, his aquiline nose, and his long dark locks unadorned in this moment by a wig. He looked younger than I had expected. Even though this most important man of all France was the same age as my mother, I had somehow pictured him older, more patriarch-like.

"She is my daughter," Maman said, looking him in the eye now.

The light from the window behind her highlighted the strands of caramel-colored hair that had escaped from under her coif. I reached up to touch my own hair, realizing in a rush of horror that my nearly raven locks were uncoifed and windblown.

"You have a child?" He seemed genuinely surprised.

"Yes." Was that a challenge in her eyes? "You must have known."

"How could I?"

"You are the king."

He grunted then offered a self-deprecating smile. "Her name?"

"Sylvienne," Maman said. "Sylvienne d'Aubert." Her emphasis on d'Aubert seemed odd.

He held me in his gaze for the longest time. There was something about his eyes. Green with flecks of gold. It was more the depth of his countenance, however, the intensity of that look. Was his smile because he found me to his liking? He was famous — infamous might be a better word — throughout the realm for his love of young women. But then, I was barely out of my childhood. What could he find enticing in me? While my breasts had begun to bud, I was anything but a woman.

"How old are you, Sylvienne d'Aubert?"

"I'll be sixteen on my next birthday."

A calculating frown settled over his brow. The moment seemed to edge into an eternity; I had to force myself not to fidget. He smiled again. "She is quite lovely, *ma cousine*."

Cousin?

"Merci, Your Majesty," Maman murmured.

"Sire." An officer spoke from the doorway. "The horses have all been watered."

The King nodded, and the man left. Louis put his hands on his knees and gazed at me again. After a moment he rose; my mother and I rose with him.

"Thank you for your hospitality, Isabelle."

How seldom I heard my mother's name spoken. And for King Louis to speak it in such a casual and familiar way. I blinked, astounded, when he put his arms around her in an affectionate embrace, bussing her on both cheeks. Then he stepped back and said with a smile I couldn't interpret, "You are as beautiful as I remember." His eyes flicked toward me. "And clearly you have found a way to replicate your loveliness."

Maman dropped into a curtsy. I followed suit.

He appraised me one last time. "Fifteen, is it? Almost sixteen?" He nodded his approval then strode out the door and across the lawn calling to his mastiffs. His soldiers fell into step behind him. The crowd in the yard applauded, bending into ragged bows and curtsies as he passed. The King acknowledged them by doffing his wide-brimmed hat then climbed into his gilded coach and settled himself across from the Queen. Next to him sat a woman in a dazzling turquoise ensemble. He raised his hand signaling his permission to depart.

"*Allons-y!*" the captain of the guard shouted, circling his hand above his head.

The command was repeated along the line of carriage and wagon drivers. Slowly, those in the front began to roll, then each one behind, until finally the royal coach pulled away.

"Maman," I asked. "Why did King Louis choose our house to stop?"

"Why does a king do anything? Because he is king." She turned and walked back into the house before the last of the carriages had rolled away.

Dust kicked up by carriage wheels and horses' hooves hung in the air. Blondeau and Tatie stood by the lane engaged in animated conversation with the last of the hangers-on, most of the crowd having drifted away once the King's cavalcade had faded into the distance.

Etienne emerged from behind the house, Maman's long-handled garden spade in hand. He stood for a moment surveying the yard. All that remained to give evidence of the royal court's visit were Maman's trampled garden beds and the piles of horse dung dotting the lane. Etienne went to work on those, shoveling and tossing the steaming piles into the ditch.

"You don't have to do that," Maman called from the doorway.

"*Au contraire*, Madame d'Aubert," he said with a grin. "It is not every day the son of a shoemaker has the honor to dispense with gifts left by the Sun King."

I looked at Maman in horror that he'd made such a jest.

"Merci, Etienne." Was that a smile she was trying to suppress? "When you finish, come inside for a cup of cider. But wash those hands first!"

I chased Maman back into the sitting room. "Maman! The King. Why did he call you cousin?"

She picked up the broom and began sweeping the floor Tatie had scrubbed spotless that very morning.

"Maman!" I begged. "Is it true? Are we descended from royalty? What are we…third cousins? Fourth? Fifth? Please, Maman. Tell me."

She paused in her sweeping, her gaze settling on me, her grey eyes so unlike my green ones. The only thing we seemed to have in common was a small cluster of freckles off to the side of each of our faces, hers on the left side, mine on the right. "My father…"

"Gaston," I said, tugging the name from memory.

"Yes, Gaston. He was…" Her knuckles whitened as she grasped the broom and began sweeping even more doggedly. "He was Louis's uncle."

I stared at her in confusion. Then it sank in. My jaw dropped. "*Le Grand Monsieur?*" Gaston, Duc d'Orléans, had been the brother of King Louis XIII.

I grabbed her broom to force her to stop. "But that makes you and King Louis *first* cousins."

She nodded, shrugged her shoulders, and turned away leaving the broom in my hands.

"Why did you never tell me this?"

She picked up the armchair *he* had sat on—the Sun King, Louis Dieudonné, Louis the God-given—and placed it under the window opposite where we usually kept it. My eyes fixed on the chair. To my dismay, there was nothing of his radiance left on it. No glow. No aura. It was just a chair.

Maman picked up the brocade stool. I followed close on her heels, jumping out of her way when she swung around, looking for a place to set it. Why not where she always kept it, under the table, next to her sewing basket? Then something occurred to me. I shoved the broom against the wall and confronted her.

"My grandmother…her name was Marie-Jeannette. *La Grande Madame* was—"

"Not Marie-Jeannette. No." Now she grabbed a rag and began polishing the spotless side table. She glanced out the window to be sure Etienne still occupied himself with the horse droppings, that Blondeau and Tatie still stood at the road's edge with the neighbors.

"My mother was not the Duc's wife." She searched my eyes, daring me to condemn her. Then she returned to her dusting and polishing.

"But why did you never tell me this?" I repeated, my voice rising in consternation. This seemed like a pretty big secret to keep. "If your mother wasn't the Duchess, who was she? Why do you never speak of her to me, even after all my questions?"

Maman's dust rag stilled. "My mother, Marie-Jeannette de Vienne, was a lady-in-waiting to Queen Anne."

Bringing my hands up to my cheeks, I recalled the confusing relationships of the royal family. Queen Anne, known as Anne of Austria, wife of Louis XIII, was the mother of our Louis and his brother Philippe. What kind of fairy tale was she spinning?

"Your mother was a lady-in-waiting?"

She nodded.

I drew in a breath. "Even so. To never tell me you have royal blood. That *I* have royal blood?" My voice took on an accusatory tone. "Why did you never live at court?"

"I did live at court. For a short while." Maman sank onto the brocade stool. "Queen Anne professed to be fond of my mother, and when she realized Mother was with child and by whom, she allowed her to give birth at the palace and to resume service afterward. I was put in the nursery with Louis. Later, baby Philippe joined us." She stopped when she noticed my gaping mouth and wide eyes.

"So it wasn't a fairy tale." I knelt in front of her, remembering the times as a young child I had begged her to tell me about her life growing up. And she would say in a teasing voice, *"I lived in a grand palace. Until one day an evil witch stole me away and imprisoned me in a convent. And there I waited for a handsome young man to rescue me."* *"Papa!"* I would exclaim. And then, *"Is that true, Maman?"* And she would smile. *"What do you think, ma petite?"* I would laugh and say, *"Non! Ce n'est pas vrai!"* Then she would change the subject, never letting me inquire any more into her past than this bit of fantasy. Or what I thought was fantasy.

Maman entwined her fingers in her lap. Her gaze drifted over my head, to a past I had never been allowed to share. "I spent my toddling years as a playmate to the princes. When I was seven, however, they sent me away. To the convent of the Cistercians at *l'Abbaye d'Argensolles* south of Reims."

Her brow furrowed as she spoke. I could only imagine how awful it must have been to be sent away from the palace, the only home she had ever known, at such a tender age and to be given into the care of nuns shut behind cloistered walls.

"Did you never return to court?" My voice a sad whisper.

Maman absently reached for her sewing basket. "Once. For Louis's coronation."

Etienne's knock interrupted her story. Maman took the opportunity to escape to the kitchen. I was loath to let him in, there was so much more I wanted to ask her. I opened the door.

"I can't stay long," he said. "But a cup of cider would be most quenching."

"Of course." I glanced down at his wet hands.

He quickly wiped them on his breeches. "I washed them at the well." He studied my face. "Are you okay?"

"Yes. No. I mean, of course I am." My mind still riddled with questions, I tapped my foot impatiently.

He must have sensed my perturbation. With a concerned smile, he reached out and traced a damp line onto my cheek but pulled back when Maman returned with a mug of sweet-smelling cider.

"This is the least I can do in gratitude," she said. "I would not have relished the smell of the royal horses lingering in the yard overnight."

Etienne exclaimed over how good the cider tasted. He glanced from Maman, whose look of relief was evident, to me with my arms crossed, my brow furrowed. "I think I should go."

Ignoring the unanswered question in his eyes, I stepped outside to see him off. When I returned to the house, Maman stood waiting.

"Sylvienne," she said. "It would not be prudent to talk about my..." She hesitated. "My story. To others."

"Oui, Maman."

The next day, I hoped to confront Maman alone. I had so many questions. What was her life at court like? Who were the people she had known and played with? What were the princes like as young boys? And the palace…? But she kept herself busy working with Tatie in the kitchen or the garden. After a while, I sat to take advantage of the light coming through the front window to do some mending. The bodice for one of my dresses needed re-stitching at a seam. Finishing that, I had an idea for freshening it up with floral embroidery.

I was concentrating on an intricate bit of stitchery when a banging on the front door caused me to stab my thumb with the needle. Thumb to mouth, I opened the door. I gasped. "Oncle?"

Up close Claude d'Aubert was taller, broader than I remembered my father being. His hair darker, his brows heavier. And he had a small, nasty-looking pockmark on his left cheek. Still, he was quite handsome in his black and grey-striped doublet and black velvet breeches. A silver feather adorned his wide-brimmed felt hat. His eyes didn't have the twinkle or mirth I had so loved in Papa's eyes, but they clearly marked him as his brother.

"Sylvienne!" His voice, rough-edged yet disarming, was nothing like Papa's. His mouth arced into a benevolent smile. "The last time I saw you, you were knee high."

I couldn't say out loud what I was thinking: *The last time I saw you, you were naked.* In truth, not the *last* time. But more than once. From the tree.

"Look how beautiful you've become." His eyes swept the room, the doorway into the kitchen. "Is your mother home?"

I bobbed my head, gave a half-curtsy, and hurried into the kitchen where Maman worked alongside Tatie, cutting up a rabbit. The pungency of raw meat assailed my nose. "Maman! He is here."

"Who is here?" The blade of her carving knife rose and fell.

"Oncle!"

Her knife stopped in midair.

"He is at the door…asking for you."

With a sharp intake of breath, she gripped the knife tighter, the veins in her hand standing out, her jaw tightening. She set the knife down next to the rabbit carcass and wiped her hands on her apron.

"Stay here." Removing the apron, she walked into the front room.

Tatie, brow furrowed, refused to put down her own knife. My eyes drifted to the cutting board. The blood on it caused me to shudder.

"Isabelle! How good to see you."

His deep, gravelly voice carried me back to another time. To the manor house on the other side of the hedgerow. Oncle, standing in the large kitchen arguing with Maman. Me, cowering behind a serving cart, shaking. Maman telling him she would not marry him, not now, not ever. Oncle, telling her she was a fool. That he would have the courts declare Papa's estate null and void, deeded to him. She would have nothing.

When she still refused, he took a step toward her, his arm raised. That's when I charged him, bit his leg. He slapped me away and was about to kick me when Maman grabbed the carving knife, her voice like grit. "Get away from her."

He stopped, clearly taken aback by her ferocity.

"Get out of this house. If you ever come near her or me again..." She raised the knife higher.

I held my breath, afraid to cry out.

He glared at her a moment longer. "Bah!" He waved her away. "You are not worth it." Walking past me, he lifted his foot as if to kick me after all. At Maman's growl he thought better of it and strode out, slamming the front door behind him.

Now he was at the front door of our cottage. His bold voice and Maman's softer one drifted from the sitting room. I crept to the doorway to peer through, Tatie tight behind me.

"It has been far too long," he was saying.

"What do you want?" She did not invite him to come in.

He brushed past her anyway and sat in the same chair King Louis had occupied. He indicated she should sit on a nearby stool. Instead, she crossed the room and chose a straight-backed chair, keeping her own back as rigid as the wood behind her.

"What is this I heard? That you had a distinguished visitor?"

She said nothing.

"King Louis paid you a visit?"

Still, she said nothing. The silence between them was so absolute I could hear Tatie breathing, her oniony breath warming my neck.

"When a relative of mine, the widow of my dear departed brother, is graced by an unexpected visit from the King—I assume it was unexpected, since I wasn't invited to be part of the welcoming delegation—it behooves me to make it my business to learn why." He regarded her with an artificial smile.

"It was a social visit. We are distantly related. He needed a place for his officers to water their horses."

Oncle Claude frowned. "That's it? A social visit? Nothing more?"

Maman shrugged.

"Regardless, I dislike being left out. This event has become the talk of Amiens."

"You have shown no concern regarding my affairs since..." She sucked in a breath. "Since after Guy's funeral."

"When the affairs of my brother's widow are of concern to the King, it is only natural I should take note."

"In case you can gain personal advantage from it?" Her voice had taken on a hard edge.

"To protect my family's interests. Your interests." He kept his voice smooth. "As head of the family, I insist you notify me should the King deign to communicate with you again."

Maman rose. "You must have other business to attend to." She opened the front door.

Oncle Claude glared at her. After a moment, he rose, forcing his insipid smile again and inclining his head toward her in acquiescence. Then a nod toward the kitchen. I stepped back, bumping into Tatie, hoping he hadn't seen me.

"Your daughter—Guy's daughter—is quite stunning. She will need a benefactor. Someone who will look out for her interests, ensures she marries into a notable family. You will do well not to ignore my patronage."

Maman stood stony-faced at the open door.

"Very well then." He took his leave, but not before turning to her one last time. "We've had our differences, Isabelle. But in this matter of King Louis, I will not be ignored."

Maman closed the door behind him, then leaned heavily against it, working to control her breathing. Tatie nudged me to go to her.

Maman wrapped her arms around me, and a single sob rose from her throat.

"Maman?"

She straightened her shoulders. "Forget he came." Her voice was husky, but with tender fingers, she pushed hair off my face. "Let's go back into the kitchen. There is work to do."

CHAPTER THIRTEEN

That night I lay under the summer coverlet in the four-poster featherbed I shared with Maman, watching the flame flicker on the bedside candle, waiting for her to come to bed. Every night she would sit and brush her hair at her *toilette*, a cherrywood table with a wood-framed mirror that had been a gift from Papa. Tonight, however, she sat, hands in her lap, eyes downcast. She seemed to be barely breathing.

I climbed out of bed and went to her. "Maman?"

She gave no response. Then I saw the framed miniature of Papa in her hands. I loved that simple charcoal sketch. His smile and the warmth of his eyes radiated from it.

"I was so young when we married." Her voice was small and distant.

I knelt down beside her. "Did you love him from the first moment?" I thought of all the heroines in the novels I adored, falling in love at the first sight of their paramours.

She shook her head. "We didn't know each other."

"What do you mean? You've never told me how you met."

"We met the day we were married."

I was speechless. Was this why she never spoke of her past, even of her marriage to Papa?

"Ours was an arranged marriage. He was much older than me."

This I knew. We had recently celebrated Maman's thirtieth birthday. If Papa were still alive, he would have been in his late forties. "Were you frightened?"

"Very much so." She reached for her ivory comb and ran it through her hair until she hit the first snarl. She seemed not to know what to do about it, so I took the comb from her and worked out the tangle.

She looked up at my image in the mirror. "He was so gentle and kind. It wasn't long before I grew to love him."

I teased out a few more snarls from her gentle waves as she talked. Maman was not Papa's first wife, she told me. He had been married to a woman named Suzanne, who had died in childbirth. The baby died a month later. Poor Papa had so much sadness in his life before Maman came along. In my mind, he was a knight in shining armor, rescuing her from the convent as if she were a princess in a tower. In truth, she gave him happiness as well. I set down the comb and wrapped my arms around her, resting my head against hers.

Maman squeezed my hands. "It's time for sleep."

Lying in bed next to her, listening to her quiet breathing, I thought about all that had changed in my life these past weeks. Leaving school, watching Perrette sail away, learning that Maman was cousin to King Louis. And now, that Papa had experienced such losses before Maman entered his life, and yet he had agreed to marry her without even knowing her. The very idea astounded me. Why would he do that? Why would she agree to it? I supposed it was the way of the nobility. And yet, they grew to love each other. It was an amazingly romantic story—as good as any in the novels I so loved. And perhaps just as tragic. If only it hadn't rained that night. If only I hadn't complained. A deep ache in my heart reminded me of how things could have been if he had never climbed that ladder.

I wished I could talk with Etienne about it. Etienne. This boy whom I'd taken for granted since the day we first met was growing into a man. Handsome, strong. Yet tender. But a shoemaker's son. I had greater ambitions than marrying a shoemaker. Still, my mother, daughter of a prince, had been born out of wedlock. What did that make me? I yawned. So glad I hadn't blurted out Maman's secret to Etienne. The look in his eyes if he knew. Did Papa know? Papa's smiling eyes, how I missed them. My eyes closed.

If I thought my life would improve because the King of France occupied our sitting room one summer afternoon or because I had royal blood in my veins, I was grievously mistaken. Of course, rumors raced rampant throughout Amiens as to why King Louis had deigned to stop at our insignificant cottage. Most agreed it was an aberration; he needed water for his horses at the very moment his entourage was passing my mother's cottage. No one but me had heard him refer to Maman as his "cousine."

Despite my persistent questions, Maman had no more to say about her life before Papa, and little even of recent events. It was Tatie who told me about Oncle Claude's insistence on marrying Maman after Papa died. Standing over the rough-hewn table positioned outside the kitchen door for work like today's — plucking chickens — she said, "He didn't give her more than a month to grieve before he came sniffing at her skirts."

With one whack of Tatie's butcher knife, the chicken carcass fell into halves. "And he was not delicate in phrasing his expectations, claiming it was his right as her husband's brother to insist she marry him." She threw the entrails into the slop bucket. "Of course, what he wanted was that big house next door and your papa's title and all the money and property included with it. But your mother would have nothing to do with him."

"What do you mean, title?" I tugged at the feathers from my assigned carcass.

"Your Papa was the original *seigneur*." She paused a moment to wipe the sweat off her forehead with the back of her arm. "The lord of the manor house and all the property from here to the river. King Louis had bestowed it upon him the first time your papa married."

I stopped plucking. "Why did Maman never say so?"

Tatie shrugged, noticing my idle hands. "When she refused to marry your uncle, he paid off a judge to re-assign the title to himself." She took the carcass from me and ripped off the skin. "The judge had the presence of mind to refuse to allow you and your mother to become indigent. He required Monsieur d'Aubert to sign a deed giving your mother the groundskeeper's house and a pension to live on."

I had only vague memories of moving out of the manor house and into this one. Mostly, I'd thought they were part of a dream. Thinking about it now, something occurred to me. "Tatie, was this your house — and Blondeau's — before Maman and I moved in?"

Tatie dumped the chopped chicken into a pot. She wiped her hands on a towel then turned to me. "*Mon ange,* this house belonged to your father as part of his estate. Blondeau and I lived here while he was alive by the grace of his kindness and generosity. We were honored when your mother invited us to remain here with the two of you."

"Oh, Tatie!" I threw my arms around her. She accepted my embrace before pulling away and straightening her skirt. With a husky voice she said, "Let's get this mess cleaned up."

I scooped up the chicken feathers and dumped them into a pail to take out to the garbage pit, wondering what else my mother had not told me.

September came and went before Maman could find a suitable tutor for me. A young man with an awkward demeanor and a long, angular face, Monsieur Ouvrard claimed to have earned a degree from the university at Strasbourg and came highly recommended by Barthelme, Maman's banker. However, after several weeks of lessons, it became evident I was more fluent in Latin and Italian than he. When he attempted to introduce me to the classics, he flailed his hands complaining to Maman that I had already read the books on his list of recommended reading.

"What I want to learn about," I said to him one day as we sat at the dining table going over sums, "is natural philosophy, how our world and everything in it works. And the heavens! I want to learn about the findings of Copernicus, Galileo, and the other star gazers."

"What an absurd idea." Ouvrard waved a hand in dismissal. "What use are those for a young woman? All they will do is fill your head with useless fiddle-faddle."

"But what fascinating fiddle-faddle!"

One afternoon when Maman was out, Ouvrard took it upon himself to teach me another kind of lesson. First, he laid his hand upon my knee. When I shook it off, he moved a lock of my hair from my neck, and, with his other hand pulled my head toward him, setting his lips upon mine.

He yelped when I slapped his face. Blondeau appeared and escorted him to the lane, the back of the tutor's collar bunched in his thumbless fist. Maman refused to pay his wages for the day's lesson. Afterward, Tatie declared it was a good thing *le grand professeur* had not deigned to enter her kitchen, for she had her butcher knife at the ready to make him *un petit professeur*. Thus, was my education interrupted for the second time that year.

Autumn turned into a long, dreary winter. I buried myself in my novels, diving into the first volume of Mademoiselle de Scudéry's dramatically long *Artamene ou le Grand Cyrus*. In between chapters, I found myself thinking of Marie-Catherine, wondering how she was doing at the convent school. Once when Etienne stopped by on his way to deliver shoes to a neighbor, he mentioned his sister had been chafing under the tutelage of the nuns, and that his parents were considering pulling her out. I penned a note for him to deliver, urging Marie-Catherine not to give up too soon, and to take advantage of every bit of schooling available to her.

Rereading my gazettes — with their accounts of King Louis and his beautiful and enigmatic mistresses, and of the King's brother Philippe, who seemed to favor men over women, even over his own wife, Princess Henriette — put me in mind of Perrette who had spent hours giggling over these stories with me.

Had she arrived in New France yet? I couldn't imagine being out on that immense, cold ocean in a wooden sailing ship, no matter how sturdily built it was. And what would she encounter in her new homeland? Savages? Wild animals? Unkempt men whose job was to tame that wilderness? And would she find friendship among the women who traveled with her to find husbands? The thought of it was dreary and disheartening. All I could do was to say a prayer that she would be safe and find happiness in her new life.

Maman became frustrated by my withdrawal into fiction and courtly fantasy and petitioned Etienne to loan me one of his mathematics books. He readily complied, bringing the book himself and going over the first lessons with me. My mind was soon twisted into happy knots puzzling over equations with him, and I lost interest, if only momentarily, in the lives of scandal-plagued women.

Our trips into Amiens became fewer and farther between as the winter rains brought ice and snow. Maman's cough worsened making shopping in cold weather distressing for her. In truth, I was relieved not to go. The thought of encountering Guillaume Boivin or Oncle Claude distressed me. Etienne was too busy at school to visit with, and the Raveau's bakery seemed empty of its usual good cheer with Perrette gone.

Christmas Eve arrived with a pretty dusting of snow. Blondeau arranged for a neighbor to lend us his buckboard wagon and horse for the drive to Midnight Mass. Maman, huddled under a bundle of blankets in the wagon bed between Tatie and me, seemed pleased to be out of the house. Riding past the empty manor — Madame du Barré spent her winters on the southern coast along the Mediterranean — made me grit my teeth at Oncle Claude's perfidy in keeping Maman and me from living there.

Back home after the Christmas service, Blondeau lit the Yule log in the hearth, and Tatie brought out a platter of meats and cheeses. As we did every year, Maman set out the miniature characters of the *crèche* Papa had given to her as a gift on their first Christmas, and we stayed up into the early morning hours enjoying our *petit réveillon de Noël* and chatting. I wondered what Etienne was doing at this moment. I missed his sweet laughter. My fingertips strayed to my lips, thinking of his even sweeter kisses.

On New Year's Day neighbors came calling, bearing handmade tokens of appreciation — embroidered handkerchiefs, candles, scented soap, candied chestnuts, and other sweets. Maman welcomed each visitor with a mug of mulled cider. My heart quickened when I opened the door to Etienne who had braved the cold on Jolie. I wanted to throw my arms around him, but of course, with a houseful of company all I did was smile and invite him in. He presented Maman with a covered bowl of sugar-coated almonds his mother had made. Later, pulling me out the back door for a moment of privacy, he presented me with a secret kiss.

That kiss would have to last, because winter dragged on with no sight of Etienne until mid-February when a warming spell offered respite in time for *Mardi Gras*. The following day, Ash Wednesday, would mark the beginning of Lent, when we set aside meat and sweets for the forty days before Easter.

Throwing on my woolen cloak, I waved to Maman and ran to join Blondeau and Tatie who waited for me out on the lane. They were as eager for Mardi Gras as I was. Blondeau hailed a passing farm wagon. Our neighbor, Jean-Pierre Garnier, invited us to ride in the back with his wife and children. The gloriously sunny day heightened our spirits, the air warm enough to leave our cloaks open to the faint, almost spring-like breeze.

A short while later, I stood with Tatie and Blondeau surveying Amiens's crowded Cathedral square looking for Etienne. Across the square, a family wove its way through the throng of people—Oncle Claude, Tante Judith, and my cousins. The eldest girl, Jeannette, waved at me, but Oncle nudged her to keep going. I supposed his visit with Maman last summer to find out why the King had come to our house still rankled.

"There they are," Blondeau said as Etienne and his family approached.

I bussed Marie-Catherine on both cheeks and greeted her parents and younger brothers and sisters, offering a shy smile to Etienne. Noting the leather satchel slung across his chest, I thought to ask him about it, but there was too much commotion. Tatie and Blondeau gave me last-minute warnings to mind my whereabouts, then drifted off to enjoy their day. After a few moments, Etienne, Marie-Catherine, and I headed off to find our own fun.

Revelers and street musicians bustled about. Children raced back and forth playing tag and blindman's bluff and chasing hoops. Gleeful crowds gathered around magicians, jugglers, and dancers. Etienne's younger brother, Robert, loomed over us, walking about on tall wooden stilts.

The aroma of freshly made *crepes* and honey-sweetened waffles drew us to a row of vendors. I fished coins from my pocket to buy *beignets*, deep-fried dough pillows dipped in honey that were a specialty of Mardi Gras. The little pastries melted in my mouth — pure bliss.

"The parade is starting!" Robert called down from his stilts perch.

Etienne grabbed my hand as the crowd of revelers surged forward. A procession of wagons came into view, decorated with immense colorful bows and carrying costumed dancers, their fantastical masks mocking the Royal court. Alongside the wagons pranced more dancers and musicians with mandolins, trumpets, and drums of every size and shape. Young men on stilts, whom Robert eagerly joined, wove in and out of the procession, trailing green, purple, and yellow ribbons behind them.

A wagon rolled by carrying the "King" and "Queen" alongside women decked out in salacious gowns and outrageous face paint meant to represent his mistresses. The crowd erupted in a roar of merriment. With an unexpected twinge of unease, I realized this was my cousin we were making fun of. I let go Etienne's hand and turned away to hide my discomfort.

That's when I saw him. Guillaume Boivin. His back was to me, but he was laughing and gesturing with a group of other young men. My stomach lurched and bile rose into my throat. Should I flee? Or find a rock and throw it at him? He turned around. Relief flooded over me. It wasn't him after all.

Etienne put his arm around my waist. "Is something wrong?"

I shook my head, reassured by his closeness. The crowd dispersed, a gaggle of revelers following the parade as it disappeared around the corner on its way to the Quartier Saint-Leu, where drinking and dancing would go on through the evening. Others rushed to get in line at the food and drink stalls. Merry-makers, already drunk, sang loud, ribald songs in the street.

The deep resonating bells of the cathedral rang out four times — my signal that I had an hour left before meeting Blondeau and Tatie for the trip home. I wished I could stay longer, but the sun over Etienne's shoulder was already low in the sky.

Marie-Catherine waved to collect the younger ones as we sat on the cathedral steps.

"What do you have there?" I asked, pointing to Etienne's leather satchel.

"He carries his sketchbook everywhere he goes now," Marie-Catherine said, keeping a watchful eye on the little boys playing leapfrog over the cobblestones.

"A sketchbook? Do you fancy yourself an artist now?"

"An artist, no," Etienne said, blushing. "But I get ideas for new styles of shoes, and I don't want to forget them."

"He scribbles in it whenever he thinks no one is looking," Marie-Catherine said, "He's actually quite good."

Etienne's blush deepened, and he kicked at his sister playfully.

"May I see?"

He hesitated, but then pulled out the leather-bound sketchbook. I leafed through its pages, amazed at the details. I pointed to one drawing, a woman's shoe with an elongated toe that curved ever-so-slightly upward. A note indicated the shoe was to be made of embroidered fabric. The stitching evoked birds and butterflies. A folded fan of fabric and a large satin bow topped the instep. The heel, perhaps a thumb's length in height, tapered to a slender point. Nestled upon the bow was a pearl-laden brooch. He had written he would trim the collar of the shoe with braided piping.

"This one," I said. "This is the one all the women will want."

"Do you think so?" His eyes lit up, pleased.

"I know so. I would love to wear a shoe this elegant. But wouldn't it be costly?"

He took the sketchbook from me. "Father chastises me for wasting time designing shoes nobody in Amiens will purchase. Of course, if I had the right buyer, someone with enough money..." He let the thought slide and slipped the book back into the leather bag just as his parents arrived to take their children home.

"I'll stay with Sylvienne until she can find Madame and Monsieur Blondeau," Etienne said.

I hugged Marie-Catherine again before saying au revoir.

A voice called out Etienne's name. Several of his friends waved from the opposite side of the square. "Join us!" one called out.

Etienne waved back. "Maybe later!"

"Do you want to go?" I asked. "I can wait here for the Blondeaus."

"I'd rather be with you." His smile was genuine, and it pleased me to hear his words. He nodded toward the cathedral. "Have you ever been inside?"

"Only once, when I was very little."

"Let's see if it has changed since then." He took me by the hand and pulled me toward the towering red entry doors.

Inside, the height of the vaulted ceiling took my breath away. "How did they build such an edifice four hundred years ago?" I asked in a whisper.

"God must have directed them." Etienne said. "Come, I want to show you something."

We crossed to the center of the nave, my eyes drawn upward again, this time to the stained-glass windows on the west wall, aglow from the setting sun.

Etienne directed my attention to the marble floor tiles patterned with intricate geometric designs. "It's a labyrinth."

We stood inside an octagonal medallion bordered with Greek lettering. He pointed to the center where four angels and four robed figures surrounded a symbol of crossed scepters. "That represents the bishop who ordered the construction of the cathedral and his three architects."

He stepped onto the thick black line leading out from the medallion. Together we wound our way along the black-and-white marble maze, back and forth, around and around until we reached the center. He stopped suddenly, causing me to bump into him, giggling. He turned, put his hands on my shoulders and leaned down to kiss me. What we were doing was sacrilegious — kissing here in the house of God — but I couldn't help myself. I allowed him to explore my mouth with his tongue. After a long moment, I pulled away, breathless.

"Would you like to see the head of John the Baptist?" he whispered, his voice husky.

"No! Yes. Really?"

He led me up the north aisle to a small wooden door set into the thick stone wall. A window in the door, protected by crisscrossed iron bars, provided a view into an antechamber. Standing on tiptoe, I peered through the window. I gasped. The shock of seeing it caused me to rock back on my heels so that Etienne had to catch me to keep me from falling. The skull, encased in some kind of crystalline material, sat on a silver platter, its eyes hollow, the broken jaw contorted into a death grimace.

I peered up at the small window, wanting to see it again, but not wanting to. "Is it truly him?"

"So they say."

A shiver of dread ran through me, the light in the church fading. "Let's go."

Stepping out into the cool air, I sucked in deep breaths. Etienne wrapped a protective arm around me. I nestled into him, my head against his warm chest.

He gazed down at me with an intensity that unnerved me. "Sylvienne, I want to marry you."

I blinked, stunned, then pushed away. Despite his luscious kisses, despite Perrette's prediction in the summer just before she left, I was caught off guard.

He held my arms. "I want you for my wife. I know I'm nothing more than the son of a shoemaker and you deserve better, far better, but—"

"Etienne, I…I am too young."

"You'll be sixteen in less than a month. And we don't have to marry right away. I can wait." His words came all in a rush. "I'll wait until you are sixteen. Or seventeen, if you like. I'll wait as long as you want. As long as need be. All I want is to know that at the end of the wait we will join our lives together."

"I…I don't know what to say." One side of me wanted to shout, "Yes!" But the other, the side that won out, hesitated. What was wrong with me that I couldn't embrace the moment and accept his proposal?

"Don't say anything. Not yet. I had not planned to ask you until after your birthday, but I leave for Rouen with Father next Sunday. We'll be gone most of three weeks. Promise me you'll think about it. We know each other well. We've been friends for a long time. I want to be more than friends. I want to share my life with you."

He bent his head to kiss me.

"There you are!" Blondeau's voice caused Etienne to jerk his head up. "We've been looking for you."

Etienne gazed down at me, his earnestness reflected in his eyes. "When I return, will you give me your answer?"

CHAPTER FOURTEEN

Maman was already in bed when we arrived home. Tatie ladled bowls of soup for Blondeau and me from the pot she kept warmed on the hearth. I said nothing to them about Etienne's proposal of marriage.

That night in bed, lying next to Maman, I wondered if I'd been a fool not to say yes to him immediately. I tingled with pleasure remembering the warmth of his lips as he kissed me in the cathedral. But did I want to be the wife of a shoemaker? I didn't know what I wanted. I tossed and turned until Maman reached over to rub my back. After a long while, I fell into a restless sleep.

When I awoke the next morning, Maman was in the kitchen listening to Tatie's stories of Mardi Gras and planning our meatless meals for the next forty days. Restless, I pulled out the mathematics book Etienne had given me and sat down at Maman's writing desk. Opening the book to a page of problems that seemed daunting and confusing, it occurred to me Marie-Catherine likely didn't know her brother had asked me to marry him. Why would he announce his proposal, even to his sister, until he knew the answer? Should I tell her? Marie-Catherine would be shocked to learn I was hesitating. I wished Perrette were here. She would give me good advice.

"You are quiet today, Sylvienne." Maman came into the sitting room with mending in hand. Her voice was low, her breathing uneven. "Did you not enjoy the festivities yesterday?"

"It was a grand celebration." *And Etienne proposed to me.* But something held me back from confiding in her. "Perhaps the best ever."

"But...?"

I shrugged. "Lent is a long time to go without."

She contemplated me with the bemused look that crossed her face more and more often lately. However, she didn't question me. And I said no more.

It turned out the forty days of Lent was to be devoid of more than just meat and sweets. Etienne had thought he would be gone for three weeks. But his father came down with a fever, delaying their departure for a week, and their meeting with business partners in Rouen took longer than planned. It was almost Easter, and I had not seen nor heard from Etienne since Mardi Gras except through Marie-Catherine.

Growing increasingly restless, I swung back and forth between missing him desperately and distressed over not knowing if I was ready for marriage. I worried about leaving Maman with her health in decline, though she would be in good hands with Tatie and Blondeau. And to be honest, I still had girlish dreams of doing something grand with my life, although I had no idea what that could be. Foolish, I knew. My love for Etienne was real. Would I be passing up an opportunity to spend my life with someone who loved me as Papa loved Maman? Perhaps that was my fear. What if something happened, and I lost Etienne the way Maman lost Papa? What if I caused Etienne harm? Papa's willingness to climb onto the roof to keep me dry still painted a dark shadow that haunted my dreams. As I helped Maman and Tatie with household chores, my thoughts were a tangled knot of what-ifs and wonderings.

On a quiet Sunday evening in early March, while the candles were still burning but after Tatie and Blondeau had said, "*Bonne nuit*," I reached for Maman's embroidered silk pouch. Sitting at her feet, I spread the stones out on the rug in front of me. They felt so familiar — some smooth, others rough or with dimples. "Maman, teach me to read the stones the way you do."

Her eyes still on the shift she was mending, she said, "Sylvienne, it is not a skill that can be taught." At the sound of my deep sigh, she looked up. "It is a gift you either have or you don't."

Biting my lip, I tossed the stones. No matter how they lay, I could not see what Maman saw in them.

She reached out and ran her fingers through my hair. "Don't despair. If you have it, the gift comes when you least expect it, but most need it."

"I don't think I am destined ever to have it." Gathering up the stones, I slid them back into the pouch.

"You have other gifts," she said. "Your kind heart. Your brave spirit. Your voice. Be grateful for what you have. Don't lust after what isn't yours."

I stood and kissed her on the forehead. "I think I will take my gifts and go to bed."

"Don't mock me, daughter."

"That was my voice speaking. Unbidden. I would never mock you." I offered a crooked smile then turned to go upstairs.

"Sylvienne, wait." She reached into the pouch and pulled out the black stone with two white stripes. My favorite. "Take this. My gift to you."

"Are you sure? Won't it change the balance of your cipher?"

"The gift is not dependent on any one stone or any number of stones. Keep this one close as a remembrance."

"To remember what?" I held the stone to the candlelight, seeing how it gleamed.

"Our time together."

Unnerved, I scrutinized her face. "Is there something wrong?"

She shook her head. "Sometimes we can know our future, most of the time we can't. We must treasure every moment together."

Still disconcerted, I climbed the steps to our sleeping loft and tucked the stone into my cedar keepsake box next to the one I'd found the day Perrette sailed away. The same day King Louis had deigned to visit our house. Remembering Etienne's efforts to clean up after the royal horses brought a momentary smile to my lips. How I wished he were here now to put his comforting arms around me and reassure me that nothing was wrong with Maman. That my life would always be happy.

In that moment, I decided I would marry Etienne.

My sixteenth birthday, the first of April, 1671 dawned with an early spring thunderstorm. Gazing into Maman's wood-framed mirror, I didn't feel any older. I still had the same untamed near-raven locks, and my green eyes still looked too big to me. I curled my lips into a half-hearted smile. My teeth were acceptable — white, blessedly uncrooked. I had taken to cleaning them with a small wood-handled brush made of horsehair that Maman had come upon in the marketplace.

This would be a year of change. Telling Etienne I would marry him meant a new life was in store for me. Come this day next year, for better or worse, I would be living a different life. And as Etienne's wife, it could only be for the better. A flash of lightning lit the bedchamber window followed by an enormous crash of thunder that sent me scurrying down the steps.

"That was a close one," Tatie said as she put me to work in the kitchen slicing turnips and carrots for my birthday stew. Rain still pattered against the window, but the thunder had already subsided to a distant rumbling.

"You seem unusually happy," Maman commented, scrubbing out the stew pot.

I realized I had been humming. With resolve, I put down my knife. "Maman, I have something to tell you."

But before I could say anything more, Blondeau rushed into the kitchen, dripping rain. "Madame! A courier has arrived. He says he has something for Mademoiselle Sylvienne."

For me? We rarely received letters. Perhaps it was from Perrette. I wiped my hands on my linen apron and went to the door, Maman and Tatie not far behind. A man, his wool riding livery soaked through, stood waiting outside. Bowing when I appeared in the doorway, he carried the scent of the open road, a man who'd been riding for some time. Behind him, his horse snorted, its dappled grey hide glistening with sweat despite the rain.

The courier held out a dripping leather satchel. "I am to deliver this to Mademoiselle d'Aubert."

I took the satchel from him, taking care not to get my own clothes wet. "Merci, Monsieur."

He bowed a second time then turned on his heel. Mounting his horse, he kicked it into action, its hoofbeats fading as they sped down the lane.

"What is it?" Maman asked, closing the door against the rain.

"Don't lay that wet thing on the table," Tatie ordered.

She put a linen towel down first. Then she and Maman and Blondeau hovered as I set the satchel on it and unbuckled its straps.

"Oh, my!" Tatie held her hands to her cheeks, her eyes wide as I tugged out a parcel wrapped in muslin and tied with silver and gold ribbons.

Maman's lips grew taut.

Blondeau removed the satchel and towel so I could set the parcel on the dry table. "Well?" he asked. "Are you going to open it?"

Blinking, I realized I had been staring at it. "Yes, of course."

He and Tatie leaned in as I tugged at the ribbons. The muslin fell away. Tatie gasped.

"Maman, look!" I held up a blue satin bodice embroidered with silver and gold threads.

Maman's face was unreadable as Tatie lifted the matching blue satin skirt, its opalescent folds shimmering with silver-and-gold-threaded vines. Floral appliques matching those on the bodice adorned the hem.

"A gown fit for a princess," Blondeau said. "Who do you think sent that?"

"I've no idea." I held the bodice in front of me, wishing I had one of Madame Trouillet's full-length mirrors.

Maman pulled out a note tucked into the muslin. She frowned at the white linen stationery with my name written in elegant script. Stamped into the gold wax seal was an insignia—a circle of vines surrounding a trio of fleurs-de-lys topped by a crown.

"Is that...?" My eyes widened as I handed off the bodice to Tatie and took the letter from Maman. "Is that the seal of the King?" I slid my finger under the wax to loosen it and unfolded the stiff paper. I read the words. Then I read them again.

"What does it say?" Tatie asked.

Stunned, I looked at the three of them. "It is an invitation to attend the royal court in Paris. An invitation from King Louis."

CHAPTER FIFTEEN

Madame Trouillet's thick brows arched in delight over her beak of a nose when Maman and I walked through the door of her shop the next day. "I didn't expect to see you for another month."

"Sylvienne is in need of a traveling ensemble," Maman said. "Wool of course. She will also require a half-dozen silk gowns."

"Silk?"

"And taffeta," I said. "And lace."

Madame Trouillet's eyebrows rose higher.

"I'm going to court!"

"Indeed?" Madame Trouillet seemed disbelieving. But when Maman nodded, she said, "Madame, I am delighted to dress your daughter. And yourself, as well?"

Maman turned to survey the bolts of fabric. "Not just yet. What about this color for Sylvienne?" She held up a swatch of mauve silk. She was not happy about the invitation from the King. She had been solemn during my birthday dinner while Tatie and I gushed over the unexpected gift and note. But she had lost no time in taking me to the dressmaker to make sure I would be properly appareled.

"It is just as well to wait on your dresses, Madame. If you will excuse my saying…" Madame Trouillet lowered her voice. "You have lost weight, *non*?" She reached out to tuck a pleat into the sleeve at Maman's shoulder. "This dress fit you perfectly the last time you were here. Are you well?"

Taken aback, I realized Maman had indeed lost weight. Why hadn't I noticed before that her dress hung on her, loose over her bosom and hips?

"I'm fine. What about this green?" Maman held up another swatch, this in the palest hue.

Madame Trouillet waggled a finger in the air. "Phfft! That color does nothing for *la demoiselle's* coloring. When do you leave?"

"In two weeks," I said. "King Louis is sending a coach for me."

"Oh, my. Well, yes, that's not very much time, is it? We'd better get to it." She scurried to grab bolts of silk in hues of turquoise, violet, and rose. As I stood before her floor-length, oval looking glass, Madame Trouillet held fabrics to my face and shoulders so Maman could inspect their effect on my skin. The rose made my cheeks and eyes shine.

Maman shook her head. "Too bright. Try the indigo. Do you have anything in russet? Or a soft grey?"

"You would send your daughter to court in grey?" Madame Trouillet admonished.

"Coral then. Or olive. Do you have some sketches for us to consider?"

With a sigh of disapproval, the dressmaker left us to fetch more bolts and her sketchbook.

Maman appraised the designs, shaking her head at the low-cut bodices, cinched waists, drop shoulders, puffy sleeves, and the oversized bows. "These won't do."

Madame Trouillet threw her hands in the air. "You might as well send her in a maid's frock."

"Maman, please," I said. "Madame Trouillet's drawings are in vogue with every fashion I have seen in the gazettes."

"I will not have you looking like a trollop in the presence of the King."

"Your daughter is a beautiful girl," the dressmaker said. "She deserves equally beautiful clothes. Especially if she is to be in the presence of the King."

Maman's eyes darkened and her jaw clenched. "She does not need a dress that exposes her breasts to every scoundrel that holidays at the royal palace. Simple but elegant will do."

With pursed lips, Madame Trouillet produced more sketches.

Moments later I stood in front of her mirror while she measured, pinned, and took notes. I imagined myself dressed in lovely gowns, dancing in the grand ballroom of the royal palace.

"Maman, what do you remember of King Louis's brother, Philippe?"

Maman sat on a nearby stool, watching Madame Trouillet's every move. "Oh, Sylvienne, we were so young then. There is nothing to remember."

"But you must recall something."

"He was a sweet boy. He loved to wear his mother's pearls and her tiara."

I sensed Madame Trouillet's ears perking up, though she gave no sign she was listening to our conversation.

"He married Henriette of England," I said.

"Yes, I'd heard that."

"It is said he wears her jewels and sometimes her gowns." I glanced down now at Madame Trouillet whose eyebrows were raised, pins between her lips as she wrapped a swatch of silk around my waist. "Even in public."

"That is absurd," Maman said. "You shouldn't be repeating such nonsense."

"It's in all the gazettes."

"The gazettes should not be printing it then." Maman stood. "Madame Trouillet, can you have these ready in time for her departure?"

"Of course," Madame Trouillet said. "But I will have to add a surcharge for priority service."

"Send me the bill when you have it prepared." Maman threw her cloak over her shoulders. "I will have Blondeau deliver the payment."

Madame Trouillet rolled up her measuring tape. "I wish you a safe journey, Mademoiselle. I am honored that you will wear my gowns at court."

The gowns we ordered were not as fashionable as I had hoped, but I smiled thinking of the blue silk and taffeta gown hanging next to our bed — the one King Louis had sent me to wear for my presentation at court. Maman had no say in how that gown would look on me, no matter how much it bothered her to see me looking courtly.

Maman had other errands to run and agreed I could stop by the shoe shop to order a pair of dress shoes and to share my news with Marie-Catherine.

"What news?" Marie-Catherine had just returned home from school and was reaching for a leather apron when I walked in. With a nod from her father, we ran up the steps and into the family's apartment with its wide latticed windows overlooking the street. She motioned me to a low cushioned settee so we could sit side by side. But I was too excited to sit.

"Something unimaginable has happened," I said.

"Tell me!"

Arching my eyebrows, I asked. "Do you remember when King Louis visited my house?"

"How could I forget? It's all anyone talks about, even now, half a year later."

I bounced on my toes, so excited I couldn't hold back any longer. "I've been invited to court!"

A look of confusion clouded her eyes. "Court? Do you mean the court of King Louis?"

"No. I mean the court of King Charles of England. Of course, I mean King Louis! Marie-Catherine, I am going to Paris!"

She jumped up and shrieked, grabbing my arms. "When? How will you get there? I can't believe it!"

The words tumbled out in a flurry. "I received the invitation yesterday. It came by royal courier. Written on royal parchment with the King's own seal. I thought I would faint."

She took my hands in hers. "What does your mother say? When will you go?"

"A fortnight from now. They will send a coach for us." I tried to sound casual. "When will Etienne and your father be home?"

"Their return has been delayed. They won't start home until mid-month."

My heart dropped. I wanted to break the news of my royal invitation to Etienne myself.

"Sylvienne? What is the matter?"

With a shake of my head, I forced a smile. "Nothing. I am just so excited."

As she chattered on about the adventure I was about to undertake and how everyone at school would be jealous, especially Claudette, the memory of my last words with Etienne weighed on me. He expected to hear my decision when he got back. And now I wouldn't be able to give it to him until after my return.

"He'll be disappointed that he missed you," Marie-Catherine was saying. "But I know he will be happy for your good fortune."

I hoped against hope she was right, and that Etienne would understand how important this was for me. "Marie-Catherine, please don't send word of this to Etienne."

"You'd rather I wait until he arrives home?"

"I will tell him myself. In a letter. I'll send it to you before I leave."

Easter this year was the Sunday following my birthday. After Mass we sat for our noon meal, relishing the lamb shank garnished with mint Tatie had roasted on a spit over the kitchen fireplace the day before. Afterward, while we sat in the front room with the windows open for the first time this spring, Blondeau presented me with a simple but elegantly made oak travel chest big enough to hold all my new clothes. Tatie appeared in the kitchen doorway, wiping her hands on her apron, her eyes moist. Maman watched from her favorite chair, a wan smile curving her lips.

Blondeau beamed as I knelt to inspect it. "I had planned it for your trousseau," he said, his voice unusually husky. "I think you have need of it now."

"You lined it!" I said, breathing in the scent of cedar. "And where did you find brass?" I ran my fingers along the smooth handles. "It is magnificent." I jumped up and threw my arms around him. "*Merci*, Blondeau. Merci! I will treasure it always. And when it's time to begin collecting for my wedding, this chest will be perfect." Then a thought occurred to me. "Maman, what will you use to carry your dresses?"

A look passed between Maman and Blondeau. He cleared his throat. "Did I tell you, Mademoiselle, that my bees received a royal invitation as well?"

"Your bees?"

"The King has need of their services in his orangerie."

Tatie clucked her tongue and bobbed her head. "It is said King Louis's orangerie has so many trees he is recruiting bees from far and wide."

Maman spoke quietly. "Sylvienne, I won't be going to Paris with you."

I stared at her in disbelief. "Maman, why not?"

But I knew why not. Her eyes were ringed with dark circles. She had taken to napping in the middle of the afternoon and had little appetite for the sumptuous meals Tatie prepared. And, as Madame Trouillet had so astutely observed, she was losing weight. The two-day journey to Paris would be more than Maman could withstand right now.

The glow of the royal invitation dimmed. "Maybe I shouldn't go. You need me here."

"Nonsense. One does not turn down an invitation to court." Maman smiled her thanks to Blondeau and Tatie and they disappeared into the kitchen. Once we were alone, her face became grave. "An invitation from the King is not a request. It is a summons." She held out her hands and I went to her, sinking to my knees. "You must go, but it is not a choice I would have made for you."

"But, Maman, you lived at court. Why wouldn't you want me to?"

"I was there for only a short while."

"As a young child. So you've said."

She sank back against the chair looking tired.

"You needn't worry so, Maman."

"Sylvienne, court is not the fairy tale life you believe it is."

"I know it isn't all pageantry and romance. And I will have to be careful. But King Louis is our cousin. He will make sure no harm comes to me."

Now she leaned forward. "Daughter, you must trust only your own heart. And you must guard your heart closely." We held hands as she spoke. "I was only four the day the old King died. Still, I remember it clearly. The Duc d'Uzès came into the royal nursery proclaiming, '*Le Roi est mort! Vive le Roi!*' And we all, children and adults alike, turned and dropped to our knees in front of my playmate Louis, the new king." She let out a deep breath and closed her eyes again, reaching for a memory. "From then on, everything changed. How we addressed him, how we played with him, how we were required to walk behind him. Forever after."

She was silent for so long I rubbed her hand. "You said you went back to court for his coronation."

"I did."

"He was fifteen. And you were...?"

"Fourteen. Not long until my next birthday." She opened her eyes now.

"After the ceremony in the great cathedral at Reims, I was allowed to accompany my mother back to the palace at Saint-Germain-en-Laye."

A million questions hovered on the tip of my tongue, but I kept my silence.

"It was intended I should stay for only a week, but my mother took ill, so I stayed for another month. Mother's condition worsened and nothing could be done for her. After her funeral, I was packed up and sent back to the convent with no time to say au revoir to anyone." Maman looked distraught for a moment. Then she straightened her shoulders and drew a deep breath. She looked at me with eyes bright with fever. "Enough of my past. It is your future we must be concerned about. You have a chest to pack. And I need to lie down."

My new gowns arrived two days before I was to depart for Paris. The colors looked bland next to the one the King had sent, but still I took pleasure in folding them one by one into my new travel chest. Madame Trouillet had added extra bows here, colorful lace there, deepened a neckline or two, ruffled a sleeve, surprising little touches that made me smile. Maman made note of the unbidden changes but said nothing.

I had put off writing my missive to Etienne, but time was slipping away and there were no more excuses. Now, quill in hand, I found it difficult to find the words. Should I answer his proposal in a letter? No. It was too great a commitment. I must declare my intention in person. I touched quill to paper.

> *Mon Coeur,*
>
> *An incredible honor has been bestowed upon me. I have been invited to attend the court of King Louis in Paris. Please be happy for me. When I return, I will give you the answer you are waiting for.*

I signed my letter *Avec toute mon amour, Sylvienne,* and gave it to Blondeau to carry into town to Marie-Catherine.

That task completed, giddy with anticipation, I gathered my personal possessions into a cloth traveling bag—a brush and comb, a book to read, my quill and sealing wax. When I glanced up to see Maman rolling my hosiery in swaths of linen, tying them with ribbons, a dread came over me, one I couldn't fathom. Taking the hosiery from her, I tucked them into the oak chest, my throat tight with unexpected grief.

That evening candles lit the room with a warm, cozy glow, their flames flickering in the breeze from the open windows. Maman and I sat together.

"You will need money for your journey." She handed me a leather pouch filled with coins. "And this to keep your complexion safe from wind and sun."

She held up a vizard mask made of buckram. I knew from the gazettes it was fashionable for noblewomen to wear such face coverings when they were outdoors. The mask was fronted with black velvet and lined on the inside with satin. "Maman, where did you get this?"

"It was given to me many years ago. You can see it has hardly been used. You might be glad to have one at court."

Holding the mask to my face, I struck a comical pose, winking through the eyeholes. Maman laughed so much it caused a coughing fit, which brought Tatie from the kitchen with a steaming cup of chicory water laced with honey.

"Mercy!" Tatie said, scowling at my masked face. "Such a sight!" With a wag of her head, she disappeared back into the kitchen.

"You might need these as well." Maman handed me a satinwood keepsake box. Inside were a pearl necklace and a pair of pearl-drop earrings. I gulped. They were quite expensive. I'd only seen her wear them once. At Papa's funeral. "I think they will go well with the blue silk gown," she said. The one King Louis had sent.

I nodded and slipped the precious jewelry back into the box.

Last, she held out two small, framed sketches, one of her and the one of Papa that she kept on her toilette table.

"Oh, Maman! Are you sure you want to part with this?" I fingered the miniature of Papa.

"His image is forever in my heart. This one is yours now." She took my hand. "Promise me you will return home as soon as you can."

"I will." I squeezed her hands. "This is where my heart belongs."

CHAPTER SIXTEEN

"Madame! Mademoiselle!" Blondeau called from the doorway. "It's here. They've sent a coach and four!"

Rushing to the front window, I let out a little yelp when I saw the shiny black carriage with the golden fleur-de-lys emblazoned on the side. Two pairs of graceful chestnut horses stood harnessed to it, their coats shimmering in the morning sun. The coachman, the postillion, a footman, and an outrider all wore red, blue, and white livery, royal colors. A dray wagon hitched to a pair of sturdy roans pulled up behind them.

My stomach twitched as if filled with Blondeau's bees. I glanced over my shoulder at Maman putting last-minute items into my travel chest. Despite the giddiness that had me dancing in circles at odd moments, my heart clutched to think I was leaving her behind.

And what of Etienne? What would he think when he read my letter? Would he be happy for me? Or offended because I hadn't given him my answer to his marriage proposal? I breathed in deeply, willing the turmoil in my stomach and head to settle.

Maman stood alongside me now at the window. After a moment, she heaved a sigh, straightened her shoulders, and turned to Blondeau. "Get one of the men to help you take the chest out. Tatie, where is the bread and cheese we prepared?"

Blondeau called to the footman, and together they carried the chest and several small bags out to the wagon. Then they fetched the bees, loading a half dozen crates of the mounded straw skeps, the men shaking their heads and swatting while they worked. Tatie carried out wrapped parcels of food with carafes of cider.

Maman handed me my cloak and travel bag. "Do you have everything? What about the money purse? Tatie, is there enough cheese in there?" Her voice rose in pitch.

I grabbed her by the arms. "Maman, it's all right. I have what I need." Throwing my cloak over my shoulders, I looked at her wan face with a moment of hesitation.

"Write to me as soon as you get there," she said.

"I will. I promise. Tatie and Blondeau will take good care of me."

"I know." She kissed my cheeks.

"Maman. I so wish you could go with me." I wrapped her in a fierce hug.

She held me tightly, then gently pushed me away, her expression stoic. "Paris awaits."

Outside, we greeted the neighbors who had come to see me off.

Marie-Barbe bobbed her head. "Don't worry. I'll watch over your mother."

"Merci beaucoup!" I gave her a quick, awkward hug.

I was moved nearly to tears when several neighbors offered me sweets or dried fruit for the journey. It had not occurred to me that my call to court would mean so much to the people who knew us.

The footman opened the carriage door. I gave Maman one last hug, before stepping up into it. Tatie, in her own new dress of black wool, climbed in after me, then Blondeau, wearing his best wool breeches and doublet. They positioned themselves on the cushioned leather seat opposite me.

A clatter in the lane caused us to crane our necks. A fiacre—a small publicly hired carriage—pulled up behind the baggage cart. Out stepped Oncle Claude, attired in an outfit of hunter green with lime green trim.

"Sylvienne!" Oncle's voice boomed. He turned to the royal footman. "Put my trunk and baggage into the cart."

"Claude, what are you doing?" Maman's eyes were wide with concern.

"My niece cannot travel to Paris without a chaperone."

Maman's expression darkened. "She has two already."

Blondeau shifted, ready to jump out of the carriage, ready to put up a fight. Tatie laid a restraining hand on his arm.

"A young lady cannot have too many escorts," Oncle Claude said. "The highway is dangerous, and the royal palace..." He twirled his walking stick then aimed it at my carriage. "Can be a bit of *le théâtre* for the uninitiated."

"Maman?" I entreated, but she was helpless to stop him as he climbed into my carriage uninvited.

Glaring at my uncle, Tatie changed seats, plopping herself next to me, forcing Oncle to sit beside Blondeau.

Once settled, Oncle doffed his feathered hat. "I am honored to escort you to the court of King Louis, ma chère nièce."

Before I could say his presence was neither necessary nor desired, the footman stepped up to provide each of us with a fur lap robe, the backing made of a kind of supple leather. Perfect for covering our legs against the early spring dampness and surprisingly soft.

"Buffalo. From the Americas," he said. He exited the coach, securing the door behind him.

Moments later the coachman shouted "Hyrrah!" and the horses lurched into motion.

I pressed my face to the glass window. Maman stood amid the throng of waving neighbors. We rounded the bend in the lane, and she was gone. I blinked. Then I remembered to breathe. Should I have left her? Did I have a choice? This was the adventure I'd dreamed of my whole life. But it wasn't just Maman I was leaving behind. Would Etienne forgive me? Would he wait for me? My thoughts were so jumbled. I closed my eyes and leaned against the leather seatback. I wouldn't be gone that long, I told myself. And this was my dream come true.

When I opened my eyes, there was Oncle Claude sitting next to the stern-faced Blondeau, his smile unnervingly broad. His fingers, entwined over the gilded knob of his walking stick, bore several thick, bejeweled rings. The tang of his lemon and lavender hair pomade mixed with oil of clove, caused my nose to twitch.

"I expect we'll have a pleasant journey," he said.

Tatie sniffed. "If the air doesn't sour overly much."

Blondeau grunted his agreement.

Oncle ignored them. He studied me for a moment. "You look nothing like your mother, but you are quite the ravishing beauty in your own right. I will have to use this…" He tapped the walking stick on the floor. "To keep the young bucks away."

Heat rising to my cheeks, I shifted my gaze to the window. I could think of nothing to say to him that wouldn't brand me as impertinent. A glimpse of the mounted outrider wearing the colors of the King and keeping pace alongside the carriage brought to mind Oncle's earlier caution. The roads could be dangerous. I was glad also for the postillion mounted on the lead horse, charged with keeping the team under control. The plodding of the horses' hooves, erratic at first, had already settled into a rhythm.

Never having been any farther than Amiens, I soaked in every nuance of the landscape—stone fences, farmhouses, cows, sheep, a deer and her fawn leaping across a field of budding clover, all under a sky mottled with thick billowy clouds that reminded me of the *neige de crème* Tatie whipped up on special occasions to top my favorite berry-filled crepes. There was so much to take in. I didn't want to miss a minute of it.

An hour later, though, I'd had enough jolting, jostling, rocking, and swaying, not to mention Oncle's incessant chatter, to last a lifetime. I heaved an exasperated sigh. "Is it long before we reach Beauvais?" That was to be our overnight stop.

Oncle Claude gave me a sidewise glance. "Our journey is still quite young. It would behoove you to exercise patience. Something to practice before you arrive at court." He offered an imperious smile.

It was all I could do to keep from sticking my tongue out at him. Likely sensing my inclination, Tatie patted my arm.

Every so often, we came up behind a farm wagon, laden with hay or crates of pigs or squawking chickens. Without slowing down, we swung around them, one time nearly running over a trio of men walking down the center of the road. Their shouted curses filled the air in our dusty wake.

Oncle dozed off, snoring, his chin bouncing on his chest. Tatie rolled her eyes. The air inside the carriage grew close, and I pulled out the vizard mask to use as a fan. Noticing my discomfort, Blondeau stood up and released a catch on the window nearest me, lowering the glass a few inches. The welcome breeze brushed my forehead.

"Merci," I said with a relieved smile.

Shortly afterward, he and Tatie both closed their eyes and soon were breathing rhythmically despite the bumpiness of the ride. Oncle's head now lolled against the back of the seat and his breath came in fits and snorts, the pockmark on his otherwise handsome face more evident than ever. He had taken off his plumed hat and hung it on a peg near the door, the jouncing yellow feather inches from tickling his nose. I studied his face, trying to find any resemblance to Papa.

He opened one eye, then the other, a smirk forming on his lips, He checked to see that Blondeau and Tatie were asleep. "This is quite an adventure you are on," he said, his voice low enough not to disturb them.

I said nothing.

"It is rather unusual that a girl from Amiens should come to the attention of the King, don't you think?"

Still, I kept silent.

"Your father, I imagine, would have been quite proud of you."

I forced myself to hold my tongue, letting my gaze drift back toward the window, hoping he would realize I wasn't interested in conversation. He persisted.

"He never spoke of how he came to be betrothed to your mother. Or why, after the death of his own beloved first wife and child, he would take a wife already...with child."

My head jerked back in astonishment. "What do you mean?"

"Ah, now you pay attention."

"What are you saying about my mother?"

He offered an ingratiating smile. "I wasn't granted the privilege of meeting the lady until after my brother's tragic death, but..."

I sucked in a breath. It still pained me to think of my father's accident.

"There were rumors."

"What kind of rumors?" I regarded him openly now.

The low rumble of Blondeau's voice interrupted his answer. "Monsieur d'Aubert was devoted to his daughter from the moment of her birth. He didn't countenance rumors then, and I won't countenance them now on his behalf." His arms crossed over his chest, Blondeau had yet to open his eyes, but there was a tone to his voice that caused Oncle to snap his mouth shut.

He glowered at Blondeau before turning to his window. I heard no more from him, but I was left wondering what his words meant.

We made one stop for a midday repast in a shaded area near the bend of a river. The men pulled hardtack from their side bags, but their eyes lit up when Tatie offered them chunks of the baguettes and cheese she had packed for our lunch, and preserved pears from Maman's orchard.

I was loath to climb back into the carriage at the end of our respite, to have to endure hours more of bumping along rutted roads, especially under Oncle's unnerving gaze. And yet, I was eager to get moving again, if only to bring our journey closer to Paris. Disquieted by Oncle's earlier words about Papa, I wondered what he had been insinuating. I suspected he was simply trying to rattle me, but I couldn't understand why.

The jouncing started again, but now my eyes drooped. Leaning my head back, I thought of Maman and her incredible story about her time at court. It was hard to believe I was on my way to Paris, that I would be a guest of King Louis, that he was my mother's cousin. It didn't concern me to learn she was born illegitimate. If anything, that circumstance made the story more chivalrous. But what was Oncle implying about her and Papa? A coldness came over me I couldn't shake, despite the comfort of the buffalo robe which I pulled closer.

The carriage lurched, jolting me out of a fitful doze. The shadows stretched long as the coachman brought the horses to a stop in the tamped-down yard of the roadhouse on the outskirts of Beauvais.

In the dining hall a serving woman in a coarse apron brought us savory bowls of mutton stew with lentils, carrots, onions, and rutabagas, along with fresh-baked bread to sop the broth.

That night Tatie and I shared a bed while Blondeau slept on a mat along the opposite wall. The drivers, postillion, footman, and the outrider crowded into a single room next door. Oncle Claude had procured a private room on the top floor, ousting the current occupant who was then forced to find refuge with our men. The words exchanged between the unhappy former lodger and the innkeeper were loud enough to rise through the floorboards.

Once things quieted down, I snuggled in next to Tatie. I wondered what kind of reception I would receive at court. What would the courtiers be like? Would I meet Madame de Montespan, King Louis's favored mistress? Were my dresses fancy enough? Would people think I was interesting, or would they find me too provincial? And there were Oncle's words again, about Maman and Papa. I shook them off as an attempt to agitate me. When I could get Tatie alone, I would ask her about it.

My eyes closed. Before I knew it, a rooster was announcing the rising sun.

"LaGrange won't be riding with us," the coachman told Blondeau as we climbed back into the carriage. "He's back in the outhouse, retching his guts out."

"Something bad in the stew?" A scowl of concern furrowed Blondeau's brow.

"Hard to say. Drank like the sluice gate was stuck open last night."

Tatie asked if we would be safe on the road without the outrider, but Oncle reminded her that both the coachman and the postillion were armed.

The sky in the east wore a rosy glow with layered clouds floating across the rising sun. Within an hour on the road, however, the entire sky was overcast. The air hung damp and heavy. I fanned the vizard mask again.

The first drops of rain splattered across the dirt-caked road. In minutes it was pounding the roof of the carriage. I worried about the men outside, but they had pulled oiled tarps over themselves, providing some protection from the torrent.

As quickly as it had started it was over, thinning to a fine mist, then stopping altogether. The sun fought to break through the clouds but with only occasional success. The road had turned to mud, a taxing slog for the horses, slowing our progress.

As we approached a heavily wooded area, the postillion shouted to the coachman.

Oncle stuck his head out the window. "What's going on?"

"An overturned wagon," the coachman said.

Oncle banged his walking stick against the carriage roof. "Keep moving! Don't stop."

I leaned to look out the window. "Shouldn't we help?"

"Sylvienne, no." Tatie tugged at my arm.

As we approached the overturned wagon, I craned my neck to get a glimpse. A hunched figure stood next to it, her head covered with a ragged shawl. "It's an old wom—"

A musket blast rent the air, causing me to jump.

The carriage came to a jolting halt. Men outside were yelling. The look of alarm on Blondeau's face sent a ripple of fear down my spine. "What's going on?"

Tatie thrust the vizard mask into my hands. "Put it on."

I jerked the mask up over my face a half moment before a man with mud-caked hair and grimy teeth pushed up against the window next to me. Tatie screamed and pulled me away from him.

CHAPTER SEVENTEEN

"Who are you?" Oncle demanded. "What do you want?"

The mud-caked bandit wrenched the carriage door open and thrust a dagger toward us, gesturing for us to get out. Blondeau climbed down first, reaching up to help me and Tatie descend the steps. He eyed the dirty man and his dagger with a wary scowl. Oncle was slow to get out, causing the bandit to growl at him.

The vizard mask still over my face, I gasped at the sight of our footman lying on the ground, his leg bleeding. Tatie put her arm around me.

The coachman and the postillion had both rushed to the footman's side. The old crone from the upturned cart strode toward us. She pulled off the shawl, revealing not a woman but another bandit, this one brandishing a pistol. Blondeau pulled Tatie and me closer to him.

"What is the meaning of this?" Oncle asked, careful to keep his distance from the brigands. "Why did you shoot our man?"

"A pretty head of hair this one has." The bandit with the dagger sidled toward me.

Blondeau thrust me behind him, Tatie closing ranks with him.

"I'll have a look at that pretty one." The bandit lurched, trying to get around him, but Blondeau kept himself between us despite the threat of the dagger.

"Let it go, Dumais," the man with the pistol said. "Just their money and jewels. We don't have time for the girl."

"Perhaps they're sewn into her skirts? I'll take my pleasure looking for them." He danced around Blondeau again, who thrust him away with a mighty push. The man came tearing at him, his dagger outstretched.

"No!" Tatie shouted. She lunged to charge the man herself, but I grabbed her arm, holding her back.

Blondeau side-stepped to avoid the dagger. The bandit sputtered with anger. He spun around to attack again, but another shot exploded from behind us. Coming to an abrupt halt, a ragged, bloody hole in his forehead, the bandit blinked in astonishment. Then he keeled over, dead.

Tatie screamed loud and long. Blondeau grabbed her and pulled her to his chest, his other arm around me, as a trio of men dressed in noble finery galloped up on horseback. The bandit who'd masqueraded in the shawl sprinted for the woods. The nobleman on horseback, spent flintlock in hand, motioned for one of his companions to give chase.

"Good man! You arrived just in time," Oncle said, his voice shaky despite his bluster. "I believe these ruffians were prepared to kill us all."

"Have you been harmed, Mademoiselle?" the nobleman asked me.

I shook my head, but his voice sounded eerily familiar. Shifting my mask to get a better look, I stiffened.

Oncle stepped in front of me. "We owe you a debt, Monsieur...?"

"Boivin. Guillaume Boivin."

I kept my face hidden as he surveyed the scene.

"One of our men has been shot." Blondeau motioned to where the footman lay on the edge of the road, his fellow journeymen squatting next to him.

"Where are you headed?" Boivin asked.

"Paris." Oncle stepped closer. "The royal palace."

Blondeau grimaced. "I've been asked to lend my bees to the royal orangerie." He motioned back toward our dray which had halted not far behind the carriage. He didn't mention me or my royal invitation, for which I was grateful.

Oncle looked as if he wanted to say more, but Blondeau scowled at him.

The man who'd given chase to the lone bandit trotted back to our group. "He's gone. Likely knows these woods too well."

Boivin nodded. "Help the wounded man into their dray." He turned to Blondeau. "We're headed to Paris ourselves. We'll accompany you to make sure you are not bothered again."

Blondeau nodded appreciatively.

Oncle bowed. "Merci, Monsieur Boivin. Your kindness will not be forgotten."

How could he be so obsequious? Anger replaced my fear. But of course, my uncle didn't know who our "rescuer" was. Or what he had done to Perrette. A pall of dread enshrouded me at the thought of being in the company of this man, beholden to him. And what if he were to see my face? Would he recognize me?

I kept close to Blondeau as Boivin's men helped lift our footman onto the wagon, a portion of the discarded shawl knotted around his bleeding leg.

Blondeau ushered Tatie back into the carriage. He was about to reach for my arm when Boivin beat him to it. In my haste to avoid him, I lost my grip on the vizard, exposing my face for the briefest of moments.

Boivin looked at me even more curiously now. "Have we met?"

"I think not." I put a foot on the first step, my heart thudding.

Boivin kept his hand on my arm. "I believe we have. If I recall, you are rather talented with a pitchfork."

I jerked my arm away and hastened into the carriage, sliding as close to Tatie as possible. Oncle pushed past Blondeau to climb in after me. Settling himself into his seat, he lifted his walking stick and waved it affably at Boivin and his men.

"What was he saying about a pitchfork?" Oncle stuck his hand into the space between the seat and the wall of the carriage.

"I have no idea." I had to work to keep my voice steady.

To my astonishment, he pulled his jeweled rings from the crevasse. I had been too distracted earlier to see him shove them out of sight. One by one he slid the rings back onto his fingers.

As the carriage lurched into motion again, I thought of how Papa had climbed onto the roof of our house to protect me from the rain.

Oncle's only care seemed to be protecting his precious jewelry. I turned away in disgust, only to see Boivin mount his horse and position it alongside the carriage.

As the sun began its late afternoon descent, my eyes grew heavy. I must have dozed because when I opened them again the road had become busy with traffic in both directions. Carriages and wagons trundled past peddlers with goods-laden wheelbarrows, men in military uniforms, families, the older children walking, the youngest in arms or riding on older boys' backs. Soldiers on horseback kicked up dirt in the faces of those on foot. Clusters of cottages littered both sides of the road.

"Paris soon! The largest city in all of Europe," Oncle said. "Easily a half million people."

"How does anyone know how many people live in a place so large?" Tatie asked.

I smirked when my uncle scowled at having his source of knowledge questioned.

Before long we passed through city gates and down narrow, crowded streets set with paving stones. The sky grew darker. Tatie gripped my hand. It wasn't safe to be out after dark in any city, much less one as large as Paris.

To my wonderment, however, men in royal raiment moved along the Parisian streets, lowering large glass lanterns from poles set every twenty paces or so. They lit the lanterns, then raised them back up. The thoroughfares glowed with a soft light. I had never encountered anything so magical.

My eyes teared up—but not from the beauty. Rather, from the stench of the Parisian air. At home in Amiens, I would wrinkle my nose each time I encountered the fetid smell of horse droppings or urine puddles. Here, however, to keep from gagging at the reek of open sewage, I had to push my face deep into the lavender nosegays Oncle purchased at a roadside stand. Was this the trade-off for having so many people living in one city?

Everywhere buildings, roads, and bridges were under construction. Despite the late hour, workmen bustled about shouting to one another. Draft horses pulled wagons full to the brim with lumber, cobblestones, and bricks, the clopping of their hooves competing with the clank of hammers against stone.

Our carriage came to a stop in front of a large, imposing edifice. Row upon row of windows framed by ornate cornices glowed with calm authority. The palace. My view was abruptly blocked by Boivin's horse. I pulled my vizard mask up over my face when Oncle pushed the carriage window down to hail him.

"We'll be taking our leave here," Boivin said, his horse prancing nervously.

"Merci, Monsieur," Oncle called out. "If we don't see you again, fare well."

"You never know when our paths will cross again. Until then..." Boivin offered a quick salute in my direction.

"So handsome!" Tatie murmured. "Perhaps we will meet him again."

Gritting my teeth, I sincerely hoped not.

We pulled into line behind a half dozen coaches and wagons, all with passengers waiting to disembark or to unload cargo in the vast courtyard fronting the Palais des Tuileries, the Paris residence of King Louis XIV. I leaned out the window, fascinated by the frenzy of courtiers and palace staff rushing to greet people, carrying baggage, dashing hither and to in the light from the courtyard torches.

After a brief wait, a liveried servant waved our carriage into place and a rush of baggage handlers descended on our dray to help our wounded footman and to unload our belongings. A palace footman stepped forward to open our carriage door, offering a hand to help me step down. A short, officious-looking man in a black waistcoat and breeches bustled up.

"*Bienvenue au Palais des Tuileries,*" he said.

I presented my invitation.

"Ah! Mademoiselle d'Aubert, I have been expecting you." Bowing from the waist, he said, "*Je m'appelle Carufel, à votre service.*"

"This is my uncle, Monsieur Claude d'Aubert. And my..." I didn't know what to call Blondeau and Tatie. Servants, I suppose, but I'd never thought of them that way. "My other chaperones, Madame and Monsieur Blondeau."

"We are here at the request of King Louis," Oncle said, pointing with his walking stick toward the paper I'd handed over.

"Of course. The men will bring your belongings along."

"I will continue on to the gardens," Blondeau said.

"Ah, yes. The bees." Carufel glanced at the crated skeps where one lone bee had escaped and was harassing the baggage handlers. "I believe the drayman knows the way to the gardening headquarters."

"How long will you be?" Tatie asked.

Blondeau shrugged. "A day or two, perhaps. No more, I would guess. Just long enough to get the bees settled. You'll stay close to our *jeune fille*?"

"As close as the ties on my apron." Tatie gave a sidewise glance in Oncle's direction.

Blondeau nodded, bowed to our little group, then headed off to the dray.

Carufel inclined his head. "If you follow me, I will show you to the guest quarters."

Tatie, Oncle, and I set off across the courtyard, hustling to keep up with him, Tatie gawking open-mouthed at the palace before us. A giddiness overcame me, and I twirled once in delight at the magnificence of it all.

Stepping into the grand foyer, my eyes were drawn to the gilded ceiling embedded with opulent paintings. Now *I* was gawking. Chandeliers and wall sconces illuminated portraits of royal ancestors interspersed amid landscapes and Old Testament scenes.

"Come on!" Oncle waved us forward with his walking stick.

We caught up to Carufel, dodging servants scrubbing floors, others polishing candelabras, lugging furniture, carrying trays of food, racing after the throng of noblemen and women who swept past us in their elegant silk justaucorps and dresses.

Carufel led us up a staircase to an expansive corridor with more doors than I had ever seen in one place. He opened one and ushered us in. "Your quarters, Mademoiselle and Madame."

Stepping into a room twice as large as my bedchamber in Amiens, I drew in a deep breath. A bed with four ornately carved posters dominated the room. It was hung with cream-colored silk valences embroidered with birds and flowers in bright blues, greens, and reds. Matching window curtains framed a view of the courtyard. In front of the window was a writing desk not unlike Maman's. At the sight of it, I made a silent promise to write to her as soon as possible.

Oncle nudged past me, surveying the room with a critical eye. "This will do for the time being. I assume my accommodations will be not far from *la demoiselle's*?"

Carufel inclined his head. "As we were not notified that you would be accompanying Mademoiselle d'Aubert, we do not have a room made up for you. But if you will grace us with your patience, I am sure we can accommodate you in one of our overflow guestrooms."

"Overflow?" Oncle seemed offended.

"Temporary, of course." Carufel turned toward me and pointed to a second, smaller bed tucked along the wall on the far side of the poster bed. "For Madame, your chaperone."

At that moment, a girl not much older than myself stepped out of the shadows.

Carufel nodded toward her. "Lisette will unpack your belongings and attend to all your needs."

"Bonjour, Mademoiselle." She curtsied. "May I take your wrap?" Lisette lifted the cloak from my shoulders, then took Tatie's. She opened a door and disappeared into another, smaller room which contained an armoire, a dressing table, and a cushioned bench.

"Lisette will bring your dinner to your room this evening. Would you like Monsieur d'Aubert to dine with you?"

Tired from the journey, the last thing I wanted was his company at dinner, but I couldn't be rude. "Yes, of course."

"Very well." Carufel nodded at Lisette who had reappeared. "In the morning, after you break your fast, you will have your first audience with the King and Queen. Do you have a gown appropriate for the occasion?"

"One was sent along with my invitation. I assume that will do?"

"Ah! Of course. I will take my leave then. Send Lisette if you have need of my service." He bowed, then inclined his head toward Oncle. "If you will follow me, Monsieur, I will get you established in your quarters before you rejoin the ladies."

As soon as the heavy door closed behind them, I spun around, taking in my new accommodations. "What do you think, Ta—" I spotted Lisette eyeing me curiously. "Madame Blondeau. Can you imagine what Maman would think to see me in such quarters?"

"I cannot." Tatie gazed about, overwhelmed.

"Mademoiselle, do you have need of the chamber pot before you change to take your rest?" Lisette asked.

"Rest?"

"You must be weary from your journey. Wouldn't you like to nap before your dinner arrives?"

"Indeed, she should rest," Tatie announced. "And I would not mind making use of the chamber pot myself."

Lisette nodded and ran to fetch a pewter pot, directing us to a small, leather-covered stool with a hole in the top. She slid the pot under the stool and invited me to sit. When I had finished relieving myself, she offered me a strip of linen to clean with.

When it was her turn, Tatie lifted her skirt with elation and positioned herself on the stool. Afterward, while she was still adjusting her skirts, Lisette grabbed the chamber pot and took it away to dispose of its contents.

"I feel like a queen!" Tatie declared, holding her hands up to her cheeks.

I hugged her. "If Maman could only be here."

"You must rest, and I will unpack." Tatie tugged the bed covering away from the pillows.

"What about you? You must be tired, too."

Despite looking exhausted, Tatie refused to lie down. By the time Lisette returned, she had ushered me onto the bed and covered me with a light throw. I had never rested my head on a pillow so soft. I lay with my eyes open, gazing up at the bed valance, listening to Tatie and Lisette whisper as they unpacked my trunk and other bags, thinking about the wonder of being in Paris and here at the royal palace. My eyes closed.

A tap on my shoulder brought me fully awake.

"Mademoiselle, your supper has arrived. As has the gentleman," Lisette said.

I had been asleep for an hour. I scurried off the bed, straightened my skirt and hair, and nodded for Lisette to open the door.

"You'd think a palace such as this would have better accommodations for their guests," Oncle said as he strode in. He had changed into a brown doublet with matching breeches. He set his walking stick aside and eyed the spread of food — cheeses, sliced pork, bread, a plate of fruit, and a bowl of sugared almonds — that had been arranged on a small table in the center of the room and set with three chairs. "I suppose this will do," he said with an affected sigh.

He waited for me to sit before seating himself. Then he eyed the third chair suspiciously. Tatie hovered off to the side, unsure what to do.

"Madame Blondeau always takes her place at table with Maman and myself," I said, indicating with my hand she should sit.

Tatie gave Oncle a wary, sidewise look, but took her seat.

Then something occurred to me. "But when will you eat?" I asked Lisette.

"When you no longer need my services for the evening, Mademoiselle."

"Oh." I looked around. "And where do you sleep?"

"In the clothes chamber, of course."

I exchanged glances with Tatie.

Oncle groused throughout the meal about his accommodations, the food, what he'd seen of Paris and of the palace so far. Tatie said nothing, eating with her eyes downcast.

I listened as politely as I could, but when he said, "And what of that annoying man, Carufel? What do you make of him?" I could not hold back.

"I find him to be quite agreeable. And as he is our liaison with all things royal, I plan to treat him with the utmost respect while I am here."

Oncle sniffed in derision. He pointed at Tatie with his knife. "I have a tear in the sleeve of my green doublet. I must have snagged it on a nail in that abominable carriage."

"No doubt when you were grousing 'round for the rings you tucked into the cushion." She glared at him now.

Oncle's visage darkened. Tatie did not back down.

Thinking it prudent to avert an altercation, I said, "I'm afraid our sewing kit is buried in the bottom of my traveling trunk. Perhaps Carufel could recommend someone who could attend to it for you."

He speared a piece of pork and brought it to his lips, all the while muttering, "What good is it to have brought her along?" He thrust the morsel into his mouth.

Tatie stood up abruptly, grabbed her empty plate, and stalked away from the table.

"I can repair the sleeve for you, Monsieur," Lisette said in a timid voice. "If you will allow me."

Oncle nodded, satisfied. "I'll have someone deliver it in the morning."

Carufel knocked on our door to ask if we would like to view the gardens.

"In the dark?" I asked.

"I believe you will find them quite illuminated." His eyes twinkled like a cat with a secret.

I nodded eagerly. I loved exploring, and I suspected this would be Lisette's only opportunity to partake of a meal. Tatie begged off, offering to help Lisette clean up after our supper.

Out onto the terrace, the sight before me took my breath away. Under the star-studded sky with the rising half-moon, the Tuileries Gardens stretched out on either side of a wide central lane with hedge mazes and lamplit promenades. Two immense ponds, each with a fountain, bisected the lane. Even at this late hour, people strolled along the paths, the hum of voices and burble of laughter rising to greet us. *Oh, Maman! How I wish you could see this.* The garden lamps below mirrored the stars above. So many couples wandering in the moonlight. I sighed, wishing it was Etienne at my side, instead of Oncle, gazing out over the gardens so alluring with the scent of magnolias on the warm breeze.

"Can we walk a bit?" I asked.

"You can explore the gardens tomorrow," Oncle said, punctuating his words against the stone steps with his walking stick. "For now, it is time for you to be in bed."

At my groan of disappointment, Carufel cleared his throat. "Perhaps your uncle is not wrong. I will be fetching you in the morning for your audience with the King and Queen."

With reluctance, I followed them back into the palace.

After bidding Oncle and Carufel, "*Bonne nuit*," I submitted to Lisette's ministering as she helped me undress and slip into my nightgown. Such an odd feeling to have someone else handle my clothes and touch my body.

Tatie waved her off when Lisette offered to do the same for her. Later, when Lisette rushed the chamber pot out of the room, Tatie turned to me. "That uncle of yours!"

"What about him?" I was weary, and he was the last thing I wanted to think about.

"Have you seen the way he looks at that girl?"

"At who? What do you mean?"

She grunted. "At Lisette. I'm surprised his tongue doesn't loll out like the dog he is."

Lisette returned just then, preventing me from questioning Tatie further. The truth is, I hadn't noticed. But I would make a point to pay attention now.

I climbed into the oversized bed and pulled the blanket up to my chin. The mattress was soft and downy, but I found myself staring up at the bed canopy, my eyes refusing to close despite my fatigue. I had shared Maman's bed for as long as I could remember. On the journey here, I shared with Tatie. Now I felt terribly alone.

Lisette had crawled onto the palette she'd made for herself in the clothes closet. I could hear Tatie rustling her covers as she settled onto the trundle near my bed. My eyes drifted to the beam of moonlight streaming in through a crack in the curtains.

"Tatie?"

"Yes? Are you still awake?"

"Will you come up and sleep with me?"

There was no response for a long moment. Then I could feel her climbing onto the bed. As she settled next to me, she patted my hand before rolling onto her side. Her gentle snores filled the space between us almost immediately.

CHAPTER EIGHTEEN

I awoke to the soft shake of Lisette's hand on my shoulder. Sunlight streamed through the open window. The aroma of fresh bread, eggs, and cheese greeted me as I stretched under my coverlet. Tatie had already risen; I was alone in the bed.

"You must get ready to meet the King and Queen," Lisette said.

"Oh!" I threw back the covers. Hurrying to relieve myself in the chamber pot, I called out to Tatie to please find my necklace and earrings.

After I'd washed my hands and face with the bowl of rose water Lisette had ready for me, I reached for a fresh chemise. Lisette took it from me and slid it over my head. Then she tied a bib of linen around my neck so I could eat my breakfast without dirtying myself. Again, it was disconcerting to let someone wait on me this way. The girl's hands were soft yet firm, and she seemed to know what I needed at every turn.

When I finished eating, she pulled my skirted petticoats over my head and down around my waist, cinching them in the back. While Tatie laid out the sky-blue gown, I slid silk leggings up over my knees, blushing when Lisette insisted on tying the braided garters to hold them in place. As she slipped the simple black shoes Tatie handed her onto my feet, I thought of Etienne in whose family shop they had been made. What would he think of me now, dressing with the help of a maid? Preparing to meet the King and Queen of France?

Lisette lifted the blue silk skirt and pulled it over my head and down over the petticoats. Last she held out the matching whale-boned bodice for me to slip my arms through, lacing it up the front—a bit too tightly, causing my breasts to bulge over the top.

I sat in front of the dressing-table mirror while she combed and brushed my hair into a bundle of compliant curls, allowing two tendrils to stray down either side of my face. Afterward, Tatie draped Maman's pearls around my neck, but I insisted on putting on my own earrings.

"Oh my!" Tatie said, a mixture of pride and worry furrowing her brow.

Lisette turned me toward the looking glass. I blinked. Except for the discomfort of the too-tight stays, everything was perfect.

Carufel arrived with flawless timing. He studied me silently, a smile creasing his face. "King Louis will be pleased."

Lisette gave me a confident nod as Carufel ushered me out the door. I was surprised Oncle had not come to accompany me this morning, but also relieved.

Carufel led the way along the *Grande Galerie* connecting the royal residences of the Palais des Tuileries with the chambers of government in the Palais du Louvre. We passed a steady stream of noisome and brightly dressed courtiers, soldiers, servants, pages, men carrying musical instruments, even priests in black cassocks.

"As a matter of protocol, it is forbidden to sit in the presence of the King or the Queen unless invited to do so," Carufel instructed. I thought of my mother, on her stool at King Louis's feet in our sitting room. "You will curtsy and not rise until bidden to do so."

So many rules. Would I remember them all? We approached a set of gilded doors. Two blue-uniformed guards stood stiffly at attention. One pulled open the door.

"You may address him as Your Majesty, Monsieur le Roi, or Sire." Carufel entered first and handed a card to a man whose black attire was offset by a squared, white collar — the Master of Ceremonies.

"Mademoiselle Sylvienne d'Aubert d'Amiens!" the Master of Ceremonies called out.

Just then Oncle appeared. The Master of Ceremonies looked confounded.

I steeled my face to hide my embarrassment. "And Monsieur Claude d'Aubert d'Amiens," I whispered.

The Master of Ceremonies looked dubious, but at Carufel's nod he announced Oncle Claude as well.

Oncle held out his hand. Reluctantly, I placed my hand on his. He twirled his walking stick once, and we entered the royal audience chamber.

A throng of courtiers dressed in a mosaic of colors crowded the audience chamber, all craning their necks. Their buzz of whispers set my cheeks ablaze. Had I committed a faux pas already? They formed a corridor of sorts through which Oncle and I traversed, hand upon hand. My nose wrinkled at the unexpected array of *parfums* wafting from the courtiers. Suddenly light-headed, I was gratified for once to be supported by the hand of my uncle as we approached the royal couple.

Sitting on a crimson damask-covered armchair laden with gold tassels, and surrounded by several large mastiffs and two small black and white spaniels, King Louis offered a welcoming smile. Next to him, on a matching chair, Queen Marie-Thérèse observed me with critical eyes.

My heart thumped wildly as I dropped into a deep curtsy, Oncle bowing next to me. The two spaniels yipped and rushed over, tails wagging, to take my measure, then retreated at the sound of the quiet but authoritative voice I remembered from last summer.

"Rise, cousine." King Louis was even more handsome than I'd remembered. His lips were full, green eyes intense. His dark hair fell in loose curls to his shoulders. I had an inkling now why the gazettes reported that women of all ages flirted with him, hoping to be invited into his bed — much to his wife's dismay.

Queen Marie-Thérèse looked at me as if she were trying to place where she'd seen me before. Could it be she remembered that awful day in the convent chapel? Or was she sizing me up as a threat? I immediately chastised myself for the thought. I was nothing of the kind, and I was sure Queen Marie-Thérèse knew that.

"My dear wife and Queen," the King said. "I present to you *ma cousine*, who was long lost to me as was her mother with whom I spent my suckling years. Mademoiselle d'Aubert's lineage is from my late uncle, Gaston, Duc d'Orléans."

The Queen said to me. "I trust your journey was comfortable?"

"Yes, Your Majesty. The coach was a pleasure to ride in."

"And who might this be?" King Louis asked, eyeing my uncle.

Claude took a step forward and bowed a second time. "I am your humble servant, Claude d'Aubert." He puffed out his chest. "Chaperone to the daughter of my dearly departed brother."

Murmurs from the courtiers rose.

"Ah. Well. Thank you for delivering her safely."

Oncle opened his mouth to speak again, but the King stood and held out his hand to me. The room fell silent again.

"Shall we walk in the garden?"

Gasps of astonishment bubbled from the courtiers. My blush deepened at this new attention. I took His Majesty's hand. It was firm and warm, if a bit delicate, his fingers clad with rings encrusted with diamonds, rubies, and sapphires. On one pinky was a simple, but elegant signet ring, silver, with three fleurs-de-lys surrounding an ornate letter L.

I glanced awkwardly at Oncle, who offered me a proud smile of encouragement.

The Queen rose and took Louis's other hand. "I am tired," she said in her heavily accented French. "With your permission, Husband, I will retire to my chambers."

"With my blessing." He kissed the back of her fingers, then handed her off to one of her ladies-in-waiting.

A swarm of Spanish-speaking women surrounded her Majesty like a cloud of bees. They floated her out of the audience chamber, their buzz-like chatter drifting behind them.

Upon the Queen's exit, a woman with hair the color of corn silk, thick and curling over her shoulders, stepped out of the crowd. To my surprise, she assumed the very place the Queen had just vacated alongside King Louis. There was no undue reaction from the courtiers. Was this the Marquise de Montespan? The maîtresse-en-titre, whom I'd read so much about? Her body was curvaceous, her voluptuous breasts swelled from the top of her bejeweled bodice. She gave me a sidelong glance, her languid blue eyes appraising me as we walked toward the door.

"Your cousin, Sire," she said in a voice just loud enough for everyone to hear. "She is quite lovely...in a provincial sort of way. How long will you keep her at court?"

King Louis squeezed my hand. "For as long as she amuses me."

CHAPTER NINETEEN

We stepped off the veranda and into the garden I had viewed the night before, King Louis taking my hand and tucking it into the crook of his elbow. Madame de Montespan possessed his other arm, her bearing imperial as she walked. A sea of people bowed and curtsied before us in an unending wave that both intimidated and exhilarated me.

"How fares your mother?" King Louis asked, leading the way down the boulevard lined with magnolia trees, the spaniels and mastiffs running ahead of us. Daffodils and tulips filled sculpted beds.

"She has not been well. I worry about her."

"What ails her?"

"She has had a cough all winter. She tires quickly and eats little."

Louis let out a long, slow breath. After a moment, he said, "I will send one of my physicians to attend to her."

"Merci, Sire." His words had touched me. "That is kind of you."

"She is dear to me," he said.

We made small talk the rest of the way to the fountain. As we walked around it, I glimpsed Oncle trailing behind us, surrounded by a bevy of women, one on each arm prattling with animated coquetry.

"It looks like Mademoiselle d'Aubert's uncle has lost no time acquainting himself with the ladies of the court," Madame de Montespan observed.

"Fancies himself a peacock, perhaps." King Louis grimaced.

"Ah, but when his plumage is all plucked away…" Her voice took on a wry tone. "What do you think we'll find underneath?"

Louis snorted. "Not much of substance, I would imagine."

I giggled.

He chuckled as he steered us away from my uncle. Apparently, King Louis had as little desire to engage with my uncle as I did. "Ah, look who's come out to join us," he said.

A group of courtiers strolled toward us, their lavender, rose, and chartreuse attire vying for attention with the flowers in the spring beds. Their chatter drifted on the air.

"Brother!" one of the women called out. She separated herself from the group and approached the King. He embraced her warmly. Unimaginably thin, she was not beautiful but somehow beguiling. "And who is this?" she asked, her eyes bright with curiosity. "The country cousin all the court is whispering about?"

Her words took me by surprise. Why would the court be whispering about me? I had only just arrived and was nobody of consequence. I offered a shy smile and a quick curtsy.

"Minette, my darling," Louis said to her. "Are you enjoying the sun? And yes, this is Sylvienne." He turned to me. "Minette— Madame—is my dear sister-in-law, Princess Henriette-Anne d'Angleterre."

Madame! I dropped into a deeper curtsy, embarrassed that I had not recognized her nor offered the appropriate respect. When I arose, she smiled and took both my hands.

"I have been waiting to meet you," she said. "I have only a vague memory of your mother, but she was always very kind to me."

"You knew my mother?" My heart warmed to her immediately.

"I was quite young, and she wasn't at court for long. She had returned for Louis's coronation. I was only nine, but she was so beautiful, and I wanted to be like her. It saddened me when she went away again. I never knew what happened to her."

"At long last we have found her," King Louis said, a certain warmth to his voice.

"And now this lovely creature. What a delight to have you with us, cousine." Her eyes brightened. "I am planning a soirée this evening. Just a few close friends. Will you join us?"

King Louis nodded his encouragement.

"I'd love to." I couldn't believe my good fortune to be invited to a social gathering so soon after my arrival.

"*Merveilleux!* And who is that?" She nodded toward Oncle, who had the ladies giggling.

"My uncle, Claude d'Aubert." I stammered. "He is my chaperone."

"Now, Minette," Louis chastised. "Don't be toying with him. It will serve no purpose but to aggravate my brother."

"Is that not purpose enough?" At Louis's look of chagrin, she laughed. "I will leave him to the ladies of the court. I have enough suitors to annoy my husband." She turned to me. "Tonight then. After the *grand couvert*." She bussed me on the cheek, then flittered off with her coterie.

"You are filling your calendar already." King Louis took my arm again. "I hope you will leave some time for me."

Back in my room, I grabbed Lisette's hand and twirled her in a little dance of joy. "I walked with the King! In the garden. We walked arm in arm."

Lisette's eyes widened as we spun around. After a moment, she pulled away. "Was Madame de Montespan not there?"

"She was there. Right alongside us."

Lisette seemed relieved.

Tatie frowned. "It is unseemly for His Majesty to walk about in the company of his...his..."

"Maîtresse," I said, trying to sound blasé.

"The King insists she accompany him." Lisette reached to unfasten my pearls. "He won't have it any other way. Will you nap?"

Nodding, I yawned, still exhausted from the coach journey.

Carufel had said he would fetch me that evening for dinner, the grand couvert. I asked Tatie to help me with the azure gown I had worn that morning.

"No, Mademoiselle!" Lisette looked horrified. "A lady must never wear the same gown for dinner she wore in the morning."

A new rule. "The rose-colored one then?"

She nodded, satisfied, and helped me dress again. She was putting the finishing touches to my hair when we heard the knock at the door.

"That must be Monsieur Carufel," Tatie said, folding my day clothes.

"Let him in." I gazed into the looking glass Lisette held for me, aware of my many flaws. When I turned to greet Carufel, I saw it was Oncle who entered, wearing yet another change of clothing, this time a deep blue velvet. I hid my disgruntlement.

"Dinner is with the royal family tonight." He attempted to buss me on the cheek.

I sidestepped. "That is what I am told."

"Excellent, excellent." But his look was critical. "Are you wearing *that*?"

"Is something wrong with my dress?"

"It's rather...bucolic. Don't you think?" His attention drifted. I realized his eyes were trailing Lisette as she moved about. His tongue flicked out to lick his lips before he turned back to me. "Are you expecting Carufel?"

"He is to escort me to the Queen's dining room." I was the one distracted now, noticing Tatie had positioned herself between Oncle and Lisette.

Another rap on the door.

"That must be him," Oncle said. "I will accompany you, of course."

Lisette scurried to open the door and immediately dipped into a curtsy. Yet again it was not Carufel, but a much taller man who stepped through the door. He wore a black wig cascading with curls and ribbons, several strands of pearls around his neck, and matching pearl drop earrings. A large circle of cerise powder highlighted each cheek, and his lips were colored with a bright red cream that matched the red of his waistcoat and breeches. Oncle coughed to hide his snigger. Tatie stared wide-eyed but managed a quick curtsy.

The visitor lifted a lace-cuffed hand to his chin and regarded me, his finger tapping a black velvet beauty patch affixed to his cheek. "You look nothing like I remember her." His voice dripped with disappointment.

"Who?"

"Your mother."

It was then I realized who he was. I dropped into a deep curtsy. "*Monsieur!*" I addressed King Louis's brother with the title he was known by at court. When he bade me rise, I added, "She told me I favor my father."

"Then he must be a rakishly handsome fellow. It translates well into the female form."

I felt the all-too-familiar heat rising to my cheeks.

Oncle stepped forward. "And you are…?" His voice startled me into an introduction.

"Oncle Claude, this is Monsieur le Duc d'Orléans — Prince Philippe."

Oncle's eyes went wide. He quickly bowed from the waist. "Monsieur. I apologize. Claude d'Aubert, at your service. La demoiselle's uncle and chaperone."

"Hmm." Philippe's gaze swept over him dismissively. To me he said, "Perhaps you would allow me to accompany you to dinner. I am curious to get to know *la jeune cousine* of whom my brother is so enamored." He extended an arm.

Unable to hide my delight, I placed my fingers on his wrist, just the tips, as I had seen the courtiers do. "You are very kind." I batted my eyelashes at him, attempting to mimic the ladies of the court.

He laughed, moving my hand to the crook of his arm. "There is no need to play the coquette, ma chérie. You will garner more attention from the men here than you'll know what to do with just by being yourself. And cause extreme vexation among the ladies."

Outside my door stood a crowd of courtiers waiting for Monsieur. A man with a mustache and long golden curls draping his shoulders leaned against the far wall looking studiously bored. The women in the group eyed me warily, dipping in the slightest of curtsies, while the men bowed with exaggerated pomp.

"I present to you…" Prince Philippe flourished his hand in dramatic fashion. "Ma cousine, Mademoiselle Sylvienne."

"Bonsoir, Mademoiselle!" The men's voices rang out in eager greetings.

All except the one still leaning against the wall. His voice was an insolent drawl. "I suppose she's pretty enough. Will likely get eaten alive at court."

Monsieur swatted at the man's head as we passed. "No naughtiness, Lorraine."

The courtiers fell into step behind us, crowding out my uncle. The man called Lorraine let several moments pass before pushing himself away from the wall and following.

Unlike Carufel, who always hastened to get from one location to another, the Prince preferred to stroll. Obviously aware of all eyes on him, he treated our journey through the palace as a pageant, he and I in the lead, his devotees trailing like bright peacocks.

Carufel, waiting at the door of Queen Marie-Thérèse's dining chamber, bowed as we approached. "Mademoiselle Sylvienne will sit with the royal family," he said. Then, pointing to a door further down, "Monsieur d'Aubert, you are welcome to join those who wish to observe."

Oncle, affronted, complained, "I am her uncle, her chaperone. She is my charge."

"Oui. But she is cousin to the King. You are not."

Oncle looked to Monsieur for help, but the Prince only shrugged before ushering me into the sumptuous room. I had a momentary pang of guilt for the relief I felt that Oncle would not be at table with us, but my discomfiture was short-lived. To my astonishment, crowded at the far end of the room stood a throng of nobles gawking at the royal table.

"Pay no attention to the flock," Monsieur said in an undertone. "One of the disadvantages of royal life."

"Why are they here?"

"A dividend granted to devotees of the monarchy. Annoying, but unavoidable."

A semi-circle of elegantly dressed dowagers perched on brocade-cushioned ottomans served as a barrier between those standing and the royal diners.

"The duchesses," Monsieur whispered before handing me off to a page. "Oodles of money. Never turned away."

The page escorted me to my seat—a cushioned stool at the farthest end of one of the linen-draped tables set to form the arms of a U-shape. Philippe strutted to the head table and stood behind an exquisitely carved straight-back chair to the left of the red velvet, royal armchairs. Other members of the royal family, who I would eventually learn were princes and princesses of the blood, drifted in and stood behind their assigned seats.

Before long, Madame de Montespan entered. A momentary hush descended as the courtiers in the gallery bowed and curtsied. King Louis's favorite took her place behind a chair next to what would be the King's.

Moments later the banging of halberds on the floor preceded a guard who called out, "Le Roi! Le Roi!" The dowager duchesses rose. A hush fell again.

King Louis and Queen Marie-Thérèse entered followed by the two spaniels. Along with the others, I dipped in obeisance. The royal couple sat, a signal to the rest of us diners to sit as well. On the King's right, Madame de Montespan smiled brightly, her blue eyes surveying the crowd of courtiers. Philippe sat to the left of the Queen, next to him a middle-aged woman I recognized from popular sketches—la Grande Mademoiselle, the Duchess of Montpensier, one of Louis's many legitimate cousins. She surveyed me with curious eyes. With a start, I realized she must be Maman's half-sister. Gaston, the late Duc d'Orléans was her father as well as Maman's. Was she sizing me up as yet another usurping bastard relative? For, of course, she had several already.

Looking out at the gaggle of observers, I realized with a shock that the crowd had grown in size and most appeared to be watching me. At the back of the throng stood Oncle, glowering. Disconcerted, I focused my eyes on my hands in my lap.

"Madame is not joining us for dinner?" King Louis asked Philippe.

I looked up now, realizing with dismay that there was no place set for Princess Henriette.

"Brother, my wife is indisposed. She sends her regrets and apology."

King Louis frowned. It was difficult to tell if he was annoyed or disappointed. My shoulders sagged. Henriette's invitation must have been no more than a polite gesture. Certainly she had no intention of introducing her illegitimate country cousin to her coterie.

"And you," King Louis said to la Grande Mademoiselle. "Are you feeling well today?"

"I am most well, Sire." She raised an eyebrow. "We have someone new at the table?"

"Our new-found kinswoman, Mademoiselle Sylvienne d'Aubert d'Amiens. Her mother, Isabelle, was a playmate in the royal nursery. Perhaps you recall her."

The Duchess sniffed. "I have a vague recollection of a third urchin adding to the racket of the playroom." She looked across the table at me, eyebrows arched. "And how do you find Paris, Mademoiselle Sylvienne d'Aubert d'Amiens?"

"Quite...s-splendid, Mademoiselle." My voice shook, heat rose to my face. But when I realized she had referred to my mother as an urchin, my hackles rose. I opened my mouth to tell her that people from Amiens appeared to have better manners than Parisians, but the majordomo marched in leading a parade of uniformed footmen with tureens of soup, thus saving me from making a fool of myself. When the footmen exited, a servant stepped forward and dipped a spoon into the King's tureen, brought it to his own mouth, and swallowed. He waited a moment then — not having keeled over from poisoning, I assumed — bowed to his Majesty.

Another servant ladled the soup into the royal bowls. And then the rest of us were served. The aroma was heavenly. I dipped my spoon into the creamy broth and brought it to my lips. It had an earthy yet sweet taste but with a hint of sage and thyme.

Before I had even finished my soup, platters of fish were set on the tables. A footman offered me a plate of shells. In a panic, I realized they were oysters. The market in Amiens sold oysters, but they were very expensive, and I had never tried them. To be honest, I didn't know how. I watched the others loosen the meat with their spoons then slurp it out of the shell. I poked at mine. The slimy look of it made me cringe.

The Marquise de Montespan smirked across the expanse of the table. "Your little country cousin appears to be unfamiliar with Parisian cuisine, Sire."

My spoon stopped half-way to my mouth as I realized everyone had turned to look at me. I set the spoon down and put my hands in my lap again, willing myself to disappear.

"Eat, cousine! Eat! Like this." King Louis lifted a shell to his lips and slurped noisily.

Philippe offered me an encouraging smile, lifted his oyster shell as if to toast me with it, then poured the meat down his throat in one quick elegant motion. No noise, no slurping.

My hand trembled as I brought the oyster shell to my lips. Tilting it, I let the meat slide into my mouth and down my throat, worried I would gag at the slippery texture. I didn't. Rather, the salty, almost buttery taste was surprisingly pleasurable.

The nobles in the gallery broke into applause. I stopped breathing for a moment, wishing to die on the spot.

But King Louis only laughed. "There is much more to come.!"

And indeed, another course was delivered to the table, silver platters heaped with roasted meats, vegetables, and breads.

Once the main course had been served, Madame de Montespan asked, "Sire, have you determined a position here at court for your little country cousin?"

I didn't know whether to be mortified that she kept calling me a country cousin or thrilled at the expectation I might stay at court for longer than a few days.

King Louis offered a steak bone to one of the spaniels, then licked his fingers. "I thought perhaps I would place her in your household."

The Marquise's eyebrows rose in astonishment. "Mine?"

"You've been plaguing me these past months, begging for a *dame or demoiselle d'honneur.*"

A quiet gasp went up from the gallery. It was well known only a queen or a princess could employ a lady-in-waiting. Offering his mistress such an office within her entourage elevated her to the status of royalty. I glanced surreptitiously at Queen Marie-Thérèse. The unhappy expression she'd worn throughout the dinner deepened to a scowl.

The Marquise de Montespan studied me openly for a long moment, then a smile curved her lips. "Yes, I think that is a lovely idea. I would be happy to take *le petit chou* under my wing and educate her in the etiquette of the court. I would hate to see such a sweet little thing embarrass you again with an unwitting faux pas such as a public hunt for oysters in their shells."

The red burned into my cheeks. Now she was calling me a little cabbage and making fun of my unfamiliarity with oysters. Murmurs wormed their way around the table, while courtiers in the gallery smirked and leaned to whisper to one another. With great fanfare, the footmen marched in with platters of candied fruits and sweetmeats. I pressed my napkin against my lips, the palace delicacies suddenly nauseously unappetizing.

Dinner over, I followed the royal family out of the Queen's dining room. My mortification subsiding, I had thought to say a few words of appreciation to Monsieur. But the insolent man with the mustache and curls had already corralled him, engaging him in intense conversation.

Scanning the crowd in the hall to see if Carufel was available to escort me back to my quarters, I caught sight of Oncle weaving his way through the press of nobles.

"Sylvienne!" If I had hoped to escape, it was too late. In the time it took to draw a breath, he was at my side. "I will walk you back to your chamber." He grasped my elbow and guided me away from the throng before I could protest. "You need tutoring regarding table manners," he said in a gruff voice. "But at least you didn't spill on yourself."

I pulled my arm from him and sped up, but he kept pace with me. "Has there been any talk of compensation?"

"Compensation?"

"A stipend. Salary. You are being awarded a position as maid of honor with the Marquise, are you not? Will there be pay involved?"

"Nothing was mentioned. Why?" I slowed my pace now.

"As your agent, it is my duty to negotiate for you."

I stopped then and confronted him. "You are not my agent."

"Someone has to represent the family."

"This is not a family matter."

He gripped my arm and propelled me into walking again. "My dear, you are young and quite naïve. I will deal with this appointment. You needn't worry. Ah, here we are at your door. I hope you have a pleasant sleep." Before I could respond, he turned and strode off.

A slow burn in my gut, I stomped through the door.

"Sylvienne!" Tatie bolted upright on the chair upon which she had fallen asleep. "Did you enjoy the dinner?"

"According to Oncle, I made a fool of myself."

"I'm sure you were a wonderful guest." Lisette emerged sleepy-eyed from the clothes closet. She had already laid my nightgown on the bed.

"I received word from Blondeau this evening," Tatie said. "He has finished setting up the beehives. He will be here tomorrow to collect me for the trip home."

"So soon? I wish you didn't have to go." As I said the words, however, I knew they weren't true. I worried about Maman and wanted Tatie to be home caring for her. More than that, I was desperate to be free of the constraints of family, and that included being out from under the watchful eye of my beloved Tatie.

"How can I leave you here with that dolt as your chaperone?" Tatie wrinkled her nose. "I don't trust him."

"You needn't worry on that account," I said. "King Louis has granted me a position here at court." An arrangement I hoped would enable me to eschew the unwelcome guardianship of my uncle.

"A position?"

"I am to be a maid of honor."

"To the Queen?" Tatie looked incredulous.

"Not the Queen." I turned away, unable to look her in the eye. "I will be serving in the household of the Marquise de Montespan."

Lisette gasped.

"A marquise?" Tatie said. "I don't understand. Who is this Montespan?" She put her hands to her mouth. "La maîtresse? No. The Queen would never allow it. Your uncle will never allow it."

"I do not think either of them have a choice in the matter. The King has decided." Yawning, I fumbled to undo the clasp of my necklace.

In an instant Lisette was at my side. She had just unhooked the necklace for me when a soft rap sounded at the door.

"Who could it be at this hour?" Tatie opened the door a crack, then wider, her frown deepening. "He wishes to speak to you."

At the door, a footman in blue livery bowed then said, "Madame has requested the honor of your presence at her soirée this evening."

"Madame?" My heart soared. Princess Henriette wasn't ill after all. The invitation was real. But why hadn't she been at dinner? And who hosts a soirée at midnight?

"She has provided a conveyance to take you to the Palais Royal."

"Oh, no, no, no." Tatie shook her head fiercely. "It is not possible. It is much too late!"

"The young lady will be quite safe," the footman said. "I will personally guarantee it."

"Will that Montespan be there?" Tatie demanded, turning on him with fierce eyes.

He took a defensive step back. "I do not know."

"Tatie, I cannot refuse an invitation from Madame." I was practically dancing on my toes with excitement. "Lisette, my cloak."

"But—" Tatie looked horrified, as if I were being arrested.

"I will go with her." Lisette reached for both our cloaks.

The footman nodded his approval and waited until we were ready to accompany him. Tatie paced in distress.

I bussed her cheek. "I shan't be long. You sleep." I hurried out the door before she could protest more, Lisette close on my heels.

CHAPTER TWENTY

In the moonlit courtyard stood a sedan chair, liveried porters at the ready front and back. I had seen such devises before in Amiens; but only the very wealthy used them. Two lantern bearers stood alongside the conveyance. In the glow of their brass lamps, I could make out painted images of floral garlands surrounding winged cherubs on the side of the gilt-edged sedan.

"Where will Lisette sit?" I asked.

"She will walk with me," the footman said. He held out a hand to help me in.

Settling myself on the velvet-covered seat, I peered out the open window hung with gold-tasseled valences. The sedan rocked once as the porters lifted it and started out across the courtyard and through the gate. The two lantern bearers walked in front, Lisette and the footman in back. I imagined this must be what it felt like to be a princess, to never have to walk from one abode to another or get one's shoes dirty in the mud and filth of the street. In less than ten minutes we arrived at the Palais Royal.

The footman escorted us to Princess Henriette's apartment in the east wing. My shoes clacked over the parquet floors as we walked past walls lined with paintings of gods and goddesses in impossible poses, most of them brazenly unclothed.

We entered an antechamber, and Lisette took my cloak. Then the footman ushered me into the salon. The scene before me was like something out of one of the paintings I'd just passed, except that everyone was reassuringly clothed. The spicy scent of fresh cut carnations adorning tables in massive bouquets heightened the thrill of seeing courtiers lounging on chairs and settees, several on the floor leaning against the legs of others. All eyes were intent on Henriette and a man I did not recognize dancing a duet to the music of a single harpist.

The footman waited until there was a pause, then he cleared his throat. "Madame," he said. "I give you Mademoiselle Sylvienne d'Aubert."

Now all eyes turned to me. The footman bowed, then exited closing the door behind him. Willing my nerves to calm themselves, I took a deep breath. "Madame." I curtsied.

"Cousine! I am so glad you came." Princess Henriette rushed forward and bussed me on both cheeks. She took my hand and led me into the middle of the room where her dance partner bowed then stepped away. "This, my friends, is Sylvienne, our cousin, from…?" She turned to me.

"A…Amiens." Flustered, I could hardly get the word out.

"Sylvienne is new to court. I know you will welcome her."

To my surprise, her guests applauded. Her dancing partner stepped forward. "Mademoiselle." He took my hand and kissed it.

"Sylvienne," Madame said, "this is Guy Armand de Gramont, Count de Guiche. By far the handsomest rogue at court. And I command you to stay far away from him." She said the last with twinkling eyes.

The Count appraised me openly. "I see before me someone who might give the fairest of our ladies serious competition."

Too tongue-tied to respond, I felt the heat once again rising to my cheeks.

"Pay no attention to him," the Princess said, tucking her arm through mine. "He flirts with every breath. But he is not wrong about you."

As the harpist began playing again, she led me around the room, acquainting me with the ladies and gentlemen of her circle, a viscount here, a lady-in-waiting there. Amidst the blur of introductions, I looked for her husband, Monsieur, but he was not there. Neither was Madame de Montespan. Tatie would be relieved.

"Sylvienne." Madame drew my attention back to her guests. "I would like you to meet René Lorgeleux, Duc de Narbonne. Almost as handsome as Guiche, but much wealthier."

The Duc shot a querulous glance at the Princess before bowing. "It is a pleasure to meet you, Mademoiselle."

"Likewise," I curtsied.

Someone rose from a velvet-covered settee so Madame and I could sit next to one another. Someone else offered glasses of wine. As we chatted, several couples took up positions in the middle of the room and cued the harpist to play a minuet.

"Would you like to dance?" Madame asked.

"I wish I could. They did not teach dancing at my school, I'm afraid."

"Ah, the convent school? I'm not surprised." Her smile expressed sympathy.

"How did you know I went to a convent school?"

"Louis has spoken much of you. He seems quite enamored to have found a new cousin." She smiled. "I'm glad he did, too."

"That is kind of you to say." It warmed me to hear her words.

"I also understand he has appointed you to the service of Athénaïs."

"Madame de Montespan? Yes." And how had she heard? He had announced it only an hour earlier. "Would it be rude of me to say I wish he had appointed me to your household?"

Princess Henriette's laugh reminded me of chimes ringing. "That is sweet of you. But I assure you Louis does nothing without purpose."

Before I could ask what she meant, the Count de Guiche approached and held out his hand to me. "Would you do me the honor of dancing with me?"

Flustered, I gulped.

"Guiche," Princess Henriette said, setting her wine glass on a tray proffered by a servant. "My cousin's feet hurt. Dance with me again." She held out her hand for him to take.

"Delighted to. Always." To me he said, "I will hope for another time."

Before walking away, the Princess leaned over and whispered into my ear, "We shall have to teach you, *non?*"

She seemed almost to glide as she crossed the room, her hand on the Count's. The harpist thrummed his strings, as the dancers performed an intricate minuet. The Princess executed the steps with grace and ease. Could I ever learn to do that? A footman offered me another glass of wine. As I watched the dancers, the music and quiet chatter around the room lulled me. I took another sip before closing my eyes for a moment to soak in the ambience of it all — the harp, the sweet-tasting wine, the pleasant company.

"Sylvienne. Sylvienne!" Someone stroked my arm.

My eyes fluttering open with a start, I squinted, disoriented. Princess Henriette's guests were putting on their cloaks, bussing each other's cheeks.

"Poor girl, you fell asleep." She smiled in amusement.

I bolted upright. "I beg your forgiveness." Suddenly dizzy, I clutched the arm of the settee, mortified at what I'd done. "I don't know what happened."

"It is quite late. Narbonne, will you see her home in your carriage?"

"Of course," the Duc said, offering the slightest of bows.

"Merci, Monsieur le Duc," I said mortified that he had seen me fall asleep at a party. At Madame's party. "But I have my maid with me. Here. Somewhere."

"There is ample room for you both." He held out his hand to aid me in rising from the settee.

Princess Henriette hooked her arm through mine for the second time that night and walked me to her antechamber where Lisette waited sleepy-eyed with my cloak.

The Princess kissed me. "Will you come again?"

"Yes. Of course. And next time I won't, I mean…"

"Ma chérie, you may nap anytime and anywhere. I, however, will endeavor to make my next soirée more entertaining so you will stay awake."

"Oh, no. I didn't mean. No, it wasn't..." If only I could disappear into nothingness.

"I'm joking," she said. She kissed me again. "The Duc will see you home safely."

Inside his carriage, Lisette beside me trying hard not to yawn, I realized the city watchmen were snuffing out the lanterns of the night before. The stars had all but disappeared and the haze in the sky held the promise of sunrise. "Have we been up all night?"

"Some of us have." The Duc's lips curled into a suggestion of a smirk. "Ah, here we are already." The Duc ordered his footman to see us to our chamber door.

"*Bonne nuit.*" I said, taking the footman's hand to step out of the carriage.

"*Bonne journée,*" the Duc replied. That smirk again.

Disconcerted, I stumbled on the first step. Fortunately, the footman tightened his grip, preventing my fall. Holding my head high, I was sure I had made a fool of myself yet again. And, as the first rays of the rising sun fell across the cobblestones in front of me, I was sure that despite her kind words, Princess Henriette would never invite me to another soirée again.

I awoke bleary-eyed the next morning. Both my head and my stomach ached. I wasn't used to staying up all hours of the night, nor was I used to eating and drinking so much. Tatie was awake and bustling about, so I got up as well. I wanted to write a letter to Maman to send with Tatie.

Before dressing, I dug out the satchel of writing papers, quills, and ink Maman had sent in my trunk, along with the miniatures of Maman and Papa, which I set on the small writing table. The sun now poured through the window.

Dearest Maman... I began... *I miss you so. I wish you were here with me.*

My gaze drifted to the window and the courtyard beyond. What had it been like for Maman to live in this palace? To play with her cousins, Louis, the future king of France? And Philippe? Had she run through these halls laughing and giggling? Played hide and seek amongst the furniture? Pestered the servants? My own Maman was that little girl, long before I knew her, long before I was born. Touching my ink-filled quill to the page again, I wrote, *I am overwhelmed by the graciousness of everyone here. The King presented me to Queen Marie-Thérèse and to his courtiers.*

Should I tell her about the Marquise de Montespan? What would she think to learn I would be in the household of King Louis's mistress? Better she hear it from me than from Tatie.

I have been given a wonderful opportunity, a position here at court.

Assuring her I would be in excellent hands, I told her the Marquise promised to teach me everything I needed to know.

I do so want to make you proud of me.

The sound of Tatie and Lisette behind me packing Tatie's few things reminded me I had to finish my letter before Blondeau arrived. I dipped the quill again. Three pages later, I folded the delicate papers, heated the sealing wax with a candle, then pressed my new seal — an ornate letter S — into the melted wax.

A knock on the door signaled Blondeau was waiting outside with the coach.

"Let me help you get dressed one last time," Tatie said, teary-eyed as she tucked my letter into her traveling bag.

I relished the feel of her familiar fingers helping me into my skirts and pulling the mother-of-pearl comb through my hair, tying my tresses into a knot at the back of my head.

"There!" she announced. "You are decent again."

Tears flowed freely as I gave her and Blondeau each a last hug before watching their carriage jolt away over the cobblestones. Wiping my eyes, I turned to walk back into the palace. A thrill rushed through me at my newfound independence. But that independence was to be short-lived. A flurry of footmen had already arrived to move my belongings into the apartment of the Marquise de Montespan.

CHAPTER TWENTY-ONE

Françoise Athénaïs de Rochechouart de Mortmart, the Marquise de Montespan—or simply Athénaïs as she preferred to be called within her inner circle—reclined on her daybed in a white silk and lace dressing gown, dangling a string over the edge. An orange cat with black spots batted at the bow affixed to the end of the string.

"What is expected of a maid of honor?" I had asked Carufel as we followed a pair of servants carrying my trunk to the south wing of the palace.

"You may be asked to give advice on wardrobe, jewelry, or even hair styles. She may request that you deliver private missives, compose a letter, that sort of thing. But your primary duty will be to provide companionship to the Marquise. Discretion will be required…at all times."

Now, in Athénaïs's salon, I leaned in to observe the cat more closely. To my astonishment, I realized it wasn't an ordinary house cat.

"She is a baby ocelot," Athénaïs said, tickling its ears with her fingers. "A gift from Louis." She scooped up the cat and handed it off to a maid. "She's hungry." The maid nodded then curtsied with cat in arm before hustling off.

My gaze swept the room, though I tried not to seem too obvious as I beheld walls draped in gold-embroidered cream-colored silk, stitched images of exotic birds and animals shimmering. Potted fig and citrus trees cluttered the corners. Vases of fresh roses occupied every table. Where did the roses come from? Who grew roses this early in the spring?

A pair of lemon-colored canaries trilled in tandem in a gilded cage. I reached out to touch something lizard-like perched along the back of a settee and startled, laughing, when it turned its head to peer back at me.

Athénaïs shrugged off the wonderment I failed to hide. "The iguana came from the Americas, as did the ocelot. I take it your quarters are suitable?"

"Yes." My attention was all on her now. "My room is quite pleasant."

Much to my relief, I would not have to sleep in the Marquise's closet. I was provided a bedchamber larger than the one I had just left with an adjoining receiving room and a closet big enough to house several Lisettes. I offered to let the girl make a pallet to sleep next to my bed, but she insisted she preferred the privacy of the closet.

"Do you have apparel appropriate for court?" Athénaïs slid off the daybed and swept ahead of me into my chamber, startling Lisette. She ordered the girl to lay out my wardrobe.

One by one, Lisette pulled my gowns from the closet where she had just finished hanging them and held each one up for the Marquise's inspection.

Athénaïs shook her head at dress after dress, the very ones Madame Trouillet had designed for me. "These won't do."

"But they are based on the fashions of Paris," I said.

"Last year's perhaps. You can wear them as housedresses. I will have my designer fit you with a new wardrobe. And Louis's *cordonnier*. You will need shoes to match."

Shoes. A wave of guilt assailed me. I'd hardly thought about Etienne since my arrival. Dismayed at such callousness on my part, I suspected Etienne would have declared the out-of-fashion garments on my bed overly grand.

Off in the distance, church bells tolled the *Angelus*, marking the noon hour. I barely registered the sound, however Athénaïs's eyes flickered toward the door. "You may nap now."

"I'm not tired."

"Regardless."

I stared after her as she disappeared into her own chamber.

"Shall I put the dresses away?" Lisette asked.

"I'll help you."

A loud knock sounded on the antechamber door just as I reached for a gown. At the door stood a young page—he couldn't have been more than twelve or thirteen—standing in full livery, red velveteen from neck to knee, white stockings with red piping, and golden curls falling past the starched white collar of his doublet. He held before him a black and gold lacquered box no larger than my hand. I looked at the boy, uncomprehending.

"For Madame de Montespan." His tone suggested I should know why he was there.

"I'll take it to her," I said.

"No! I always present it myself." He brushed past me and hurried to Athénaïs's chamber door, knocking again.

Athénaïs opened the door, took a ring from the box—the silver signet ring I'd seen on King Louis's own hand—and slipped it onto her thumb. "Merci, Jérôme."

The boy bowed, then turned on his heel and walked out, clutching the now empty box. Athénaïs had already closed her door. Confused, I went to finish helping Lisette.

We had only hung half the dresses when another knock sounded, this one quite soft. Before I could answer it, the knob turned, and the door opened.

To my astonishment, King Louis walked in, still dressed in his hunting garb—breeches and a doublet of green velvet trimmed with brown leather. He wore wide-cuffed leather boots and a wide-brimmed leather hat with falcon feathers in the brim. The two spaniels trailed after him, tails wagging, noses working overtime as they rushed to explore the room.

"Bonjour, cousine." He doffed his hat at me and then at the wide-eyed Lisette.

We sank into deep, belated curtsies.

"I trust you understand the benefit of discretion?"

"Oui, Sire. Of course."

"And your maid?"

"Oui, Sire." Lisette's voice was barely a squeak.

"Will you allow Filou and Hera to keep you company?"

"Of course, Sire," I said, rubbing the ear of the spaniel that was already making my acquaintance.

He ordered the dogs to sit, then proceeded into Athénaïs's chamber. As soon as the door shut behind him, the spaniels jumped up and rushed me, tails wagging.

I put my hands over my mouth as I turned to Lisette, my eyes as wide as hers. Lisette hid her giggles behind one of my whale-boned bodices.

"We must say nothing," I admonished.

"Oui, Mademoiselle. Of course."

We delivered the last of my out-of-fashion dresses to the wardrobe. I glanced at the door to Athénaïs's boudoir. According to the gazettes, she had two children whom her husband would not let her see as long as she resided at court. I couldn't imagine what kind of woman abandoned her own children even to gain the favor of the King.

The dresses put away, I didn't know what to do with myself while the King was "in residence." Reaching for a book to read, I sat at the cherrywood writing table, the spaniels crowding my feet. Unable to focus, I set the book down and pulled out my small porcelain ink pot, a quill pen, and several sheets of fine linen paper. Who to write to? Marie-Catherine.

Oh, that I could whisper in her ear about my journey to Paris, dinner with the King and Queen, moving in with the Marquise, needing all new gowns, waiting for King Louis to leave Athénaïs's boudoir. I picked up the quill. Was the mail service safe enough for me to bare my heart?

> *Dearest Marie-Catherine, my Friend, my Confidante! There is so much to tell. I have been warmly received by the King and court. And I have come into the most unusual position in service to, of all people — you will never believe this, but it is most true — Madame de Montespan herself! King Louis's favorite. Athénaïs, for that is what she allows me to call her, is incredibly beautiful, like the Greek goddess. I—*

The door to Athénaïs's room opened, startling me so that I dropped my quill. The dogs jumped up, tails wagging as King Louis emerged, his face flushed, and still buttoning the last of his doublet buttons. I rose and dropped into a curtsy.

He kissed my hand. It was then I realized he had the silver signet ring back on his little finger. "Until dinner then," he said. Positioning his hat on his head, he snapped his fingers for the dogs to follow before striding out the door.

He had invited me to the grand couvert again! I scrambled to pick up the quill, groaning in dismay at the inky mess on the tiled floor. Lisette found a rag to clean it and shooed me away.

Athénaïs's languid voice called, "Sylvienne…"

I hurried to her room. "Oh! *Pardonnez-moi*, Athénaïs."

She lay across a swath of pillows, naked except for a string of pearls around her neck and a bit of silk sheeting draped carelessly over her midriff, seeming indifferent to my startled expression. "Call my serving girl to fill the tub. Let us soak awhile in rose water."

"Us?"

"You do bathe? Or is the practice looked down upon in the provinces?"

"I…I love bathing."

She rose from the bed and sat at her toilette table. Picking up a brush, she ran it through her blond tresses. A large oval mirror with a gilded frame reflected her naked body. Apparently, it also caught my reflection. "Close your mouth, *ma chère*. It is unbecoming."

I brought my hand to my lips to stop the giggles that threatened to erupt. "The serving girl…I'll fetch her." I hurried from the room.

My skin tingled as I stepped into the marble bathtub. Fragrant oils, rose and lavender, made the water feel slippery and sensuous. Athénaïs, already seated, swished her hands back and forth causing little ripples to wash toward me as I sank into the water. Lisette had pinned my hair up to keep it from getting wet, and now I turned my head to hide my embarrassment at having my naked body so exposed to the Marquise's frank scrutiny. A gaggle of serving women bustled around us, apparently seeing nothing unusual about two women bathing for the sheer pleasure of it. I sank further until the warm water covered my breasts.

"Louis dislikes bathing." Athénaïs lolled with her head against a small silk pillow, her breasts fully exposed. "I dislike bathing alone."

I hadn't realized until I saw her climb into the tub that I was taller than she — the distinctive gowns she wore and the poise and confidence with which she commanded a room served to magnify her person. Whereas I was thin, my legs too long, and my breasts small round buds, her body was curvaceous, perfectly proportioned, her breasts large and full. Her glistening skin was incredibly fair, her nipples pink, her private hair as blonde as that on her head. A jealous shiver ran through me, thinking of my own body which I had always been too willing to allow the sun to shine upon and darken. It was by force of will that I kept my hands from covering my dark thatch down below.

My embarrassment quickly dissipated as I reveled in the decadence of the bath water, subtle fragrances rising from the bath oils. Only now did I take in the opulence of Athénaïs's *salle de bain*, dominated by the basin in which we soaked. Gold pipes carried the water from…I didn't know where. Spigots, also of gold and fashioned as swans from whose mouths the water flowed — one for hot, one for cold — operated upon the twist of a lever. The walls surrounding us were covered in a lavender fabric edged with gold braiding. A fire crackled in the fireplace against one wall.

A maid brought a dome-covered silver platter and placed it on a lacquered table next to the tub. She lifted the cover to reveal sliced cheeses and grapes. A second maid offered flutes of a translucent amber liquid. Bubbles rose from the bottom of the tall, thin glasses.

Athénaïs held her glass aloft. "*A ta santé.*"

"*A la vôtre.*" Feeling brave, I took a sip. The bubbles tickled my nose and throat. I hiccupped, making me giggle. I sipped some more.

Athénaïs offered a languid smile. "Mon petit chou likes champagne?"

"Mm…tasty." I hiccupped again.

Athénaïs drank from her own flute before saying. "I don't suppose you can read?"

"Oh, but I love to read!" I hiccupped again.

She regarded me with skepticism. "What sorts of things do you read?"

"The classics primarily." I eyed the cheese platter. "They were required at the convent school." Of course, I couldn't eat before my hostess did. "I have a small collection of novels I trade with my friend Marie-Catherine." My stomach rumbled. "And the gazettes! I love reading the gazettes. When I can sneak them past Maman." Politeness be deviled, I popped a bite-size square of cheese into my mouth with a wet hand.

"Your mother disapproves of court gossip?"

"Very much so." I reached toward the cheese platter again.

The corners of Athénaïs's lips curved upward. "I wonder what she will read about you?"

My hand stopped in mid-air. I jerked it back. A maid took our empty champagne glasses. Another held out a tray with an envelope on it.

Athénaïs held up her hands for another maid to dry with a cloth before taking the missive and opening it. "Mademoiselle de Scudéry is inviting us to a salon in her home."

A *salon*! A gathering of the most intellectual of Parisians. I had read about such soirées in the gazettes. "Us? I am included in the invitation?"

"It would seem the noblesse are curious about our petit chou." She held the letter aloft. "I suppose you will have to wear one of your country frocks. It will take a week before we can have a proper gown ready for you." A maid returned with the tray to retrieve the letter. "You can wear something from my wardrobe. I have dozens of dresses I'll never wear again. With a ribbon here, some lace there, no one will know they were mine. Well, of course, it will take a bit more than that—my dresses are singularly unique—but we can make it work ..." She prattled on.

I nodded pleasantly, my eyelids drowsy, my head heavy. I sank lower into the warm water, a tickle against my chin, when—

A scream ripped the air!

I sat bolt upright, alarmed.

"Get it out of here!" Athénaïs shrieked.

Three serving girls ran in with towels and batted at something dodging back and forth across the tiled floor. A mouse. It dashed around the side of the tub and up a leg of the table that held the cheese tray. Athénaïs shrieked again and scrambled out of the tub, splashing water everywhere. Maids rushed to wrap towels around her.

The mouse had discovered the delectable treats. I could not help but laugh at its good fortune—and mine. I grabbed the domed cover from the woman holding it and slammed it down over the tiny creature. "Got you!"

Lifting the covered tray, I handed it to the wide-eyed maid. "It's just a mouse. It won't hurt you."

Clasping the lid tightly, the woman scooted out with the tray and the mouse.

Athénaïs recovered her composure. "How fortunate we are today. Our country mouse saved us from the palace mouse." She unfurled her towel and thrust it at the nearest maid. "Bathe as long as you like," she said to me. "I'm going to nap." She strode out, naked, her attendants close on her heels.

I stared after her a moment before sliding back into the water. Breathing in the scent of the bath oils, I was too restless now to enjoy it. I stood up. Lisette appeared with a towel to help me out.

"Do you wish to nap as well?" she asked.

"No," I said. "Help me get dressed. I wish to walk."

I chose an amber skirt with a cream-colored bodice from my wardrobe. It may have been last year's fashion, but I liked the way it hugged my hips and accentuated my waist. It would be fine for a quick, solitary stroll around the garden.

After fastening me into the dress and helping me with my hair, Lisette took her own cloak from a hook in the closet.

"Are you going out, too?" I asked.

"Of course."

I must have looked baffled, for in the next breath she said, "Mademoiselle, you can't go out alone."

"Why ever not?" I was used to coming and going as I pleased in Amiens.

"It…it just isn't done. A young woman walking alone. In Paris. It's not safe."

"But I will only be in the palace gardens." I reached for one of the bamboo-handled parasols nested in a large floor vase near the door.

"All the more reason you should have a chaperone." Lisette paused in the middle of tying the ribbons to fasten her cape. "Would you rather I called Monsieur Carufel to accompany you? Or your uncle?"

"*Non*! No. I'm being rude. I'm sure you would like fresh air as much as I would."

She curtsied then held open the door.

The warm breeze teased as Lisette and I strolled along the lane. I hadn't realized how stuffy Athénaïs's apartment felt. Adjusting the parasol to keep the sun off my shoulders, I breathed in the fresh air.

"Cousine!"

I swiveled to find myself face to face with the King again. He had changed out of his riding clothes and was accompanied by a half dozen courtiers and his troop of dogs. The spaniels rushed to greet me as I dipped into a curtsy, Lisette following suit.

"A glorious day, don't you think?" He extended his hand for me to rise. "Do you enjoy walking?" He offered me his arm.

I laid my gloved fingers on the crook of his elbow. I had no trouble keeping up with his quick step, but I noticed the group behind us, including Lisette, fell further and further behind.

"Did you enjoy your morning hunt, Sire?"

"The ride was quite pleasurable. Unfortunately, the catch was for naught."

"I'm sorry."

"Don't be. Do you ride?"

"I…have ridden. But I do not claim to know how to control a horse."

"Would you like to learn? I can teach you."

"That is most generous of you, Sire." My heart pounded with disbelief. Not only was I walking through the palace gardens again on the arm of King Louis, but he was offering to teach me to ride.

"Good. We leave for Fontainebleau in a few days. I'll instruct my stablemaster to choose a horse for you there."

Fontainebleau? I was just getting acclimated to Paris and Athénaïs's apartment, and now we were to move to another palace?

"Will you be joining us at the tables this evening?"

It took me a moment to realize he was not talking about dinner; he was referring to the infamous gaming tables, something else I had read about in the gazettes.

"I...I don't know."

"Of course, you will. Athénaïs wouldn't dare leave you behind." We had come to the end of the lane, the nobles and hounds rushing to catch up. "For you, ma chérie, are the talk of the court."

CHAPTER TWENTY-TWO

Lisette followed me into Athénaïs's salon, the sound of groaning and grunting from her boudoir bringing us up short. Her door was open, and after a moment we heard, "Tighter, by the love of God. Can't you do any better than that?"

Lisette shook her head and backed away, but I crept onward, peering around the corner and into the room. Athénaïs stood grasping a bedpost, holding on for dear life. Martine, one of her maids, struggled to tie the laces on the back of her mistress's corset. She had one knee up against Athénaïs's spine, a grimace on her face, her hands knotted from the effort.

"*Fini!*" the maid declared, stepping back triumphantly.

Athénaïs let out a slow breath, released the bedpost, and stood for a minute, before nodding her head in acceptance. Her creamy breasts bulged so much I feared they might burst. She looked glorious. Apparently, I not so much.

"Mon Dieu! You wore that out of doors?" She scowled.

"I was only going for a walk in the garden."

"Pray no one saw you."

I bit my lip.

"Martine, get the burgundy and blue ensemble from my wardrobe. The one I wore to the opera last month. They are not exactly her colors but will have to do." She turned to me. "Mon chou, take off that rag. We must get you ready for *le grand appartement* this afternoon."

Martine hustled out to find the designated dress.

"Le grand appartement?"

Lisette helped me out of my dress.

"The card games," Athénaïs said. "In the King's residence. It is *the* place to be seen. And incredibly fun."

Lisette and Martine redressed me, taking in the waist here, adding lace there, pushing up my bosom until I could barely breathe. After her hairdresser finished with Athénaïs's famous finger-length curls, she turned to me, while yet another maid applied powder, rouge, and lip paint to my face. Martine held out a lacquered jewelry box from which Athénaïs chose a diamond-and-pearl necklace and matching drop earrings for herself and a ruby necklace and earrings for me. I stood in front of her full-length looking glass. There before me stood a woman I didn't recognize, glamorous and quite…beautiful.

Athénaïs regarded me with a satisfied smile. "Louis will be pleased with my artistry. Do you have money?"

"Money?" I attempted a few shallow breaths in the confining bodice.

"The stakes can be quite high." She packed a miniature silk purse with coins and a small silk handkerchief.

"But I don't know how to play."

"The courtiers will love you all the more. They are always looking to increase their winnings."

"I have a small amount my mother gave me."

She fluttered a hand. "Keep it. Louis will cover your losses."

"He would do that for me?"

"He will if I ask him to." She tucked her purse into the sash at her waist, taking a last glance into the mirror.

As we approached the game room, I could hear the excited babble of people groaning, laughing, laying bets, arguing. However, all chatter ceased when Athénaïs appeared in the doorway. She smiled, nodded her head once in acknowledgement, and the throng of courtiers took up their bets again. We meandered from table to table, courtiers standing to bow or curtsy to her. Athénaïs greeted all who sought her attention.

An army of servants bustled about the room delivering drinks, removing empty plates, replenishing food on the buffet—cold meats, pâtisseries, and mouth-watering fruit, both fresh and sugared. A quartet of musicians strummed lutes and drew bows across violins. Candlelight from sconces and crystal chandeliers set players' hair ashimmer and made the tapestried gods and goddesses gracing the walls seem to come alive.

"Cousine!" Prince Philippe called out. He sat at a table with three other men, one of whom was the golden-haired swain. "You look exquisite. Have you come to lighten your purse?"

"Monsieur." I dipped into a curtsy. "You will have to forgive me as I am new to this. I have never played cards before."

"A virgin in more ways than one, she would have us think," the golden-haired man drawled. "I refuse to believe her. She is much too ravishing in that gown."

I recoiled. Was he mocking me? The heat of embarrassment rose to my freshly powdered cheeks.

"The Chevalier de Lorraine," Athénaïs said to me. "Ignore him." She took my arm, led me away. "Monsieur's pathetic lover." Her voice a half-whisper meant to be heard by all. Then she called out, "Madame de Sévigné!"

We stopped before a pleasant-looking, middle-aged woman whose deep blue gown was knotted at her bosom with crimson silk flowers. "Are you collecting gossip to share with your daughter?"

"Always, my friend. These gatherings are rife with titillating news. Including His Majesty's new little country cousin." She turned to me. "Although, it would seem you've managed to leave the country behind. That gown becomes you in untold ways. How are you finding court life?"

"Mademoiselle d'Aubert, I'll have you know, is a real-life heroine," Athénaïs said before I could speak. "She has a way with small creatures." Her lips turned up in an impish smile, and she moved us on to the next table before Madame de Sévigné could question me further. "Always leave them desiring more," she said to me. "Offer a tantalizing tidbit, then walk away. Ah! Monsieur Jourdan." She greeted a tall, slender man at another table. "How is your lovely wife this evening? Is she not here? Have you left her at home to wonder whose eau de parfum will grace your hair when later you climb into her bed?"

As Athénaïs chatted with Jourdan, I glanced around the room. Blinking, I had to bite my lip to keep from gasping. Two tables over sat Guillaume Boivin. He looked up from his cards and winked, seeming not at all surprised to see me. I pivoted, every sinew in my body tensing with disgust. Willing myself to breathe normally, I pretended to engage with Athénaïs and Jourdan. When, moments later, I chanced a peek over my shoulder, Boivin had leaned over and was speaking to a man whose back was to me. The man turned and nodded with familiarity. My eyes widened. It was the Duc de Narbonne. I swiveled, only to discover Athénaïs had moved on. I hurried to catch up with her, my cheeks hot.

"Athénaïs! Cousin Sylvienne! Come, join our table." Princess Henriette waved us over to where she sat with three men.

"Madame, we missed you at dinner last night," Athénaïs said. We dipped into curtsies. Two of the men jumped up, offering their seats. One caught flutes of champagne from the tray of a passing footman and handed them around the table.

"Merci, Langlée." Henriette smiled at him. "Dangeau, you roué, stop ogling my young cousin and deal the cards."

Dangeau blushed as he dealt. I squinted at my handful of cards, clueless as to what to do with them.

The courtier behind me leaned close to my ear. "It's called l'Hombre, a trick-taking game."

"Ah. Merci, Monsieur...?"

"La Vaquet. Edmund de la Vaquet. The plays are easy to learn."

He happily offered to teach me the rules, leaning close over my shoulder to pluck cards from my hand. His very presence felt like a shield between me and Boivin who sat just three tables over.

I sipped my champagne as we played. When it was my turn to lay down cards again, I giggled over the jumble of unfortunate combinations in my hand, causing a chuckle from la Vaquet despite my losing the round of play. I looked to Athénaïs, embarrassed because she had advanced me the money to join the game, but she seemed not at all concerned.

I glanced over at Boivin. He and Narbonne chatted with two provocatively dressed women who shared their table. After what must have been a particularly auspicious play, Narbonne reached out and swept the pile of winnings into the mound already in front of him.

"I'm afraid you haven't much left to lose," Princess Henriette said, drawing my attention back to our table.

Before I could respond, the sound of halberds pounding on the floor drew everyone's attention to the door. "Le Roi! Le Roi!" a guard shouted out.

The entire room rose as King Louis entered, Queen Marie-Thérèse on his arm. Louis offered a polite bow. We all bowed or curtsied in return, then everyone sat down, and the chatter and laughter continued. The King delivered the Queen to a table of women who had left a chair open for her, her wide-hooped skirts nearly knocking the cards off the table as she sat down.

"She looks positively passé in that farthingale." Athénaïs's lips curled in derision, but her voice was low so only our table could hear her.

"It is a Spanish fashion," I said in defense of the Queen.

"All the more reason to burn it."

Princess Henriette hid her smile behind her cards.

Watching King Louis wend his way through the room, I was impressed that he took the time to respond as courtier after courtier offered greetings. However, unlike Athénaïs who had something to say to everyone who hailed her, the King offered few words in return, mostly listening, occasionally smiling, often nodding before moving on. Finally, he stopped at our table.

He kissed his sister-in-law on both cheeks. "Are you prepared to lose to me again, sister?"

"Losing to you is always a pleasure," she said with a sly smile. "But perhaps today I will turn the tables."

King Louis grinned. "I wish you luck." He turned and kissed Athénaïs, then came around and bussed me on my cheeks.

Dangeau had already risen to give up his seat. The King nodded his thanks and sat across from me. "Cousine, I trust you are refreshed after your walk in the sunshine?"

Athénaïs arched a questioning eyebrow at me.

"Yes, Sire. It was a pleasurable excursion."

He nodded his head in agreement. He turned to Athénaïs and, taking her hand, kissed it most tenderly. "Shall we commence the game?"

A footman brought plates of pastries and fruit to the table.

"Did you bring a large purse?" Athénaïs asked the King. "I plan to replenish my coffers at your expense."

"You don't need to win at cards to do that," Henriette said with a knowing smile.

"It's more fun this way." Athénaïs shuffled the deck of cards. "Will you fund your country cousin's purse, Sire? I am determined to initiate her into the evil ways of court, but all she has to offer, I'm afraid is her virginity."

I coughed, nearly choking on my champagne.

"I assume you have that at least to offer?" she said to me.

I bobbed my head like a fool. King Louis laughed.

Henriette swatted at Athénaïs with her fan of cards. "Leave the poor girl alone."

"And poor she is. Unless her royal cousin intervenes on her behalf," Athénaïs said.

"I am happy to do so." King Louis signaled a footman, who stepped up with a small leather sack. The King poured out a pile of coins for me, keeping the rest for himself. "Are you practiced at cards?"

I shook my head no.

"Ah, then I shall win my purse back forthwith. Let's play!"

Another footman presented a tray of champagne. I helped myself to another flute.

King Louis played for about twenty minutes, losing most of his purse to Athénaïs and Henriette. The remainder he gave to me. "Please continue. Enjoy yourself."

I bobbed my head again, too late realizing I looked like a mophead doll. "Merci beaucoup, Your Majesty." Did my words sound slurry?

"And mind the champagne," he said with a wink. He stood, and the card players all rose in tandem. At the door he turned back toward the room and bowed gallantly. "Carry on."

Staring at the cards in my hand, I could make no sense of them. Was I not clever enough to learn the game? Or perhaps it was the champagne. Before long, I lost my entire purse.

"I think I should lie down before dinner," I said to Athénaïs.

As I rose to go, a glance at Boivin's table told me he had already left. So had Narbonne. With a curtsy to Henriette and Athénaïs, and a thank you to la Vaquet, I wove my way around the tables. In the grand hallway, I stopped to get my bearings.

"Do you enjoy games of risk?"

A jolt ran down my spine at the sound of Boivin's voice. I swiveled to find myself face to face with him. I took a step back, but he matched my movement, forcing me against the wall.

"Excuse me, but I think you have mistaken me for someone else." Looking him in the eye, I willed my voice not to shake, nor my legs.

"I think not." He put a hand against the wall, trapping me with his outstretched arm. "I believe we've had more than one encounter. How is your pretty little friend back in Amiens?"

"I don't know who you mean." My nose twitched at his overbearing parfum.

"I like the look of you better without your sun mask." He reached for my hair with his free hand.

"Please, don't."

"I think you mean, please do."

Panic rose within me, and I pushed against him but to no avail. He leaned closer to my mouth.

"Boivin."

The commanding voice caused him to jump. He turned and bowed. "Monsieur."

Philippe observed Boivin with calculating eyes, but said to me, "Mademoiselle d'Aubert. I do believe you promised to walk along the gallery with me."

I had no memory of such a promise, but he proffered his arm, and I took it with gratitude. "Oui, Monsieur. I always keep my promises."

A glance at Boivin caused me to shudder. He smirked like a cat, even though forced to let go of the mouse.

"Bonsoir, Boivin," Philippe said, waving him off. "Go find someone else to torment. This young lady has better things to do than consort with the likes of you."

Boivin bowed again and returned to the gaming room.

"Merci, Monsieur," I said to Philippe. "How can I thank you for your...intervention?"

"I'm quite sure an opportunity will present itself. Until then, shall we walk?"

CHAPTER TWENTY-THREE

At that evening's grand couvert, my eyes were heavy with desire for sleep. All my life I had been in bed and sound asleep by now. I found myself blinking at the throng of courtiers crowding into the Queen's dining chamber, jostling to position themselves to see better. Was it a special event tonight? Nothing about the table signified anything different from last night. Except my seat had been changed. A footman escorted me to a chair much closer to the royal couple.

As unobtrusively as possible, I searched the faces of the courtiers for Boivin. Apparently, he had taken heed of Philippe's warning. There was no sign of him. The tension ebbed from my body. I didn't see Oncle either. Another relief. The banging of the halberds drew my attention to the door.

"Le Roi! Le Roi!"

King Louis, Queen Marie-Thérèse, and Athénaïs entered, followed by Monsieur and, tonight, Madame, smiling at friends among the courtiers. The royal spaniels scurried behind them and circled the table several times before nestling near favored legs, Hera lying across my feet.

The footmen paraded in carrying covered trays of food. As one, they lifted the domed covers and stood off to the side. I nearly swooned from the aromas, realizing how hungry I was. As soon as the royal taster had sampled the King's food, and Louis in turn took his first bite, I helped myself to poached cod spread with a butter glaze, asparagus in a silky cream sauce, and egg halves filled with an artichoke paste. When I couldn't eat another bite, my eyes began to droop. I pinched myself to keep from nodding off onto my plate.

"Sire, I have the most amusing story." Athénaïs's voice caused me to jerk to attention. "Your little country cousin performed an amazing rescue today."

The room fell silent, all ears attuned to her. I cringed. Only Henriette turned to look at me, curiosity in her gaze.

"Whom did she rescue?" King Louis asked, smacking his lips over a succulent partridge leg, sauce dripping from his fingers. He offered a piece of the bird to one of the spaniels.

"Why, me, of course." Athénaïs patted her lips with her linen napkin. "We were lounging in the bath…" She stopped and picked up a nugget of pineapple to nibble. "When an enormous rodent scurried across the floor."

The crowd gasped. Athénaïs furrowed her brows, pretending to dredge up the horrid memory. "My serving women were in a panic, not a one of them with the least idea of what to do, dashing here and there, screaming, chasing the rabid creature with towels." She paused again to let the image sink in, motioning to the nearest footman to step forward with his domed cover. "Our brave Sylvienne, murmuring words of encouragement, wooed the creature onto a platter laden with cheese. Then, with the utmost calm…" She took the lid from the footman. "She reached for the cover and…" Athénaïs slammed her lid down over the King's plate of partridge, causing him to jump. "Trapped the beast with the cheese."

The room stayed silent, all eyes wide, everyone watching for the King's reaction. He stared at the lid for a long moment, then slapped the table and chortled. Laughter erupted around the table and from the throng of observers.

"What did she do then?" King Louis asked, casting a delighted grin in my direction.

Athénaïs puckered her lips and to my horror mimicked my voice. "'S'il vous plaît,' your country cousin begged. 'Do not kill the little thing. It is but a poor, harmless creature.' She convinced a serving girl to take the platter with the trapped mouse out of doors." With that, Athénaïs lifted the cover from King Louis's plate, took a morsel of his partridge and popped it into her own mouth, licking her fingers.

The courtiers applauded again. Several of the men banged their walking sticks against the floor, the countesses seated in the front row whispered behind their fans. Philippe flashed me a smile and winked.

"Are you a witch, then?" Queen Marie-Thérèse, in her Spanish-accented French, caught the courtiers' attention. "An enchantress?" All eyes turned toward me.

"No. *No!*" I blurted out. "It was just a mouse."

Philippe grinned at me. "It takes a brave country girl to defy a Parisian mouse." He and the King both laughed.

"Just a mouse." The words echoed throughout the room. "Just a mouse."

My ears burned, my dinner souring in my stomach. I wanted to run from the room. Instead, I lifted my napkin to my lips and stared at my plate.

The next morning, Athénaïs swooped into my bedchamber followed by a bevy of serving women. Bleary-eyed, I scrambled out of bed and curtsied. "I'm sorry, I didn't realize you were awake, or I would have—"

"No time for chitchat. The fabric vendors will be here any moment. The dressmaker, too." She ordered Lisette to throw open the curtains.

The sun caused my eyes to squint and water. Fortunately, Lisette had a cup of chicory water ready to ease my throbbing head.

"All you need to wear is your chemise and a robe. Don't tarry." Athénaïs dashed out in a swirl of silk and chiffon, her entourage disappearing through the door in her wake.

Lisette hustled to get me washed and to fix my hair. She slid a silk robe over me to cover the thin chemise.

By the time I entered Athénaïs's receiving room, the fabric vendors had gathered, a half-dozen merchants in solemn black standing in a semi-circle. Behind each stood a line of assistants bearing swatches and bolts of the most sumptuous fabrics in the most luscious colors and designs I'd ever seen.

Athénaïs stood over a table inspecting a panel of brocade patterned with tiny butterflies and vines. "No. It looks like a bramble bush."

A man in a black doublet with gold piping and gold buttons signaled the vendor to take his bramblebush fabric away and another to step forward. This one held aloft a lengthy swatch of an opalescent rose-colored satin.

Athénaïs's breath caught for the briefest of moments as she fingered the fabric. Then she spotted me. "Ah, you're here. Monsieur Delacourt, this is Mademoiselle Sylvienne, King Louis's cousin."

Delacourt eyed me with one raised eyebrow, then dipped his head in acknowledgement. "It is my pleasure to dress you, Mademoiselle." He turned to Athénaïs. "Shall we start with the rose satin?"

She seemed to hesitate, considering the fabric with an almost wistful gaze, then with resolve declared, "Yes. It will go well with her complexion."

"Ah, that *is* perfect!" Princess Henriette entered, entourage in tow. "I'm surprised you didn't snatch it up for yourself, Athénaïs."

"Mmm, well, Louis has ordered le petit chou to look presentable for the ball he'll give at Fontainebleau." Athénaïs handed the fabric off to Delacourt, who handed it off to one of his assistants.

"Yes, we wouldn't want her to look bucolic, would we?" Henriette smiled at me, her eyes twinkling. She traversed the room examining the fabrics, her ladies-in-waiting trailing behind her. "This one is lovely, don't you think?" She fingered a panel of embroidered jade silk.

Her ladies nodded, chirping their approval.

Delacourt held out a hand for me to step onto a small footstool, putting us at eye level. "If you please, the robe."

Lisette hastened to take the wrap from me as I shrugged the silk from my shoulders. I stood in my chemise.

"Bien. Hold out your arms." He took a notched leather thong from an assistant and proceeded to measure me—my arms, my neck, my shoulders, my waist, my back, my hips—all the while murmuring numbers to the assistant who scribbled into a notebook.

"Hold your hands above your head, like thus." He demonstrated, and I raised my arms, linking my fingers together. Then he wound his leather thong around my breasts. I gulped.

"Excellent," he said.

A single person clapping drew my attention to the doorway. "Excellent, indeed," Philippe said.

Delacourt bowed from the waist, still holding the thong aloft. I yelped. His grip had tightened, pinching my nipples.

"Don't be gauche, husband," Henriette chided. "She is being measured for gowns. Why are you here?"

"Please. Don't stop on my account. I came to lend my celebrated fashion sense." He approached, his robin's-egg blue justaucorps flaring out over his cream-colored breeches and silk stockings. His long black hair was pulled back to showcase a pair of opal earrings and a pearl and opal necklace strung about his neck. A heart-shaped dot adorned a spot above the corner of his red-painted lips.

Delacourt, flustered, dropped his thong. When he stooped to pick it up, Philippe smacked him on his bottom, causing the dressmaker to yelp. With a mischievous smirk, Philippe strutted across the room to examine the bolts of fabric.

Henriette sighed. "Can't you leave well enough alone?"

"But I wish to commission the talented Delacourt to make something for *me*." Philippe held up the fabric with the butterflies and vines. "Ugh! What cretin thought this was suitable for a gown? Surely you don't plan to use this for ma petite cousine?"

"Of course not." Athénaïs signaled for me to step down from the box.

Lisette hurried over with the silk robe.

"Ah. Bon." He turned toward me. "I am sure, Mademoiselle, that you will be the loveliest rose at court in whatever rags they deign to dress you in."

I curtsied, wondering if he meant his words to be a compliment or a jest.

"Carry on then. The young lady must have proper clothes, mustn't she?" He winked at me, then strode out of the room like an actor exiting the stage.

A sigh of relief escaped Delacourt's lips. At Athénaïs's nod, he clapped his hands twice. "Back to work, everyone."

"My dear niece! I trust you had a good dress fitting this morning." Oncle bussed my cheeks later that afternoon. On his cheek he wore a black velvet beauty patch, much like the ones Philippe wore, but larger to cover his pockmark. "Have you been in the gardens yet today?" He spoke to me, but his gaze followed Lisette as she lit extra candles before going out to run errands. "It's quite lovely outside." I didn't like the look in his eyes.

Once she was gone, his attention focused on me again.

"It went well." I didn't invite him to sit, hoping he wouldn't stay long.

He sat anyway, tapping his walking stick against the floor between his legs. "I understand you were at the gaming tables yesterday."

"I was in the company of the Marquise de Montespan." I lifted my chin in defiance. "Now that I am part of her household, I go where she goes."

He pointed his stick at me. "You lost a considerable sum, I hear."

"I've much to learn about cards, apparently."

He sniffed. What would he say if he knew it was the King's money I had lost? "I would like you to procure an invitation to the tables for me."

I blinked in surprise. "You wish to engage in gambling?"

"I've had some practice at cards." He thrummed the head of his walking stick with his fingers. "The people here are all fools with their money. It will be easy for me to relieve them of some of it."

"I…I can't promise." The last thing I wanted was Oncle in the same room when I was losing money. "I don't know the protocol."

"You have the eye of the King. Use it to our advantage." He stood. "We are family after all."

"What do you mean, the eye of the King?"

"Don't pretend to be naïve. You are young. You are fresh." He regarded me with a carnal smirk. "You have a stunning figure and eyes that beckon to the bedchamber."

"That is untrue!" My fists clenched. "How dare you suggest such a thing."

Oncle lifted my chin with his finger, his eyes darkening. "You know very well why you are in this palace, in the service of His Majesty's maîtresse-en-titre. He has entrusted his whore of a mistress with training you."

I staggered backward, "Get out of here."

He pointed a finger at me. "A place at the games. Or..." He rapped his stick on the table for emphasis. "I will make sure that young shoemaker who is so enamored of you knows exactly what King Louis has in store for you." He strode out the door.

Stunned, shaking, I sank into the chair he had just vacated. My eyes were drawn to Athénaïs's door. Could Oncle be right? That there was a nefarious purpose in my being here? Or was it another of his lies—like the one about Maman already being with child when she met Papa? Henriette had said King Louis does nothing without purpose. I shivered even though I wasn't cold. And what should I do about Oncle's demand for a seat at the gaming tables? What could I do? I closed my eyes against the headache that threatened to engulf me.

CHAPTER TWENTY-FOUR

The next afternoon, Oncle's words niggled at the back of my mind as Athénaïs helped me choose another of her cast-off dresses—my new wardrobe would not be ready for several weeks—this time to wear to the salon hosted by my favorite author, Madeleine de Scudéry. I selected a dress with a lemony-colored satin embroidered with yellow and green vines. The bodice, which needed to be taken in to accommodate my flatter chest, was trimmed with a row of pearl buttons fastened with delicately embroidered eyelets.

Lisette lifted my hair into cascading curls with pearl-studded bows holding my locks in place. She fastened Maman's pearl necklace around my neck. I slipped on the matching pearl-drop earrings. A glance in the mirror caught me by surprise. How sophisticated I looked. Perfect for my first salon—the one place I could be assured Oncle would not venture.

Mademoiselle de Scudéry welcomed us into the salon of her century-old Italianate townhouse in the Marais district of Paris. "Madame de Montespan, always *so* delightful to have you grace our little get-togethers!" Lounging on a yellow damask-covered divan, our hostess opened her arms toward me. "And you must be Mademoiselle d'Aubert, the new *saveur charmante* all the court is talking about."

I stopped mid-curtsy to look up at her. Did she just call me a charming new flavor?

She beamed, the wrinkles on her face not quite hidden by a thick paste of white powder or the cascades of faux blond ringlets that framed her cheeks. Her dress, a bright violet, seemed at odds with the mound of green and orange pillows surrounding her.

"I am pleased to meet you," I said. "I have read several of your books."

"Merveilleux! Now I am doubly pleased that you have joined us today."

The status of the guests clustered around our hostess on the hodgepodge of upholstered chairs set my nerves ajumble. I recognized several, others I didn't, but all appeared quite erudite. During the carriage ride over, I had obsessed over what might be the topics of conversation among such well-read people. Perhaps we would discuss the novels of our hostess. Or would we critique the plays of Molière and Corneille? I'd only seen a few. Or the essays of Racine? I rued that I hadn't read him yet. Perhaps poetry. I loved poetry. In fact, I had rehearsed several stanzas in case I was called upon to offer a favorite.

Princess Henriette's eyes lit up when she saw me. I curtsied happily to her, then to la Grande Mademoiselle who gave me the barest of nods. Across the circle, Philippe leaned casually against the back of a chair occupied by a woman I did not know.

"Sylvienne, come meet Gabrielle." Athénaïs bussed the cheek of the woman who had captured Philippe's attention. "My sister is the Marchioness of Thianges." She settled onto a chair next to her sister, a beauty in her own right but whose dark features contrasted with Athénaïs's fair ones.

I offered a quick curtsy. "I am pleased to make your acquaintance."

Philippe gestured for me to take the seat on the other side of the Marchioness.

"Are you the mouse enchantress everyone is talking about?" she asked, opening her fan and waving it languidly in front of her face.

I winced, remembering Athénaïs's recounting of the tale at the grand couvert.

"There are not many people who can impress my sister the way you did."

Her tone was not unkind, but was I never to live down that episode?

"I dare say, my young cousin has many talents," Philippe said, leaning against the back of the lady's chair again. "Sadly, winning at l'Hombre turns out not to be one of them." His smile was teasing.

"I do love a good game of l'Hombre." Madame de Thianges closed her fan and tapped my hand with it. "Perhaps you'd like me to teach you some strategies."

"That would be wonderful." I smiled my gratitude to the Prince for changing the subject so adroitly.

"There's Madame de Sévigné." Athénaïs waved, then hid her lips behind her fan, speaking *sotto voce* as the lady approached. "She's still mourning the wedding of her daughter. I think she would have preferred had the girl never married." She smiled up at the woman and folded her fan. "My dear Marie, how is your sweet Françoise-Marguerite and her new husband?"

Madame de Sévigné's amber dress was set off at her bosom by an enormous ruby pendant that bounced as she walked. "Bonjour again, Mademoiselle," she said to me. Then her eyes filled with tears. "Her husband, the Comte de Grignon, was just appointed lieutenant governor of Provence."

"That is admirable news," Madame de Thianges said.

"Yes, a high honor. But now my sweet Françoise must stay in Provence with him. I thought their visit there would be temporary." She dabbed at her tears with a laced handkerchief. "I am desolate. I fear our correspondence will continue ad infinitum, when I would so rather converse with my daughter arm in arm."

"An excuse to gather more gossip," Athénaïs said, the wicked delight in her eyes belying the sympathetic smile on her lips.

Listening to Madame de Sévigné's woe, I resolved to write to Maman again as soon as I returned to the palace.

A dozen of us had gathered by now. Seated next to Princess Henriette was another of my favorite authors, Madame de La Fayette. I had been reading her novel, *La Princess de Cleves*, when I was dismissed from the convent school.

Another woman arrived, her simple but elegant dress the color of cinnamon in blunt contrast to the garden of dazzling colors adorning the rest of us. Her dark brown hair was pulled back into a soft chignon, with two tendrils left loose on either side of her face. She offered

Madame de Thianges and Philippe a polite curtsy then greeted Athénaïs with a hug.

"My dear friend, Madame Françoise Scarron," Athénaïs said to me.

Madame Scarron offered me a warm smile. "I'm so glad you could join us. I hope you will enjoy our conversation. It can get quite lively at times."

The late husband of Athénaïs's friend, I learned, was the writer Paul Scarron, whose humorous novels and poems Marie-Catherine and I had taken great pains to hide from the nuns because of their burlesque nature. This gathering was going to be delicious.

At the last minute, the Duc de Narbonne slipped in and positioned himself on the other side of Princess Henriette, kissing her hand. Was it my imagination or did Philippe, still standing behind Athénaïs's sister, suddenly stiffen?

"Where the hell has Lorraine gotten himself to?" Philippe muttered under his breath.

Madame de Thianges reached over her shoulder and patted his hand.

Athénaïs raised her fan again and whispered to me, "René Lorgeleux, Duc de Narbonne. One of the wealthiest men in France."

I thought better of mentioning that I had already met him. A servant offered us cups of a steaming, fragrant beverage.

"I don't believe he truly cares for the conversations at our gatherings, but he's on the hunt for a wife. And what better place to inspect his options than at salons full of women of means?"

I sniffed the creamy brown liquid in my cup. Chocolate! Bringing it to my lips, I winced at the heat, but delighted at the taste.

Our hostess rang a small bell, and the side conversations abated. "I had the happy occasion to receive a copy of the newly published *Letters of a Portuguese Nun*," she announced.

"Have you read it?" Madame de Sévigné asked, tears now dried. "I understand it is so popular the bookstalls of Paris cannot keep it in stock."

But so controversial the booksellers of Amiens would not carry it, I knew.

"Ah, Marie, it is quite passionate, if not outright salacious," Mademoiselle de Scudéry said.

"I don't think it salacious at all." Athénaïs closed her fan with a snap.

Agog at the idea they were discussing such a book, I had to will my body to sit still.

Athénaïs continued with her defense. "The feelings this writer had for her lover were painfully raw, but incredibly honest. She is to be admired."

"But was her lust for him not a sin before God?" la Grande Mademoiselle asked. "She was a woman of the cloth, after all."

"Do you truly believe those letters were written by a nun?" Philippe's tone dripped with skepticism.

I stared up at him, blinking. It had never occurred to me the passionate letters of the anonymous Portuguese nun written to a French military officer might not be authentic.

Madame de Thianges leaned over and said to me, "Of course, he has not read the book himself. Monsieur never reads. I think he simply enjoys instigating quarrels."

Philippe winked at me when I glanced up at him again. Stunned, I almost lost the thread of the conversation.

"Of course the nun wrote them," Madame de Sévigné said. "No lay person could have that depth of feeling. Such passion arises from being prohibited from love by one's vows to God."

"Any woman caught up in a marriage of political arrangement knows what it means to be prohibited from love," Henriette said archly.

"Ah, but such a woman can always find love." Was Monsieur taunting his wife? "She just needs to exercise discretion."

The tension in the room became palpable. Thankfully, the Duc de Narbonne redirected the conversation. "Nuns and forbidden love aside, a question was posed to me the other day." He stretched his legs out in front of him and crossed them at the ankles. "Once two lovers have known each other in a carnal manner, can they ever go back to having a purely intellectual friendship when the affair has ended?"

Philippe snorted. "Hardly."

A murmur of anticipation bubbled from behind a flurry of fans.

"And why not?" Madame de Thianges squared her shoulders for a challenge she appeared to relish. "A relationship between a man and a woman doesn't have to be based solely on their...amorous congress."

"Yes," Philippe countered, "but once it has risen to the point of — "

"Isn't that a presumption?" Athénaïs cut in. "That there is a hierarchy within relationships? That carnal intimacy is of a higher order?"

"I'd say it is of a baser order," Madame de La Fayette said. "In my novel *La Princess de Cleves* — "

"I read your book!" I clapped a hand over my mouth as all eyes turned to me.

Mademoiselle de Scudéry offered an amused smile. "And what did you make of it, dear?"

I dropped my gaze, my hands twisting helplessly in my lap. "I...I enjoyed it." Looking up again, I chastised myself for such silly words. "I mean, I thought the characters were...well drawn, and the plot...well I..." My heart began to thump, but I forced myself to look at our hostess. "I think the Prince of Cleves was a character to pity. He was so madly in love with his wife, the Princess. But, of course, she was in love with another. I...I have to wonder..."

"Yes?" Madame de La Fayette leaned forward.

I looked around nervously. Henriette smiled her encouragement. Bolstered, I said, "Is it a worse fate to be married to someone who doesn't love you? As was the case with the prince in the novel. Or to love someone whom you can never marry, as with the princess...and...and the Portuguese nun?"

"An excellent question to ponder!" Mademoiselle de Scudéry clapped her hands approvingly. "Do go on, child."

"Well, I...that is, if you think about it — "

The doors to the salon burst open and all heads pivoted as the Chevalier de Lorraine strode through, a pamphlet in one hand, a devilish grin lighting his face.

Mademoiselle de Scudéry pursed her lips. "You're late, Lorraine. You know I don't tolerate tardiness in my salons."

Lorraine swept his wide-brimmed hat from his head with a flourish as he bent into an exaggerated bow. "My sincerest apologies,

Mademoiselle. But I have procured a copy of this morning's *La Gazette* and thought it would bring a delightful bit of levity to our little symposium today."

"How so?"

He tossed the pamphlet at Philippe. "Your country cousin has managed a showing on page two."

I blinked in disbelief. They were writing about me in the gazette? Philippe glanced at me with a puzzled look before opening the pamphlet.

"There's even a funny little sketch." Lorraine leaned an elbow on the back of Henriette's chair. She swatted it away, so he sauntered over to stand next to Philippe. Smirking, Lorraine grabbed the pamphlet from him and handed it down to me. "I don't think the caricature favors you a bit."

I stared in horror at a sketch of a girl naked in a bathtub, one hand holding a domed platter aloft, the other clutching an oversized mouse by the tail. Too stunned to react, I closed my eyes to blot out the room. What would Maman think if she saw this? And Etienne. Oh, God, Etienne. I prayed he would live by his declaration never to pay attention to the gazettes.

"Lorraine, why do you have to be such a cad?" Philippe growled.

"She might as well get used to it," Athénaïs said.

With rising desperation, I fought the tears that threatened. I must look the fool in front of these people.

"Sylvienne. Cousine." A tender hand touched mine.

I looked up into the face of Henriette who now stood before me.

She gently removed the pages from my shaking hands. "Ma chérie, we have all been lampooned in the gazettes at one time or another. There is not one of us in this room who has escaped the vicious quill of the satirist." She lifted my chin, forcing me to look up at her. "We learn to hold our head high and ignore the jealousy of the uncouth." She glanced pointedly at Lorraine, then back at me. "You will learn to do that, too."

I nodded. But I didn't believe it.

CHAPTER TWENTY-FIVE

The carriage ride back to the palace worsened a headache that had begun at Mademoiselle de Scudéry's townhouse. Grateful for the pomander I held to my nose, breathing in the scent of ambergris and lavender, I thought again about the horrible sketch in *La Gazette*. I was confident that if Tatie came across the pamphlet, she would go to great lengths to keep it from Maman. But what of others in Amiens? Marie-Catherine would think it hilarious. There was no hope for my reputation if Claudette got her hands on it. And what if Etienne were to see it? I let the pomander fall to my lap and closed my eyes against the throbbing in my head, taking small comfort in knowing that he couldn't be bothered with the gossip papers.

The late afternoon shadows were long when we arrived at the palace. I grabbed Athénaïs's sleeve in a panic. "You won't tell His Majesty about the gazette, will you?"

"I'm quite sure he won't need to hear of it from me. But no, I won't say a word."

Lisette greeted me in my bedchamber with an eager smile. "Did it go well, the salon?"

"I met some lovely people, and we had a grand discussion," I said through gritted teeth. I jerked off my wrap and threw it at her.

She regarded me a moment, her eyes questioning the veracity of my words, but as she hung my cloak she said only, "You have a letter."

She presented me with a silver tray on which lay the missive. The handwriting and the wax seal with a single initial, *I*, caused my heart to skip a beat. Maman! I took the letter to a chair near the window to read.

My dearest Sylvienne,

I was comforted to receive your letter today. You will be glad to know Blondeau and Tatie returned safely from Paris and reported no incidents on the road. I thank God your trip was uneventful.

A sigh of relief escaped my lips. My chaperones had not informed her of our encounter with the bandits or even Boivin.

Your descriptions of Paris and the palace bring back memories. However, I am curious about your new position as Demoiselle d'Honneur to the Marquise de Montespan. I must confess I am not entirely happy about the news. However, if the King believes it to be appropriate, then I will not attempt to intervene. I do advise you to behave with caution. You are a young woman of strong character and good moral judgment, but you are young and in a situation that is foreign to you. You will encounter people whose intentions are not always apparent nor honest. Guard your heart and do not judge people by what they say or promise. Rather, judge by how they behave. ~Your Most Loving Maman

Only a single page, but I held the missive to my heart as I gazed out the window at the carriages coming and going in front of the palace. I missed her now more than ever. *Judge by how people behave.* I judged Lorraine a cad. I grabbed up my quill and a piece of writing paper.

Dearest Maman,

Today I attended my first salon. The famous authoress Madeleine de Scudéry hosted us in her home!

My hand halted. What if I were never invited back after that awful caricature? My headache throbbed worse than ever. I pushed aside the quill and paper. The letter would have to wait. I made my excuses to Athénaïs for not attending the evening's gaming tables with her. Instead, I laid on my bed, a wet cloth on my forehead. I groaned remembering that Oncle expected me to garner him an invitation to the tables. How was I supposed to manage that when my own reputation was all of a sudden so tenuous? I closed my eyes.

A noise from my antechamber stirred me, the sound of a chair scraping the floor as it was pushed aside. A woman's voice sounded distraught. "Please. Don't."

A disconcerting image of Perrette flashed before me. I scrambled off the bed and thrust open the door to discover Oncle Claude pushing Lisette up against a corner, one hand grasping her breast, the other fumbling with her disgusted face as he tried to kiss her.

"What are you doing?"

Oncle let go of her and stepped away. "Sylvienne! I thought you were out with the Marquise. The gambling tables. I...a misunderstanding. She...she asked for a kiss. Begged, actually."

"No! I didn't." Lisette moved behind a chair. "I swear. I would never."

"Get out." I picked up his walking stick and threw it at him. "I don't want to see you in this chamber again. You are a beast. You've been a beast ever since I've known you."

"How dare you speak to me that way!" He tugged on the hem of his doublet. "You will remember your place, Mademoiselle, and my role as your chaperone."

Lisette sobbed behind me.

My voice hardened. "Does Aunt Judith know the type of recreation you engage in while serving as my 'chaperone'?"

He glared at me. "You leave my wife out of this."

"You leave my friend alone."

"Friend?" He snorted. "She is a serving wench. You had best learn the difference if you want to maintain your place in society." He tapped his walking stick once, then strode out.

I wrapped my arms around Lisette. Trembling, she wept into my shoulder. It was a moment before I realized I, too, was shaking.

"I am so sorry, Mademoiselle," she said when her cries had reduced to a whimper.

"It is not your fault."

She wiped her eyes. "Mademoiselle, is it true you think of me as a...a friend?"

I hadn't thought about it one way or the other until I had uttered the words moments before. "Yes," I said. "A dear friend."

She smiled gratefully, but only for a moment. "I am honored that you think so. And I will be faithful to you forever. But please, Mademoiselle. Be careful. If the Marquise or anyone else were to think I was acting above my station..." Her voice wavered. "I could lose my position here. If that happened, I would have nowhere to go." Tears flowed again.

My heart broke for her. I hugged her tightly, then stood back. "I promise I will never let that happen. And as for my uncle, I will make sure he never bothers you again."

A word to Athénaïs, who in turn spoke to the King, was all it took. The following day, the dust from Oncle's carriage wheels hung in the air long after it had left the courtyard. Maman could deal with him now. And a postscript on my next letter home would ensure she'd never allow him back into our home again either.

After the Angelus bells had announced the noon hour, a knock sounded on my antechamber door. Lisette opened it to Jérôme who stood with the lacquered box in hand. By now I understood the King's visits to be a daily occurrence. Before long, Filou and Hera were nestled at my feet. Hera barked when another rap sounded.

"The palace courier." Lisette handed me a letter.

The paper was coarse, its edges frayed, likely having passed through many hands. It was addressed to *Mlle S. d'Aubert à Amiens France*. Under that, in Maman's familiar handwriting, was the instruction to deliver it to the *Palais des Tuileries à Paris*. There was no indication who the original sender was.

I held the letter to my nose. It bore a damp, earthy scent, a faint tang of sea brine. Sliding my finger under the plain wax seal, I unfolded the single page, smoothing the paper as best I could. The handwriting was shaky, childlike. *Ma chère amie Sylvienne,*

It couldn't be! I dropped my gaze to the bottom of the page.

Ton amie dévouée Perrette

Perrette! Elated, I pored over the scribbled words.

September 5, 1670 Ma chère amie Sylvienne, I write to you from my own hand. I am on ship le Prince Maurice. We are at sea for many days and many more to go. So much rain and wind. Not much food. I have a kind friend who teaches me to read and write.

The words blurred, and I wiped a tear from my cheek, my eyes unexpectedly brimming.

September 25, 1670 Bonjour again

Now the handwriting had changed. She had procured the services of a scribe, the letter said, so she could say more.

I survived the ocean as you can guess. It seemed we sailed forever, but it was only seven weeks. Quebec is a small village and quite backward. The Sisters met us at the dock. They call us les Filles du Roi! Can you imagine? King Louis's daughters because he has been so generous to pay our way. They took us to their convent to give us baths, warm beds, and bowls of rabbit stew. Two weeks after we unpacked and cleaned our dresses, we met the men hoping for wives. You should have seen their eyes when we walked into the hall all dressed up. They fell on their knees with their fur hats in their hands.

I chose a very sweet man to wed, Jean Bordeleau. He is a wheelwright, and he owns land and a small cabin. Anything I ask for he will build for me. We have a table and chairs and a bed with a goose down mattress. Sylvienne, I am with child already! I must end now because there is so much work to do on our small farm and I must get our cabin ready for the cold and snow to come. Please write to me.

She signed her own name with bold letters. How different her life was now. To choose her own husband. Unheard of. Though perhaps not a bad thing. I couldn't imagine having to carry and raise children in such a harsh and savage land.

Grabbing my quill, I reached for a sheaf of fresh paper. An hour later, I stood, my shoulders aching, my fingers cramped. I had written six pages, telling Perrette everything about my unexpected move to Paris and my new life.

I signed the letter and folded the pages. As I reached for a stub of sealing wax to hold over the candle flame, the door to Athénaïs's boudoir opened and King Louis stepped through, a satisfied smile on his lips. I jumped to my feet and dipped into a curtsy.

"Writing letters home, cousine?" he asked, nodding toward my pages.

"To a dear friend, Sire. In the colonies."

"New France?"

"Yes, Sire. Québec. She is newly arrived there. Grateful for your sponsorship."

King Louis's eyes lit up. "And did she claim a husband?"

"Most certainly, Sire. She is already with child."

"Excellent! Colbert tells me the colony is growing. That pleases me." He bussed my cheeks then strode out, the dogs bounding after him.

Later that afternoon, at the gambling tables, I puzzled my way through *Triomphe*, a new game introduced to me by a handsome young courtier who was extraordinarily patient with my inability to follow suits and claim tricks, especially after I'd had two glasses of champagne. To my great relief, no one mentioned the caricature in *La Gazette*. I suspected Athénaïs had something to do with that.

Afterward, the King invited us all for a promenade through the gardens to enjoy the early evening air. I needed to avail myself of the chamber pot, so I made my excuses to Athénaïs and rushed back to my bedchamber. When I made my way outdoors again, most of the courtiers had wandered to the far side of the expansive lawns. For a moment, I hovered at the edge of one of the gazing pools, enjoying the cool, jasmine-laden breeze.

"Mademoiselle, are you lost?"

The hairs rose on the back of my neck at the sound of that voice.

CHAPTER TWENTY-SIX

Guillaume Boivin sat astride a handsome bay, the setting sun at his back, the feathers in his broad-rimmed leather hat lit by the last of its rays.

"I am not lost, thank you." My boldness surprised me. "I am on my way to join King Louis in the garden."

He trotted his horse in a circle around me, cutting off my escape. "Is it wise to be out here without an escort?"

Fighting panic, I moved to walk past him, but the horse snorted and stomped, jittery about being so tightly reined in. I backed up to avoid its hooves. Boivin circled again.

"I assure you I am not in need of an escort. If you will let me pass—" My heart thrummed in my chest despite my bravado. Dogs barked on the other side of a hedge.

"And how will you reward me for the privilege of passing?" His lips curled into a lascivious smile.

I clenched my fists, fighting the urge to charge the horse. Could I unseat this awful man? Was it worth the attempt to endanger my life? I took a deep breath and girded myself.

"Cousine!"

Relief washed over me as I turned to greet King Louis with a smile I hoped belied my distress. I dropped into a curtsy. "Your Majesty."

The bay's harness jangled behind me as Boivin slid off. "Your Majesty," he echoed, bowing.

The King strode up to us, his dogs chasing back and forth around him. "Ah, Boivin. I take it you've met my cousin. She is a refreshing addition to court."

"I couldn't agree more, Your Majesty. She is a vision of loveliness."

"Come, ma chérie." King Louis offered his arm. "The Queen and the others have gotten ahead of me. I had a bit of unexpected business to attend to, but now I want to enjoy the sunset and the cool air."

I put my hand on his sleeve, my heart calming down.

"If you will excuse us," he said to Boivin.

"Of course, Sire." Boivin slipped his foot into the stirrup and remounted his steed. "Mademoiselle." He tipped his hat, his horse prancing backwards. "It has been my pleasure." He tugged on the reins, clicking his tongue, and trotted off.

King Louis guided me in the opposite direction. "The man is an ass, but harmless, I would judge. I trust you and Athénaïs are getting along?"

"Exceptionally well, thank you."

"Good. I hope you will plan for your stay at court to be a long and fruitful one."

My heart did a flip. King Louis wished me to stay at court. My spirits were buoyed. And I need not fear that awful man, Boivin. The King, my cousin, would see to my welfare. As we walked in the sunset, I decided to write to Etienne, to let him know I would be at court a bit longer than I had first anticipated.

Entering the Queen's dining chamber with Athénaïs that night, I surveyed the crowd in the spectator gallery. To my dismay, Boivin stood amongst them. He smirked. I set my jaw and continued to my seat at the table, vowing not to let my distress show.

The first course was served, but my stomach was in such a knot I could do little more than nibble at the array of cheeses offered. *Mimolette. Brie de Meaux.* The pungent *Livarot.* And the nutty goat cheese they called *Crottin de Chavignol.*

My gaze swept out over the gallery again, surprised at how large the assemblage had grown. I could no longer find Boivin among the faces. Perhaps he had left. The knot in my stomach loosened a bit.

The second course, lamb stew, was so aromatic my appetite returned.

"Most delectable," King Louis said as he scooped chunks of the tender meat with his fingers. The Queen used a spoon to lift bits of carrots and turnips to her lips.

Athénaïs studied her bowl, a look of consternation clouding her face. She held up a hand to summon the majordomo hovering nearby. "I wish to have a fork."

All conversation stopped. Spoons halted in mid-air. The lamb between the King's fingers dripped sauce midway to his mouth. The majordomo, disconcerted, looked to him for guidance. Without even glancing in Athénaïs's direction, King Louis sighed and nodded. The majordomo hurried to the door where he whispered to a waiting footman who hustled off.

Disgruntled, Louis returned the meat to his bowl, wiped his fingers on a napkin, then folded his hands in his lap. The rest of us did the same, sitting with our hands folded, saying nothing until the footman returned holding aloft a gilded platter. He handed the platter with great ceremony to the majordomo, and the majordomo with even more ceremony presented it to Athénaïs. She took the small silver fork from the platter and held it up for all to see, its pearl handle glimmering in the candlelight.

With a smile, Athénaïs poked the fork into her stew, picked out a chunk of lamb and brought it to her lips.

"Satisfactory?" the King asked.

"Oui. Merci." Athénaïs offered her most alluring smile then dipped her fork again.

Louis nodded, then scooped the almost certainly cold meat from his bowl with his fingers. La Grande Mademoiselle, with a grunt of disapproval, reached for her spoon, so I picked up mine.

When the dinner was over, King Louis stood and whispered something into Athénaïs's ear. Did he hand her something? I couldn't be sure; it was such a private gesture. He held out an arm to the Queen and together they left.

I was determined to avoid another encounter with Boivin, and so stayed close to Athénaïs and her retinue of favored courtiers back to her apartment. Was that the King's signet ring on her finger? Later, alone, I helped Athénaïs remove her jewelry — all but a simple strand of pearls — before she dismissed me.

Another letter lay on the silver receiving plate in my antechamber. This one had been composed on fine linen paper with the outline of a dove pressed into the wax seal. In elegant script was written a notation to deliver it to *Mlle Sylvienne d'Aubert au Palais du Louvre.* Above that, the name of the sender: *Marie-Catherine Girard d'Amiens.* My heart soared. Sitting at my toilette table, I broke the seal on the letter and unfolded the linen paper while Lisette took off my jewelry.

Ma très chère Sylvienne, Amiens is not itself without you.

Lisette began untying my stays. I groaned with impatience as she pulled off my bodice, skirts, and chemise. In one swift motion, she pulled my nightgown over my head. Settling back into my chair, I picked up the letter again.

I stand corrected — the convent school is the same as it ever was, except Mère Abbesse has gotten even more strict. She has forbidden us to read anything except the Bible and the classics. I miss finding delicious novels hidden away in the crannies of the wall.

I couldn't help but smile at the memories as the first strokes of Lisette's brush pulled through my hair.

Your mother and I spoke the other day at the market. She is always so kind to me and her greeting was warm, but there is a certain sadness in her eyes. I think it has been difficult for her to accept your absence.

A heaviness settled in my heart. Oh, Maman. I never should have left you. Closing my eyes for a moment, I said a quick prayer for her.

Marie-Catherine's next words caused my eyebrows to arch with curiosity.

I must tell you the news about Claudette. She, too, has —

A soft knock sounded on the antechamber door, startling me. I slipped into a curtsy as King Louis passed through on his way to Athénaïs's boudoir.

"You look lovely as ever," he said to me. "That nightgown becomes you." He smiled then disappeared through her door.

I blinked, not knowing how to take his compliment. While his nighttime visits were not as regular as those of the noon hour, they were often enough that I had stopped being embarrassed to be caught in my nightclothes. Lisette had told me it was common knowledge that, regardless of how late the King stayed with Athénaïs, he always returned to the Queen's bed before the sun rose. Would I ever get used to the rules of love and marriage here? I shook my head then returned to Marie-Catherine's letter.

I must tell you the news about Claudette. She, too, has left the convent school. She claims her parents became disenchanted with the education the sisters provide, but I think it must be something more than that, although I cannot imagine what. They have also withdrawn their funding for the convent. That is making it difficult for those of us still here. My father is not happy with the rise in fees since Claudette left. I wonder how much longer he will allow me to stay.

Such an odd state of affairs. I hoped Marie-Catherine would not have to quit her education before she was ready. I read on.

My news of Etienne is most worrisome. He has become distant and surly recently. He no longer meets with our clients. Instead, he spends all his time in the back of the shop scribbling in his sketchbook and working on shoes. Papa had plans to send him to the university in Rouen, but Etienne seems to have lost all enthusiasm for anything except working with the leather. And that is a shame, because Papa has high hopes of seeing him take over the family business one day. I have tried talking with him. However, he avoids me. I don't know what is wrong with him.

A dread settled over me as I put the letter down and climbed into bed. Marie-Catherine had no way of knowing Etienne's malaise was my fault, that he had been expecting I would marry him. I think if I had stayed in Amiens I would have. I loved him. But now? I was enjoying my new life at court, serving as maid of honor to Athénaïs. I relished the attention of the King and of Monsieur and Madame. If only Etienne had been born into privilege. Still, Marie-Catherine's letter reminded me how much I missed him. The sweetness of his lips. The warmth of his arms around me when we sat together on Jolie. Sometimes at night I found myself dreaming he was a courtier enjoying palace life with me.

Yawning, I decided my response to Marie-Catherine would have to wait until morning. Curling up under the covers, I didn't notice when the King passed through on his way out, or when Lisette blew out the candles.

The sun was high before I awoke the next morning. After I broke my fast and while Lisette pinned my hair into tight elongated coils — a court fashion my unruly curls too often resisted — another missive arrived for me.

"La Grande Mademoiselle's seal," Lisette observed as she handed me the letter.

Puzzled, I broke the wax and studied the note.

> *Mademoiselle d'Aubert, S'il vous plaît, join me at my table for cards today. Cordialement, Anne Marie Louise d'Orléans, Duchesse de Montpensier*

She was the last person I expected an invitation from. Perhaps her heart had softened toward me. After that business with the caricature in *La Gazette*, I could use another ally at court.

The pastry buffet in the game room was most tempting as I walked past it looking for la Grande Mademoiselle. Greeting courtiers at this table and that, I noticed something odd. In front of each, alongside their hors d'oeuvre plates lay...a fork. Pewter forks, silver forks, forks with etched scrollwork or spindled handles, some with two tines, some with three.

At la Grande's table, I curtsied first to Prince Philippe and then to the Duchesse herself before taking my place. When a courtier sidled up thinking to avail himself of the last empty chair, la Grande offered a barely perceptible frown, and he scuttled away.

"Why so many forks?" I asked.

Philippe cocked his head. "Our Athénaïs does not wish to eat with her fingers anymore, thus we..." He wiggled his fingers. "Shall not eat with ours anymore either."

"And the King...?" I asked, suppressing a giggle.

"The King shall continue to do as the King wishes to do," la Grande said as Philippe dealt out the cards. "But I expect eventually he, too, will acquiesce."

"Yours is quite lovely," I said to her. A highly polished mahogany box held a three-tined silver fork with a mother-of-pearl handle and a matching knife.

"I dare say, the cutlery vendors have had a profitable day." She sniffed and closed the lid.

"And yours, as well, Monsieur."

Philippe picked up his gold fork with its scrollwork of hearts and grape clusters and stabbed a candied pear from his plate. "One must always eat with the utmost of elegance." He thrust the pear into his mouth and, after pulling the gold implement from between his lips, smacked them noisily.

I chuckled as I plucked a card from my hand.

"You've made yourself quite at home here at court,"la Grande said.

My hand stopped mid-way to the discard pile. There was something in her tone that set me on edge. With careful deliberation, I finished my play. "Perhaps not. I do not yet know where the cutlery vendors park their carts."

Philippe smirked at my attempt at a witticism, but it seemed la Grande was not in the mood for coy banter.

"I will be direct with you," she said. "I was not pleased to learn, upon your arrival at court, that I had competition for my estate in the person of your mother. A supposed half-sister."

I sucked in a breath. She dared suggest my mother to be a usurper?

"Come, come, ma grande cousine," Philippe said. "I am quite certain neither our dear Sylvienne nor her mother has designs on your inheritance." He looked at me with a mischievous twinkle in his eye. "Or do you?"

"Inheritance?"

La Grande spoke to Philippe but kept her eyes planted on me. "As the bastard child of a bastard child, this urchin has no right to inheritance of any sort, whether mine or anyone else's in this family."

I slammed my cards down on the table. "I am not a..." Aware of heads turning in our direction, I lowered my voice. "I am not illegitimate. My father was a nobleman. Guy d'Aubert d'Amiens. Granted he was only a lesser nobleman and granted my mother and I lost our house to his awful brother, but my standing in life is quite legitimate."

Philippe clapped his hands. In support or to mock me? More heads turned.

"You think so, do you?" La Grande stood up. "We shall see just who you are. And why you have presented yourself to my cousin's court. My advice to you is to know your place, and not to take your cues from that woman who usurps the Queen's rightful place in her husband's bed." She snatched up her cutlery box and stormed off.

It seems I had stopped breathing in that moment, for I exhaled all at once.

"Pay no attention to la Grande," Philippe said, scooping her abandoned coins into his own pile. "She is only jealous that someone new has caught Louis's eye."

"Surely you jest."

He shook his head. "She once had hopes herself of being his queen. But our mother, who of course was Louis's regent at the time, would have none of it." He picked up the cards, shuffled them once, then set the deck in front of me, tapping them for me to cut. When I'd done so with a shaky hand, he picked them up again, then leaned in close. "My advice to you — if you wish to have a position of influence here — is to exercise discretion. Be constantly observant. And perhaps, at times, even a little cunning." He spread the cards out in an arc in front of me. "Choose one."

I blinked. I wasn't striving for a position of influence. All I desired was to experience a life grander than the one I'd known at home.

"Go ahead, choose one."

I lifted a card. The Jack of hearts.

"Ah, good choice!" He took it from me. "I predict you will find love here at court."

My heart beat a little faster. Could he read my thoughts? But I was betrothed to Etienne. Or almost so.

"Remember." He scooped up the cards. "Discretion and cunning." Tapped the deck on the table. "Skills you will need if you are to survive." Rose and bowed. "Until next time, my beautiful little cousine." He waggled his fingers over his shoulder as he walked away. "Au revoir."

Lisette greeted me upon my return, clutching a small parcel. "A courier delivered this."

The package was wrapped in a floral silk fabric and bound with gilt ribbon. I opened it to find an enameled cutlery case, inside of which was a silver fork, its handle inlaid with mother-of-pearl and topped with silver scrollwork. Puzzled as to who would send me such a gift, I opened the folded card nestled inside the case.

In disgust, I thrust the box, silk wrappings and all, back into Lisette's hands. "Take it! I don't want it."

"I don't understand, Mademoiselle." Lisette's startled eyes widened as she looked from the box to me.

"You can have it. Do with it what you will. Keep it. Sell it. I don't care. It's yours." I began to pace.

"Mademoiselle, please, is something wrong?" Lisette begged.

"I wish to go out." But I couldn't go out. The fork was from Guillaume Boivin, and I had no wish to encounter him in the garden again or anywhere. "No. I will go to the chapel. Will you accompany me?"

"Of course, Mademoiselle. If you have need of prayer, we will go immediately." She thrust the box with the gilded fork into the closet where she slept. She draped my shawl around my shoulders, then reached for her own. "What will we be praying for?"

"For my very soul," I responded. Because in that moment I wanted to thrust that fork into Guillaume Boivin's heart.

CHAPTER TWENTY-SEVEN

"Of course you'll go to the salon," Athénaïs said, rummaging through my wardrobe the next day. "A second invitation from Mademoiselle de Scudéry is not to be taken lightly." She pulled out a sapphire and white ensemble with a contrasting stomacher and full paneled sleeves cinched with yellow garters below the elbows. "This one. It sets off your eyes." She held the dress out for Lisette to take.

The Angelus had rung at noon, but still I lay in bed, cocooned under the down coverlet so warm and comforting, the world outside so cold and mean-spirited. The King was off hunting, and Athénaïs was eager to take advantage of her freedom. I tried making excuses, but she wouldn't hear of it and ordered Lisette to get me dressed.

Later, in Princess Henriette's carriage—she had invited Athénaïs and me to ride with her—I twisted a sachet of citrus-scented leaves and shut my eyes to the discomfiting sights of the Parisian streets. How could I face those people again after that caricature in *La Gazette*? And then la Grande Mademoiselle accused me of trying to steal her inheritance. And now, Boivin mocking me with that fork. The morning breeze did nothing to allay my disquiet on what should have been a joyous May Day.

Henriette leaned across and patted my hand. "Fretting doesn't become you, Sylvienne. Hold your head high and let the world know you will not be cowed by a silly cartoon."

I looked across at her and nodded, but I could not bring myself to smile.

"I promise you, it will not be mentioned," she said.

"Truly?" Who could control the vicious wit of people such as that prancing Chevalier?

"Madame speaks with verity," Athénaïs said. "Mademoiselle de Scudéry decides what is discussed in her salon, and she has no interest in prolonging the public humiliation of one of her inner circle."

"Her inner circle? Me?"

The ripple of Henriette's laughter lightened my mood. "Ma chérie, you would not be in this carriage on your way to her salon if she did not consider you one of her intimates. She told me herself you are her favorite newcomer."

My eyes were wide and my smile genuine as we pulled up in front of the *salonnière's* townhouse. When the footman opened the carriage door, Henriette took my hand. "Remember, head high, chin up."

Surveying Mademoiselle de Scudéry's salon, I noticed with disappointment that the handsome Duc de Narbonne was not among the guests today. Nor was the Chevalier de Lorraine. Of that, I was glad. Philippe was instead accompanied by a pretty-faced young man I had never seen before. He introduced his friend as Antoine Coëffier de Ruzé, the Marquis d'Effiat.

"I am pleased to make your acquaintance," I said, dipping into a polite curtsy.

"Mademoiselle, the pleasure is all mine. Monsieur speaks highly and at great length of your beauty and your cleverness. Of the former, I can see with my own eyes. Of the latter, well, let's just say I look forward to a rollicking and convivial discourse this afternoon." He bent forward to kiss my fingers.

"Merci," I said, extracting my hand. "You are far too kind." I couldn't tell if he was sincere or being impertinent. Sitting down next to Athénaïs, I glanced over to see d'Effiat surreptitiously stroke Philippe's leg.

A servant held a platter in front of me with a cup of chocolate, served this time with a dollop of Chantilly cream and a splash of hazelnut liqueur. The steaming drink calmed my nerves.

Mademoiselle de Scudéry, sitting amongst her bright pillows—today wearing a turquoise gown with a matching turban—rang her little bell. "Mademoiselle d'Aubert, welcome back." Murmurs of agreement rose from the circle.

After a reading of a new poem by Jean-Baptiste Racine, Henriette opened her fan and fluttered it. "I understand the Prince de Condé made a most unusual wager at the card tables this week."

"Yes," Athénaïs said. "He lost several plots of land he owned in Nouvelle-France."

"To whom did he lose them?" Madame de Sévigné asked.

"To Lorgeleux."

"The Duc de Narbonne?" Mademoiselle de Scudéry said.

"Yes. I don't imagine the Duc is happy with his acquisition, though," Athénaïs replied.

"Then he's a fool," Philippe said. "There is a burgeoning trade business in furs from the colony, if one wishes to take advantage of it."

"But is it sustainable?" d'Effiat asked. "The place is a wilderness. It takes people to create a business."

"Have you not heard of my brother's initiative to recruit marriageable young women to help populate the colony?"

"What woman would sail across an ocean on a king's whim?" Madame de Sévigné asked, reaching for a plate of *petit fours* offered by a servant.

"Quite a few, it would seem," Philippe said. "The program has been an astounding success, from what I understand."

"And the incentive?" Madame de La Fayette asked.

"Besides the King paying their passage and dowries?" Athénaïs said, her tone implying that should be enough.

"They say the young ladies are allowed to choose their husbands from among the available men." Philippe waved away the servant with the plate of treats.

"Oh, that can't be true!" Madame de Sévigné stopped licking her fingers.

"It is true," I said, instantly regretting having drawn attention to myself again. There was nothing to do, however, but go on. "I have a dear friend who married in Quebec under the sponsorship of His Majesty."

"What an odd circumstance." Madame de Sévigné brows furrowed. "Who would allow a young woman to choose her husband? So much can go wrong."

"Is your friend happy with her choice?" Princess Henriette asked, holding up her chocolate cup for a servant to take away.

"Quite happy, so she says. But I can't picture what it must be like for her there. New France is a primitive and barbarous place to raise a family."

"And what does it say of a man's character that he allows himself to be chosen, as it were." D'Effiat crossed his arms over his chest.

Philippe scoffed. "They live in the woods with wild animals and savages. Character isn't much of a concern."

"Character is always of concern," Henriette countered, holding his gaze pointedly. "Regardless of one's circumstance."

I wasn't sure if she was speaking in general or implying something about her husband and their own marriage. Regardless, thinking of Perrette, I hoped the man she chose had character worthy of her.

"Congratulations!" Henriette said as we bumped over cobblestones on our way back to the palace.

"For what?" I asked.

"You held your head high."

I smiled. "I suppose I did."

Henriette patted my hand. "It is only two days until we depart for Fontainebleau. You will love the château."

"Everyone says it is lovely," I said.

"I don't suppose you have proper dancing shoes?" Athénaïs's fan had slowed.

"Dancing shoes?"

"Have you not heard?" Henriette said. "There is to be a grand fête while we are there. Lully is composing a new score for the ballet."

"But why would I need dancing shoes?" I grabbed at a bar on the carriage wall as we lurched around a corner.

"So you can dance, silly!" Henriette said. "All the ladies of the court dance in the chorus with the King."

"King Louis dances?"

I must have sounded the dunce, for Athénaïs scoffed. "Of course, he dances."

"Louis is a marvelous dancer," Henriette said. "Exquisite, in truth."

"Madame will dance the lead opposite him," Athénaïs said. "The rest of us take supporting roles."

"Queen Marie-Thérèse does not dance the lead?"

Both women stared at me astounded, then broke into gales of laughter. I frowned in frustration over my apparent faux pas.

"The Queen does not dance," Athénaïs said, snapping her fan closed.

"Never?"

"Never."

Nor did I, as Henriette already knew. My convent school education had introduced me to the classics, I could do sums in my head, my stitches were neat and tidy, and like the other girls, I could sing in both French and Latin. However, the one thing the nuns did not teach us was to dance.

As our carriage passed through a market just blocks from the palace, a movement caught my eye, a commotion in the street. I leaned forward and shouted, "Stop! Stop the carriage!"

Startled, Henriette banged on the carriage wall. "Driver! Stop! Sylvienne, what is it?"

I was out the carriage door and fairly jumping down the steps. I ran toward a stall where Guillaume Boivin had Lisette by the arm, dragging her along. She protested but looked too frightened to scream.

I pounced on him, beating against his back. "Unhand her, you cur! What are you doing?"

He sidestepped and scowled at me but did not let her go.

"Mademoiselle." He feigned great regard for my concern. "This wench has stolen from you. I was about to deliver her into the custody of the local gendarme."

"No. Mademoiselle, please, I did not steal. I would never do so. Not from a fr—" She stopped herself. "From you."

"What is it you think she stole?" I could not believe the girl would do such a thing.

Boivin held up the little wooden box he had sent me, flicking it open to reveal the pearl-handled fork. "I caught her trying to sell it here at one of the second-hand merchant stalls."

My eyes narrowed in disgust. "I assure you she did not steal that fork from me."

"Then how did she come into possession of it? Hmm?" He shook her. "And why is it every time I ask you about it, you go mute?"

My poor Lisette. Her eyes filled with tears, and she trembled in his grasp.

"I gave her that fork. I told her to do with it what she will. She has chosen to sell it, and that is fine with me. I do not wish to own it."

Boivin stared at me in disbelief for a moment. Then he shoved Lisette away. I managed to catch her before she fell to the ground.

"What is going on? Is there a problem?" Henriette pushed through the gathering onlookers, her security guard and Athénaïs in tow.

"Madame." Even though I had just been in her company, I dropped into a curtsy to alert those around us that she was a woman to be reckoned with.

"Madame." Boivin bowed. He, of course, knew immediately who she was. "Marquise." He bowed toward Athénaïs. "There has been an apparent misunderstanding."

"Of what nature?" Athénaïs asked.

"Of a personal nature. A gift that was unappreciated made its way to the sellers' stalls. It is of no consequence." He tossed the small box into the air and caught it like a ball. Then he pitched it into a nearby dung heap. He turned to me. "My apologies, Mademoiselle. I underestimated the depth of your antipathy." He smiled, but his eyes glinted cruelly. He lowered his voice. "Rest assured, one day you'll be required to change your mind about me."

A chill passed through me.

He bowed again then brushed past the guard and strode off through the crowd. The guard waved the onlookers away.

"Are you hurt?" Henriette asked.

I shook my head.

"And you?" She asked of Lisette, who dissolved into tears again. "You must ride with us in my carriage. I insist."

Putting my arm around Lisette, I glanced at Athénaïs. She nodded. Lisette balked as we approached the royal carriage, but Henriette reassured her, and Athénaïs motioned for the girl to sit next to me.

She accepted the linen handkerchief I offered. I felt bad about the fork. Not that it had ended up in a dung heap, but that Lisette could no longer make use of it.

CHAPTER TWENTY-EIGHT

The sun had yet to crest the hillside when a cavalcade of wagons laden with royal furniture and baggage set out for Fontainebleau, each pulled by a pair of hearty draft horses. An hour later, I climbed into a coach along with six of the Queen's ladies-in-waiting. A throng of bleary-eyed courtiers climbed into the hundred or so other carriages.

Queen Marie-Thérèse, Henriette, and Athénaïs, along with the spaniels, traveled in the royal coach pulled by six white stallions with braided tails and feathered plumes on their heads. King Louis and his brother cantered alongside, Louis on his favorite white Andalusian, Philippe on a lively black gelding. Bringing up the rear were the courtiers' baggage carts and wagons loaded with servants.

A full day's journey ahead of us, Lisette had warned me not to drink along the way. It seemed an odd admonishment, but I soon came to realize why. The King did not allow his retinue to stop for anything, not even for his ladies to take care of their personal needs. We ate bread and cheese while bouncing along the rugged roads. I sipped cider to quench my thirst.

By the time our caravan rolled up the potted-tree-lined avenue leading to Fontainebleau, the setting sun was bathing the château's façade in a golden glow. A befitting arrival for the Sun King. However, as soon as our carriage came to a halt, I leaped out and ran for the nearest bush, the Queen's ladies not far behind me. My business finished, I hurried to find Athénaïs who was just emerging from behind a bush of her own. Her face had a grey cast to it.

"Are you not well?" I asked.

"I'm fine." She mopped her brow with an embroidered linen handkerchief. "The motion of the carriage and the Queen's perfume overwhelmed me."

The King dismounted and removed his plumed hat. "How was the ride?" he asked.

Athénaïs offered her usual, captivating smile. "The Queen was delightful company, as always. She enthralled us with her enlightened conversation."

Mortified at Athénaïs's choice of words—Queen Marie-Thérèse was famous for her poor French and lack of personality—I watched for the King's reaction. To my surprise, he only chuckled.

"What do you think?" he said to me, sweeping an arm across the vista of the château and its grounds. He seemed particularly energized.

"*C'est magnifique*, Sire."

"I'm glad you like it. Tomorrow you learn to ride." He put his hat back on. "I'll see you both at dinner." He kissed the back of Athénaïs's hand before loping up the horseshoe-shaped steps, his elegant form disappearing into the building.

"He's so handsome!" I blurted.

Athénaïs regarded me with a look I could not discern. Irritation? Consternation? I chided myself for thinking it might be jealousy. I didn't have time to puzzle it out, however. She smiled and entwined my arm in hers. "Shall we find our apartment?"

Dinner that first night at Fontainebleau was a small, intimate gathering. Unlike at the Louvre where anyone who could afford to dress appropriately was allowed to attend, here only a chosen few were present to watch the royal family dine. To my relief, Guillaume Boivin was not among them.

The next morning, I rose early, well before Athénaïs, Henriette, or any of the courtiers. After dressing with the help of a sleepy Lisette, I headed out to explore the grounds of the château.

Finding my way to the center of the manicured garden, I gazed up at the Fountain of Diana, the Roman goddess of the hunt. Appropriate, given King Louis's love of the sport. Inhaling deeply, I took delight in the fresh air, the gentle breeze carrying the fragrance of peonies in bloom. Cardinals, bright red and trilling to each other, flitted along the boxwood hedges that edged the garden path. A hawk flew overhead, silent on the breeze, then dove toward a distant field.

An arched gateway nestled in the hedge beckoned. Curiosity was one of my faults, Tatie had always admonished. True to form, I couldn't resist investigating. On the other side of the hedge, I discovered the stables. The tang of fresh hay and horsehide, the sting of manure slopped out of the barns and into waiting carts, reminded me of the barns in Amiens. Grooms, who must have been up at the first crowing of the cock, led horses to various paddocks. A stableboy brushed a chestnut mare. Unlike the vacant courtyard garden surrounded by apartments full of sleeping courtiers, the stables compound was busy, purposeful, full of life.

"Have you forgotten your riding boots?"

Swinging around, I dipped into a curtsy. "Your Majesty. I didn't think you'd be up and about at this hour."

He swept his brown leather hat from his head and bowed, looking gallant in green riding breeches and a matching doublet. His dogs rushed to sniff my hands. I reached down to scratch the ears of my favorite, Hera.

"You had better hurry and change," King Louis said, thrusting his hat back onto his lush, dark hair. "I believe we have a lesson to accomplish this morning."

My heart soaring, I curtsied again and rushed off to find Lisette.

Fortunately, when the dressmaker designed my new wardrobe, Athénaïs had thought to order a set of riding clothes for me. A handsomely tailored olive-green jacket with lemon and apricot trim over a cream-colored silk chemisette and a green wool skirt. The outfit was topped with a matching narrow-brimmed hat, two apricot-colored feathers tucked in its band. Lisette soon had me outfitted, and I bounded back out to the stables where King Louis was feeding bits of apple to a dappled mare.

"Ready to ride?" He stroked the mare's nose. "This is Phoebe. She's quite gentle. Up you go." He motioned for a stableman to help me into the sidesaddle.

I had never been on a horse by myself, only ever behind Etienne or tucked safely in his arms. And certainly never sidesaddle.

"Hook your right knee over the pommel," King Louis said. "Yes, like that. Now tuck your other knee up under the horn. That will help you balance and give you more control over the horse."

I positioned my body as instructed, adjusting my skirts to fit.

He guided my foot into the slipper stirrup then handed me the reins. "Comfortable?"

Upon my nod, he took the halter lead and with a cluck of his tongue guided Phoebe into a slow walk. Startled, I grasped the pommel with a nervous laugh. Soon, however, I found my balance and began to enjoy the feel of the horse under me.

"What do you think?" he asked.

"I'm riding!" I said, unable to hide my foolish grin.

He laughed. "Indeed, you are."

He handed the lead to the stableman who led Phoebe around the paddock several more times, trotting alongside to allow the mare to go a little faster each time.

The King beckoned for his own horse, not the Andalusian but a tall black steed he called Atlas. With the help of the groom's handhold, he swung into the saddle. Atlas pranced for a moment, eager to be off, but the King reined him in. The stableman led Phoebe out of the paddock.

"Click your tongue when you're ready to go," King Louis said. "Tug the reins to tell her which direction to turn. Pull back when you want to stop. She'll do the rest."

Clicking my tongue, I grabbed the pommel again when she began to walk but thrilled at the feel of her under me. King Louis led the way out onto the lane. We ambled side by side between rows of linden trees, the mastiffs and spaniels rollicking alongside.

"You take to riding quite naturally," he said. "Soon you and Phoebe will be galloping in the fields."

At the end of the lane, we turned our horses around. I wished we could ride longer, but I dared not say so. The King had been quite generous with his time already. As we approached the château, he shouted, "They're here!"

He kicked his steed into a fast trot. I urged Phoebe to follow.

In front of the grand staircase stood an ornate carriage pulled by four plumed horses. Two men climbed out. King Louis pulled to a halt and slid off his horse, the dogs bounding up to greet them. The men bowed, doffing their hats.

He grabbed each man in turn by the shoulders. "It's good to see you again."

I pulled Phoebe up next to Atlas. A groom rushed to grab her halter, and a stableman helped me down.

Louis beckoned me forward. "Ma chère Sylvienne, come say bonjour to Messieurs Molière and Lully."

My knees nearly buckled at the names of the most famous playwright and musician in all of France. I took a breath and curtsied. The men bowed back—to me!

Louis smiled expansively. "Sylvienne, Lully has composed a new ballet for us."

The taller man nodded in agreement.

Then the King said, "This will be Mademoiselle d'Aubert's first time dancing with our little troupe."

"Is that so?" Lully asked.

I blinked. "Me? But, Sire, I do not dance. I mean…I would love to, but…I do not know how." Out of the corner of my eye I could see Molière enjoying my discomfort.

"Nonsense," King Louis said. "Anyone can dance. You will be merveilleuse. Lully, don't you agree? She just needs to be taught a few steps."

"Of course, Sire." Lully inclined his head in assent, but I could tell by his forced smile—and Molière's broadening smirk—that he did not appreciate having to add yet another impossible task to his roster of responsibilities. I hated the thought that my inadequacy would burden this great man.

I needn't have worried. That afternoon, Lully turned me over to Pierre Savard, the royal dance master who, after one look at my attempts to dance, assigned one of his protégés to be my instructor.

CHAPTER TWENTY-NINE

"*Non, non, non!*" André Beausoleil, the assistant dance instructor, held out his hands in exasperation. He was a tall, slender man, his dull brown hair cropped to his shoulders. "Step forward, step forward, step back. Then twirl. This movement is the *courante*. Try it again."

My first dance lesson was turning out to be a miserable failure. It was as if I had two toes on one foot and too many on the other. My rhythm didn't match the music. I stumbled through the steps.

King Louis peeked in once, his brows knit. "Perhaps a different instructor?" he asked Lully.

I missed my step and tripped again.

The sound of retching interrupted my morning breakfast. Alarmed, I crept to Athénaïs's door and peeked in. The Marquise, still in her nightgown, knelt over her chamber pot, Martine holding a damp cloth to her mistress's forehead.

"Are you ill?" I asked, stepping in.

"Something I ate last night disagrees with me." She turned her pallid face and vomited into the pot again. When she came up for air, she waved me away. "Get dressed. We start rehearsals for the ballet today."

I rushed to take her arm as Martine helped her back to her bed. "Will you be able to dance?"

"Of course. It's a stomach upset. Nothing more."

I suspected it *was* something more, however. One could not be intimate with the King on a daily basis without consequence.

However, there was no time to dwell on Athénaïs's condition. I had another worry this morning — another dance lesson with Beausoleil.

Courtiers gathered to watch my progress in the chandeliered ballroom as he attempted to teach me the *allemande*, which required me to hold my fingertips up to his while we performed three tandem springing steps forward and a hop backward. By the end of the hour, I had managed to learn the steps. I was neither nimble nor graceful, but my tutor seemed satisfied I would not be an embarrassment to him.

After my lesson, I noted a cluster of dancers hovering around Princess Henriette in front of the arched floor-to-ceiling windows. The late morning sun shimmered through the diaphanous folds of her pearl-colored gown. Her admirers hanging on her every word, she seemed to be making a point of ignoring the group huddled with Philippe. He stood at the opposite end of the room near the enormous fireplace guarded on either side by larger-than-life bronze statues.

I wavered, unsure of which group to join. Philippe wore a flowing pink satin tunic and a garland of white carnations in his near-black hair. I owed some allegiance to him — he had been my champion here at court. Still, the joyful chatter around the Princess was too intoxicating to resist.

I had just melted into her crowd when Athénaïs swept into the room, her gauzy lemon-colored skirt flowing around her legs. All but the two royals turned to pay their obeisance. She acknowledged each of the clusters with a nod, then sought Lully and dance master Savard who stood consulting with the quartet of musicians.

King Louis, brilliant in his white and gold dance tunic and leggings, strode into the room with Molière. Lully signaled everyone to gather around.

Molière waited for the group to quiet before speaking. "The new ballet, *La Naissance d'Apollon*, dramatizes the birth of Apollo, god of music, dance, and poetry, god of sun and light. It begins when Hera, Zeus's wife, discovers her husband's mistress, Leto, is with child."

I glanced at Athénaïs, who casually adjusted her dancing skirt.

Molière explained that Hera banned Leto from giving birth anywhere on Earth. "But the voice of her unborn child, Apollo, tells her of a floating island called Delos. Leto flees to Delos where a flock of goddesses disguised as swans welcome her. Leto gives birth, first to Artemis, Apollo's twin sister. Then Apollo emerges from his mother's womb clutching a golden sword in one hand and a golden bow and arrow in the other."

The troupe burst into applause, King Louis clapping loudest of all. "Excellent! Excellent!"

After a dramatic pause, Lully announced, "His Majesty, our own King Louis will dance the role of Apollo."

A roar of approval erupted as the King bowed. "Merci, mes amis. Merci." He bowed again, this time toward Lully and Molière.

On King Louis's signal, the room quieted, and Lully continued. "Madame de Montespan will dance as Leto."

Princess Henriette looked surprised but joined in the applause. Athénaïs dipped into a theatrical curtsy.

Lully then assigned the role of Zeus to Philippe. Henriette was to be Artemis, Apollo's twin sister. Lully awarded the parts of Hera and Eileithyia, the goddesses of childbirth, to Madame de Polignac and Mademoiselle de Baude. I was to be one of the seven swan goddesses. King Louis beamed, smiling his delight with me.

The dancers stretched and took practice steps, chattering among themselves. I did my best to mimic some of their stretches. The movements were foreign to me, but I could feel the tension in my body loosening.

After a few moments, Lully clapped twice. "Shall we commence?"

He and Molière strode back to consult with the musicians, while dance master Savard took King Louis and the other primary dancers off to a corner of the ballroom. Beausoleil motioned for the swan goddesses to begin our rehearsal.

I tried in earnest to reproduce the steps he had taught me. The other swan goddesses took few pains to hide their smirks at my clumsiness. Their mirth didn't last long. One glance from the King in passing stopped their giggles. I was keenly aware, however, of how experienced they were, how quickly they acquired the new steps, and how dreadful was my dancing.

The next day wasn't much better. To my chagrin, my rhythm was off. I *pliéd* right when the other swans *pliéd* left. And I stumbled more than once.

"Mademoiselle d'Aubert, it is three steps forward, then you turn," shouted Beausoleil.

After a few trials, I managed to complete the steps in the correct sequence, but still my movements were awkward, not fluid like the other swan goddesses. When Beausoleil permitted us a brief rest, I drifted across the room with the others to watch King Louis rehearse with Athénaïs, Henriette, and Philippe. They were so accomplished, their feet performing intricate movements, their bodies seeming at one with the music.

I marveled as King Louis took three leaps across the stage, twirling after each. On the last step, however, he stumbled, lurching into several bystanders. We gasped as one. Someone caught him, but not before he'd fallen to his knees, biting his lip in pain. The heel of his right shoe had broken, causing his mishap.

Though he protested he was not hurt, when he stood, he limped. After examining his ankle, his personal physician declared His Majesty had only twisted it. He ordered the injured limb to be wrapped in wet compresses and the King to stay off his feet for the remainder of the day.

Lully signaled for the rest of us to take our positions again. With the King gone, the courtiers drifted to where we swans were practicing. A few pointed and smirked. My cheeks burned. Athénaïs, who had stopped to watch as well, threw her hands up in annoyance and stalked out.

"Again! Do it again." Beausoleil's voice droned.

I stepped, I hopped, I twirled. And landed on my derrière. The other dancers and the courtiers laughed openly now. I covered my face in shame.

"Enough!"

The crowd fell silent as Philippe, today dressed in black leggings and a simple black tunic cinched with a gold belt, stepped forward and held out a hand to help me up. He gestured toward the door. "Everyone out! Go. Now!"

The room cleared of onlookers and dancers alike. The musicians set their instruments down, prepared to flee.

"You stay," he said to them, then turned to Lully, Savard, and Beausoleil. "Messieurs, if you would give yourselves a respite. Perhaps a glass of wine in the garden."

The men nodded and left. Only the musicians, Philippe, and I remained. Tears rolled unbidden down my cheeks.

Philippe pulled a white linen handkerchief from his sleeve and offered it to me. In the gentlest of voices he said. "Sylvienne, compose yourself."

After I'd wiped my eyes and awkwardly tucked the handkerchief into my own sleeve, he signaled the musicians to resume playing. Stepping around me, graceful as a cat, he stood close behind me and put his hands on my shoulders. "Close your eyes," he said. "Listen to the music."

I could feel his body swaying, and after a moment I began to sway with him.

He took my hands and held them out on either side. "Feel the music."

My heartbeat slowed under his touch.

"Count to four with me then move to the right. Un, deux, trois, quatre…" He stepped to the right, I moved with him. "Now to the left. Un, deux, trois, quatre…" We stepped together. "This way…and back again…Turn around, but keep your eyes closed."

He guided my hands so that my body did as he bade. When at last I opened my eyes, we were facing each other.

"Don't worry about the steps." His voice was soothing but insistent. "Just feel the music. Un, deux, trois, quatre…" We stepped to the right, then back. I felt the rhythm. Still, he held my hands. "Two steps to the right, then to the left."

I followed his lead.

"Now forward, listening, feeling, don't pay attention to your feet, only the music."

Soon, I was doing all the steps. At the end of the movement, he twirled me around with a flourish. I looked up into his smiling eyes. "I did it!"

"*Vraiment.*" He squeezed my hand. "Ignore everyone. Listen to the music."

I nodded.

"Let's try it again." He signaled the musicians. This time, he held only one of my hands, dancing alongside me.

"This is fun," I said.

"That is the purpose. Not to impress others. To enjoy yourself."

He let go my hand, and I danced, moving with the music, my steps fluid, instinctive.

"Fetch Lully," he said to the flutist.

The musician, instrument in hand, ran out of the room. The others kept playing, and I danced, Philippe alongside me.

When Lully returned, with Savard and Beausoleil in tow, I demonstrated my steps. At the end of the movement, Lully nodded, satisfied. "We'll resume tomorrow."

Philippe bussed my cheeks. "You are going to be marvelous. I promise."

The next afternoon, with the King still out, Savard and Beausoleil put us through our paces, rehearsing the movements over and over. Relieved that spectators had been banned from the ballroom, I relaxed into my role, enjoying the rhythm of the music.

A short while later, Louis limped in. "I apologize for my tardiness, but a distressing situation has arisen. I just learned my favorite shoemaker has been laid low by apoplexy."

The dancers murmured their sympathy.

"I am sorry, Sire," Lully said. "Will he survive?"

Louis shook his head. "Not likely. Now I have no one to make me a new pair of shoes for the ballet."

Etienne! Should I mention him as a potential replacement? Before I could speak up, however, Savard said, "Sire, with your permission, I can introduce you to my shoemaker. He is quite good at his craft."

"I would like that. Thank you. How goes the rehearsal?" He looked around the room, his eyes settling on me. "I am told you have been practicing."

I nodded.

"Show me."

Beausoleil ordered the swan goddesses into position. Wracked by a sudden onset of nerves, I took several breaths to steady myself. Lully signaled the music to begin. I glanced over at Philippe. He touched his heart once and smiled. I closed my eyes for a moment, listening for the beat, then stepped out with the other swans. Murmurs of approval from Beausoleil filled me with elation. When I'd completed the routine, Athénaïs nodded her approval.

A collective hush settled over the room as King Louis tapped his chin before breaking into a broad smile. "This will be one of our best ballets ever."

Henriette rushed over and hugged me. "You were marvelous, ma chérie."

Two weeks later, we performed our ballet on a freshly painted stage in front of a crowd of several hundred courtiers. Our costumes had been designed by Henri de Gissey, our makeup and hair created by an army of artists presided over by Mademoiselle de Canilliat, the official *coiffeuse* for all court ballets.

Philippe, in a flowing black tunic embroidered with silver lightning bolts, danced the role of Zeus nimbly and with dark emotion. In stark contrast, Athénaïs's light, airy movements as his mistress were uplifting; her costume of white satin, cinched under her breasts with a simple gold braid, flowed as if blown by the wind as she turned and leaped. Her movements took on a sad, then torturous mien as Hera banned her until, at long last and with the help of the seven swan goddesses — in short gossamer frocks with flowing winged sleeves, white slippers, and garlands in our hair — she danced onto the island of Delos.

Henriette's *glissades* and *arabesques* as Artemis, Apollo's sister, were willowy, graceful, and elegant. Dressed in pale gold, she looked fragile, ephemeral.

But it was King Louis's dance with Athénaïs that mesmerized me. He stepped onto the stage attired in gold from head to foot, a crown of gold fanning out from his head, gold dust in his hair. As they performed their mother and unborn child *pas de deux*, their bodies entwined, twirling, leaping, coming together, pushing apart. Until Athénaïs, *en pointe*, pirouetted one last time then collapsed into a dramatic heap, while Louis performed a celebratory *grand jeté*, his legs outstretched as he leaped. At the end he settled his gold-clad body into a deep motionless reverence in front of her.

The audience, as one, stood and applauded, shouting their approval. But as the curtain slid down in front of the King and Athénaïs, I noticed one person in the front row still as stone, her unsmiling gaze fixed on a spot above the two dancers — Queen Marie-Thérèse. On either side, her ladies-in-waiting sat as well, for if the Queen did not rise, neither could they.

Someone nudged me from behind, reminding me to line up with the dancers. When the curtains opened again, we grabbed hands and bowed, the audience still cheering wildly. The Queen's chair was empty now.

CHAPTER THIRTY

"You danced beautifully tonight, Mademoiselle." Lisette helped me out of my swan goddess costume in my chamber.

"I was *so* nervous!" I grabbed her by the hands and danced her about the room humming the theme from the ballet as we twirled and giggled. When we stopped, I said, "Madame is hosting a party to celebrate. Tonight!"

Lisette chose a silk gown for me, one drenched in shades of plum and violet, trimmed with tulle and organdy. Its bodice, stiffened with whalebone, pushed my breasts up and out.

I grabbed her arm. "Lisette, why don't you attend the party with me? You could wear one of my dresses!"

"Don't be silly." She blushed, but I could tell my suggestion had pleased her.

A short while later, I joined Athénaïs whose gown of scarlet and gold perfectly complemented her honey-colored hair. When we entered Henriette's apartment, King Louis and all the guests applauded Athénaïs.

The King held a glass of champagne aloft in her honor. "To our talented goddess, Leto."

"A la vôtre!" we called out holding our glasses up as well.

Then he turned to me. "And to our newest member of the royal troupe."

I curtsied as they cried out, "Santé!"

Philippe approached with gleaming eyes and bade me twirl. "Your transformation is coming along nicely, cousine."

Lilting strains of violins punctuated the chatter as I wandered the room on Philippe's arm. Vases of deep purple lilacs adorned every table, filling the air with their intoxicating scent. Servants kept the buffet filled with every kind of sweets imaginable and held out trays with filled wine glasses.

When Philippe stepped away to talk with another guest, Mademoiselle de Baude, who had danced the part of Eileithyia, sidled up, touching my elbow. "With a gown like that, you'll want to be careful when you curtsy."

Accepting another glass of wine from a passing footman, I laughed. "Your advice is noted. What's going on there?"

The guests had formed a circle around Henriette and King Louis. They were singing the popular *"Sur le Pont d'Avignon,"* about a fabled bridge upon which lovers walked in the moonlight, kissed, then quarreled. De Baude and I joined them. By the time they got to the third verse, we were all singing along.

As the song ended, Louis pulled me onto his lap. "Tell us what you enjoy most about court life, ma chérie."

By now the wine and high spirits had taken over my tongue. "Parties! I love parties!"

The courtiers laughed. All except Athénaïs, whose sulky eyes sent a shiver through me. After a moment, she composed her face and turned to engage a young nobleman in conversation, laughing delightedly at some remark he had made. Which in turn made Louis grimace.

He leaned in close, whispering into my ear, "Your dancing was superb tonight. More wine?" Something about his arch tone confused me.

Henriette tapped a spoon against a glass bowl to get everyone's attention. "I wish to go for a swim in the pond. Who will join me?"

"I will!" I turned to the King, my eyebrows raised, beseeching. "May I, Sire?"

"Of course." He laughed as I slid off his lap and ran to join the group rushing out to the garden.

"Will you not come, Monsieur?" I asked Philippe who hung back with the Chevalier de Lorraine and several others. He shook his head no but waved for me to go have fun.

The night was unusually warm for May. Stars glimmered in the inky sky, the crescent moon playing peek-a-boo through tendrils of clouds. The pond shone like a fairyland, its edges lit with torches and lanterns. Eager men threw off their clothes and plunged, naked, into the water, creating ripples set ablaze with torchlight. The women took off all but their chemises, tiptoeing in.

"It's not polite to stare." Mademoiselle de Baude laughed, reaching for the laces on the back of my bodice. Tipsy with wine, I did nothing to dissuade her from undressing me.

"Come in! Come in!" the men called.

Untying de Baude's laces, I realized I had not seen Athénaïs for some time. "Where is Madame de Montespan?"

"She went back to her chambers."

"Without me?"

I must have sounded petulant for de Baude gave me the oddest look saying, "With the King."

"Yes, of course. How silly of me." I stood in the moonlight in nothing but my chemise, my arms crossed over my chest.

"Don't be shy, Sylvienne. Come in," Henriette urged. "The water is wonderful."

When I hesitated, de Baude, her breasts visible through her creamy chemise, grabbed my hand and pulled me into the pond, giggling and splashing. The water was surprisingly warm, but still I hugged my arms to my body.

"Have you never gone swimming in your little village?" Henriette asked before leaning back to float with her face to the night sky, her golden hair fanning out around her head.

I pushed onto my back, relishing the water as it embraced me. Floating alongside the Princess, gazing up at the stars and moon, I didn't tell her I grew up swimming in the river alongside Etienne. She shrieked with laughter when one of the naked courtiers swam alongside us like a whale spouting water.

Beausoleil swam up next to me, only his head and chest visible above the water. "Are you enjoying yourself?" the dance instructor asked.

"Immensely."

"You danced extraordinarily well tonight."

"Merci." I kicked my feet then swiveled to stand upright. "I fear I have much to learn, however."

"Perhaps you would like me to continue your instruction." He sucked in water and blew it out in a spout. Something about his voice reminded me of the lecherous tutor back in Amiens.

"That is kind of you." I turned to seek out Henriette again, but she had floated off.

Beausoleil grabbed my wrist and pulled me close to him so I could feel his manhood under the water. "Would you like a lesson right now?"

Before I could pull away, his other hand reached up behind my head and he covered my mouth with his own. I pushed at him as hard as I could. When he wouldn't move, I stepped on his foot and ground mine into it.

He spluttered in pain and let go.

I splashed away just as Henriette called out, "I'm cold. Let's go back inside."

Relieved at the opportunity to escape, I sloshed toward the pond's edge. The men bobbed about in the water as the women waded out of the shallow end. When I glanced back, Beausoleil was watching me. Uncomfortably aware of how my wet chemise clung to my body, my breasts, I hurried to catch up with Henriette and the other women. I gathered up my clothes and, holding them tight against me, ran into Henriette's chamber. There I slipped out of my wet underthings, dried myself, and pulled on my skirts and bodice, my hair hanging limp down my back.

Henriette kindly summoned a page and a serving maid to see me safely back to my chamber. With Lisette's help, I changed into my night clothes and climbed into bed, shivering.

"Did you have a good time at the party?" Lisette asked, tucking a warming brick under the covers close to my feet.

"It was a wonderful evening." I shook away the memory of Beausoleil grabbing me under the water. "Quite illuminating."

My head throbbed on my pillow in the morning. The sight of breakfast turned my stomach. Lisette prepared a hot, steaming tea made of hyssop and fennel. The concoction eased my churlish stomach and lessened the tension in my head. Before long I was able to eat a bit of toasted bread with goat cheese.

Later that morning, I found Athénaïs leaning over her chamber pot again. By the time Louis arrived for his noontime visit, however, her cheeks were pink, and she was glowing.

As I settled onto my favorite chair to read with the spaniels nestled at my feet, a courier arrived with a letter. I unfolded the thin paper.

> *Dearest Daughter,*
> *Your latest letter was heart-warming to read. And while I am pleased, I am also concerned about your newfound passion for the salons of Paris. I have no doubt the coterie with whom you engage are well worth your time and acquaintance. However, I fear you are of an age in which ideas and intentions are easily misconstrued, and I am concerned you may be inappropriately influenced in matters of morals and principles. Guard your mind and your soul as well as your heart when you attend these gatherings.*

I set the letter on the table and closed my eyes. Maman was right to warn me about guarding my soul and my heart. But it was not the salons that needed guarding against. My head began to throb again, and I asked for more of the hyssop and fennel tea. When the pain subsided, I took up my quill.

> *Dearest Maman, I think you will not believe this, but I have learned to dance!*

I smiled, thinking of the performance and my insignificant role in it. How I wished Maman could have been here to see it. Had she ever danced? I had never seen her do so, not even in the village square during Mardi Gras. I told her about King Louis dancing as Apollo.

Maman, he is a glorious dancer!

And my role as a swan goddess. I described how agog I was to be in the company of Lully and Molière and took great pains to describe the costumes and the scenery. I did not mention Princess Henriette's party or my dance instructor, Beausoleil.

King Louis stalked out of Athénaïs's boudoir while I was sealing my letter. A fierce frown marring his face, he left without acknowledging me. Concerned, I rushed into her room.

"Athénaïs?"

She stood looking out the window. When she didn't answer, I went to see what held her attention so. Down in the courtyard a man dressed in a black coat of the type worn to funerals paced back and forth.

"Who is that?" I asked.

"The Marquis de Montespan."

A shock ran through me. Athénaïs's husband. Beyond him stood a black carriage with four sets of monstrous antlers attached to the top, one at each corner.

"Did the King see him? Why is he here?"

"He wants the world to know he is in mourning." Her voice sounded oddly indifferent.

We watched as a pair of guards rushed over to talk with him. He gesticulated in an agitated manner, but then allowed them to escort him to his carriage. One of the guards called up to the driver, who whipped the horses into action as soon as the carriage door was shut.

"Who is he mourning?"

"Me." She turned from the window. "Call the chambermaid to make up the bed. And Martine to help me dress. Sylvienne, we will not speak of this to anyone."

"Of course."

Later I would learn, despite Athénaïs's order not to speak of it, that her husband had refused the usual gratuities bestowed on the families of women favored by the King. And that the antlers atop his carriage were his public notice to King Louis and his court of his refusal to accept his cuckold status. Now that he was gone, I hoped he had the sense to stay away.

CHAPTER THIRTY-ONE

A flurry of parties took place in the days following the ballet, various courtiers and members of the royal family hosting. Despite the morning headaches afterward, it was a heady time for me. I felt accepted. I had proven my worth in the ballet, despite the insignificance of my role. Young men sought me out to dance or to share a glass of wine and conversation, though I was careful not to allow myself to be led off to one of the many private nooks in the palace.

At the end of the week, King Louis made a stunning announcement. He had asked Princess Henriette to sail to England as his ambassador to the court of her brother, King Charles II of England. He wanted to strengthen the alliance between England and France. The request surprised the entire court.

A public row broke out between Madame and Monsieur over her acceptance of Louis's assignment. She argued she missed her brother whom she had not seen in years, and she yearned for the opportunity to spend time with him, even if only for a week. "And…" she said, "I am duty-bound to serve at the pleasure of the King."

Philippe accused his wife of having experienced too much pleasure at the behest of his brother. "And furthermore!" he bellowed. "Don't deny you've been flirting with Guiche again!" It was common knowledge Henriette had had an affair with Guy Armand de Gramont, the handsome Comte de Guiche, after the King's attention had drifted from her to Athénaïs. Henriette, in turn, declared Monsieur was only jealous because he wanted Guiche for himself.

"Want him?" Philippe yelled at his wife during afternoon cards in Madame's own salon, the guests awkwardly silent. "I *had* him. And you stole him away." At which point, he stalked out of the room yelling all the while. "We'll see whether you go to England. Louis hasn't heard the end of this." The door slammed behind him.

All eyes turned surreptitiously toward Henriette sitting two tables away from mine, no one yet daring to speak. With an exaggerated sigh, she picked up her cards and said to the courtiers at her table, "Whose turn is it to deal?" A flurry of cards passed back and forth on all the tables.

"Sylvienne, dear, don't stare," Athénaïs admonished in an undertone, making a point to study her cards, even though she had only two left in her hand. The men playing against us examined theirs just as closely.

After a few minutes, Henriette set her cards down. "I have lost enough for one day." She pushed away from the table, and we all stood. "Play as long as you wish." Followed by her ladies-in-waiting, she exited through the gilded door separating the salon from her private study.

Sitting again, I picked up my cards. "Will she be refused the visit to her brother?" I asked in a whisper.

"Oh, she'll go." Athénaïs threw a card onto the table, which one of the men quickly scooped up. "Monsieur can rage all he wants. It is Louis who makes the decisions."

On a balmy morning in late May, courtiers and their servants boarded the parade of carriages and wagons that would take us on the four-day trip from Fontainebleau through Flanders to the port of Dunkerque. There we would bid our Princess *bon voyage*.

Athénaïs, of course, would ride in the royal coach along with the King and Queen. I worried for her because she hadn't yet told the King about her condition.

"There will be plenty of time when we return," she told me while supervising the household staff packing her trunks. "You must swear he won't find out from you."

"But Athénaïs, surely he will change his plans in your regard if you tell him. You must tell him."

"Louis never changes his plans once he has made them. And it would only complicate the situation with…her." She gave me an arched look then said no more.

Henriette had invited me to ride in her coach along with two of her ladies-in-waiting, Madame de Châtillon and Madame de Vivonne, whose company I found to be quite agreeable. Philippe, apparently in a pout over the whole affair of his wife going off to England, chose to ride in a separate carriage with the Chevalier de Lorraine and the Marquis d'Effiat.

When the driver called to our quartet of horses, "*Allons-y*," the carriage jerked and started to roll. Henriette, sitting across from me, clutched her stomach and drew in a ragged breath.

"Are you unwell, Madame?" I asked.

Gritting her teeth, she nodded and offered a wan smile. "I have a sour stomach. It will pass." But her face seemed uncommonly pale. Could hers be morning sickness as well?

Madame de Châtillon extracted a jar of goat's milk from a covered hamper. After a few sips, the color came back into Henriette's cheeks and her smile was more genuine. "Tell me, Sylvienne. What was it like growing up in Amiens?"

I pondered a moment. No one had asked such a thing of me before. "I had a peaceful childhood. Except for when my father died."

"Were you quite young?"

"Not yet five. However, the memories still linger."

She offered a sad smile. "I was near the same age when my father was…when he died."

With a sudden rush of horror, I remembered that Henriette's father, King Charles of England, had been beheaded.

Before I could murmur my apology for inciting such awful memories, she asked, "And what of your mother? My memories of her are faint. She never remarried after your father died?"

I shook my head. "It wasn't from lack of offers. I suppose in her eyes, no one could measure up to Papa."

Henriette smiled at that. "He must have been a good father."

When we stopped for the night, she joined the Queen and King. During our days on the road, however, she asked me questions about Amiens and its cathedral, wondered where I had gotten my education, seemed fascinated by my stories of festivals and village life. She was so easy to talk with that I found myself admitting I'd been expelled from the convent school, something I had not told anyone at court.

"You poor dear," she said. "How awful for you."

She encouraged her ladies to recount stories of their childhood as well. And she told us of her life growing up in France after her father's death. She and her mother had been forced to flee England during the civil war when she was barely two. King Louis, still a child himself, and his mother, the Queen Regent, had graciously taken them in. She spoke of feeling like an outsider because she was English, and how her brother, the current King of England had nicknamed her Minette. He wrote to her often, she said, always in English, so she wouldn't forget her home language. She was terribly excited to be going back, even for such a brief visit, though she worried her English was limited and she would appear the fool.

"I am sure you won't have to worry," I hastened to say.

"Your English is impeccable, Madame," de Vivonne assured her. "You will make both Kings quite proud of you."

Before long, the conversation turned to the affairs, foibles, and social faux pas of various courtiers, gossip I took guilty pleasure in.

When finally, on the fourth day, we passed through the gates of Dunkerque, the cloud-covered sky had an ominous cast to it. Henriette was only to be gone a week, but still I was anxious for her. Crossing the channel was a dangerous undertaking, and on the other side she would be in a foreign land despite it being the country of her birth and she in the company of her brother, the King of England.

At the harbor, King Louis spoke intimately and at length with Henriette before hugging her warmly. Philippe made a grand show of bussing both her cheeks, then walked away and climbed into the carriage carrying Lorraine and d'Effiat.

After saying au revoir to the Queen and Athénaïs, Henriette gave one last wave to the rest of us then strode up the ship's broad boarding ramp, followed by her throng of ladies-in-waiting, secretaries, bodyguards, and servants.

At last, the ship slipped away from the dock, towed by two rowboats. Out in the harbor, it bobbed on the waves until the sails unfurled and caught the wind. A dread I couldn't explain washed over me as I watched Henriette's ship sail out into the narrow sea.

We'd only been back at Fontainebleau a few days when King Louis announced we would move to Versailles. He wished to survey the palace's reconstruction progress. Some whispered he planned to move his seat of government there permanently. Not now, but soon. The packing began again in earnest.

Only a half-day's journey from Paris, Versailles was a mosaic of buildings, gates, and gardens. And, I was to learn, constantly under construction. The building had been the late king's hunting lodge, a surprisingly immense château. Still, it wasn't large enough for Louis. He had ordered an entire new palace to be built around the former edifice, with service wings extending out on either side creating a vast courtyard. Current construction was centered on extending the main wing, creating new gardens, and building the vast array of outbuildings that would house the kitchens, stables, workshops, and the legion of servants, artisans, and workers who serviced the palace, as well as the courtiers who serviced the King and his family.

As we rode through the royal gate, its golden crown motif glowing in the midday sun, I found myself in a world that was almost as deafening as Paris. Supply wagons rumbled past, sledgehammers pounded, shovels clanked, men shouted. Scaffolding enveloped most of the building, workers scurrying up and down. Inside the palace, the commotion was almost as bad, if not as noisy. Interior craftsmen were busy painting and wallpapering. Workers hung chandeliers, tapestries, and paintings mounted within sumptuous sculpted frames. Servants and courtiers flowed like a river along the maze of corridors, a challenge to navigate.

Athénaïs's apartment — she hinted it was larger than the Queen's — was located on the second floor, above King Louis's. I soon learned a secret spiral staircase had been constructed to connect the two. The day of our arrival, the King's noontime visits to Athénaïs began again.

Yet, even with all the hustle and bustle at Versailles, court life seemed listless without Princess Henriette's presence. Of course, the gambling tables continued, and I was glad for the distraction they provided. By now I was becoming addicted to a new game, Faro, with its fast-paced betting against the dealer's cards. The Crown provided me with a small monthly stipend for my services to Athénaïs, so I no longer needed the King's gift of a purse to play.

One rainy afternoon, a group of us gathered in Athénaïs's salon to play cards. She had invited Edmund de la Vaquet, and a friend of his, Jean-Leon Campion, to play at our table.

When the men excused themselves to fill plates from the sideboard, I took the opportunity to ask Athénaïs about Campion. "He seems quite enchanting."

"Oh, mon petit chou, non. Don't even consider him. As charming as he is, his family is of the bourgeoisie, not the noblesse. They are *nouveaux riches*. Tax collectors. That sort of thing. He is only at our table because he has a large purse to lose."

La Vaquet and Campion returned before I could ask more. I had just placed another bet against the bank, the round dealt by Campion, when a footman approached followed by a courier bearing a burlap-wrapped package.

Without taking her eyes from her cards, Athénaïs replied, "Take it to my library."

"I'm sorry, Madame, but the package is not for you." The footman's eyes flicked toward me. "It is for la demoiselle."

"Mademoiselle Sylvienne? Fine. Leave it then."

The courier offered me the parcel. I gave him a coin from my winnings. He bobbed his head and scurried away as if afraid someone might insist he give it back.

"Open it," la Vaquet said.

"Yes, do." De Baude's eyes lit up at the prospect of a surprise.

With trepidation, lest it be something like underthings from Maman, I tugged on the knot in the twine and let the fastenings fall away. Inside the burlap was a velveteen bag. And inside that was a pair of the most beautiful shoes I'd ever seen.

The courtiers exclaimed when I held up the plum-colored footwear etched with silver stitching and topped with a rosette of lavender lace. "Merveilleux!" "Who sent them?" "Try them on!"

La Vaquet took the shoes from my hands and, to everyone's delight, knelt in front of me. He slipped first one and then the other onto my feet. But—

"Ow!" I jerked my foot out of the shoe.

"What is it?" he asked? "Is there a loose nail?" He reached in and pulled out a stone—a semi-polished bit of amethyst, the same color as the shoes. My heart skipped a beat.

"How odd," he said, holding it up for all to see. "A pebble in her shoe."

I took the stone from him and let him slip the shoe back onto my foot.

"They are incredible. Who made them? Who sent them?" Athénaïs did the asking now, but everyone wanted to know.

La Vaquet shrugged. "There's no letter. No name on the package. No way to know who the shoemaker is."

But I knew who the shoemaker was. I cradled the stone in the palm of my hand as I paraded among the tables modeling my new shoes. Outwardly, my smile bespoke my pleasure on receiving such a gift; inwardly, my heart soared.

Athénaïs, apparently having had enough of the diversion, shuffled the cards. "Shall we play?"

And as quickly as the distraction had begun, my shoes were forgotten in the courtiers' lust for wagering. Picking up my cards, I wondered if the shoes were a sign of forgiveness or a rebuke.

Back in my chamber, I slipped off my new shoes, ran my hand over the soft leather. Bringing one after the other to my nose, I inhaled deeply. The scent of him. Leather and lanolin. Etienne. I closed my eyes, pressing a shoe against my cheek.

After a moment I pulled the amethyst from my skirt pocket, turning it this way and that, enchanted by the way the light glistened on its surface. I brought the stone to my lips for a moment, then tucked it into the embroidered silk pouch that held the other stones I had collected.

That night, I fell asleep with my new shoes tucked under my arm.

Princess Henriette's return from England the second week of June was the buzz of the palace. As soon as word came that her entourage was within a mile of Versailles, King Louis mounted his steed. Followed by a slew of courtiers, he rode out to greet her. The only ones to stay behind were Philippe and the Queen.

I was torn. Should I keep my mentor company or go with the King? Philippe waved me off. "Go. Go! She enjoys your company far more than mine."

Mounting Phoebe, I chased after King Louis and his retinue. A cheer went up from the crowd when Henriette's carriage came into view. Not long thereafter, it stopped in front of the King. She stepped out and curtsied before Louis. He slid from his horse and overwhelmed her with his embrace.

She looked exhausted and held her side as she walked. Still, she declared her mission to be a grand success, and the smile she flashed my way as she climbed back into her carriage appeared genuine.

Back at Versailles, Henriette and Louis locked themselves away in his council room for hours at a time, sometimes with various of his ministers, at other times alone. But always excluding Philippe, who paced the galleries of the palace becoming more irascible by the day.

I was thrilled when Athénaïs announced a private welcome home party for Henriette at the Trianon de Porcelaine, a cluster of decorative pavilions Louis had commissioned specifically for Athénaïs's pleasure.

Sitting at my toilette preparing for the party, I sniffed the tiny ceramic jar of lip cream Athénaïs had given me to try.

"It's called carmine," Lisette said. "It's made of crushed cochineal."

"Bugs?"

"It's what all the ladies use. It won't hurt you."

I wasn't sure about that. Regardless, I dipped a finger and applied the bright red substance to my lips, smacking them for effect.

Princess Henriette looked pale but lovely sitting next to King Louis in the largest of the pavilions. Athénaïs sat on his other side, Queen Marie-Thérèse having decline the invitation preferring a visit to her favorite convent. The maze of flowerbeds and potted orange trees gave up their heady scent in the early evening breeze.

Philippe sat drinking and looking bored as guests fawned over his wife.

"Are those the new mystery shoes I've been hearing so much about?" Henriette asked when it was my turn to welcome her back. "Oh, please do let me see."

I couldn't hide my delight as I pulled up my skirt to hold out my foot.

"Extraordinary! Have you discovered yet who made them?" she asked. "They make mine look dull and ordinary."

"No. Forgive me. I didn't mean to —" I pulled my foot back and dropped my skirt.

Henriette laughed. "I must have a pair designed for me. Don't you love a mystery?"

The next day, Philippe announced he and Madame would be departing for their château at Saint-Cloud the following morning. King Louis was said to be furious at his brother's impertinence, but he did not stop them.

Two weeks later, on the last day of June, I accompanied King Louis and Athénaïs as he inspected work on a new fountain he had commissioned for Versailles — the Fountain of Apollo. The statue being installed depicted the sun god rising from the sea in a chariot pulled by four horses, commanding the sun to rise.

"C'est merveilleux!" I said, astonished at the complexity of the artwork.

At that moment a horseman galloped onto the terrace shouting for the King. Guards quickly surrounded the rider.

"What is it, man?" King Louis demanded.

"I've been sent to fetch you, Sire!" he cried, gasping for breath. "Madame is dying!"

Had I heard correctly? No. This was a horrid, cruel joke.

Louis turned on his heel, shouting as he strode toward the palace. "Saddle my horse!"

Within the hour a bevy of carriages was on the road, the King racing ahead on Atlas. At Saint-Cloud, the sound of Henriette's screams caused the hairs on the back of my neck to rise.

"What is it?" Louis demanded, barging into her bedchamber, the Queen and Athénaïs close on his heels. I hovered with the others near her door, peering in.

Philippe, pale as a wraith, stood at her bedside. "She was fine yesterday. She bathed in the river and took a promenade with her ladies in the garden. They say she asked for a cup of chicory water before bed to help her sleep. An hour later, she complained of stomach pains."

By now her screams had faded into pitiful moans.

"I don't know what to do." Philippe wrung his hands. "The doctors are of no help."

King Louis reached out to touch Henriette's forehead, but she screamed again, clutching her belly and pulling her knees up to her chest in agony. After a moment she opened her eyes and looked about wildly, not seeming to recognize any of those hovering over her. Then she saw the cup on her night table. "Have I been poisoned? Did my husband poison me?"

"No! I did no such thing!" Philippe gestured frantically.

"Do you have an antidote?" the King asked the doctors.

They reached for their bags, pulled out vials and bottles, argued over what to do for her.

Helpless, I looked on as she cried out again and again, writhing on top of the bedsheets.

"What of the water she drank?" King Louis asked. "Is there any left? Give it to the dog. See if it was poisoned."

One of the maids scrambled to do his bidding. The small terrier I had seen occasionally following Henriette around eagerly lapped at the water in the cup. I held my breath. The dog whined and pawed at the bed, but he showed no ill effects.

The doctors administered their potions and powders. One set leeches on her stomach. Another bled her arm. Yet the harder they worked the more she writhed in pain. In between bouts of screaming, she lay deathly quiet.

Philippe paced back and forth at the foot of the bed now. He confronted one of the doctors. "Why can't you do something?"

"Patience," the doctor said.

Philippe threw his hands in the air. "I have no patience! My wife is dying!"

"Brother, come. Let the doctors do their work." Louis took his brother by the arm and led him away from the bed.

"Their work is for naught, can't you see?" Philippe wailed.

In the doorway, I could no longer suppress the sob that rose in my throat. Athénaïs signaled to de Baude who guided me to a chair out of sight of Madame's bed, but I could still hear her moans and Philippe's anguish.

Then she became eerily quiet. I ran back to the door. Henriette's breathing was shallow, her face the color of the satin pillow on which she lay. The doctors stepped away from the bed, shaking their heads, making the Sign of the Cross.

"Send for the priest," the King said, his voice filled with quiet resignation.

Madame de Châtillon rushed from the room. Several minutes later she returned with a robed priest. He held a crucifix in one hand, a bottle of oil in the other. Once the anointing was done, a line of people led by the Queen shuffled to Henriette's bedside to kiss her and wish her farewell as Philippe held her hand. When it was my turn to offer my kiss, she lay so still I feared I was too late, that she'd already taken her last breath. But her eyes fluttered open for a moment, a sad smile on her lips as she gazed at me. Then they closed again as if the world was too weary a place for her to exist.

The last to say *adieu* was King Louis. Tearfully, he kissed his sister-in-law, told her he loved her, then left the room. A monarch is never to be in the death chamber. Only her husband and her priest were at her side when, at three in the morning, our dear Princess Henriette took her last breath.

The priest stepped out of the bedchamber. "Madame is dead," he solemnly intoned.

With the other women, I collapsed onto the floor, sobbing.

CHAPTER THIRTY-TWO

The unforgiving sun pierced the morning sky as our caravan arrived back at Versailles the next day. All the way back I could think of nothing but how full of life Henriette had been. Yet in the blink of an eye she was gone, her now cold body awaiting the autopsy knife of the team of royal surgeons. To rid myself of such morbid thoughts, I let my mind drift back to that first night when she had invited me to her apartment, and I had fallen asleep during her soirée. She had never chastised me for such rude behavior. Instead, she took me under her wing, introducing me to so many people at court. She had become not just my cousin, but a friend and confidant. And now she lived no longer.

Stepping out of the carriage, exhausted and with swollen eyes, I sensed something was amiss. The grounds were silent. The ever-present scaffolding along the sides of the building stood empty as did the work sites scattered about the estate, giving the palace grounds the air of an abandoned village. There were no wagons delivering construction materials, no forge fires, no clank of iron nor thud of bricks, no men shouting.

"Where have they all gone?" I asked Athénaïs. "The workers."

"They've gone home to mourn. They'll return after the funeral."

Inside the palace, my throat constricted at the sight of servants silently enshrouding the windows in black. Memories of another house engulfed me. Another time. Another version of myself. *Papa is dead.* Averting my eyes from the black silk that covered the portraits and mirrors and hung in ribbons from the wall sconces, I hurried to my quarters to weep some more.

The Queen cancelled the grand couvert, the royal family taking their meals in private. The gambling rooms were shuttered. King Louis's visits to Athénaïs became somber affairs with little said between us as he passed through to her chamber.

The first week in July we laid Princess Henriette to rest within the Basilica of Saint-Denis. Our somber procession followed the funeral chariot through the streets of Paris, and by the time we entered the church, my bodice clung with perspiration.

Fanning myself, I gazed at the reliquaries preserving the remains of previous kings and queens of France, a congregation of royal effigies, their hands clasped in eternal prayer. Princess Henriette was about to join them. Her coffin, draped with a gold pall edged in ermine, was mounted on a canopied bier. A halo of candles surrounded it. Remnants of the setting sun lit the rose window above her for a moment, a sad reminder of the fleeting beauty of her life.

A cadre of bishops in purple vestments lined the altar. Philippe sat with his brother, King Louis, and other members of the royal family at the front of the assemblage. Athénaïs and I sat behind them in an area reserved for the nobility. Civil servants, bankers, artisans, craftsmen, and merchants stood in the middle of the church. At the very back, commoners crowded in, with the infirm occupying low benches along the walls.

Bearing torches, members of the Princess's household staff filed silently up the center aisle to pay homage at her casket. Lully directed a choir of boys whose perfectly pitched voices echoed *a cappella* off the vaulted ceiling. During the *Requiem* Mass, the eye-watering clouds of frankincense overwhelmed me as I watched the archbishop walk around the casket swinging an intricately sculpted incense burner from a chain. A crushing sense of déjà vu and a deep, unsettling sense of loss weighed heavily on me.

After the sumptuous funeral banquet in the great hall of the Louvre Palace, Philippe gave me a silver ring engraved with Princess Henriette's initials. He'd had several commissioned to give as remembrance gifts to those of us closest to her.

The next day King Louis ordered the court back to Versailles. In the month following the funeral, all entertainments at the palace were abandoned. The King continued the moratorium on gambling. Small groups of courtiers clustered in the gardens and in private quarters, reminiscing in hushed tones, trading gossip. The rumor that the Princess had been poisoned persisted and, in some instances, embellished upon.

I refused to believe Philippe had anything to do with Henriette's death, and I was heartened when King Louis, upon receiving the autopsy report, declared his brother innocent. The physicians pronounced the cause of death to be something they called *cholera morbus*, which I understood to be an infection in her bowels. However, I couldn't put out of my mind the terrible pain and agony she had endured the days and hours leading up to her death. The thought of it caused me to weep at unexpected moments.

With little to do but listen to idle gossip, my heart grew heavier until I could barely breathe. I needed to be outdoors. Wandering by the stables, I requested a saddle for Phoebe. We rode out past the gardens and along a path skirting the forest, finally coming to an open meadow. I gave Phoebe her head. She picked up speed and was soon galloping. For the first time since Henriette's death, I felt my lungs expand. Eventually, the horse slowed, and I directed her toward a large, lily-pad-ladened pond. As we came around a tall juniper bush, I was surprised to see someone sitting on a log, gazing out over the water. With a start, I realized it was Philippe. Thinking not to intrude on his solitude, I clucked at Phoebe to turn around.

Philippe stopped me with his words. "The water lily was her favorite flower."

I held Phoebe in check and waited.

His voice seemed far away, lost. "She loved to float among them."

"She loved swimming under the night sky," I said. "Under the stars."

"She was only twenty-six." He plucked a piece of grass. "You may not have known it, but we loved each other once. She was a beautiful bride."

What he left unsaid was that Louis had come between them not long after the wedding, inviting the beautiful young bride into his bed. From all accounts, their affair had not lasted long. Louis had moved on to Louise de La Vallière and then to Athénaïs. However, their affection for one another had never waned. I suspected that was something Philippe had never been able to abide.

He sat silent for so long I didn't know whether to dismount and go to him or leave. Before I could make up my mind, he rose. "Are you returning to the palace?" He wiped a bead of sweat from his brow. "I've walked a long way."

I held out my hand, and he climbed up behind me. Phoebe, a bit nervous at first with the extra weight, settled onto the trail and headed home without complaint. At the stables, Philippe slid off then helped me down.

"Madame thought the world of you," he said.

I looked into his eyes, my own tearing up. "I miss her."

"People won't believe me, cousine, but I do, too." He kissed me on the cheek then strode off toward the palace.

CHAPTER THIRTY-THREE

The hot, leaden days of July blended into August. When at last King Louis traded his black mourning coat for a bright red and white doublet and a red-feathered hat to wear on the hunt, the court eagerly revisited their wardrobes. The daily gambling ritual renewed as intensely as ever. I had little taste for cards anymore but found myself unable to stay away. One afternoon, shortly after I had lost my entire purse for the day, a page came running up to me in the grand hallway declaring that the King required my presence in his council chamber.

Having never visited the royal offices, I had a moment of apprehension. Why was I summoned now? When I arrived, a pair of guards opened the great doors. In the same moment, several men in the traditional black garb of counselors pushed past me on their way out, large rolls of papers tucked under their arms. Sketches and blueprints, I assumed.

The council room was large and airy. Windows stretched from floor to ceiling, sapphire and gold brocade curtains pulled back to reveal a sunlit view of the sumptuous new gardens. King Louis stood near a large marble-topped table conversing with Bontemps, his personal valet, and another man, perhaps an architect or a master gardener, who rolled up a set of blueprints then bowed before leaving.

Athénaïs stood near the window looking bored. Across the room, Philippe sat dozing in a brocade armchair, one leg sprawled out in front of him, his other foot thrown up over his knee. Above his head hung an over-sized painting of a frighteningly bloody cavalry battle.

The King hobbled around the table to greet me. "Sylvienne, I'm glad you've come."

"I am honored to be invited, Sire." I curtsied. "But you are limping."

Bontemps gave me a sharp look, and I immediately recognized my faux pas. One does not mention a monarch's shortcomings, regardless of how well-intentioned. I bowed my head in shame. "Forgive me, Sire. I misspoke."

He waved off my apology. "It's those damnable shoes I wore yesterday. I can't seem to find a craftsman who knows how to make shoes that fit without causing blisters. I've dismissed two already for lack of talent."

"Sire, if I may, I can recommend an accomplished shoemaker." I gave a quick glance in Bontemps's direction to see whether I had crossed another boundary, but he only watched with one eyebrow raised.

"The one who sent you those marvelous plum-colored slippers?" King Louis said. "Did you learn who he is?"

"He is from Amiens, Sire. His family has been making shoes for generations."

"Verily? Give his name to Bontemps before you leave."

Bontemps inclined his head in my direction, a sign of approval. He led me to a cluster of chairs before retreating to stand unobtrusively near the door.

The King limped over and batted his brother's foot off his knee, nearly causing him to fall off the chair. Without looking back, Louis hobbled over to where I stood waiting. Philippe pulled himself out of the chair and followed, his annoyance unhidden. Athénaïs joined us.

"It's time we find you a new wife, brother." King Louis flipped the tails of his waistcoat and sat down.

Was that why I was invited? Surely, he didn't mean to propose me as a candidate. I sat nervously next to Athénaïs. Philippe settled onto a lovely cherrywood chair and immediately threw one leg over the other again. I had come to love this man, but as a cousin. I could never countenance living with him as his spouse, especially knowing his...proclivities. He and Henriette had been miserable in their marriage. I wanted a husband who would be faithful to me, a husband who would love me unconditionally as I would love him. A husband like Etienne. No, not *like* Etienne. I wanted Etienne and no one else.

"I don't wish a new wife," Philippe said, holding a hand up to examine his painted nails.

"But you do wish more heirs," Louis challenged. Philippe and Henriette had two surviving daughters but no male heirs.

"I suppose so."

I listened to their exchange, wide-eyed, trying not to look too astonished.

"We'll discuss potential candidates another time," Louis said.

Philippe all but rolled his eyes. I suspected that would be a gesture too far in the eyes of the King.

His Majesty turned to Athénaïs and me with a pleading sigh. "*Mes belles*, I am in need of entertainment."

My relief was palpable. I was not to be offered in marriage to the Prince. At least not immediately.

"Did you invite us to play cards?" Athénaïs asked, sounding dubious. "We would be better to be seated at the table."

"No. I'm tired of games." Louis thrummed his fingers on the arm of his chair. "I am thinking of a ballet. To honor our dear Henriette. I've asked Lully to revive the one we did on her seventeenth birthday."

Philippe looked pleasantly surprised. "*Poseidon and Amphitrite?* God and goddess of the sea. She loved dancing that."

"I'd be happy to reprise her role with you," Athénaïs said, her eyes lighting up.

"Not with me," King Louis said. "I won't be dancing."

We all gaped at him.

"Brother," he said to Philippe. "Would you dance the lead role in my place?"

"If it is your wish." Philippe sat up straighter. "Of course. But why aren't you — ?"

"Louis, I don't understand," Athénaïs looked alarmed.

He offered only a sad smile. "My feet hurt."

"We can commission new shoes for you. Sylvienne said she knows of a skilled shoemaker."

Louis shook his head. "My heart hurts."

Athénaïs touched his arm. I wondered, had the King never stopped loving his sister-in-law after all?

Philippe's brows rose as if an idea was dawning. "And Sylvienne. She will dance as Thetis?"

King Louis nodded, a smile curving his lips again.

"Who is Thetis?" I asked.

"Thetis was leader of the sea nymphs." Athénaïs's voice had brightened.

King Louis leaned forward. "She helps Amphitrite transform from a sea nymph into the wife of Poseidon."

"I would love such a part. But I am not skilled enough. I have only —"

"You will be perfect," Philippe said. "You have a natural talent for dance. Of course you must be Thetis."

Athénaïs nodded in agreement.

King Louis smiled. "Then it is settled."

Stunned, anxious, and elated, I wondered, could I really dance such a role?

Rehearsals commenced later that same week. A group of eager women auditioned to be my fellow sea nymphs; a dozen selected. The daily regimen proved curative for my soul. I especially loved watching Athénaïs rehearse. Her condition was not yet showing despite being into her fourth month, and her movements were exceptionally graceful and fluid. Sometimes, when alone, I mimicked her dance steps.

By the end of the week my body began to rebel. I was exhausted and my muscles ached. Athénaïs, looking drained herself, declared a day of rest. We spent the morning in her study looking over fabrics for our costumes. After the King's noontime visit, she bathed while I wrote letters to Maman and Marie-Catherine. Then we headed off for a round of Faro. This time I managed to win back most of my losses from earlier in the week. Athénaïs won a large purse and was in a generous mood, giving small gifts of coins to her staff and to Lisette. Afterward we napped in our separate bedchambers.

A fierce pounding on the door to the apartment woke me from a delicious dream I'd been having about dancing with Etienne. Lisette opened it no more than a crack, but was shoved backward when a tall, angry man dressed all in black pushed through.

"Where is she?" he bellowed, his face livid, his mouth contorted into an awful scowl.

"Who?" Lisette cowered against the wall.

Wrapped in a robe, I stepped forward to put myself between her and the man I recognized as Athénaïs's wild-eyed husband. "How did you get in here?"

"I want my damned wife!" he thundered, stepping toward me, one fist raised, the liquor on his breath evident even from a distance.

The door to Athénaïs's room opened, and she stepped through wearing nothing more than her chemise. Her expression was a combination of annoyance and alarm. "Monsieur de Montespan, you are frightening my household."

"As well they should be frightened!" he shouted. "It is a grave sin to be in the employ of a whore!"

I flinched at the word, despite having become accustomed to court life in which the rules of propriety were suspended, particularly when the favor of the King was involved.

"I am here to take you home!" the Marquis de Montespan declared.

Athénaïs's face grew pale. "You cannot."

"You are my wife. And I damn well can!" He stepped toward her.

Athénaïs did not cower. She faced him squarely. "I — we — need the King's permission. No one leaves court without his permission."

Nudging Lisette who had turned to stone against the wall, I whispered, "Go fetch the guard."

The terrified girl inched her way around the door, watchful lest this behemoth turn on her. Once in the hall, she ran screaming for help.

The Marquis seized Athénaïs by both arms, jerking her to him. "If the King thinks he will cuckold me without consequence, he is sorely mistaken." His words were slurred.

"Let go of me!" Athénaïs twisted, trying to free herself. "You're drunk."

"More than drunk," he hissed. "I've come with a *gift* that you can pass onto your royal lover."

I edged toward the fireplace and grabbed the iron poker Lisette had earlier left lying with its tip in the hot cinders.

"What are you talking about?" Athénaïs turned her head as if to avoid his awful breath.

"I've come from the brothels, those with the worst reputations for the diseases they spread. Let that royal brat kill himself if he wants you so badly." He smothered her mouth with his own. She flailed against him as he pushed her up against the table, fumbling to lift the hem of her chemise.

"Get away from her!" I charged at him with the fire iron. He swung around and grabbed at it, howling when his hand touched the burning end. But the pain seemed only to increase his rage. Gripping Athénaïs by the arm, he kicked at me, growling.

Shouts at the door heralded the arrival of the royal guards. Two drew their swords, the third pointed a musket at the crazed man.

"Monsieur Marquis!" he said. "Unhand the lady."

"Go to hell," Montespan snarled. "She is my property."

"She is a guest in the King's household. You will let her go." When the musketeer shoved the firearm into Montespan's back, the man grunted and let go his wife, shoving her hard.

She immediately put the table between her and her husband, eyes narrowing. "Go," she hissed. "Or I will tell his Majesty to throw you into the Bastille."

"Whore." Montespan spat, waving her off. "That's what you are. That's what you'll always be. You are dead to me as of this moment. And dead to your children." He turned on me then, shaking a finger in my face. "And this one! This one is no better."

I clutched the fire iron and glared at him, but my hands shook, my heart thumping wildly. The guard closest to me reached out and took the iron from me, setting it aside.

"Bah!" Montespan stormed out, followed by two of the guards.

"Have you been harmed, Madame?" the remaining officer asked.

Athénaïs hugged her arms to her chest and shook her head. "Please, see he does not come back."

"Of course, Madame." He bowed then took his leave.

Lisette shoved the door closed and threw the bolt. Athénaïs's knees buckled; I rushed to keep her from falling.

"Lisette, pour some brandy." I helped Athénaïs to a chair in front of the fireplace, wrapped a blanket around her shoulders. She shook uncontrollably. I forced my own hands to be steady as I lifted the goblet to her lips. Angry welts formed on her arms where Montespan had seized her. "Please, don't say anything to Louis." Her pleading tone took me by surprise.

"It won't be kept from him," I said. "The guards will make a report. The King will have him arrested."

She shook her head. "It is not illegal for a husband to beat his wife."

I knew that. And I suspected as well that King Louis would not do anything that might bring a fight over Athénaïs to the attention of the Queen. "Perhaps he will assign bodyguards, then. That man must not be allowed anywhere near you again. Especially now that…" I let the words hang in the air, but my eyes drifted to her midriff.

Athénaïs instinctively covered her belly with her hands. Her eyes became steely. "He can't know."

"The King?"

"My husband. If he finds out I am carrying a baby, he can claim it as his own."

"But the child. Isn't it…?"

"Of course it is Louis's. But in the eyes of the law, any child a woman bears belongs to her husband."

Shocked, I said, "And King Louis? You said you would tell him."

"I will. After the new ballet. I don't want him to think me too frail to dance. Please, Sylvienne, not a word. Promise me."

Begrudgingly, I promised — again. Her trembling abated. "Athénaïs, your children with the Marquis?"

She pulled the blanket tighter around her. "A girl and a boy."

"Why are they not here with you?"

She gave me an exasperated look. "At the palace? You expect me to have children under foot when I am in service to the King?" Now she gazed into the fire. "They are well provided for." She took one last sip of brandy then stood.

I stared at her back as she disappeared through the door. How could she so easily leave her children in the care of that monster? Athénaïs was proving to be like one of the many diamonds she wore — of multiple facets, not all of which shone perfectly in the light of day.

CHAPTER THIRTY-FOUR

During our rehearsal the next day Athénaïs seemed subdued, but she held her chin high and focused on her dancing. I, on the other hand, had trouble keeping proper time with the music, bumping into one water nymph after another. After several sharp rebukes, dance master Savard called our session to a close. Relieved to be dismissed, I slipped out of the ballroom and hurried outside, making my way to a small garden with a pond I'd recently discovered. In the center of the pond a sculpted wood nymph spouted water from its mouth.

Savoring the solitude, I sank onto a stone bench at the edge of the water. The incident with Athénaïs's husband the night before and her behest to keep her condition a secret weighed on me. What would King Louis do when he found out? Surely, he wouldn't send her away. Would he? I pulled off my dancing shoes, little more than brocade slippers perched on raised heels. Then, after making certain I was alone, I gathered up my skirt, tugged my silk stockings down over my knees and all the way off. I dipped my feet into the cool water, frightening the large orange koi that swam in the pond.

When my toes started to feel chilled, I gathered my things and retraced my steps back up the garden path. Strolling alongside the hedgerow, I delighted in the softness of the grass under my bare feet. A clopping sound drew my attention to a groom leading a horse over the cobbled path, beads of sweat on its flank and neck. Reflexively, I rubbed the muscles of my own thigh under my silk dancing skirt. Something about the horse looked familiar—the chestnut coat, the blaze of white on her face. Jolie?

I ran through the gap in the hedges that led to the stables. "Boy! Boy, wait!"

The groom paused, his eyes shifting uncertainly to my bare feet.

"Where is the rider of this horse?" My heart quickened as I reached out and touched Jolie's face. She nuzzled me with unmistakable familiarity.

"He's gone into the palace, Mademoiselle."

I bolted back to the palace, running through corridors with their cold marble floors, and along the gallery until I came to the Great Hall. I rushed past a bewildered guard and threw open the doors. The hall was empty.

"Where...?" I asked, gasping to catch my breath. "Where is the King?"

The guard shook his head. "Not here, Mademoiselle."

Of course not. A shoemaker would not be received in the Great Hall as I had been. Where would they meet? I rushed toward the royal offices.

"Mademoiselle?" The voice came from behind me. Bontemps.

Confounded, I turned to tell him I had no time to stop. But he wasn't alone. Next to him stood a tall, handsome young man.

"Are you missing your shoes?" Bontemps asked, looking concerned.

My dancing slippers dropped to the floor as I gazed upon Etienne, the faintest hint of amusement crinkling his eyes. I thrust myself into his arms. He held me tightly, nestling his face in my hair. I could feel the ferocious beating of his heart matching my own, his ragged intake of breath before he pushed me away.

Bontemps's expression turned to consternation. A noblewoman does not throw herself at an artisan. I did not care.

Etienne bowed. "Mademoiselle d'Aubert."

"It appears you are already acquainted," Bontemps said.

I nodded. Etienne was thinner than when I'd last seen him. How long ago had that been? And taller. But his frame only served to accentuate the breadth of his shoulders. He wore a new jerkin and breeches, tawny-colored, and the most handsome leather shoes. His dark blond hair—unlike the courtiers whose locks fell around their shoulders in curls—was pulled back into a neat tail, emphasizing the firmness of his square jawline. A serious, inquiring gaze replaced the teasing twinkle in the blue eyes that I had always loved. He seemed more mature but also more distant.

"You look well," he said.

"I am. Merci. And you...?"

"In truth, I am...disconcerted to find myself here." A furrow crossed his brow. "I am told you had something to do with my summons."

Flustered, I blushed. "I only mentioned to King Louis that you are talented in your craft."

"That's all it took?"

"That and the shoes. You sent me shoes."

"I did." He glanced curiously at the ones on the floor.

Scooping them up, I thrust them behind my back. "I wear the ones you sent. Quite often. They are admired by the entire court."

"Then my purpose has been fulfilled."

My exhilaration melted, confusion washing over me. What was he insinuating? "Will you be staying in the palace?"

The look he gave me was one a parent gives a child speaking foolishly. "I have been assigned quarters above the shoe shop."

"Of course." My cheeks burned with embarrassment. The awkwardness between us grew like a hedge of brambles.

Bontemps cleared his throat. "The King will be asking for his new shoemaker."

Etienne bowed once more. "Until we meet again, Mademoiselle." He strode down the hall after Bontemps.

Watching them go, my befuddlement—at the wall he put between us, at the way my heart raced—quickly turned into annoyance. He was here. At court. Didn't he realize how wonderful an opportunity that was? Did it matter that I had made it happen? I balled my fists in anger and stomped off in the opposite direction. Back in my anteroom, I hurled my dancing slippers across the room, sending a vase of fresh flowers crashing to the floor and bringing Lisette at a run.

"Mademoiselle...?" She stared wide-eyed at the mess.

CHAPTER THIRTY-FIVE

That night I sent a message entreating the King to excuse me from attending the grand couvert, complaining of a volatile stomach, which was not far from the truth. I could not bear the possibility of seeing Etienne standing among the observers, watching me sup with the royal family. Would the look on his face be one of hurt? Or one of disdain? I suspected the latter.

Of course, I couldn't stay away forever. The next night, after a long rehearsal and an evening of musical entertainment in Queen Marie-Thérèse's quarters, I took my place at the table. Only after the King and Queen had arrived and we were all seated did I scan the faces in the gallery. I was both relieved and disappointed not to see Etienne among them. Nor did he come the next night, nor the next. Eventually, I stopped looking for him.

Curiously, King Louis never came to observe our progress with the ballet.

"Do you think it saddens him to not dance?" I asked Athénaïs when we were alone in her chamber.

"Very much so." She held out several rings, ruby, sapphire, and diamond, for me to put into the black lacquered armoire she had received as a gift from her sister. The chest was decorated with mother-of-pearl inlays depicting tropical birds and flowers, its drawers lined with velvet padding.

"Then why won't he dance?" I pressed.

"I don't know. He is different since Madame's funeral. It worries me."

It worried me as well. He still took meetings with his privy council, still hunted, and of course still visited Athénaïs daily, sometimes twice a day. Yet he lacked the joy he usually exuded.

He had begun the search for a new wife for Philippe, dispatching ambassadors to all the domains harboring eligible young royals. Philippe showed no interest in the process other than to glance at miniature portraits of the candidates, dismissing them offhandedly, much to the consternation of his brother. Athénaïs and I, on the other hand, took great pleasure in debating the merits and faults of each candidate.

I heard nothing more from Etienne, nor did I see him about the palace. One afternoon, after a particularly intense rehearsal, I changed into a blue skirt with yellow trim and a matching bodice that accentuated my figure and ventured out, telling myself I was only going for a walk. However, where I ended up was an enclave of cottages occupied by the royal artisans—potters, glass blowers, woodworkers, weavers, saddle makers. And the shoemakers whom Etienne now supervised.

When I peered through the open door of the shoe shop, the familiar scents of leather and lanolin transported me back to Amiens, and I had a moment of longing for that simpler life.

Several men were bent over cluttered workbenches tapping hammers, scraping sanders, conversing in low tones.

"Bonjour, Mademoiselle!" one of them called out. The tapping, scraping, and voices stopped, the others looked up.

Etienne, leaning over a sketchbook, rose. "Sylvienne." He signaled the others to carry on with their work and, taking off his thick leather apron, stepped outside. "What are you doing here?"

"I was…curious. About your accommodations. Are they adequate?"

He indicated the building behind him. "My father would be envious."

"And you have workers to help you?"

"Yes. Good men. Accomplished."

An awkward silence ensued. After a moment he said, "I hear you have learned to dance."

I offered a coquettish smile. "I suppose you hear all kinds of gossip."

"More than you would care to know."

"Like a spider hugging the corner?"

"Excuse me?"

Flustered, I tried to explain it was a comment he had made when we were children. He raised an eyebrow. I blurted out, "We perform ballets. On a stage. With costumes. It's quite... quite...glorious."

"No more dancing in the streets with the common folk for you?" His tone biting.

Heat rose to my cheeks. "I enjoy dancing of all sorts! The dance master says I am quite good."

"I've no doubt you are. If you find yourself in need of dancing shoes, send one of your servants to let me know. Excuse me, I have work to do." He strode back into his shop.

I stared at his back, confounded, fighting tears that threatened. The sounds of hammering and sanding continued within the workshop, but no voices. I turned away, regretting ever having come, promising myself I would not seek him out again.

To banish Etienne from my thoughts, I doubled my focus during rehearsals. We had just days to go before the performance. A stage had been constructed at the north end of the grand ballroom, the orchestra nestled below.

Athénaïs and Philippe rehearsed their duet from the second act, the sea nymphs and I poised at the far end of the stage awaiting our cue. Philippe executed several leaps, ending in a *tour en l'air.* Athénaïs pirouetted across the stage to meet him. Suddenly, she grasped her belly and crumpled to the floor with a groan. A cry went up from the nymphs. I rushed forward, but Philippe and Savard were already leaning over her.

"I'm all right," she gasped, holding them at bay with an outstretched hand. But her face was contorted and drained of color.

"Help her to a chair," I said.

Philippe picked her up and carried her to a settee near the window. The dance master dismissed the sea nymphs and the musicians for the rest of the day and sent a page to summon the King and the royal physician.

"*Mon coeur*, what happened?" King Louis asked rushing through the door.

Athénaïs put on a brave face. "Just a stomach ailment." She looked up at Philippe and Savard hovering anxiously. Several of the musicians lingered in the orchestra pit. In a low voice, Athénaïs said, "Louis, we must talk."

He frowned, perplexed, and signaled to clear the room. I stood up to go as well.

"Sylvienne, stay," Athénaïs said.

I nodded, sat back down, barely daring to breathe.

"What is it, ma chérie?" Louis asked, kneeling in front of her.

Athénaïs twisted her hands in her lap. "Louis, I..." She took a deep breath, closed her eyes for a moment, then gazed into his. "I'm with child."

"With child?" He seemed not to comprehend.

"Your child."

He stared at her for a long moment. Then his face lit up, and he broke into a broad smile, grasping her hands. "*Mon amour*, this is the best gift you could give me!" He kissed her hands, then pulled her to her feet, hugging her.

Athénaïs took a step back. "But...the Queen."

Louis touched her cheek. "The Queen doesn't need to know."

"How will she not?"

He brushed a ringlet of hair from her face. "There is much the Queen chooses not to be made aware of. And...we will be discreet."

Discreet? I almost barked out a laugh. I held my tongue, though, and made my face a mask as I'd seen Bontemps do many times, even as my mind spun. What if the Marquis de Montespan learned of the baby? As Athénaïs's husband, he had the right of law to claim the child, regardless of who fathered it. Even if the true father was the King of France. Misery engulfing me, I stared at a painting of the Virgin Mary on the wall behind them.

Unfortunately, my efforts to seem unobtrusive did not keep me from King Louis's scrutiny. "You knew of this?"

"Yes, Sire." My voice barely a whisper.

He nodded. "Good. I am glad to know you can keep a confidence."

I breathed my relief. Athénaïs smiled at me.

"But now, Sylvienne," Louis said, "you will bear a greater responsibility."

I looked at him, perplexed. Was there more to the secret?

"For Athénaïs must not dance in her condition. You will prepare to learn her part."

Dumbfounded, I gaped at him.

The King's physician examined Athénaïs in her bedchamber, saying privately her pains were nothing more than cramps that accompany many pregnancies. Publicly he announced that Athénaïs suffered from gastric upset. He ordered bed rest for a few days and declared she should not dance until her condition cleared.

Both terrified and exhilarated, I determined I would make King Louis proud when I danced Athénaïs's role as Amphitrite opposite Philippe's Poseidon. Fortunately, I already knew most of the movements. One of the sea nymphs was promoted to take my place as Thetis.

I practice my steps at all hours, not just with the dance troupe, but even when I was alone. Sleep evaded me at night. During the day, Lisette had to remind me to eat.

The day of the final dress rehearsal, Athénaïs and King Louis came to observe. When we finished the final act, while taking our bows, a page rushed into the ballroom and presented a parcel to me.

"Aren't you going to open it?" Philippe asked, wiping his sweat-laden brow with a cloth.

The sea nymphs clustered around as I untied the ribbons and pulled back the plain linen wrap to reveal a lovely pair of silk dancing shoes. They perfectly matched my costume of sea green and ivory taffeta with a gossamer veil. The dancers exclaimed over the shoes—the silk padded toes, raised heels, lace accents, satin bows, and silver stitching. I recognized the workmanship but assumed King Louis or Athénaïs had ordered them. Both denied it.

Monsieur? "Not me," he said.

Athénaïs encouraged me to try them on. As I slipped my foot in, I felt it. A pebble.

The stage was ready, the backdrops painted to resemble the mythical island of Atlantis surrounded by a stormy sea. Final touches had been added to Henri de Gissey's costumes—ribbons, pearls, gilded seashells and starfish. Mademoiselle de Canilliat had designed wigs in the same theme. Garlands of floral fish hung from the walls. Sconces and candelabras, made to look like coral and conches, waited to be lit.

The day of the performance, my nerves were like a sputtering candlewick. I hadn't slept for several nights. Despite Lisette's urgings, I couldn't down anything more than a cup of tea in the morning.

Costumed and wearing my new dancing slippers, I wended my way among the cast backstage looking for Philippe. Chatting with several sea nymphs, his thigh-length skirt of blue and gold silk and his chest-hugging tunic with billowing sleeves emphasized his muscular legs and arms.

I pulled him aside. "This was a mistake."

"Nonsense. You are a marvelous dancer. I have every confidence in you." He leaned down and kissed my cheeks. His affection only made me more aware of the disgrace were I to dance badly.

My heart pounded wildly as I stood poised in front of the Atlantis backdrop. Philippe took his position opposite me, near a rock constructed of wood and fabric. The curtain parted, and the audience gasped in appreciation, breaking into applause. I noted that Athénaïs sat in the front row on a simple but elegantly upholstered chair. Next to her were two gold damask-covered armchairs, in front of one a small matching footstool.

The halberds pounded. The audience stood as the doors to the ballroom opened. King Louis and Queen Marie-Thérèse walked in, her hand on his arm. He glowed in his white justaucorps with gold trim, gold buttons, and white leggings. A single, sea-green carnation graced his lapel. Queen Marie-Thérèse, by contrast, wore a dark purple gown with black trim and a pearl brooch at her bosom.

The royal couple took their places, the King positioning himself between his Queen and Athénaïs. Marie-Thérèse, never looking at her rival, sat with her short legs dangling. A footman pushed the stool under her feet. Once she was settled, King Louis sat, the rest of the audience following suit.

Lully stepped onto the stage to give a short speech. I scanned the audience, the courtiers seated on chairs, local merchants and tradespeople on narrow benches, palace staff and servants lining the walls or squatting along the edge of the stage. Boivin sat in the third row, next to the Duc de Narbonne. The knot in my stomach grew tighter.

"I present to you *The Marriage of Poseidon and Amphitrite.*" Lully bowed to King Louis, then moved to stand in front of the orchestra. With a lift of his hand, the music began.

I smoothed the skirts of my costume and counted the beats, waiting for my cue. In a moment of panic, I lost track of the rhythm. Frantic, I looked toward Philippe. He gave me a reassuring nod, his toe tapping. There it was. The beat. And my cue. I took a deep breath, lifted my foot, and twirled into his arms. And then back toward the sea nymphs. As I danced, I became one with the music, the audience fading into the background.

When the ballet came to its conclusion, Philippe took my hand and we bowed. The King stood and the audience, too, clapping thunderously. Breathless, I could scarcely believe it was over, the sound of the crowd's adulation thrumming in my head, pounding.

The thick velvet curtain dropped in front of us, and the dancers shouted, "Brava, Sylvienne, brava!"

Philippe crushed me in his embrace. The sea nymphs surrounded me. I reached out to hug one of them, but the pounding in my head grew fiercer. The room began to spin.

CHAPTER THIRTY-SIX

I gasped at the sharp scent of hartshorn and opened my eyes to find King Louis's physician leaning over me, holding a small filigree box of smelling salts. Lisette hovered next to him. She placed a cool, wet cloth on my hot forehead. Athénaïs, King Louis, and Philippe crowded at the foot of my bed, their brows crinkled with worry. Across the room stood…Etienne. My pulse quickened. Why was he here? In my chamber.

"She's awake!" Athénaïs touched my leg.

"Is she unhurt?" Louis asked.

The doctor snapped his box shut and shoved it into the pocket of his waistcoat. He placed his fingers on my wrist. "How do you feel?"

"What happened?" I was still in my ballet costume.

"You fainted after the performance," Philippe said.

"I don't see any bruising." The doctor laid cool fingers along my neck. "Does your head hurt?"

"It throbs a bit." I glanced up to see that Etienne had moved farther back, hovering near the window, blending in with the curtains.

Athénaïs shifted to the side of my bed and took my hand. "Had you eaten before the performance?"

Lisette spoke up. "I tried to get her to eat, but for the past two days she would do nothing but nibble on apples and pears."

"I believe you succumbed to exhaustion due to excess exertion and lack of nourishment," the doctor proclaimed. "Do you hurt anywhere else?"

I shook my head. He put his ear to my chest, listened to my heart, felt my forehead, and manipulated my limbs.

"You gave us quite a scare," King Louis said.

"Nothing more than a fainting spell." The doctor wiped his own brow with a cloth. "Bed rest. Perhaps some hot broth and a little brandy. If you will give permission, Sire, I will take my leave."

King Louis nodded, and the physician backed out, bowing. Athénaïs directed Lisette to fetch the broth along with bread and cheese.

"I am sorry to burden you so," I said.

She squeezed my hand. "The doctor is right. You need rest." Her corn-silk hair shimmered in the light from the candle on the night table. "We should go now. See that you eat everything Lisette brings you."

Philippe kissed my forehead. Louis lifted my hand and kissed my palm. They left, brushing past Etienne without seeming to see him.

Once we were alone, he stepped closer to the bed, his brow furrowed with worry.

"How did you get in here?" I asked.

"When you fainted, I was the one who caught you. I carried you here." He gave me a wry smile. "I remember now how it feels to be that spider on the wall."

"You were at the performance? I never saw you."

"I watched from behind the stage," he said.

Of course. Like the other craftsmen, he would be backstage in case his services were needed; he wouldn't be sitting out in the audience with the courtiers.

My eyes welled with tears. "Thank you."

He grabbed the chair from the writing desk to sit next to my bed, unsmiling.

I touched his hand. "You're still angry with me."

"You left Amiens without saying a word."

I looked away. "I was summoned. By the King."

"I asked you to marry me. You promised me an answer." He looked down at his hands, folded—nay twisted—in his lap. "I could have accepted a no." His voice hardened. "But to receive no answer..."

"I'm sorry."

He stood suddenly, almost knocking the chair backward. "And then to be summoned here. To this palace."

"I thought you would be pleased."

"To work as a common hireling?" He clenched his fists. "While you flaunt your royal position? Dressed in silk and jewels, your hair done up like a...a...harlot? I've not been here three weeks and already the serving staff are filling my head with whispers of you flirting with every young cock of marriageable age, one who is not even available to make you his wife."

"What?" I sat up now. "Who would say such things? And with whom am I flirting so much?"

He glared at me. "The King?"

"*Non!*" I bolted out of bed wrapping the blanket around me. "How could anyone say such a thing? Why would they say it? You are listening to evil people." I confronted him face to face, but he did not back down.

"You are not the same Sylvienne I knew in Amiens."

"And you know this from seeing me for all of five minutes in the palace corridor? And out by your workshop?"

"I've watched your rehearsals. And I was backstage during the performance. Sylvienne, I am not blind." His voice filled with bitterness as he spoke. "I saw a beautiful girl I used to know, who was kind and caring, but who now puts on affectations, engaging in court gossip, not seeming to care if it hurts others."

My cheeks burned. I clenched the edges of the blanket in my fists. "That's not true! Why would I do such things?"

"To position yourself, I can only assume."

"For what purpose?"

"For marriage and fortune."

The blanket dropping, I reached out to slap his face. But he caught my wrist. Stared down into my eyes. Pulled me to him, covering my mouth with his, and kissed me. Deeply. Longingly. My body seemed to melt into his as I returned the kiss. I think, in that moment, if he had thrown me upon my bed and pressed his body onto mine, I would have given in. Willingly. Longingly.

But he didn't. He pushed away, his eyes full of hurt. "You never gave me an answer. I assume it was because I could not offer you a fortune." He let go of my arm and strode out of the room.

Unable to move, I stared after him, refusing to think. Until finally I sank to the floor, breathless but dry-eyed. All I knew was his kiss. The way he had held me, the heat of his mouth, the force of his tongue pushing my lips apart, filling my mouth, the scent of him, the crush of his claim over me. We had kissed before. A lifetime ago, in Amiens. But never had he kissed me the way he did this night. With such hunger, such passion…such disdain. And never had my body responded the way it did tonight, with equal desire.

Lisette stepped into the room bearing a tray with food. "Mademoiselle?" She set the tray on the table and rushed to my side. "Did you faint again?"

"No, I…I just…I…"

"You're shivering." She grabbed the blanket from the floor and wrapped it around me.

"Was there mention of brandy?" I asked, my voice shaky. "Perhaps you can help me out of this costume then find some."

Lisette bobbed her head in assent and scurried to retrieve my night clothes. She dabbed a cool cloth on my forehead and cheeks then brushed out my hair. Afterward I sat in my nightgown, sipping a thimbleful of the burning brandy, gazing out the window but seeing nothing. Filled only with the memory of Etienne's touch, his scent, his kiss.

Two weeks passed before I saw him again. I was on my way to a late summer salon hosted by Athénaïs's friend Madame Scarron, when I spotted Etienne leaving the King's wing of the palace, carrying a leather shoulder bag with, I presumed, his measuring instruments, perhaps fabric samples, or even shoes for King Louis to try on. He did not see me, and I did not call out to him — even though my heart ached to do so. What could I possibly say to him? I loved him and hoped someday to marry him — if he would still have me. Now was not the time, however, and Versailles certainly not the place.

The day after my fainting spell, Athénaïs hosted a party to celebrate my successful performance. Her choice of location, the Trianon de Porcelaine, made me think of the last party Princess Henriette had attended before her death. How I missed Henriette. I desperately wanted to swim in the pond under the night stars. But nobody at Versailles swam anymore.

When King Louis arrived, he bussed me on both cheeks. I was overly conscious of his attention now that I knew people were accusing me of flirting with him. I cringed inwardly when he expressed his pleasure at my choice of gown for the evening, saying it accentuated the "loveliest parts" of me.

The young men in attendance crowded around me, complimenting my dancing, my costume, tonight's gown. Jean-Leon Campion and Edmund de la Vaquet stumbled over each other in their efforts to fetch drinks and food for me. The women were exceedingly polite, likely gritting their teeth as they congratulated me.

Philippe whispered in my ear as he hugged me. "It's okay to smile, cousine. It's a party."

Alone in my chamber the next day, I pulled out the embroidered silk pouch I kept tucked in my keepsake box. Loosening the drawstrings, I let the stones tumble onto my writing table—the glassy black stone with white stripes Maman had given to me; the grey one with pink crystals I'd picked up the day Perrette sailed away; the amethyst Etienne had put into the first pair of shoes he'd made for me. And the pebble from the dancing slippers. There were others, too, pretty stones I'd picked up in the gardens of the Tuileries in Paris and at Fontainebleau. I pushed them around with my finger, wishing I could find answers in them, some clue as to what to do with this pain in my heart.

"What are you doing, Mademoiselle?" Lisette's brows crinkled with apprehension. I hadn't heard her come in.

"Nothing." I scooped up the stones and slipped them back into the pouch. "They are pretty stones. Nothing more."

She turned away, but as she headed toward the closet, she touched her forehead and shoulders, crossing herself.

At long last, the cooler days of September arrived. My skills as an equestrian had improved with practice, and I was learning the trails through the forest and meadows surrounding the Versailles complex. I rode early, before Athénaïs got out of bed.

When she was awake, we took walks together in the garden, often in the company of the King. It soon became evident to me that Athénaïs's body was changing. She had a glow about her that made her more beautiful than ever. It would not be long before others noticed her condition, but she took that as a challenge. She sent for Monsieur Delacourt and locked herself away with him for several hours. When, finally, they emerged, he sent for the fabric vendors.

One afternoon, Athénaïs appeared at a concert in the Queen's apartment wearing the first of a dozen new dresses she had commissioned. Constructed of gold and crimson chiffon, the gown was loose in the front, showing off a floral stomacher and matching petticoat. In the back, a length of chiffon fell from her shoulders in long flowing pleats.

Her "*robe battante,*" as she called it, concealed her growing stomach. Instantly becoming the fashion *du jour* at Versailles, noblewomen begged their dressmakers to sew robes battantes for them. And well before the first leaves of the season had begun to turn, ladies strutted the halls and galleries of the palace showing off their new, loose-fitting gowns.

I was wearing my own robe battante — a pale grey riding dress with black trim — on the day I came upon Etienne exercising Jolie on a forest trail just beyond the gardens. My heart did a little flip — it had been almost a month since we last spoke. To my surprise, he pulled alongside and slowed Jolie's gait to match Phoebe's. The awkwardness between us hung in the air like heavy frost.

After a moment he said, "You have learned to ride side saddle."

"The King insists upon it." I kept my eyes averted, a dam of tears threatening to burst.

"Not as much fun as the way we used to ride."

I glanced up to see him grinning in his old teasing way, the sun emerging from behind a storm cloud.

"But now I can race you." With an impish giggle, I kicked at Phoebe. "Hya!"

Etienne's laughter mingled with Jolie's hoofbeats as they raced to catch up and then flew past. He stopped and waited for me. When we turned to head back, we let the horses amble at their own pace.

"I'm sorry I was so harsh with you that night after the ballet," he said.

"No. I'm sorry. I've been unfair to you. It's just that…" I reached out and stroked Phoebe's mane, thinking about all those times we rode Jolie together. "So much has changed. In my life. In yours. Between us."

"You are living the life you've always wanted." His voice sounded stoic.

Tugging the reins, I brought Phoebe to a stop. Etienne pulled Jolie alongside us.

"Etienne, I don't know what I want anymore."

"If we were back in Amiens, what would your answer have been?"

I didn't hesitate. "Yes. It would have been yes."

"But we are not in Amiens."

"No. We're not."

He leaned toward me, his leg pressed against mine. I found myself reaching for him, the steeds conspiring to linger. The taste of his kiss was warm and sweet, the fragrance of the forest engulfing us, the alluring scent of horsehide beneath us.

At long last, we pulled apart. He drew in a deep breath. "When you figure out your dream, will you promise not to dismiss me from it altogether?"

Again, I didn't hesitate. "I promise."

CHAPTER THIRTY-SEVEN

Etienne and I began riding together most mornings, always before the palace awoke. Of course, the workmen were out, carpenters, bricklayers, stable hands, gardeners, but they largely ignored us.

One crisp October morning, as we climbed into the saddles, I asked, "Have you seen the Menagerie?" Phoebe and I led the way through the gardens to the southwest corner of the palace grounds to show him the King's private zoo.

As we rode, Etienne asked, "Has the King settled on a wife for Monsieur?"

I glanced over at him, surprised. Etienne had never seemed interested in the social business of court life. "He has made an offer to the Princess Palatine of Germany," I said. "Elizabeth Charlotte, though they say she prefers to be called Liselotte. He is waiting to hear her terms."

"You are quite fond of him."

"Monsieur? Yes, I suppose I am. He was the first to befriend me at court."

When Etienne did not respond, I continued. "He is…I don't know how to say it. Genuine, perhaps. I can trust that what he says, he means."

"Do you have feelings for him?"

I looked at him in disbelief. "Do you mean like a lover?"

He blushed at my frank words.

"Heavens no." I laughed. "And even if I did, he would never look at me that way."

"I've heard that he is…that he likes…he sometimes dresses…"

"It's true, he has unusual tastes. I've no doubt everything you've heard is true."

"Even that he had his wife poisoned?"

Pulling Phoebe up short, I glared at him. "No! How could you say such a thing?"

Jolie pranced in a circle, forcing Etienne to rein her in. "Everyone talks of it."

"Well, they shouldn't. The physicians examined her. And King Louis declared it untrue."

I kicked Phoebe, sending her into a gallop.

"Sylvienne, I'm sorry," Etienne called out.

We raced, my anger building, until we reached our destination. The Menagerie.

Etienne slid off Jolie and helped me down. "Honestly. I am sorry. I won't mention it again."

A curt nod was all I would give him.

He tied the horses to a hitching post outside the gate, and we made our way inside in silence. The Menagerie was a large domed pavilion surrounded by a series of enclosures fanning out like the spaces between spokes of a wheel. Etienne's eyes grew wide with astonishment as we approached the first pen.

Around a pond stood several dozen pink birds with long necks and long spindly legs, some standing only on one leg, the opposing limb pulled up tight under their bodies. The tall birds chattered noisily as ducks and swans waddled and swam among them. Watching them helped quell my agitation. "They are *flamants roses*," I said.

"I've read of them. They come from the Spanish Americas."

I let him take my hand as we strolled to the next paddock, a grassy area with zebras grazing. Ostriches clustered nearby pecking at the ground, several peering over the fence at us. Another enclosure held an elephant tossing sand and dirt over its back with its trunk. Large clumps of its dung baked in the sun. Next to it, a glass wall surrounded a large tree with thick branches upon which playful, screeching monkeys romped.

But the animals I most wanted Etienne to see were still to come. A lion with a majestic mane lay sprawled across a large flat rock in its enclosure. On the ground at his feet, sat a lioness panting in the sun. In the next enclosure a golden-coated leopard, its fur marked with black rosettes, paced back and forth, eyeing us with wary interest. The last pen housed a tiger which paced in and out through its shed door, in and out, in and out.

"Aren't they marvelous? Did you ever think you would see such animals in your life?" I looked up at Etienne, expecting awe that mirrored my own. Instead, he was quiet, almost sullen. "What's wrong?"

"To be penned up like this. It must be awful for them."

"They know no other life."

"They must have come from somewhere." He reached out and ran a finger down one of the vertical bars separating them from us. "Trapped. Unable to come and go as they wish, to live the life they were meant to live. Not unlike you and I."

"What do you mean? You came here of your own accord."

He shrugged. "Not any more than you did."

I sucked in a breath. It was true. I had felt I was accepting a prized invitation; but no one refuses a summons from the King. And no one leaves court without the King's permission. I didn't know how to respond. I didn't have to. He was already striding out of the compound.

"Etienne! Wait!" I chased after him.

He stopped near the horses. "Sylvienne, this whole place, Versailles, it's nothing more than one large…what did you call it? A menagerie. Everyone here lives their lives solely at the pleasure of the King. Doesn't that bother you?"

"I never thought about it that way."

He lifted me up onto Phoebe's saddle.

"And anyway, what choice do I have?"

"That's my whole point." He put his foot in the stirrup and swung his leg over Jolie's back. "A life without choice is no life at all."

We rode back to the palace in silence. Nearing the stables, we encountered mounted guards riding ahead of the King and his entourage on their way out to the hunt, a dozen hounds swarming around them. Etienne pulled back, positioning himself several paces behind me. As the hunting party passed us, King Louis on Atlas doffed his hat toward me and nodded at Etienne, though with a look of curiosity in his eyes. What must he think? To my relief, at that night's grand couvert he did not mention our encounter.

The next day, Athénaïs and I sat in her salon playing with a pair of baby foxes she had adopted. She said, her voice casual, "You have a fondness for that shoemaker you recommended to Louis."

Startled, I said, "We are old friends."

She rubbed the tummy of one of the kits. "Do be careful. It is important you not enter into any improper liaisons while in the service of the King."

"I would never—" I bit my tongue to keep from blurting out the irony in her words. That *she* should warn me against engaging in an improper affair. And how did she know I'd been seeing Etienne? Then I remembered. The King. His notice of us had not gone unaccounted for.

"Etienne's only wish is to keep me safe when I am out riding," I said.

"See it remains that way." She held up the tiny fox and examined it for a moment. "And remember, at court perception is everything." The kit began to squirm and nipped at her hand. "Merde!" She thrust it away from her. "Martine, come take them away."

After Athénaïs's admonishment, I suggested a change of route for our morning rides to avoid encountering the King's hunting party again. Etienne agreed. Soon the grey November skies pelted rain, ending our morning rendezvous altogether. Or perhaps the King had a hand in it? Etienne was suddenly so busy, having been tasked with crafting shoes for the Queen, Athénaïs, and the nine-year-old Dauphin as well as those of the King, that he couldn't find time for even brief encounters near the stables. For my part, I had to content myself with taking advantage of a new tutor in the palace to learn to play the lute.

December turned the drizzling rains into snow flurries. I had been writing to Maman faithfully twice a week, but her return letters came less often and were shorter. Her handwriting had lost its firmness. I worried about her health, but she seldom mentioned it.

Christmas found me longing for home. *Le réveillon* after midnight Mass was filled with the richness of the royal larder — goose, ham, duckling, sweetmeats, candied fruits — but lacked the intimacy I was used to with Maman, Tatie, and Blondeau. Staring at my *foie gras,* served with spicy anise seeds and honey, I wondered what Tatie had prepared. Christmas Mass in the palace was a long burdensome affair, the bishop intoning a lengthy sermon on the rewards of living a saintly and virtuous life, obviously directed at Louis and Athénaïs. They sat through it unperturbed, and no one dared comment on it.

New Year's Eve was more festive, marked with gambling and champagne in King Louis's quarters, hosted by Athénaïs, the Queen having retired well before midnight.

The first morning of 1672 I awoke with a dry mouth, my head pounding. Lisette prepared a cup of the popular café au lait, a bitter drink tempered with honey and milk and a heavenly aroma. Soon my head felt better.

A messenger arrived bearing an unsigned note: *Les tigres sont tristes et solitaires.* Etienne's handwriting. But what did he mean about the tigers being sad and lonely? Then it dawned on me. The Menagerie!

I bade Lisette to help me dress. Wearing my heaviest wool cape with a fur-lined hood, I ran out into the cold January air. The stable boys, bleary-eyed from their own celebrations, were dutifully mucking out the stalls. One obliged me by saddling Phoebe. Despite the nippy wind, I urged her into a gallop through the empty gardens.

At the Menagerie, I slid off Phoebe's back and into Etienne's arms. He held me tightly, kissed me in that sweet, urgent way of his.

"The gates are locked," I said, disappointed.

"It doesn't matter. I have something for you." He held out a parcel.

I laughed with delight. "I have a gift for you!"

From the leather satchel attached to Phoebe's saddle, I withdrew my parcel — a copy of a book by a natural philosopher we had discussed in one of the salons. "He is a writer named Descartes," I said as he unwrapped it.

"The World or A Treatise on the Light." His eyes shone. "My professeurs spoke of it when I was still at school. I never thought to possess a copy of my own."

"And I made those for you."

He pulled out the two strands of satin ribbon I had stitched into the binding to mark the last page read. He bent down and kissed me.

With hands shivering from the cold, I unwrapped his gift. A pair of satin morning slippers, the color of fresh peaches. The soles were fashioned from kid leather. A simple satin ribbon adorned the instep.

"They are lovely," I said. "So soft."

"When you walk in them, you will feel the touch of my hands." He ran his fingers along my cheek.

I threw my arms around him, no longer feeling the cold, only the warmth of his lips against mine.

CHAPTER THIRTY-EIGHT

The next day King Louis ordered the court back to Paris, and after a jarring journey over frozen roads, we settled into the Tuileries Palace, shivering in its dampness until the newly stoked fires could warm the stone walls. Though her robes battantes were successful in hiding Athénaïs's condition, it was fair knowledge throughout court that she was with child and due soon. No one spoke of it, however. At least not in public.

At long last, Athénaïs began her confinement. The King had rented a house for her on rue de l'Echelle, just blocks from the palace. We settled in with Martine, Lisette, a cook, a housekeeper, and a footman to await the birth. Restless, Athénaïs bade me run to the bookshop one day, the *parfumerie* the next, the *pâtisserie* each day. She inspected my purchases the minute I returned, devouring the pralines and fruit-filled meringues right from the basket. Her appetite was ravenous. I prayed this was a good sign, that the baby would be wholesome, born with its own healthy appetite. When I wasn't running errands, she pressed me to play my lute as she lay resting. While I strummed and she dozed, I thought about the joy this child would bring. A new, innocent life, adding warmth to a court I found to be increasingly cold.

The first week in February, Athénaïs was sitting at her toilette trying on earrings, when she gasped and stood up, clutching the table with one hand, her stomach with the other. At her feet was a puddle.

"Are you in pain?" I asked, setting aside my stitching.

She shook her head. "Only briefly. You must inform Louis."

"I'll send Lisette."

"No! You must go yourself." She unpinned an ivory brooch from her bodice and pressed it into my hand. "Give this to him. You need not say anything."

I sent Lissette to fetch the midwife, then ordered the footman to summon a sedan chair. When we pulled into the palace courtyard, I scrambled out and, clutching the brooch, ran to the royal apartments. My heart pounded as I approached the guards at the door, my breath coming in gasps. "I need to see the King."

They glared at me, impassive, their halberds crossed to prevent my entry.

"Madame de Montespan sent me."

The guard on the right glanced at his partner, eyebrow raised. The other, older, nodded. They withdrew the halberds, then reached for the doors and pulled them open. King Louis stood at his war table with members of his privy council, a model of a battlefield in front of them.

Forgetting to curtsy in my haste, I thrust the brooch at him. "Madame de Montespan told me to give this to you."

Louis immediately waved the men away. "Tell her I'm on my way."

I rushed back to the house on rue de l'Echelle to find the midwife, Madame Henault, had already arrived, grey strands peeking out from under her white coif. Her simple black dress and clean white apron rustled as she moved about. Athénaïs had been changed into her birthing gown and was propped up against a bank of pillows, Martine hovering.

"Have faith, my dear," Madame Henault told Athénaïs. "With God's grace, you'll soon have a beautiful, healthy baby."

"If God had awarded me grace, I wouldn't be in this situation," Athénaïs grunted.

Martine, Lisette, and I all crossed ourselves. The midwife only chuckled and went about her business. Even though the weather was mild, she ordered the windows shuttered and the fire stoked to burn bright. The smoke made my nose itch and my forehead ache. Martine moved about snuffing out candles, leaving one lit on either side of the bed.

I had some knowledge of childbirth, of course, but no firsthand experience. Athénaïs was a strong woman, and this wasn't her first time in the birthing bed. Still, I worried for her; so much could go wrong.

"I am sorry you have to do this here," I said. I wished she could have had this baby in the comfort of her own apartment at the Tuileries or, even better, at Versailles.

"Be glad, as I am at this moment, that I am not queen."

When I raised a questioning eyebrow, she said, "This inopportune circumstance —" She stopped and groaned, closing her eyes until the pain passed. "Would be much more of a bother with the entire court in attendance and gaping."

I shuddered. Queens were required to give birth in public. It was a tradition meant to ensure the veracity of the royal succession. At least Athénaïs did not have that to worry about.

Madame Henault handed Martine a small, stoppered vessel. "Stir this into a mug of hot cider. It will soothe her and give her strength to push."

The maid bobbed her head and ran to do the midwife's bidding.

"And you," she said to Lisette, "a bowl of water and some clean linen."

Lisette hurried off to fetch the needed items. When she returned with the water, the midwife instructed each of us to clean and dry our hands. Athénaïs sipped at the herbal mixture, then lay back on her pillows until the next round of pains began.

A knock so soft I almost didn't hear it sounded on the door. A man wearing a dark wool cloak with its hood up brushed past me. At first, I thought an intruder was upon us, but King Louis's worried voice said, "How is she?"

"The pains are coming more often," I said.

He nodded and went immediately to Athénaïs. "*Mon amour.* Are you in pain now?"

"No thanks to you." She groaned, clutching her belly.

A moment later, Lisette opened the door to a man with a finely combed beard and a smudged waistcoat. There was a faint odor of brandy when he spoke.

"Who is that?" Athénaïs asked warily.

"The surgeon." Louis pulled his hood low over his head again and took her hand. "He will make sure you are delivered safely. Put this on." He handed her a mask to conceal her eyes.

The surgeon threw off his outer garment. "We'll need more light," he said with a startled look at Athénaïs's masked face.

"This will have to do," the King replied in a low voice. "Go about your business."

The surgeon shrugged and pushed past me. Approaching the bed, he tugged off his waistcoat and thrust it at Martine. Madame Henault stepped to the other side of the bed.

"How long since the pains started?"

"About three hours ago," I told him.

"Prop her legs up. Let's take a look." He pushed her gown up, exposing her private area for all to see. "Could be hours yet," he pronounced after a cursory examination. "Do you have anything I could eat?"

"She will begin pushing soon," Madame Henault said, tugging Athénaïs's gown over her legs again.

Louis looked up at her startled, then at the surgeon, seeking confirmation.

The surgeon shrugged. "I smell ham."

Lisette brought a platter of ham and bread and set it on the table. He rubbed his hands in anticipation. No sooner had he taken his first bite than Athénaïs let out a loud groan. He ignored her, breaking off a chunk of bread, shoving it into his mouth.

Then Athénaïs screamed.

"It's time," Madame Henault said. "The baby's head is showing."

The surgeon rolled his eyes, pushed his plate away and stood, wiping his hands on his pants. "Move her to the chair."

"Louis. No!" Athénaïs pleaded, frantic.

I winced looking at the birthing chair in the corner opposite the bed. The arms were leather padded as was the horseshoe-shaped seat, but still it looked horrid.

"She'll stay in bed." Louis traced a finger across her forehead.

The surgeon huffed his acquiescence.

"Put a blanket under her with a towel," Madame Henault ordered. "No need to ruin a good mattress."

Lisette scurried to do her bidding.

As Athénaïs writhed in pain, the surgeon stood, legs apart, at the foot of the bed, waiting. Madame Henault instructed Martine to prepare linens and another bowl of water to clean the baby afterward.

"Ours will be the most beautiful infant God could ever grant a man," Louis whispered, caressing her cheek.

Athénaïs groaned and arched her back. "And perhaps the most painful." She screamed again and grabbed at the bedsheets.

"Hold her legs!" the surgeon ordered.

Madame Henault grabbed one knee and I took the other, holding them apart. Moments later, in the midst of Athénaïs's screams, a beautiful baby girl emerged. The surgeon swooped her up, and the infant gasped her first breath. He gave her over to the midwife and set to cutting the cord. Madame Henault took the babe away to clean and swaddle. Once he had delivered the afterbirth, the surgeon declared himself done.

While the surgeon wiped his bloodied hands on a coarse towel, King Louis slipped me a pouch heavy with coins. "Tell him there will be more as long as he keeps his mouth shut."

At the door, I handed over the pouch and passed on the admonition. The surgeon strode out, never looking back. Athénaïs removed her mask, and King Louis came out from the shadows, ordering the maids to relight the candles.

He took the infant from the midwife's arms and held her up to the light from the window to study her face. "We will name her Louise-Françoise."

Athénaïs gave him a disparaging look—that was the name of her predecessor, the prior maîtresse-en-titre. However, she said nothing.

When he offered her the baby, she waved them away. He turned to me.

I nodded eagerly and reached for her. Cradling Louise-Françoise's little body, I nuzzled her face. The sweetness of her filled me with indescribable joy. She hiccupped then yawned. She gazed up at me, her eyes a sea of dark blue. Her sweet pink bow of a mouth curled on the verge of crying, but she calmed and dozed off. An overwhelming desire to protect her washed over me.

"Madame Scarron will be here for her soon," King Louis said. He noticed my look of shock. "The baby will be well cared for. You know we cannot bring her to court."

I nodded, nuzzled her again, not wanting to let her go.

He paid the midwife handsomely, sending her on her way with a reminder to keep her tongue. "I must go now as well." He leaned over and kissed Athénaïs on the forehead.

"Don't you want to hold her?" I asked when he'd gone.

"Does she look like Louis?" she asked, her eyelids heavy with exhaustion.

Gazing at the infant's face, I smiled. "Immeasurably so."

"Nothing amiss? Fingers? Toes?"

I lifted the swaddling. "All accounted for."

"I'll see to her when I've regained my strength." Her eyes shut.

"Why must you let them spirit her away?" I asked. "Mademoiselle de La Vallière's babies were all recognized by the Crown. There are even whispers that King Louis might legitimize them."

Eyes still closed, Athénaïs murmured, "You forget. Louise de La Vallière was never married. She had no husband to complicate the situation."

The memory of Montespan bursting into our chamber that day caused me to shudder. "How can you bear it? Giving her up?"

"Madame Scarron will be an exceptional governess."

Drinking in the essence of the tiny babe, I sighed, Perhaps Athénaïs was right. Madame Scarron was kind and gentle. She reminded me of Maman.

"And she knows how to be discreet," Athénaïs said.

The sharp rap on the door made my heart lurch. Lisette opened it to Madame Scarron who was followed by a fierce-looking member of the royal guard. She pushed her hood from her head and smiled in recognition. "I've come for the infant."

I took a step back, tightening my grip on the baby.

Seeing my angst, she nodded her head in understanding. "I will take good care of her, you needn't worry." She held out her arms.

I shook my head firmly. "The Marquise will want to say au revoir first."

Martine spoke up. "The Marquise is sleeping."

"She must be exhausted," Madame Scarron said. "It is best to let her sleep." Indeed, Athénaïs was snoring softly now.

"Then I will carry her out," I said.

"Of course." Madame Scarron shepherded me toward the door. The guard stepped aside to allow us to pass.

Baby in arms, I walked into the damp night.

CHAPTER THIRTY-NINE

A cradle moon rode through cloudy tendrils in the inky sky over Versailles. Curled up on the cushioned window seat, I gazed out, the memory of Athénaïs's baby whisked off into the night still haunting me. The infant had awakened at the last moment, hungry. By the time I handed her to Madame Scarron, she was squalling as if she knew she was being taken away from the one who loved her most.

Desolate, I pressed my fingers against the cold glass. Life at court was nothing like I had dreamed as a child or read about in the gazettes. The backbiting and the baiting, the constant positioning to be close to power, the false friendliness. The expectation to serve entirely at the pleasure of the King. It was too much.

I had expected we would stay at the house on rue de l'Echelle while Athénaïs purged the blood that had built up during her pregnancy. But the very next day she had gotten up, fitted herself with a girdle and a sling filled with wool batting to fit between her legs, and ordered the footman to summon the carriage.

When I protested, asking what the King would think, she said, a blunt edge to her voice, "This is what he demands."

And indeed, Louis had welcomed Athénaïs home by hosting a dazzling Mardi Gras ball. In a gown of cascading teal silk edged with diamond-encrusted lace, she danced as if nothing had changed these past nine months, the past two days. The morning after the ball, Ash Wednesday, she couldn't get out of bed, even to go to Mass to get ashes on her forehead.

Lent had begun. With nothing social on his agenda, Louis left on a week-long hunting expedition, leaving Athénaïs to us ladies. I think my relief was greater than hers.

As I gazed out the palace window, my thoughts drifted to Etienne who chafed so under the strictures of the King. I realized he was right. This was no life. The moon floated out from behind a gauzy cloud lighting a path through my room. A new resolve settled over me. Reaching for paper, quill, and ink, I wrote —

Dearest Maman,
I want to come home. I fear I am ill-suited to court life. To be honest, I don't even know why I am here.

I unburdened myself, telling her that life at court was at odds with everything she had taught me about being a good person, an honest person.

I understand now why you were so reluctant to let me come. If you will give your blessing, I will seek an audience with the King and beg his permission to leave. I am quite sure he would readily grant it, for I must be an albatross around his neck, considering the many faux pas I commit on a daily basis. Maman, please do not be disappointed in me, but welcome me home with all the love and patience you've always directed my way.

I sealed the letter and left it on the silver tray to be picked up for the morning post.

The week dragged by. The King was still hunting. Athénaïs was still in much discomfort. The midwife sent a potion to help her sleep. Now I sat on the window seat again, a book in my lap, tracing raindrops on the pane with a finger, wondering where Etienne was at this moment.

A soft knock at the door roused me from my reverie. Likely a page delivering the day's posts. Lisette had gone to the market looking for ribbons and notions for a dress she was making, so I opened the door myself. To my surprise, Etienne stood in the doorway holding a parcel.

"What are you doing here?" I asked.

He shuffled awkwardly. "I have shoes for the Marquise." He stepped inside and cocked his head toward Athénaïs's door. "Is *he*...?"

"Not today. She is...indisposed. I can give her the shoes later."

He set the package on the table. Then he took me into his arms, his lips warm, hungry. I thrilled at the taste of him despite the risk.

Finally, reluctantly, I pushed him away. "Lisette will return at any moment."

He nodded, composed himself. "You were gone a long time."

"We visited with the Marquise's sister." My pretext was partly true. The Marchioness of Thianges had come to the little house twice during the weeks of Athénaïs's confinement. Etienne gave me a skeptical look. Ever since we were young children, he could tell when I was not being truthful with him; but Athénaïs's situation was a confidence I couldn't risk sharing, not even with him.

Another rap sounded.

"Lisette," I said. But why was she knocking?

Etienne stepped out of sight, behind the door. Standing where he had been moments before was the gangly red-headed page, Jérôme. A blush stained his freckled face as soon as he saw me. In his hands he clutched the small, lacquered box.

"I thought the King was hunting," I said.

"He has returned a day early."

"I'm sorry but Madame de Montespan is not available. Please give her regrets to the King."

Jérôme put out a hand to stop the door from closing. "It is not for her, Mademoiselle."

I raised a questioning eyebrow.

"The King said to deliver it to you."

"Me?"

He bobbed his head, his blush deepening, He lowered his voice. "You are summoned to his chamber." He thrust the box at me then turned abruptly and loped away.

I had no need to open it. I knew what lay inside. Athénaïs had accepted that same silver ring with the embossed L many times, slipping it onto her middle finger, preparing herself for a visit from Louis. What could it mean that he sent it to me?

"Is anything amiss?" Etienne whispered from behind the door.

"A messenger from the King asking after the Marquise's welfare." Thrusting the box behind me, I stepped back into the room. "I'm sorry, Etienne, but I have duties to attend to."

"Perhaps we can ride again now the weather has become agreeable."

"I would like that."

He kissed me one last time before taking his leave. My hands trembled as I sank onto the chair and, with great apprehension, lifted the lid of the box. *Mon Dieu!* What was I to do?

The door opened again, startling me.

"Mademoiselle?" Lisette, her shopping basket over her arm, regarded me with concern. "Is something wrong?" She saw the box in my hands, her eyes widening when she recognized the ring. "Is he coming here?"

I shook my head. "I'm to go to him."

She sucked in a breath. Without a word she went to my wardrobe and pulled out the rose chiffon that brought out the color in my eyes, enhanced my breasts, and drew the most compliments.

As she dressed me, I weighed the consequences of the King asking for me. If I acquiesced, how could I possibly face Athénaïs afterward? Or Etienne? Could I even do what he wished of me? Other than Etienne's kisses, I had no experience with men. None that would help me in this situation, that is. I still recoiled when I thought of Boivin panting over Perrette.

Box in hand, I took a deep breath. I couldn't refuse to go, but I could refuse anything I wasn't ready to do. I slipped the ring onto my thumb.

Lisette accompanied me as far as the royal apartments. My high-heeled shoes—the ones Etienne had made—clicked on the marble tiles, a counterpoint to the thumping of my heart. Clusters of courtiers stopped in mid-chatter to stare at me. Others leaned together to whisper as I passed. Did they know? Did they suspect I had been summoned by King Louis himself? My mouth went dry.

At the entrance to the royal wing, the two uniformed guards looked steadfastly ahead as Lisette fussed over my hair, straightened my pearls, my skirt. I tried to breathe, but my chest pushed against the bodice of my gown, forcing my breasts to bulge in a way that made me only too aware of the purpose of my summons. Lisette offered a reassuring smile then stepped back. I must go in alone.

The guards opened the doors.

Bontemps waited on the other side. "Mademoiselle."

Struggling to keep my voice from quavering, I held out the empty box. "Bonsoir, Monsieur Bontemps."

He took the box from me, then led the way through the antechamber, through the council chamber, a small library, and a room with a dining table looking out over the garden. I had to force myself not to turn and run away, remind myself I didn't have to do anything I wasn't prepared to do. Louis was King, but he had a reputation of never forcing himself upon a woman. That he never had to. At least, that's what the gossip whisperers intimated. Was it true?

At the door to the King's private study, I clasped my hands in front of me, twisting the signet ring on my thumb. Bontemps ushered me in. Louis stood at the window looking out over the palace's expansive lawns.

When he turned, I bent into a low curtsy. Bontemps backed out of the room, shutting the door behind him. His Majesty bade me rise and kissed me on each cheek. Then he took my hand, regarding me with an odd smile. I forced myself to breathe, my heart beating uncontrollably.

"Come," he said, and directed me to a gold damask settee in the center of the room.

I fidgeted with a curl that brushed my cheek, then forced my hands together, remembering the signet ring. Should I take it off? Give it back to him now?

"Would you care for a glass of wine?" he asked.

"No, I...oui. Merci."

He poured red wine from a crystal carafe into matching crystal glasses, then sat down next to me. Close. Very close. Heat rose to my face as I took the wineglass.

"Sylvienne, you are trembling." He put his hand on mine. His smile lit his eyes. So caring. So...intense.

I fought the urge to withdraw my hand from his grasp. "Your Majesty, I know not why you summoned me." My voice barely a whisper, he leaned in to hear me, the musk of his orange blossom parfum, the powder in his hair filling my senses. My breathing became shallow. "You must know I have very little...actually, no...experience with men."

He pulled back, a quizzical expression on his face. Then the corners of his eyes crinkled. "Do you think I summoned you to seduce you?"

"I...I know not." The heat in my cheeks deepened.

His smile turned to gentle laughter. "Ma chère, how old are you?"

"I'll be seventeen soon, Sire."

He chuckled. "Ah, to be young again." Letting go of my hand, he reached to push an errant lock of hair out of my eyes. "I am not going to seduce you. Though I must say I am completely enamored of you."

I stared at him, stunned, relieved, confused. Why was I here then?

He took my chin in his fingers and ever so gently lifted it. "Look into my eyes. What do you see?"

I studied his eyes. "Love." It was true. His eyes were filled with an indescribable warmth. I tugged the ring off my thumb and held it out to him.

He slipped it onto his little finger, but his eyes never wavered. "What has your mother told you about her time at court?"

"My mother?" How did Maman come to be part of this moment? "She...she doesn't speak of it."

He nodded then reached for a letter stamped with a wax seal I recognized. Maman's. He held it out to me. "You should read this."

I took the letter from him, more confused than ever as I examined the handwriting I knew so well. Was that her scent I detected?

> *Ma chère Sylvienne,*
>
> *I trust you are well and thriving at court. His Majesty tells me he desires you to know the truth about your parentage. I would prefer to protect you from the consequences of my past, but Louis is determined and promises he will see to your welfare. Please listen to what he has to say with a heart colored with compassion, forgiveness, and love. And know that, regardless of the circumstances, Guy d'Aubert, my loving husband, your devoted Papa for such a short time, truly loved you. I cherish the day we will be together again. ~ Maman*

I drew in a breath. Of course Papa loved me. Why would she mention him? What had Maman done? Why did it take the King to tell me the truth about her past?

Louis took both my hands in his. "When I was fifteen, a year, nay almost two, younger than you are now, there was a girl who caught my eye in a way no other had. I fell in love with her in an instant." His gaze drifted to the window. "We were both virgins. But we were caught up in such passion." His gaze returned to me. "And, yes, I did seduce her. Or perhaps it was she who seduced me. Who can know when it is first love? We were eager to experience each other. To learn the measure of our hearts. We kept our love-making a secret, though it lasted not more than a month. Then one day she was gone. Vanished. I was in torment to think she could leave me. With no forewarning. No au revoir. I wept. Tears of anger, rage."

"It must have been awful for you." I thought of how sad Etienne had been at my leaving Amiens, his anger when we first met at Versailles. "But...Sire, it is commonly whispered about court that your, um, deflowering, was accomplished by a friend of your mother's. One-eyed Catherine." I clapped my hand over my mouth, realizing how inappropriate my utterance had been.

He laughed. "The Baroness de Beauvais. That was a rumor put about by the Queen Regent to deflect attention from the girl." Then he sobered. "That girl —"

I knew what he was going to say even before he said it.

"Was Isabelle."

"Maman?"

"Oui."

"But she…she is your cousin. She told me she spent her toddler years in the nursery with you. That she was forced to leave court, given over to the convent when she was only seven."

"She came back. Once."

"For your coronation." Now it began to make sense. Louis became king at the age of five, when his father, Louis XIII died. However, he wasn't officially crowned until he was fifteen. I felt dizzy. It seemed my entire family history was being re-written. It was too much to take in all at once.

"Sylvienne, your mother and I—"

"No!" I pulled my hand away from his.

He didn't resist, settling his hands in his own lap. "I remember the half-moon rising the night of my coronation, like a cradle in the sky. On the night of the full moon, I went to look for Isabelle as I had each of the nights before. But she was gone." He stopped for a moment, and it was as if he were lost in time. He twisted the signet ring back and forth. "I was told she had fled in the middle of the night. That when she learned she could never be my queen, she wanted nothing to do with me."

"And you believed it?"

"I was young." He let out a deep sigh. "I thought my heart would die in my chest." He was silent a moment. "I've had many loves since then, but I've never forgotten your mother."

Looking into his eyes, I saw my own, mirrored. The same green irises with gold flecks. The same curious, always questioning arch of his brows. "She was the daughter of the late King's brother, Gaston, Duc d'Orléans." A fact I had learned the day Louis visited us in Amiens.

"Yes."

"But her mother, my grand-mère, Marie-Jeannette de Vienne was…"

"Gaston's mistress."

"A lady-in-waiting to the Queen Regent, your mother," I said.

He nodded. "I know now that Isabelle did not leave of her own choosing. We were caught together one afternoon. I was young and had no say with whom I should spend my time."

Again, he took my hand. This time, I didn't resist.

"It was only recently that I learned the truth. When my mother discovered our tryst, she sent Isabelle away without telling me. When she learned Isabelle was with child, she arranged the marriage between her and Guy d'Aubert."

I did the math in my head. My mother was only fifteen years older than me. I whispered, "When you came to our house that day..."

"I swear I did not know about you until that moment in Amiens." He fingered a small, intricately carved gold ring on his other hand. "Or I would have made sure you and Isabelle had what you needed to live the life you deserve. That is why I summoned you tonight." He slipped the gold ring from his finger. "And why I cannot, would not, despite how beautiful you are, ever try to seduce you."

He took my hand and slid the gold ring onto my thumb. "Sylvienne, *mon coeur*, I could never seduce my own daughter."

CHAPTER FORTY

When I emerged from the King's inner sanctum, dear loyal Lisette was waiting for me. She had kept vigil in the corridor not far from the stern eyes of the royal guards. She ran to me and began taking stock. My hair, my jewelry, my gown. She seemed perplexed that nothing was amiss, nothing in disarray. When she spotted the gold ring on my thumb in place of the King's silver signet ring, her eyes widened.

"We'll talk in my chamber," I whispered, steering her away from the guards and the courtiers who inevitably lolled about. Of course, I couldn't tell her the entire truth. King Louis had bidden me not to speak to anyone of his disclosure until he himself made the announcement. He would recognize me as his issue, he had told me, and in the future, he would legitimize my birth. For now, my first duty was to pay homage and swear fealty to Queen Marie-Thérèse, my stepmother.

Stepmother! My thoughts tumbled like leaves caught in a whirlwind. King Louis is my father. I am indeed of royal blood but illegitimate. Why did Maman not tell me herself? All these years, letting me believe Guy d'Aubert was my father. Papa! I still cherished the man who held me so tenderly when I could barely walk, who told me I was beautiful and precious. What did it mean that I wasn't his true daughter?

"Mademoiselle d'Aubert, are you all right?" Madame de Chatillon stopped me in the main gallery. After Henriette's death, de Chatillon had been accepted into service as lady-in-waiting to Queen Marie-Thérèse. "You look flushed."

"*Je suis bien*. Merci." I hurried on, wondering if I could still claim the name d'Aubert. If not, then what was I to be called? I couldn't very well take the name of my royal father, Bourbon, could I? Maman, what have you done? I remembered all those times I asked about her childhood, the stories she'd told of living in a grand palace and being imprisoned in a convent—stories I had thought were make-believe, stories to entertain me. But they weren't make-believe. I can only imagine the shock Louis felt when he'd first laid eyes on me that day in Amiens. And now I understood the curious looks the Queen often gave me.

Stopping in front of a gilded hall mirror, the resemblance was evident to me now. King Louis and I had the same thick brown-almost-black hair. The same green eyes. And our faces…no wonder I found the portraits of the young King so fascinating. I had been seeing myself in his countenance. My face so unlike Maman's.

Maman! My letter asking to come home. What would she think when she read it? I groaned.

At the apartment, I sought out Athénaïs. She was awake, lounging upon her divan, thick embroidered pillows supporting her back and arms. She wore a loose nightgown that revealed her still swollen bosom encased in cabbage leaves—thought to reduce the pain of unsuckled breasts—and bound with a swath of silk.

"Martine, take these off me," she ordered.

Martine unwound the silk and removed the cabbage leaves.

"*Mon Dieu*, this is horrible." Athénaïs massaged her nipples before pulling her gown over them. "Did you have an enjoyable visit with the King?"

I froze. How to answer? Did she think I went to seduce her lover? I hid my hand with the gold ring in the folds of my skirt.

"If you think you have risen above me in station—"

I stifled a hysterical giggle at the idea she thought I meant to replace her.

" —as one of Louis's bastards." She looked at me pointedly.

I gaped in astonishment. "You know?"

"I guessed. Louis confirmed my suspicion this morning. Are you pleased to learn you are a royal bâtarde?"

"No. I mean...I...I am overwhelmed. It is difficult to fathom."

Now she spotted the gold ring on my thumb. "You may be the oldest of his lot, but you are certainly not his only."

She meant her own new baby, spirited away in the middle of the night. It occurred to me then that sweet little Louise-Françoise was my sister. Perhaps that explained why I felt such a fondness for her. And then there was the young Dauphin, whom I seldom saw. And the two children of Louise de La Vallière. I blinked, dumbfounded at the notion of so many half-siblings.

Athénaïs picked something up off the table next to the divan. A letter. "I understand you no longer wish to be at court."

I inhaled sharply. "Where did you get that?"

"Louis asked me to take possession of it."

"He knows? But how?"

"All letters are read before they leave the palace. His security detail takes their charge quite seriously."

My legs trembled. I sank onto the nearest chair in fear they would fail me.

"I dare say this letter is why he chose this moment to reveal his paternity to you." She fanned herself with my letter to Maman.

"To keep me from leaving? But why? What difference does it make to him if I stay or go?"

"My dear, every child of his makes a difference. You are part of a royal cadre now. You are needed as he negotiates alliances critical to him politically, financially." She turned the letter over in her hands. "I can still send it, if you wish."

"*Non!* No. Please." I gripped the arms of the chair to keep from lurching and grabbing it from her.

She held the page toward a burning candle but waited. I stared at it for a long moment, then nodded. The corner of my heart-felt words to Maman caught the flame. Athénaïs held the burning page aloft, the tang of singed linen wafting across the room. After a moment, she tossed it among the logs in the fireplace.

"What must he think of me for writing that?" I asked.

"Don't distress yourself," she advised. "It is no longer important."

The next day a member of the royal guard stood outside my door, ready to accompany me to the Queen's wing of the palace whenever I should be summoned.

When His Majesty told me I would visit the Queen as his acknowledged daughter, I must have blanched, for he said, "She is not as forbidding as all that. She will be heartened to learn that at least one of my issue was from the time before we were wed."

However, Queen Marie-Thérèse was not available to receive me that day. She had come down with a fever. Nor the day after when she went to visit one of the convents she sponsored. I spent three days stewing about my new status at court and what the news of my paternity meant for my future—not to mention what the Queen would say when she did consent to receive me. I desperately wanted to talk with Etienne. To confide in him. To tell him everything I now knew, and to hear his reassurance that my life hadn't really changed.

When I asked Athénaïs about the guard at my door, she said, "As Louis's daughter, you naturally merit a high level of protection." I suspected only half of the guard's mandate was protection. How would I be able to meet with Etienne now? I decided to find out.

Lisette helped me dress for riding, When I walked out the door, the guard did not stop me, instead following at a discreet distance. Approaching the stables, I spotted Etienne heading in my direction. My pulse quickened. His face lit up on seeing me. But as he strode closer, I sensed over my shoulder that the guard was closing in as well. By the time Etienne reached me, the guard was right behind. Etienne doffed his leather hat and kept on going, his face a mask, only his eyes betraying his confusion. I nodded, walked on, my heart sick with disappointment.

I ordered Phoebe to be saddled. A second horse was saddled at the same time. As I rode out, my royal guard mounted the other horse and rode a respectful distance behind. I considered heading into the woods and trying to outrun him. Phoebe was quite swift, but there was no point. Another guard would simply show up at my door later. I guided Phoebe around the gardens, past the menagerie, the kitchens, the icehouse. Something on the order of five thousand people lived and worked at Versailles, all of them serving at the pleasure of the King. All of them, including me, I realized, nothing more than puppets in a grand theatre designed to amuse my newfound father. Princess Henriette's words that first night at her salon came back to haunt me. *King Louis does nothing without purpose.* I yanked on Phoebe's reins and turned her back toward the stables, kicking her into a run, my ever-present guard a dozen paces behind.

When the Queen finally sent word for me to present myself in her chamber—she had an opening in her schedule right before that evening's dinner—I scribbled off a short note: *Ignore rumors. Tonight's grand couvert will yield the truth about the tigress.*

Entreating Lisette to go with all haste, I instructed her to put the note into no one's hands but Etienne's. I prayed he would come, though he had yet to attend a grand couvert. I knew the rumors about me were rife, and I desperately wanted him to know the truth of my birth. If there was any way I could tell him myself, I would. But that had already proved to be impossible. Perhaps if he heard it from the King's lips, Etienne would understand my position.

I chose a red and gold brocade gown I hoped befitted a royal child but without being ostentatious. Knowing Queen Marie-Thérèse's religious proclivities, I hung a small crucifix around my neck. Outside her private reception room, I fingered the gold ring on my thumb, my trepidation worse than the afternoon I thought the King's summons meant he intended to seduce me. At last, I was ushered in. King Louis stood behind his wife, one hand on her shoulder. He had obviously told her the news, for she wore a resigned if wounded look.

Rising from my curtsy, I touched the crucifix at my neck. "I beg your indulgence, Your Majesty."

Her hands lay folded in her lap, her eyes scoured me. "I trust you will do nothing to embarrass or imperil this court."

"Of course, Your Majesty." I curtsied again for good measure.

She turned her head away. Our audience was over.

King Louis inclined his head, smiling at me. "We look forward to your presence at dinner."

Following the royal couple to the Queen's dining chamber, I wondered if she knew about Athénaïs's child. Or had I been positioned to be a distraction in that regard? I felt the eyes of the courtiers in the gallery following me. The buzz of their whispers floated like a haze over the room. The footman directed me to a chair next to the King's. Athénaïs's chair. I hesitated.

She leaned in close and purred into my ear. "Take your seat, my dear. Enjoy it. For this one evening." Then she took the chair next to me.

Looking out over the growing horde of observers, I felt as a hare must when sighted in the crosshairs of a hunting bow. Around me, members of the royal family chatted in muted tones, the Prince de Condé with la Grande Mademoiselle, the Queen with Prince Philippe. Next to Philippe sat young Louis, the Dauphin, playing with his spoon and knife. I studied his face, so like his father's. So, I now realized, like mine. But pouty. Our father, King Louis, never pouted.

The Dauphin looked up and stuck his tongue out at me. I smirked, resisting the urge to return the gesture. I surveyed the crowd of observers. There he was. Etienne. Slipping in through the far door. My nerves were suddenly ajumble. He wore his best doublet and looked quite handsome, but I could tell he felt ill at ease, hovering near the back wall, his expression one of cautious curiosity. When at last I caught his eye, he dipped his head in acknowledgement.

Moments later, the King nodded at Bontemps who lifted a small bell and rang it once. The room fell silent.

King Louis stood and, extending a hand to me, bade me rise. "I am pleased to present to the court Mademoiselle Sylvienne d'Aubert de Bourbon, whom I acknowledge as my daughter."

A great buzz of surprise coursed through the room. A dizzying thrill of pride and elation coursed through me. Bontemps rang the bell again. The courtiers quieted again.

"Mademoiselle d'Aubert's mother, my dear cousin Isabelle, was someone I knew and loved long before I met our beloved Queen." King Louis turned and smiled at his wife. She produced a rigid token smile in return. "I hereby recognize the lovely Sylvienne as my issue, and I require she be regarded and respected as such from this moment forward."

The silence was ominous. Then Athénaïs clapped. A heartbeat later, Philippe joined her, then other members of the royal family and the courtiers followed suit. The King bussed me on both cheeks. I twisted the gold ring on my thumb as I sank back onto the cushioned chair.

Bontemps signaled for the food to be served. After the final course, but before the dessert was brought in, the King again motioned for him to ring the bell. Expectant curiosity hung thick in the silence. My searching eyes found Etienne still at the back of the room, his face now unreadable. I offered a tentative smile.

The King, my newfound father, beamed at me. "I have further news for the court and for my daughter."

I raised my eyebrows in Etienne's direction and shrugged my shoulders ever-so-slightly.

"Our beautiful Mademoiselle Sylvienne's hand has been requested in marriage."

CHAPTER FORTY-ONE

Dumfounded, I wondered if I had heard correctly. A proposal of marriage? The King had mentioned nothing about a proposal in all our recent conversations. A cauldron bubbled in my stomach as a murmur of surprise filled the room.

King Louis was clearly enjoying the moment. "A nobleman by the name of Guillaume Boivin de Laudin approached the throne several days ago, expressing his desire to negotiate a marriage contract."

I gasped audibly. This couldn't be. King Louis knew of Boivin's reputation. My heart thumped wildly. Athénaïs laid a hand on my trembling arm, preventing me from rising and shouting my objection.

"Did you agree to the union?" Philippe asked, leaning forward, frowning.

"I considered it." The King reached for his wine glass.

My heart stopped. Closing my eyes, I dared not breathe. And I dared not look at Etienne.

"For all of a moment or two." Louis lifted the goblet to his lips and took a slow, deliberate drink before setting it down. "I told him…no."

A rush of air from my lungs started my heart again. I caught Etienne's eye. He scowled, his look one of skepticism.

A murmur of disappointment rose from the courtiers. Philippe nodded and sat back.

The King smiled again, mischievously. "The next day, the Duc de Narbonne approached the throne to propose his own marriage contract with our lovely Sylvienne."

René Lorgeleux? My eyes widened in astonishment. I put a hand to my throat. Surely, he was toying with me.

"As with Boivin, I told him I would consider it." Louis picked a truffle off a silver plate and popped it into his mouth.

I clenched my hands until they hurt, not daring to look at Etienne now.

King Louis chewed the morsel dramatically before swallowing. "And so. I considered it." He wiped his lips and hands on a linen napkin held out to him by a footman. "For all of a moment or two."

The courtiers chuckled, but my heart raced. Again, my breath stuck in my throat.

King Louis grinned, enjoying his own joke and his great dramatic performance. He looked at me with bright eyes. A sense of dread overcame me as he took my hand, pulling me to my feet. "Ma chère fille, the wedding is to be held the second Wednesday after Easter."

The courtiers broke into applause and delighted cheers.

King Louis held his wine glass aloft. "I propose a toast. To the future Duchesse de Narbonne."

The royal family raised their glasses. "Santé!"

Stunned, I could only blink. Then, in a panic, I searched the crowd for Etienne. I caught only a glimpse of his back as he stormed out the door.

By the time the courtiers in the reception line had all congratulated me — the women bussing me on both cheeks, the men gallantly kissing my hand — I was dizzy with exhaustion. The Duc de Narbonne had not been in attendance this evening, and for that I was grateful. Nor was he at the King's apartment for a small family reception afterward.

Later, in our own quarters, I sank onto an armchair next to Athénaïs's toilette table. She wiped the rouge from her cheeks in front of her gilded mirror. Still stunned by the evening's announcement, I sat staring at nothing, wondering how I could get Etienne to understand this wasn't my doing. And how could I reverse the events of this evening?

"Are you listening?" Apparently Athénaïs had been talking to me. "You've been distracted all evening. You are not harboring a secret lover, are you?"

I looked up in alarm. "Do you think the King noticed my agitation?"

"You hid it well. But I am quite aware of your moods."

Moods? I had never thought of myself as having moods.

"Are you…" She surveyed me, one eyebrow raised. "With child?"

I shook my head furiously. She knew very well I was a virgin.

"Then what has you so distraught?"

My voice quavered. "How could he do this to me?"

"How could who do what?" She leaned toward her mirror and wiped her lips.

"The King. How could he accept a marriage proposal without consulting me?"

"I thought you favored the Duc de Narbonne. Help me with this necklace."

I stood behind her. "He is handsome, to be sure. But to give me away thus. And to announce it to the court before telling me. What if I did have someone else whom I loved?"

"But you said you don't." She dipped her head for me to unhook the necklace. "And why would that matter anyway? You are a daughter of the King of France."

"A bastard daughter." I returned the necklace to her jewelry armoire, then pulled the jeweled pins from her hair.

"It makes no difference. He has acknowledged you. Any marriage you enter into must be for the benefit of the Crown."

"But I was never consulted."

"Don't be absurd. There is no reason to consult the bride. Louis arranges all marriages for members of his family. They are negotiated contracts for economic and political advantage."

My hands hovered over her hair. "So, I am nothing more to him than one of the pieces on his prized chess board?" My eyes met hers in the mirror. "But what of love?"

"If it is love you require, don't look for it in marriage. Take a lover." She tugged a diamond pendant from one ear and held it out to me.

"Cannot two people who are married be in love?"

"I suppose it is not impossible." She removed the other earring. "But personally, I can't think of any instances of it."

I put the earrings into a small drawer above the necklace. "The Queen. Doesn't Marie-Thérèse love the King?"

"If you call infatuation love. But to what end? Louis has me to turn to for romance. Sylvienne, you must stop this pouting. There is nothing to be done about the situation. Louis has decided. And tomorrow we will begin planning the ball to celebrate. I know, let's make it a masked ball!"

Athénaïs lifted her feet to let Martine remove her shoes, all the while rambling on about whom to invite to the ball, what orchestra should play, and whether extra cooks and waitstaff would need to be contracted for.

Contracted for. Was that to be the tenor of my marriage? A contract for the state. And what of Etienne? Was he no longer to be part of my life? Could I live without him? I drew in a ragged breath. I had attained the life at court I had always wanted, but at what expense?

Athénaïs dismissed me, and I bade her a good night's sleep, glad to retreat to my bedchamber where Lisette waited to help me with my own jewelry.

She curtsied deeply. "Mademoiselle."

She somehow already knew of the evening's events. "Please, Lisette. I am still the same girl you have been serving all along."

"*Mais non*, Mademoiselle." Her voice was filled with awe, her eyes shone with pride. "You are the daughter of his Majesty, the King of France. And soon to be a duchesse."

I took her hands, my voice trembling. "Oh, Lisette. I don't know what to do. Must I marry without love? This is not what I had bargained for."

"It is your fate." She squeezed my hands. "Love will find its own way. Don't despair. Fate sometimes changes its path when love insists."

Throwing my arms around her, I held her tight. She laughed in surprise but didn't resist.

After a moment she said, "Mademoiselle, you must get ready for bed. The days ahead will be filled to exhaustion."

I nodded. In that, I knew she was right.

The palace was a hub of activity for the next two weeks. Gardeners, cooks, and household staff hustled to prepare for the masked ball, which was to be held three days after Easter—on my birthday. Monsieur Delacourt was called in to design an appropriate ball gown, as well as the wedding gown, and dresses for after the wedding. For the wife of a duc must always be lavishly dressed.

To my consternation, Etienne assigned one of his assistants to design and make the half-dozen pairs of shoes I would need. The unfamiliar shoemaker knelt before me, taking measurements of my feet, then presenting me with an assortment of pearl-and-diamond-encrusted buttons and bows to choose from.

Poking at my breakfast one morning, it occurred to me I hadn't seen Guillaume Boivin at court these past several weeks. A relief to be sure. Court gossip confirmed he had been banished from the palace for being so bold as to request the hand of the daughter of the King of France in marriage—regardless of my illegitimacy. I shuddered thinking of all the poor peasant girls on whom he would take out his humiliation. I was glad Perrette was far away across the ocean and out of reach of the disgraced nobleman.

The first day of April. My seventeenth birthday. Light from a thousand candles shimmered upon the glittering costumes of the masked ball guests. I paused at the door to the ballroom, peering through my gold-embossed mask, fighting the urge to flee. The stays of my bodice—a lovely burgundy velvet trimmed with gold needlework—pushed my breasts into little half-moons. Black and white woodpecker feathers surrounded by plumes of burgundy-dyed swan feathers rimmed the mask. Only my chin and lips were revealed. My shoes, despite the careful measurements of Etienne's assistant, pinched my feet. I took a deep breath. Heads turned as I walked through the door and curtsied before the King and Queen.

"Ravishing!" King Louis kissed my hands as my cheeks were inaccessible and wished me a happy birthday. He wore a gold doublet with matching breeches. Golden sunrays framed his masked face.

Queen Marie-Thérèse, clad in a red and silver gown designed to accentuate her latest pregnancy offered half-hearted wishes for a prosperous year ahead. She wore a silver mask with red, pearl-encrusted plumes, Behind her clustered her ladies-in-waiting, masked in matching colors but without the pearls.

As guests approached to pay obeisance to the royal couple and extend their congratulations and birthday greetings to me, King Louis took two glasses of champagne from the tray proffered by a footman. He handed one to the Queen and one to me.

"Merci, Sire." I sipped gratefully, overwhelmed by the dizzying array of brightly colored costumes.

Moments later, Athénaïs swept into the room, her gown a cascade of aquamarine and ivory chiffon shimmering like a waterfall. Her mask, elegant in its simplicity, was inset with diamonds, sapphires, and opals. She curtsied before the King and Queen.

King Louis escorted Queen Marie-Thérèse to her chair on the dais. Immediately her ladies surrounded her. Louis turned to me. "May I request the favor of your first dance?"

I took his hand, and we stepped out onto the dance floor. Other couples followed, lining up for the first minuet of the evening. I couldn't imagine anything more fairy-tale-like than dancing with my father, the King of France, at a masked ball in my honor.

When the dance ended, he bowed, and I curtsied. "It seems my brother wishes to be your next partner," he said before striding off to claim Athénaïs for the next dance.

I turned to find Philippe in shades of violet, his lavender mask a large, bejeweled butterfly that looked as if it had lit upon his face. We took our places in the minuet line. As he held my hand high, I asked, "Is the Duc here?"

I had yet to meet with my prospective groom, the Duc de Narbonne. I had not spoken with him since the last salon. He was handsome and gallant, knowledgeable and well-read but, really, I knew nothing of him. Not the way he spoke in private conversation, nor the foods he preferred, the company he kept, the touch of his hands, the feel of his lips. I knew only one man's lips.

"Indeed, he is. But I won't give him away," Philippe teased. "You'll have to discover him for yourself."

We stepped out in time to the music.

"But how will I know who he is?" I asked, irritated. Was I not to know which of the dancers was my intended until the unmasking at midnight?

"That is the game, ma chérie." Philippe twirled me once then handed me off to the next dancer.

From behind my mask, I examined the eyes of every courtier who stood tall enough to qualify as the Duc de Narbonne. When the dance brought me back to Philippe, I asked, "What do you know of him?"

"I know that he once proposed to my Henriette."

Stunned, I stopped in the middle of the dance. Fortunately, Philippe had my hand and pulled me along. "Did he love her?"

"Very much so, from what I was told. He was quite upset with me for taking her away from him. A month or so after our wedding he began to come around to court again, seeking to woo her, I suppose. However, my brother had his own designs on her by then. He commissioned poor René as an officer in his Royal Regiment and sent him off to deal with some silly border dispute."

I was again handed off to another dancer, who in time handed me to King Louis.

"I understand my betrothed was an officer in your army," I said.

"A very accomplished soldier and even better leader. He had no taste for the savagery of war, however, and sold his commission after only a couple of years. An unfortunate circumstance."

"For him or for you?"

Before he could reply, he handed me back to Philippe in time for the dance to conclude. Immediately, Edmund de la Vaquet was at my side hoping for the next dance, a lively *bourée*. I smiled and took his hand.

When the dance ended, a page rushed up, bowed low, then handed me a card. A summons from Queen Marie-Thérèse requesting my presence in a small antechamber off the main ballroom. When I looked up, the page had already melted into the crowd.

Building up my nerve, I reached for a glass of wine from a passing footman, took a long drink, then handed back the glass. I found the Queen sitting on an armchair, still masked. Her ever-present ladies looked for all the world like a covey of harpies, waiting to devour me. I sank into an awkward curtsy.

"Are you enjoying the evening?" she asked, her voice sounding tired.

"Very much, Your Majesty."

The harpies scrutinized me, my gown, my jewels, my posture, my reactions.

"I'm happy for you." She waved a hand, and the harpies rose as one and filed out of the room, looks of disdain hiding their disappointment at not being allowed to stay and watch the *mêlée*. The Queen motioned to a stool in front of her. "Sit."

She removed her mask and indicated I should do the same. When I did, she regarded me for a long moment. "You favor him. It is most evident in your eyes." She was speaking of King Louis, of course.

"Merci," was all I could think to say.

"You are alike in other ways as well." Despite her Spanish accent, she had no trouble finding words. "The way you walk. The way you hold your head. But it is more. Your jaw, it clenches — like his does — at having to listen to a truth you do not want to hear."

I touched my jaw, an unthinking reaction. Indeed, it was tight, the muscles knotted.

"But there is one trait in which you differ from him greatly."

My eyebrows rose at that.

"You lack discipline. The King of France knows that the way to stay in power is to be disciplined. You…appear to disregard power. That puzzles me. I wonder if it is a…" She fingered the mask in her lap, seeking the right word. "A façade." She held my gaze. "The circumstance of your birth was different from his other spawn. Long before the contract for our marriage had been negotiated. I accept that."

I realized she knew about the babies. Athénaïs's. La Vallière's. The King's bastards were the worst kept of all court secrets. The Queen was not as naïve as she was thought to be. I also realized she was quite adept at maneuvering her token on the chessboard of state.

"I can accept that you have a special place in his heart," she continued. "But I will not abide any attempts to displace his rightful heirs, *my* children."

"Of course, Your Majesty. I would not think to—"

"You are no different from any of the others here at court. You have ambitions, whether you admit to them or not. And I have been watching you, watching how you have changed from a country mouse to a coquettish feline, learning to use your wiles and your beauty to play the games all courtiers must play."

"Your Majesty, please. You must not think so of me."

"You wish me to believe you have no designs on the throne? Yet you maneuver to marry a wealthy duc."

"I didn't...I never..."

"You might claim to know your place as a bastard. You might even believe it. But I guarantee your husband-to-be will not care about the issue of legitimacy. He will use you and will angle for any advantage he can muster." She paused, her face hardening. "It will not be tolerated."

"Of course, Your Majesty." I forced myself not to tremble, not to look down, not to look away from those eyes fierce as daggers.

"I am glad we understand one another. You may go."

Fumbling to replace my mask, I stumbled from the room, past her ladies-in-waiting, their eyes alight, challenging. Were they aware of what the Queen planned to say to me? How could she think I would try to undermine the royal household? I had only, just days before, learned of my relationship to King Louis, to his royal children. My head swam with the implications of it all. I felt caught in a vise.

Bolting through the corridor, I was grateful for the mask that hid my tears, my burning cheeks. I pushed against the nearest door leading to one of the many balconies edging the palace, yanking off my mask as I burst into the cold air.

"Well, if it isn't our country mouse." The voice was familiar, taunting. There stood a man with his arms wrapped around another, both unmasked. I recognized the Chevalier de Lorraine and —

I dropped into a curtsy. "Forgive me, Monsieur. I didn't mean to intrude upon your…" What word to use? "Privacy." My cheeks aflame for an entirely different reason this time, I turned to go.

"No, stay." Philippe inclined his head toward the door. "You," he said to Lorraine, "leave us."

"But there is drama to be had, and I love a good drama. What irks you so, little mouse?"

"I said, leave us." Philippe's voice was quiet but firm.

Lorraine rolled his eyes, offering an exaggerated sigh. Reluctantly he pushed away from the balustrade, brushed past me, and ambled into the building.

Philippe touched my arm. "What has happened? Why are you not with your guests?"

I fingered the mask in my hands. "The Queen summoned me."

"Ah. No doubt to warn you away from any designs you might have on her brats' right to the throne."

"You, too?" My fists clenched. A pulse throbbed in my neck. "How could you think I —"

"Don't be naïve. No one is free of ambition. Especially those of us with Bourbon blood coursing through our veins. You may not recognize it in yourself, but it's there."

"Even if I wanted to, the law is clear. I have no claim to the throne."

"The law only protects those who survive. And if you wish to survive, it's time to start thinking like a Bourbon."

I was speechless. He'd never spoken to me like this before.

He took my hands in his own warm ones. "Sylvienne, I don't mean to be cruel. The King is the arbiter of your fate, just as he is mine."

His words brought to mind the portrait of the German princess Philippe was slated to marry and whom I had mocked. I regretted my callous reaction now as he continued.

"You are stepping into a life for which you are ill prepared. You are kind and caring. You believe the best in people. It's clear you have not yet learned to see through their masks, to judge what is truly in their hearts. I fear you are creating a storm with this marriage."

Hairs rose on the back of my neck. *A storm.* I'd heard those words before. Somewhere.

Philippe looked into my eyes the way I remembered Papa doing — the man I used to believe was my father. "I wish you would never have to change from the wonderful, innocent child you are today. But if you are to survive in this world and not be ravaged by it, you will need to accept that courtiers want only to advance their lot in life, and they will use anyone and any means to do so."

I closed my eyes against his words. I did not want to hear them, to admit to their truth. He lifted my chin forcing me to look at him.

"You can keep your kind heart. Your soul need not desert you. But you must develop a shield around both. And a cunning eye for perfidy and malevolence. Be continually wary. Sylvienne, you are smarter and more determined than anyone I know. If you pay attention, you will learn." He touched my cheek. "The Queen is only protecting her own, as you will someday protect *your* own. Now put your mask back on and let us go and fool those people at the ball into believing you are embracing your destiny with aplomb and elation."

Tucking my arm into his, we walked back into the ballroom.

At the stroke of midnight, the orchestra stopped playing, and a masked musician clad in military garb performed a drum roll. King Louis stepped to the middle of the room. The dancers cleared a circle around him. The drummer's rat-a-tat quieted to a faint but steady beat.

"Mesdames et Messieurs, the time is upon us." The King motioned for me to join him. Then he signaled for a tall man dressed in black and wearing a black mask with small white diamond-studded lightning bolts radiating from the sides, and whom I had danced with twice, to stepped forward. I held my breath.

The drumming grew louder, then receded again. King Louis raised his hands. "Reveal yourselves!"

As the drummer hit a single loud beat, the Duc and I slipped off our masks. A cry of satisfaction went up from the crowd as he smiled then bowed to me, and I curtsied in return. I examined the familiar handsome face of my betrothed with his square jaw, his dark eyes. But there was no thrill in seeing him. No butterflies in my stomach. He wasn't Etienne. Could I go through with this? Did I have a choice? Short of fleeing from the country or taking my own life, I had no options other than to do the bidding of my father, the King.

King Louis removed his own mask with flourish, followed by the Queen, then Athénaïs, and then all the courtiers. Excited chatter ensued as people recognized one another or confirmed their suspicions.

The Duc held out his hand to me, but said to the King, "With your permission, Sire."

King Louis nodded. The Duc walked me to the head of a quickly forming column to dance the *pavane.*

"You are quite lovely tonight, Mademoiselle," he said.

"Merci, Monsieur le Duc," I responded, but I felt no pleasure in hearing his compliment.

When the dance was over, he placed my hand on his arm and walked me over to a group of courtiers who were new to me. "Mesdames, Messieurs, my betrothed, Mademoiselle d'Aubert de Bourbon." He pronounced *Bourbon* with extra emphasis.

The courtiers curtsied and bowed. I forced myself to smile. Just then a boy, balancing a tray full of empty glasses as he wobbled by, inadvertently bumped my elbow, causing my champagne to spill a bit.

"*Pardonnez-moi,* Mademoiselle!" The boy struggled to right the tray without losing its contents. "I am so sorry." He glanced up at the Duc with frightened eyes.

"It is of no concern," I whispered.

But the Duc turned on him. "Boy! What are you doing?" He let go my arm, grabbed the boy by the ear and dragged him, the boy still desperate not to topple his tray onto the floor, toward the side of the room where he gave him a good tongue lashing. I followed, miserable and embarrassed.

"Please," I said to the Duc. "He meant no harm."

The Duc offered a forced smile. "My dearest, it is my job to discipline unruly staff. I see la Grande Mademoiselle. Go chat with her about the wedding dress you've commissioned." When I did not walk away, he said, voice low, stern, "Mademoiselle, if you please."

The boy's tray wobbled wildly in his hands now, and I decided it was better to let my husband-to-be finish with him so the boy could go, than to stand my ground and make matters worse. I stalked away. Is this how it was to be? My husband would "discipline" the staff, expecting me to chat with guests about fashion?

I set my empty glass on the tray of yet another servant and sought the King's cousin. After I had done making polite chitchat with the haughty la Grande, I helped myself to more wine and made the rounds of the room engaging in conversation, avoiding the company of my betrothed. Better to let the situation cool, I decided, as I was feeling exceedingly hotheaded.

When the ball ended, sometime in the predawn hours, King Louis beckoned me to join him and Athénaïs—Queen Marie-Thérèse having long since gone to bed—in walking the Duc out to his carriage.

"It was a splendid evening Your Majesty, Madame de Montespan," the Duc said. "Please accept my gratitude for your kindness and generosity toward myself and my lovely betrothed." He reached over and bussed me on the cheek.

"I am delighted you found the evening enjoyable," King Louis said.

"And what about you, dear?" the Duc asked, turning to me. "Did you enjoy the evening?"

"I always enjoy the King's entertainments," I said, stepping away from his touch. "The unmasking tonight was especially notable."

"Then it was a success," King Louis said, beaming.

The Duc climbed into his carriage. A footman shut the door smartly, and the coach took off with a lurch. Watching it go, I gave a sigh of relief. I looked forward to kicking off my horrid-fitting shoes.

CHAPTER FORTY-TWO

I had not seen Etienne since the night King Louis announced my betrothal to the Duc de Narbonne. I was desperate to find a way to speak with him, to let him know this circumstance was not of my making, that I'd had no say in it, that I would give anything to turn back those jeweled clocks in the salons of Versailles and return us to the days before the King's visit with Maman in Amiens. But I was given no opportunity. My ever-present guard, silent but foreboding, made sure of that.

Several days after the masked ball, upon returning from a long, lonely ride on Phoebe, my royal guard riding a dozen or so paces behind me, I noticed a coach pull into the courtyard in front of the palace. A familiar figure climbed out. Claude d'Aubert. My stomach tightened.

He hailed me. "Sylvienne! Ma belle nièce."

Bringing Phoebe to a stop, I looked down at him. "Oncle, what are you doing here?" It was difficult to let go the familiar title, even knowing now he was not my blood relative.

"I have a meeting with the King."

"For what purpose?" I slid off Phoebe and handed her reins to a stableman.

He cleared his throat. "We have business to discuss. Regarding your impending nuptials."

Tugging off my riding gloves, I glared at him. "What business could *you* have regarding my marriage? You must have heard, I am not your actual niece."

He took my arm and walked me toward the palace and away from a nearby group of courtiers, the guard following at a discreet but ready distance.

"Yes," he said in a low voice. "But you must appreciate that my brother took you and your mother in under his roof and fed and clothed you." A footman opened the door, and we stepped inside. "You are here because of my brother's devotion and care, and by the grace of the pension he left to your mother. The Crown owes compensation to our — my — family."

I stopped and faced him. "How dare you! Papa sheltered me out of love."

He grabbed my arm again. "My dear, your *papa* is the King of France." His face was inches from mine, his voice a snarl. His fingers dug painfully into my flesh. "And I will have the settlement due as sole heir to my brother's estate." He noted the guard stepping toward us and backed off. "You will not impede me."

"Mademoiselle?" the guard asked. "Are you in need of assistance?"

Claude turned and hastened off to the royal offices.

Stunned, I watched him go. "No," I said after a moment. "I'm fine." I took a deep breath and strode off with a new determination. Claude might think he had a case to make to the King, but I had a powerful intercessor. Within minutes I pushed into Athénaïs's private study.

She looked up from her writing table. "Sylvienne, what is it?"

"My uncle...Claude...that man...he is back. He is meeting with the King."

"Whatever for?" She set her quill down.

"He says he wants money for my previous upkeep."

She laughed. "Well, that won't happen. Louis will send him away again."

"Are you sure?" I unclenched my fists.

She considered for a moment then signaled to her maid. "Martine, my shoes." Slipping into them, she said to me, "You stay here."

Waiting for her return, I paced the apartment, the nightingale in its gilded cage near the window annoying me with its song.

When she came back Athénaïs went directly to the birdcage. "That man won't bother the King or you anymore."

"His Majesty sent him away again?" I fought to constrain my voice.

"Better." She opened the door to the cage and stroked the bird who went suddenly silent. "He sent him to the Bastille."

"Oh." The Bastille. I thought of Judith and the children. What would happen to them if he never returned?

Athénaïs set a bowl of seeds on the floor of the cage. "I reminded Louis that the penalty for extorting the Crown was beheading. His Majesty chose to be charitable, considering d'Aubert is the brother of your late stepfather, to whom His Majesty is eternally grateful." She closed the birdcage door.

Immediately, the bird began to sing again.

I was beholden to Athénaïs in more ways than I could count. This last favor, dispatching Claude for the second time, put me forever in her debt. But at what cost? I vowed to make sure Judith and her children would never be destitute. However, right now, I had one more request for which I dared to beseech my mentor's largess.

The next day, after Mass and King Louis's noontime visit, I found my opportunity. Athénaïs and I strolled alone through the orangerie. Except, of course, we were not totally alone. My guard strolled a dozen paces behind. The scent of pomegranate, lemon, and orange buds drifted in the breeze.

"Louis has been in an extraordinarily good mood since the announcement of your wedding. Have you heard from the Duc?"

"Not since the ball."

She nodded sympathetically. "Men are in the habit of making themselves busy at the most inopportune moments." She shooed away an inquisitive bee.

"Athénaïs, I am in need of another favor." I hesitated. "I need a few moments without…" I inclined my head toward the guard.

She glanced at me, eyebrows raised. "You aren't, perhaps, desiring a new pair of shoes, are you?"

I bit my lip.

She stopped walking and studied me for a moment. "It does no good to torture your heart, you know."

"I cannot leave him wondering about my intentions, my feelings." I looked into her eyes. "You know better than most people that love is complicated, especially when it cannot be requited."

"My love for Louis is more than requited."

"Is it? You can never marry him. Just as I will never marry..."

"The shoemaker." She nodded, drew in a breath, then stepped toward the guard who was now only a half dozen paces away. She spoke quietly to him. He eyed me in alarm but nodded, falling in step behind her.

Before turning back to the palace, she said to me, "Do not abuse this gift I give you."

Hovering in the doorway of the workshop, I breathed in the scent of leather and shoeblack. Laughter emanated from one corner where three young men in leather aprons worked at a wide bench. Others stood at various workstations around the long, low-beamed room. One of the men cleared his throat. The room fell silent, all heads turning to look at me. Losing my nerve, I stepped back. Only to bump into Etienne.

"Are you looking for me?" He grabbed me by the elbow to keep me from toppling.

"No. Yes. I...but I'm sure you are busy."

"It's hot in the shop," he said, his face impossible to read. "Let's walk."

He directed me away from the prying eyes of the artisans and other palace workers and down a stone path. In a deserted part of the garden, we stopped near a small pool. A wretched silence filled the space between us.

"I suppose you expect me to congratulate you," he said after a long moment.

I said nothing, my heart aching beyond words.

He shuffled his feet. "I think I always knew I could never marry you." His usually vibrant blue eyes betrayed his hurt. "Even back in Amiens. There was something about you, as if you were meant for a life grander than mine."

"Etienne, I am so sorry. I didn't mean for any of this to happen." Grasping his sleeve, I said, "I'll decline the marriage." I was earnest. In that moment I meant it.

He grasped my arms and looked down into my eyes. "I just want to know that you loved me once." His eyes beseeched mine.

"I did. I do."

He drew me to him and kissed me passionately, longingly. I came away gasping for air, tears rolling down my cheeks.

"Run away with me," he whispered.

"I want to. You know I want to."

"But I am no longer good enough for you." Hurt deepened his voice.

"You are better than any man I know. But I am..." I loathed to say it. Still, it was the truth. "I am the daughter of the King."

He shook his head and scoffed. "One of his many..." He let the word hang.

I sucked in a breath, glaring at him, daring him to say the word — *bâtardes*.

"Let's just say you lack the legitimacy of the Dauphin."

I reached out to slap his face, but he caught my wrist in mid-air.

"Don't fancy yourself anything other than one of his baubles, Sylvienne. Even had you been of legitimate birth." He let go of my wrist and stalked away.

"Where are you going? How dare you walk away from me!"

He stopped and turned. "You forget, Mademoiselle. I have shoes to make for your wedding."

My anger mixing with despair, I seethed as I watched him stride past the guard who had returned to ensure my safety.

CHAPTER FORTY-THREE

The second Wednesday in April, René Lorgeleux, Duc de Narbonne and I signed our marriage contract in the King's chambers, with Philippe and Athénaïs as witnesses. King Louis provided a dowry of seven hundred thousand livres and another four hundred thousand livres worth of jewelry, a sum that stunned me in its extravagance.

Further, he pledged he would legitimize me as his daughter no later than my twentieth birthday. Of course, I yearned to be legitimate. But now I wondered what the cost of that promise would be.

The Duc, for his part, promised to provide the Crown with no less than five hundred soldiers recruited from within his duchy, along with a hundred and fifty arpents of huntable forest land near Versailles that belonged to the Lorgeleux family. After signing the marriage contract, the Duc and I renewed our oaths of fealty to His Majesty, King Louis XIV of France. What was Etienne doing at this moment? I pinched my wrist to keep the errant question at bay, for it insisted on manifesting itself at the most inopportune times. There was no use in pining over what I could not have. Or whom. So I told myself.

The wedding ceremony took place in the recently constructed Royal Chapel located in the Queen's wing of the palace. With its vaulted ceiling and altar trimmed in gold, above which was mounted the immense pipe organ, this chapel made Saint-Michel, the church Maman and I had attended, seem miniscule.

I had written to Maman, even sent the letter by express courier, begging her to come to my wedding. She wrote back that it broke her heart to have to decline. She counseled me to be ever faithful to my husband, to be a good steward of his home, and reminded me that even as a duchess, I must remember that in the eyes of God, I was no better than any of His other servants. After she had signed her name, she wrote an addendum saying she understood I might believe my heart belonged to someone else, but that sometimes fate has another plan for us. And to open my heart to the possibility that I can learn to love anew.

I put her letter under my pillow that night. I didn't want to love anew. But if Maman could do it after her heart was broken regarding Louis — I knew how much she had come to love Papa — perhaps, at the very least, I could learn to be a good wife. Because it appeared that was my fate.

Now I stood nervously in front of the altar in my wedding gown of blue and ivory Egyptian silk, its bodice so stiffened by sapphires, diamonds, and pearls I was barely able to breathe. A matching ermine-edged train trailed out behind me.

René — once we were married, he invited me to address him by his given name — looked more handsome than ever in his simple black velvet waistcoat and breeches, the ivory trim accentuating his height, his slender waist, his broad shoulders.

Standing before the King and Queen, Athénaïs, Philippe, la Grande Mademoiselle, the Duc's three brothers and their wives, and two hundred favored courtiers, we recited our vows. Then René placed the blessed ring on my left thumb and repeated after the bishop, "*In nomine Patris...*" He moved it to my index finger. "*Et fili...*" To my middle finger. "*Et Spiritus Sancti.*" We ended the prayer together. "*Amen.*" Lastly, slipping the ring onto my fourth finger, he said, "*Devant Dieu et mon Roi, je t'épouse.*"

And with those words my life was changed forever. Like a character in a Madame de La Fayette novel, I had walked into the chapel une bâtarde from Amiens in love with the son of a shoemaker, and now I took communion as the newly married Duchesse de Narbonne.

The royal couple honored us with a wedding banquet followed by a ball. Afterward, King Louis invited my new husband and I out to the moonlit garden. There awaited a gilded two-wheeled chariot decorated with silver banderoles and ivory plumes and harnessed to a single white steed. René handed me up into the chariot, then climbed in next to me and took up the reins. He guided the horse along the grand canal where violinists stood at every juncture filling the night with romantic melodies. Courtiers and palace staff filled the avenues, applauding and cheering as we rode by. We rounded the bottom of the canal then drove back up along the other side before veering off toward the front courtyard of the palace.

René took my hand and suddenly I was nervous about the impending first night of our marriage. As the chariot rolled over paving stones, the warmth of his body helped stave off the coolness of the night air. What kind of a lover would he be? Unbidden, my thoughts strayed to that time in the forest with Etienne, the thrill of his touch, the warmth of his lips. But we had never done more than kiss. I thought of Athénaïs with King Louis, the sounds of their pleasure evident even through a closed door, and the times I had inched the door open to spy on them, unclothed and entangled in passionate embraces. I began to tremble.

"Are you cold?" René asked. He put an arm around me. At his touch, I worried even more. Would he find me a clumsy lover? Would I be able to please him?

Two footmen waited to escort us to our quarters. The King had assigned a spacious apartment for our use during our residence at Versailles. During the banquet, Lisette had supervised the packing of my personal possessions and my growing wardrobe and moving it from Athénaïs's apartment to my new quarters.

A handsome man dressed in black met us at our apartment door.

"My dear, this is Ignacio, my valet," René said.

"Bonsoir, Madame la Duchesse." Ignacio bowed.

When we approached the bedchamber, my legs began to shake. What should I do? What was I expected to do? My breath caught when

I glimpsed the peignoir Lisette had set out for me on the bed, a gift from Athénaïs, white silk and chiffon. A fire had been lit in the fireplace.

"I will leave you to prepare." René bowed and stepped back.

Lisette, waiting on the other side of the door, smiled at me. She closed it gently. I wrung my hands. "What am I to do?"

"First you must change into your nightgown. Then you should lie on the bed. He'll be back shortly and will instruct you, I'm sure."

While she unfastened the ties and clasps to loosen my bodice and stays, I doubted I would have needed "instruction" from Etienne. Chastising myself for even thinking it, I stepped out of my skirts, then sat so she could untie my garters and slip off my stockings. Standing naked in front of her, I found myself trembling again. She held the peignoir as I slipped my arms through. The diaphanous fabric clung to my body exposing my shoulders with only three silk bows to close it over my breasts and midriff. As she let my hair down, I wanted to ask her to take it off, find one of my own nightgowns for me to sleep in, but it was too late. The door opened. René entered, and Lisette slipped out.

A heat rose in my cheeks and then between my legs as I anticipated his touch, his fingers on my breasts, his lips caressing mine, the way Etienne's had always done.

His eyes roamed my body, his fingers tapped his leg.

"Is something wrong?" I asked. Were my breasts ungainly? My hair unruly?

He shook his head as if waking from a dream. "You look quite…beautiful." He stared a moment longer, then reached out and untied the top bow of my nightgown. I trembled. He kissed my neck, then released the second bow and the third. The nightgown slid off my shoulders and onto the floor. He ran his fingers down my breasts. I shivered.

He kissed me on the lips then lifted me and laid me on the bed, my head atop the silk pillow. He removed his doublet and his breaches. leaving on his fine cambric shirt. He blew out all but the candle on the night table. A moment later the bed squeaked, and then he was on top of me, his body warm, his muscles taut. His breath, still spiced with wine and brandy, was hot on my face as he kissed me, first on the lips, then my neck, and down to my breasts. I wanted to enjoy it. To be a good wife and pleasing to him, but there was an urgency to his caresses that I didn't understand. He nibbled on my nipple, then bit it. I yelped. A tone to his chuckle set me on edge.

He started to kiss me down my belly, toward my maidenhead. In a panic, I pushed his head away.

"Is that how it's to be then?" He pushed my legs apart and thrust himself into me. I gasped in shock. The pain was brief, but the discomfort continued as he grunted, thrusting, three times, five. I held my breath, willing this moment to be over.

"Stop, please. You're hurting me." I pushed against his shoulders.

But he went on. And on. Until at last, with a groan he gave one last thrust. I could feel his wetness seeping out of me as he lay on top of me, crushing the air out of my chest. Then he rolled off and onto his back. No words passed between us. Moments later the sound of his snoring rasped against my ear.

CHAPTER FORTY-FOUR

Lying in my marriage bed next to my new husband, I stared into the darkness. I could feel his essence oozing out of me and down my leg. My thighs hurt. I squeezed my eyes shut to keep the tears from falling onto my pillow.

When I was confident he was sound asleep and not likely to awaken, I crept out of bed and over to the washbasin lit by a glint of moonlight coming through the window. I found a bit of cloth and washed my private area. The opening to my womanhood stung as I wiped the mess from it. Then I crawled back into bed and curled up with my back to the Duc de Narbonne.

In the morning, after Mass with the King and Queen, René and I boarded our carriage for the trip to Paris where he owned a townhouse. King Louis and Athénaïs came out to bid us au revoir. Philippe had departed already, leaving even before the church service. A disappointment for me. I knew he much preferred the Palais-Royal on rue Saint-Honoré in Paris, where he had lived with Princess Henriette and where his favorites were said to be frequent visitors. I hoped we would see one another once René and I were settled in our residence in the Marais district, not far from Prince Philippe's palace.

As we left Versailles, a tangle of thoughts crowded my mind. I looked forward to establishing my own home. But could I manage a large household full of servants? One side of me felt relief at leaving court, leaving the gossip, the pressure, the competition for the King's favor. The other side of me hated leaving Versailles, the people I knew, the parties, Etienne. Would I ever see him again? The hurt in his eyes when he learned I was to marry someone else still haunted me. I—

"Did you hear me?" René's voice cut into my musings.

"I'm sorry. Did you say something?"

"I asked about your maid."

"Lisette?" She and the valet Ignacio were riding in the covered wagon along with our trunks.

"Is that her name? I have no objection to you keeping her for your personal care, but is she discreet? I will not abide a gossipmonger in my house."

"Yes. She is exceptionally discreet." She had proven that many times over.

"Very well then." He returned to the papers he'd been studying.

"And your man, Ignacio?"

"What about him?" His focus was still on the papers.

"Is he equally discreet?"

René gave me an odd look, brows furrowed. "Why would you ask such a question?"

Because you did. I shrugged. "The rain is about to begin." I peered out the window at the heavy sky. Drops pattered on the carriage roof. The farm fields began to blur. "I don't know Narbonne," I said after a while. "Is it far?"

His eyes were on the pages again. "It's in the south of France. Not far from the sea."

"It must be lovely. Will we go there often?"

He shook his head. "I'm required to go once a year to collect the taxes, but the trip is ungodly. I wouldn't go at all if I didn't have to. The locals are immensely dreary."

"Perhaps not so much dreary as they have different interests than you do." I smiled to show I meant nothing more than to put a positive perspective on the situation.

René gave me a skeptical glance then grunted. He turned back to his paperwork. Little more was said the rest of the trip.

René, a dozen years older than I, was worldly, but also distant. Why had he married me? Most likely to get closer to my father, King Louis. I squirmed on the goose-down cushion René had thought to outfit the carriage with and for which I was grateful; one small comfort on an otherwise immensely uncomfortable journey. It was several hours before the first buildings on the outskirts of Paris came into view.

As we traveled through the city, I remembered why I liked Versailles so much despite all the fervor of construction there. The odors from the Parisian streets and the river assailed my nose. I dug in my travel bag for my orange pomander. Even René held a finger under his nose for a while but soon seemed able to ignore the fetid air.

Our carriage lurched and careened, dodging people dashing across the road. Draymen cursed at our driver when we edged too near their carts. Barking dogs chased our wheels. At last we came to the Marais district, a quieter part of the city. I recognized Mademoiselle de Scudéry's Italianate townhouse when we drove past it.

We drew up in front of an elegant three-story townhouse with a wide stairway leading to the front door. Mullioned windows on both the ground floor and the floor above had wrought iron balustrades.

A footman trotted down the steps to open the carriage door for us. Inside the house, dozens of domestic servants from scullery maids to the majordomo lined up to form a corridor as we entered. Partway up the grand staircase the Duc stopped, and we stood before the staff.

"Madame Lorgeleux, la nouvelle Duchesse de Narbonne," he said, introducing me to his household staff.

They applauded, causing heat to rise to my cheeks. Never had I been so aware of my inexperience. I spotted Lisette standing off to one side. She gave me a smile of encouragement. I took a deep, calming breath.

"Merci," I said. "I am delighted to be in my new home."

René smiled his approval then took my hand, and we climbed the long stairway to the bedchamber. When he threw the doors open, my eyes lit up. The room, decorated with a rose Persian carpet and rose-colored bedding, was even larger than my sleeping chamber at Versailles had been. I loved it immediately.

"This will be your room. Mine is down the hall."

Separate bedchambers. Relieved that he would not be in my bed all night every night, I thanked him for the beautiful accommodations.

After René excused himself, Lisette helped me out of my traveling clothes and into a dress appropriate for a late afternoon luncheon. Then she set herself the task of unpacking my trunks while I went to meet my husband in the dining room. Approaching the stairway, I wondered how I would find him in a house this large. I needn't have worried. A maid even younger than Lisette awaited me at the top of the steps.

"I will show you to the dining room, Madame," she said with a curtsy. *Madame.* Would I ever get used to being called that? I was now on a social par with Maman and Athénaïs.

"What is your name?" I asked the girl.

Surprised, as if no one had ever asked her such a thing, she curtsied again. "Fleurance, Madame."

Fleurance led me down the long, curved staircase, through a wide hallway, and into an elegant room with amber walls and windows dressed with floral drapes and valences. Dominating the center of the room was a double-pedestaled walnut dining table that sat ten on velvet-padded chairs the color of claret.

René rose from where he sat at the head of the table. He'd been reading a business gazette. A footman seated me opposite my husband, then took the papers René held out. Another footman entered from the opposite door with a tureen of soup and served us our first course. Two tall brass candlesticks were spaced along the center of the table and between them a shallow bowl of roses floating in water.

"Are you tired?" René asked. "Perhaps I should have delayed our luncheon so you could rest?"

"No. I'm fine."

"I have arranged for Ignacio to give you a tour of the house when we have finished eating."

"You won't do it yourself?"

"I'm afraid I have to go out. I have business to attend to." He smiled apologetically.

"I see. What kind of business, may I ask? As your wife, are there affairs I should know about?"

His hand stopped in mid-air, soup threatening to spill from his spoon. He smiled. "Nothing you need to be concerned with. Financial affairs. Legal affairs. That sort of thing." He brought the spoon to his mouth and downed the broth.

The footman brought in sliced meats, cheeses, and breads, a simpler fare than the elegant meals served at court. It reminded me of what Tatie would prepare for Maman's table. A pang of homesickness swept over me, and I reached for the wine glass to hide my longing.

"Managing a household of this size can be quite daunting," René said. "But you needn't worry. You'll learn as you go. For now, all you need do is approve the lunch and dinner menus each day." He paused to wipe his chin with a linen napkin. "Is there anyone in particular you wish to invite as our first dinner guest?"

"I hadn't thought about guests. I would love to invite someone. Perhaps Monsieur?"

"Monsieur?" He seemed taken aback at first but recovered quickly. "Is he in Paris at the moment?"

"I understand he is in residence at the Palais-Royal." Then I remembered what Philippe had told me about René's love for Henriette. Perhaps I should suggest someone else.

"I think Monsieur would be an excellent first guest." He set his napkin on the table. "Shall we make it a dinner party? We'll keep it small. Eight or ten at the most."

He held up a hand for the footman to clear our dishes. "If you would write out the invitations, I will see they are delivered. Is a fortnight from today too soon?"

"Two weeks should be perfect." How did one go about planning a dinner party?

"Well then." He stood. "I'll leave you to it." He dipped his head in a polite bow before leaving. Our first meal together in our new home was over.

I set my napkin next to my plate, stood, then hesitated a moment, at a loss as to where to go, what to do. Fortunately, Ignacio appeared at my side.

"Would you care to inspect the residence, Madame la Duchesse?"

"S'il vous plaît. I would like that."

He led the way from the dining room to the main salon, a large room styled in shades of blue and gold, and introduced me to past members of the Lorgeleux family whose portraits stared down from the walls. From there we visited several smaller, more intimate sitting rooms with pastoral paintings. A great room, regal with chandeliers, was large enough to hold a moderate-sized ball. The solarium, filled with plants and lit by southern exposure windows, also served as the breakfast room Ignacio said.

The room that was to become my favorite was René's library. Once I recovered from the shock of the painting hanging above the fireplace — a semi-nude Aphrodite lounging on a rock in a tide pool, a gossamer swath of silk drenched in seawater clinging to her — I delighted in the floor-to-ceiling bookshelves that graced the walls. I was in heaven, imagining myself spending hours here, indulging my passion for reading.

Ignacio waited patiently near the door as I perused René's collection, running my hands over spines of dog-eared works of Descartes, Racine, and Cyrano de Bergerac. I discovered books of poetry by Paul Scarron whose wife was now governess to Athénaïs's baby. And the novels of Mademoiselle de Scudéry and Madame de La Fayette. On the opposite side of the room were books by mathematicians and natural philosophers from all over Europe: Francis Bacon, Galileo Galilei, Johannes Kepler. And some I had never heard of. Blaise Pascal? Christiaan Huygens? My husband did not shy away from controversy in his choice of reading, Perhaps, one day with his patronage, I could host a salon of my own.

On the top shelf, I found his copy of *Letters of a Portuguese Nun*, that scandalous book we discussed at my first salon, hosted by Mademoiselle de Scudéry. I had been so tongue-tied that day. I smiled at the memory. Yet, something niggled at the back of my mind, something about René. What had he asked that afternoon at the salon? He had posed a suggestive question about lovers. *Once having known each other in a carnal manner, can they go back to having an intellectual friendship?* I hoped that didn't mean he expected a wife to lack intellectual curiosity.

Ignacio's polite cough reminded me we had more rooms to inspect.

When the tour of the house was completed, I asked Ignacio where I could purchase stationery to write dinner invitations. I had already decided to invite Mademoiselle de Scudéry and Madame de La Fayette. And perhaps Madame de Sévigné, though I worried that her constant tears over her daughter's move to Provence would sour conversations at the table.

"I will entreat his Lordship's permission to put in an order for you from the *papetier*," Ignacio replied.

"I must prepare the invitations. To do that, I need stationery."

"Of course, Madame. However, all expenditures must be approved by his Lordship."

Any thought that marriage and becoming a duchesse would provide me with some sense of self-governance crumbled. René was now the master of my finances and my life. There was no point in taking umbrage with Ignacio. Once he took his leave, I wandered back to the library to select a book of poetry by Paul Scarron to read.

At dinner that evening, René informed me he had approved my expenditure.

"Thank you," I said curtly.

René did not so much as glance up, my irritation at needing to have my purchases approved apparently not of concern to him.

Later that night, he came to my bed. The experience was no better than our wedding night. As he took his pleasure, I closed my eyes and pictured the tomes by Galileo I looked forward to exploring. When, at the end, he rolled off me and his ragged breathing slowed to a soft snore, I thought again about his question at Mademoiselle de Scudéry's salon. The intimacy he had referred to would require getting to know someone through the joys of mutual lovemaking. I rolled onto my side with a sigh, my back to my husband. If that was the case, I need not worry about losing an intellectual relationship with the man in my bed.

When the stationery arrived a day later, I wrote out the dinner invitations. Afterward, I wrote a letter to Marie-Catherine to tell her of my wedding and to invite her to visit me and my new husband in Paris. I placed my letter on the silver tray set on the mahogany console in the foyer for the post.

Two weeks later, we hosted our first dinner party with Prince Philippe as the guest of honor. Madame de Sévigné had sent her regrets due to a malaise brought on by the change in weather. Mademoiselle de Scudéry and Madame de La Fayette both accepted as did René's guests, the Duc de La Rochefoucauld, and his wife, and Jean de Coligny-Saligny, a nobleman and military commander of renown, along with his wife.

Christophe, the majordomo, had worked with me to plan the menu: a course of cold meats and cheeses served from the sideboard, followed by a seafood bisque, braised lamb set in a sauce verte, a fricassee of early asparagus à la crème, and pastries. Peach preserves in a caramelized sauce and marzipan would do for dessert. He also helped me work out seating arrangements and choice of plateware.

That afternoon, I was a bundle of nerves making sure everything would be perfect for our guests. Finally, to calm myself, I took a book by Mademoiselle de Scudéry into the morning room and sat near the window. Before I'd completed a chapter, shouts and the pounding of hooves in the street outside drew my attention. Peering out, I was astonished to see a garrison of mounted soldiers thunder by. Ignacio was coming up the front steps, having posted a letter I'd written to Maman.

I met him at the door. "What is going on?"

He frowned. "There is word of a duel. The King's men mean to put a stop to it."

"A duel?" I shuddered. Such fights were forbidden. The penalty was hanging for those who survived, both the combatants and their seconds. "Who...?"

"Two gentlemen by the names of la Vaquet and Boivin."

I sucked in a breath. I did not care what happened to Boivin, but the charming Edmund de la Vaquet had been my favorite of my Faro partners. We had danced at numerous balls.

"I'm afraid I have no more information, Madame." He bowed and left me to my mulling.

I was anxious to ask René what, if anything, he had heard of the duel, but no opportunity presented itself. At nine that evening. our guests arrived. An awkward moment threatened to derail my careful planning when Philippe arrived in the company of the Chevalier de Lorraine whom, I learned, my husband disdained as much as I did. I had not planned on an extra seat at the table, but Christophe came to my rescue and made sure the extra place setting was accommodated without anyone knowing the difference.

The conversation around the table, thankfully, remained polite, if constrained. René had the good grace to focus the discussion on literature and the theatre, and Philippe and Lorraine had the good grace not to veer from those topics, except to gleefully mention the duel that had everyone talking. My ears perked up.

"You know Boivin, don't you?" I asked René.

"I've played cards with him on occasion. La Vaquet as well."

Lorraine took delight in telling us that the gossipmongers were saying Boivin had gone on a drunken spree after the King banished him from court.

"Whatever he did to get himself banished, I've no doubt Boivin deserved it. He's a nasty fellow," de Coligny-Saligny observed.

"He molested a serving wench la Vaquet has been prowling after," Lorraine continued. "And, when he abused her, la Vaquet beat the drunkard with his fists,"

Good for la Vaquet, I thought, favoring my Faro partner in any match between the two, but aware this had all started because Boivin dared ask the King for my hand in marriage. I glanced up briefly to see René's lips set in a grim line. He, of course, knew of Boivin's proposal.

"Boivin took exception to the beating," Lorraine said, clearly relishing the story. "The duel was set for dusk at Pré-aux-Clerc."

When I shook my head in bewilderment, René said, "A popular dueling grounds near the Seine. They are both fools as far as I'm concerned. It's too bad they didn't kill each other during the fist fight."

"What was the outcome of the duel?" I asked, forcing my voice to remain calm.

"Boivin lost," Philippe said.

At my questioning look, Lorraine said, "Shot dead."

"A deserving end." Philippe stabbed his lamb.

I set my fork down. "And la Vaquet?"

Lorraine picked up his wine glass and held it under his nose for a moment, inhaling. "It seems la Vaquet and both seconds managed to flee before the soldiers arrived. Word is he's on his way to Austria where he has relatives."

"I am so glad he got away," Madame de La Fayette said. "Though I do wish King Louis could put a stop to these awful duels."

I hid my own relief behind my glass of claret. It saddened me that I would likely never again see la Vaquet, now banished from France on pain of death. However, I felt no guilt over my elation that Boivin had been banished forever from this earth.

The next day, I was still basking in the glow of our first successful dinner party and René's compliments regarding my choice of guests and the menu, when I received a reply from Marie-Catherine saying she would be delighted to spend a week with us. I was ecstatic! She planned to arrive the first week of May. Preparing for her visit distracted me from the fact that René was gone for longer and longer periods during the day and even some evenings.

After he had not appeared in my bed for four nights in a row, I asked Lisette if she had become acquainted with any of the household staff well enough to inquire, discreetly of course, as to Monsieur le Duc's habits during the day.

"Oui, Madame," she said, brushing my hair. "But are you sure you wish this? You might not like what you will hear."

"Please, just be discreet."

"Of course."

The morning Marie-Catherine was to arrive on the public coach I directed the staff to build a cozy fire in the daffodil bedchamber, give the bedding a proper airing, and set out vases of freshly blossomed daffodils from our garden. Spring had been slow to make itself known, so even this first day of May daffodils were plentiful.

Lisette followed me as I rearranged the vases. "Madame la Duchesse," she said, twisting her fingers in front of her. "I have the report you asked me to provide."

"Report?"

"Regarding the Duc. If you'd rather wait until after your guest has come and gone…"

"No. Tell me."

She closed the bedchamber door. "It is widely reported that he enjoys gambling."

I rolled my eyes. "As do most men." And of course, I could not condemn him for that, as I had enjoyed the diversion myself.

"He has been known to imbibe a bit too much, even in mixed company."

I nodded. Something to be wary of to avoid embarrassment. When she hesitated, I asked, "Is that all?"

"No. He…the Duc…he has…um…a companion with whom he spends an exceeding amount of time."

I raised my eyebrows. "A companion?"

"A woman he enjoys visiting when he is not at the offices of his banker or his barrister."

"I see." I steeled myself. "And who is this woman?"

"Her name is Madame Hélène Cloutier."

I grimaced. "Is she a…a—"

"*Non*, Madame. Not…not that kind of woman. She is the wife of one of the Duc's bankers."

"The wife of a banker?"

"They are a very wealthy couple. She has no children and much time on her hands."

"But her husband. What must he think?"

"I am told he is so busy with his bank he does not notice who his wife spends time with." She lowered her voice to a whisper. "Or perhaps he doesn't care. The Duc is his wealthiest client."

I closed my eyes and willed my breathing to steady itself. René's question—as to whether an intellectual friendship must end when a relationship moved into the realm of the carnal—echoed in my head. "I don't suppose she enjoys reading?" I muttered.

"Madame?"

I squared my shoulders. "Merci, Lisette. You have done me a great service."

Fleurance's soft knock alerted me to Marie-Catherine's arrival.

CHAPTER FORTY-FIVE

Racing down the stairs to the foyer, I threw myself into Marie-Catherine's arms. Our tears of joy mingled as we kissed each other's cheeks. Suddenly she pulled away and swept into a deep curtsy.

I grasped her hands and pulled her back into my embrace. "No, please, Marie-Catherine."

"You are a duchesse now. And daughter of the King."

"When we are alone, I am just me. Sylvienne. The girl who put frogs in the convent's cistern and scrubbed the chapel floors with you."

She laughed. "Ma chère Sylvienne. Queen of the frogs. But only when we are alone." She squeezed my hands.

I hardly dared to believe my cherished friend was here in Paris. More than a year had passed since I had seen her last. In her traveling dress, with her hair tucked up under a modest lace-edged coif, Marie-Catherine appeared so much more mature than I remembered. Her blue eyes, so like her brother's, sparkled, but I could see the weariness in them.

"Are you tired?" I asked. "Would you like to rest?"

"No. But I would shed these dusty clothes."

Indeed, her grey wool skirt and jacket were covered in a layer of grime. I locked arms with her, and we climbed the grand staircase to the daffodil room. A houseboy had already delivered her traveling bag and small trunk.

I sat on the bed while she washed and changed into a pretty, plum-colored skirt and bodice, all the while chattering about her trip and her escorts. Madame Trouillet, the dressmaker, and her husband had invited Marie-Catherine to share a coach with them as they traveled to Paris to shop for fabric and scrutinize the latest fashions. I reveled in the familiar lilt of her voice, the way her simple stories became amusing adventures, remembering why I loved her so.

"Did you visit my mother before you left Amiens?" I asked, brushing her hair in front of the oval looking glass that adorned the toilette table.

Sadness clouded Marie-Catherine's eyes. She lifted a hand over her shoulder and touched mine. "Her health continues to worsen, Sylvienne."

A heaviness grew inside me that I had been ignoring since I had received Maman's letter saying she could not attend my wedding. "You made mention in your correspondence that the King's physician has attended her." My voice sounded hopeful.

"He is doing his best," Marie-Catherine said. "Weekly bloodletting. Leeches. Not much helps, though. She doesn't leave her bed."

"I will petition my husband to let me visit her."

Marie-Catherine stood and pulled me into a hug. "That would be good." We held each other quietly for a moment, until finally she stepped back, her face brightening. "I have written to Etienne and asked him to join us in Paris."

I masked my disquiet. "Do you think he might?"

"I hope so. I miss him terribly. Did you encounter him whilst at Versailles? I understand he is kept quite busy in the royal shoe shop."

Not able to look her in the eye, I busied myself straightening the combs on the vanity. How much to share? How much did she already know? "I saw him on occasion. His skills are much appreciated by King Louis and the Queen."

She beamed with pride. "Who would have thought my brother would become premier shoemaker to the King?"

"A monarch could have no better. Would you like a tour of the house?"

"Yes!" She clasped her hands together.

Arm in arm we started out.

"You know, I always wished you and Etienne would fall in love."

I nearly stumbled, but she didn't notice.

"Silly, I know. But I so wanted you to be my sister-in-law."

We started down the stairs.

"The two of you would have made a grand match. That is, before anyone knew you were a royal." She squeezed my arm with affection.

I was especially excited to show Marie-Catherine the library. As I expected, her eyes lit up when she saw the shelves of books and furniture designed for the sole purpose of reading.

"Oh, my!" she said gazing up at the painting of Aphrodite over the fireplace.

"She's quite beautiful, don't you think?" I tried to sound nonchalant.

"Quite...something!"

We both giggled.

"Sylvienne, you are living your dream!"

I must have looked nonplussed for she continued, "This is all you ever talked about when we were in school. Living in a big house. Marrying a nobleman. And here you are." She swept her arm around. "You have married a duc."

I managed a tight-lipped smile. Pulling her onto a brocade-covered settee next to me, I asked, "And you? What is new in your life? You said in your letters you are no longer at the convent school."

"Papa said I'd had enough of that sort of education. He needed me in the shop." She pressed her lips together as if hiding a secret, then broke into a wide grin. "Sylvienne, I am engaged to be married."

"Marie-Catherine! How wonderful! When? Who?"

"Do you remember Michel Gérôme?"

"Etienne's friend? His father is a cabinetmaker."

"Michel has been apprenticing to follow in his father's trade. Oh, Sylvienne, I love him so. And I am at long last going to be free of my father's rules and restrictions. I'll be able to set up my own household like you have. Well, not *just* like." She laughed, a bright, gay giggle.

I hugged her. "I am so happy for you. Truly I am." How could I not be? For Marie-Catherine would have everything I did not—love and freedom.

Later, at dinner, I was glad René seemed to enjoy Marie-Catherine's company. She exclaimed over every room of the house, but especially the library. "I have never seen so many books! Not even in the bookseller's shop. You must be very learned to have read them all."

René laughed. "Not all of them, at least not yet. Do you enjoy reading?"

"Yes. Very much so. Though I have little time for such pleasure anymore. When we were in school, Sylvienne used to find the most tantalizing books." She lowered her voice to a conspiratorial tone. "Sometimes, naughty ones."

I was shocked! How could she say that to my husband? I gave her a look imploring her to stop, but she ignored me. "Of course, the good sisters would never allow us to read anything but the classics, so Sylvienne would finish a forbidden book then hide it in a crack in the convent wall for me to discover. I called them her hidden treasures."

René glanced at me. Amused or perplexed? I couldn't tell. He smiled. "You are both welcome to read anything you like from my collection."

"Thank you," I said. "That is generous of you." I didn't tell my husband I had already been helping myself to his books without asking his permission.

René offered his carriage and driver for the next day so I could take Marie-Catherine on a tour of Paris. "I've arranged for you to lunch at the home of a friend on the left bank of the Seine. It's near the Hôtel de Sens, a private residence once inhabited by Marguerite de Valois, the first wife of Sylvienne's great-grandfather, King Henri IV."

The pride with which he said the name of my great-grandfather embarrassed me.

"That is very kind of you," Marie-Catherine said.

The next morning, before we left on our tour of the city, René handed me a small coin purse with enough livres to pay for lunch and buy a few trifles. I appreciated the gesture, as I had no currency of my own at this point.

"If you were to bring home some sweets, I wouldn't object," he said with a smile.

With the whole day to ourselves, Marie-Catherine and I toured the Tuileries Garden, then rode past the new astronomical observatory. Marie-Catherine was especially enthralled with the cathedral of Notre Dame, smaller than our cathedral in Amiens, but steeped in history. We stopped at a spice shop, then at Athénaïs's favorite parfumerie. We finished up at my favorite bookseller on rue Saint-Honoré. Marie-Catherine delighted in it all, which delighted me.

Our late lunch was simple but filling — roasted chicken served with glazed carrots and crusty white bread still warm from the oven.

Marie-Catherine gushed over the sights and shops of Paris. "I envy your life," she said, sopping up the last of the plum sauce with her bread. "You must be incredibly happy."

When I didn't answer she looked up. "Sylvienne?" Seeing my lip quiver, she put a hand on mine. "Dearest friend, are you not happy at all? What is wrong?"

I took a moment to compose myself. "If I say, you'll think me arrogant and ungrateful."

"Never."

I offered what I hoped was a reassuring smile. "Let's just say that life at court, and now as the wife of a duc, is not what I thought it would be."

She tried pressing me for more, but I had learned from my time at court to be guarded with my words. "We have one more stop to make," I said, forcing a bright tone to my voice. "I mustn't disappoint my husband."

The visit to the confectioner's shop lifted our moods again.

"This must be what heaven smells like!" Marie-Catherine exclaimed as we walked through the front door, the hanging chimes announcing our arrival. We tasted samples of chocolate nougats, sugar-coated anise seeds, and *calissons*, small oval-shaped treats made from crushed almonds and candied melon. I requested a handful of each to be wrapped for René.

It was late afternoon when we returned to the house, laughing and giddy from our day of sightseeing and shopping. As we entered the foyer, I spotted a letter on the console table. I picked it up and turned it over. My heart lurched. "This is for you." I held it out to Marie-Catherine. It was all I could do not to bring it to my nose and inhale his essence.

"It's from Etienne!" she said, breaking the seal and eagerly perusing the contents. "He says he's coming to Paris, and we can meet."

"How wonderful for you." I feigned neutrality. "Did he say when?"

"He has accepted an assignment to work on loan for the King's brother. He will be in Paris on Wednesday." She looked up at me, her eyes shining. "Sylvienne, that's the day before I leave for home, but I'll get to see my brother. It's been almost a year since we were last together." She reached out and touched my arm. "You'll go with me, of course."

It was an effort to speak the words. "Wednesday? I'm so sorry. I have an appointment on Wednesday. With one of our attorneys." The ease with which I lied to my best friend dismayed me.

She looked at me, bewildered, but didn't question me. "I understand. I'll hire a carriage..."

My heart was breaking, but I spoke as casually as I could. "No. You can use our carriage and driver. I insist. The Duc will insist."

She threw herself at me, hugging me in the warmest of embraces. "You have always been so kind to me. I am so sorry you can't accompany me. I know Etienne will miss seeing you."

We dressed for dinner; I had given Marie-Catherine several of the numerous dresses that hung unused in my wardrobe. All the while, I wondered how I would get through a season in Paris with Etienne so near.

Marie-Catherine and I huddled together deciding which of her new dresses she would wear to meet her brother.

"This one. Definitely. The color brings out the blue in your eyes," I said of a deep indigo dress I was confident Etienne had never seen me wear.

"Thank you!" She hugged me, then hugged me again after she had put it on and preened gayly in front of the looking glass.

I ordered the carriage to come around and waved as Marie-Catherine rode off for the afternoon. A deep lethargy enveloped me as I walked back into the house. I approved the menus for the day then wrote a short letter to Maman which I would entreat Marie-Catherine to deliver for me. I tried to read a book by the philosopher Descartes but couldn't focus long enough to make sense of it. Should I have gone with Marie-Catherine after all? No, of course not. There was no point in torturing myself or Etienne with what could never be.

In the library, returning the Descartes book, I noticed a copy of *La Gazette* on René's writing table. How odd. My husband had several times expressed disdain for such publications, decrying their tendency toward gossip and titillation. I examined the sketches and headings. One heading made my blood run cold: "A Pen Portrait of a Duchesse of Dubious Royal Sanguinity."

Sinking onto the settee, I read the piece with shock and dismay. The character in the portrait, a young duchesse who insinuates herself into the life of an overlord and his mistress, was named Charlatynne. She attempts to seduce the overlord, but he discovers her to be his very own daughter. "But is she?" the writer asks. Or is she a changeling, a mythical creature who set out purposely to disrupt the household of the overlord? In the vignette, Charlatynne bewitches not only the overlord in question, but his brother and other members of his household "with eyes as green as the forest reflecting the slant of the morning sun and hair of dark luscious curls." It described her "sitting astride her steed as if she owns the world" and "donning dresses lovely as a spring morning while wearing shoes that magically transport her through time and place."

My pulse quickened as I reread those final words. "*...wearing shoes that magically transport her...*" Why the mention of shoes? Had someone taken note of my rides with Etienne? I scanned the page to see who had dared to write such a piece, but the author was listed only as *Inconnu.* Anonymous.

I closed my eyes, willing my heart to calm itself. Could I be misinterpreting who this Charlatynne was meant to represent? No. It was clear who she was. Had I been that indiscreet? And had René read the piece? Of course he had. I dropped the pamphlet onto the writing table and ran from the library.

Marie-Catherine returned in the late afternoon, pink-cheeked and exhilarated. We sat in what had become my favorite salon, a small, intimate room with sunny south-facing windows opposite a white molded fireplace. We shared a plate of figs and sliced pears, though I had little appetite. "Did you have a good visit with your brother?"

"It was glorious. He is doing so well. Papa will be pleased." She nibbled a fig, then became unusually quiet. After a moment she said, "Sylvienne, why didn't either of you tell me of his feelings for you?"

Startled, I searched her face for a clue as to what they'd discussed. "Why? What did he say?"

"He didn't have to say anything. It is written all over his face."

"Did he...? Did he ask after me?"

"Yes." She reached out and touched the back of my hand. "Do you love him as well?"

I glanced toward the door ensuring we were alone. "Would it make a difference if I did? This is my life now."

She nodded. "I am so sorry. For both of you."

The next day, saying au revoir, Marie-Catherine and I hugged and promised we would see each other soon. René had invited Marie-Catherine to share his carriage. He would see her safely to the public inn where she would meet the Trouillets and board their coach for the two-day trip back to Amiens.

In the house, alone except for the servants who padded about doing their work quietly, I found myself more bereft than ever. At dinner that night I told René how happy I was to have had Marie-Catherine's company all week.

"I'm pleased you found her diverting. However, I do hope you don't plan to make a habit of inviting every sort of opportunist from your past into this house whenever you are bored."

"Opportunist? Marie-Catherine is not an opportunist. She is my dearest friend. And if you are worried about her economic status, her family owns a successful and profitable business."

"Nevertheless, they are of the bourgeoisie."

"Many of the *bourgeoisie...*" I said, "are wealthier than some of the nobility."

"That may be true but remember that you hail from royal blood. And now you are a duchesse. We have a certain status to maintain."

My dinner untouched, I sat, a slow burn growing inside me.

He went on as if nothing he had said was untoward. "I received a missive from His Majesty earlier today. He has expressed a wish for you to remain as lady-in-waiting to Madame de Montespan when we are in residence at court."

I brightened. "Has he?"

"Obviously that is not acceptable. I will send a message demanding he put you into the Queen's retinue instead."

Now I cringed. Life with Queen Marie-Thérèse was one of prayer, needlework, and the rare visit to area convents. Queen Marie-Thérèse did not favor many of the entertainments that were so popular at court. "But I like serving Athénaïs, I mean Madame de Montespan. We get along well together."

He snorted. "The wife of a duc should not be waiting on the King's consort. Being in the Queen's company will shelter you from the worst of the debauchery that goes on at court."

I put my fork down. "I do not need sheltering." My ire rose, but I forced my voice to stay calm. "I am quite capable of maintaining my virtue without being minded like a child, whether by the Queen or anyone else."

"Don't be impertinent. You are my wife now, and you will do as I say." He motioned for the servant to take away his plate, his food half-eaten. "There is a pen portrait that showed up in *La Gazette* this week."

I blanched. "Yes. I read it. I can't imagine who would write such a thing."

"All the more reason to be careful concerning your choice of guests, and to whose company you will allocate your time while at court." He wiped his lips with his napkin. "And now that you are my wife, you will conduct yourself in a manner that is discreet and designed not to draw undue attention to either of us." He addressed me as if I were a child needing education.

Before I could say anymore, he set his napkin down, then pushed back his chair. "I will take my brandy in the library. Have a good night, dear." He strode out of the dining room, leaving me staring at my cold plate.

That night, he came to my room. I had just blown out the candle when the door creaked open. I slipped under the bedcovers hoping he would think I was already asleep.

René set his own candle on the bedside table and pulled the covers back. He made no conversation, simply lifted my gown and climbed atop me. His breath reeked of the brandy he had enjoyed after dinner. I gritted my teeth until he was done. To my dismay, when my husband was finished, he rolled off and curled up next to me, his snoring keeping me from the refuge of sleep.

Several days later, the sun shining cheerily through the east windows, I wrapped a shawl around my shoulders and took a walk in the cool morning air, observing the massive houses along the boulevard. I missed walking in the gardens at Versailles, but I was glad to no longer be followed by the Royal Guard. The guardianship of my person had been transferred from my father to my husband. Fortunately, René did not feel the need to have me guarded all day long.

Sometime after the noon Angelus bells rang out, I sat in the smaller, sun-drenched salon mulling over menus for a half dozen dinners René was eager to give for friends of influence. Before long, I wearied of the task, my eyes roaming the pleasing brocade curtains woven with delicate blue, green, and russet floral patterns. Was it my husband who had such good taste? Or had he appointed someone to dress each of the rooms for him? I loved the way the sun played over the fabric patterns.

A knock at the door brought me up short. Had René caught me daydreaming? No, he was out for the afternoon, likely with the wife of his favorite banker. Fleurance stood in the doorway.

"Yes, what is it?"

"Madame la Duchesse, there is a man at the servants' entrance, who wishes to deliver a parcel to you."

It must be the boy from the stationery shop again. "Tell him to leave it."

"I'm sorry, Madame. He insists on surrendering it personally."

"Why are these hirelings so vexatious?" Immediately I chastised myself for harboring such a haughty notion. "Please, ask him to wait. I'll be there shortly. If he's hungry, give him something to eat."

The girl curtsied and hurried out. I shuffled the guest lists, giving them one last glance, and rechecked the menus. Finally, I ordered them by date. Stopping by René's library first to leave the dinner plans on his table, I made my way to the servants' entrance.

A man stood looking out the window at the garden, his back to the hallway. My pulse quickened when I recognized his silhouette. "Etienne?"

He swung around, hesitated, then stepped toward me, a package in his hand. "I've brought you the shoes you ordered, Madame," he said.

"But I didn't—"

He put a finger to my lips to hush me.

"Expect them so soon." I glanced back as Fleurance scurried out of view.

He held out the linen-wrapped parcel, his eyes searching mine. "I hope they meet your expectations."

Grabbing him by the arm, I pulled him into a storage room lit only by a single small window and shut the door behind us. Amongst the barrels, crates, brooms, and mops, I threw myself into his arms. The sweet saltiness of his lips, the crush of his ribs against mine were all I wanted in this world. We kissed long and ardently until we had to push away just to breathe.

After a moment, I rested my head against his chest. "I've missed you so." My voice was husky. "But you shouldn't have come."

"Marie-Catherine said you are unhappy." He lifted my chin and gazed into my eyes.

"How can I be happy without you?"

He raised an exaggerated eyebrow. "Why? Do your feet hurt?"

I burst out laughing, then clapped a hand over my mouth. "Be serious."

He picked up the parcel he had dropped when we first embraced. "A shoemaker is always serious, Madame." He tucked the parcel into my hands and said suggestively, "How do you wish to pay me?"

"You may put it on my husband's account."

He looked at me askance. "Are you sure of that?"

"Very sure. Will you come again?"

"Whenever you require a new pair of shoes."

I pulled back a corner of the linen wrap to see a bit of blue satin with a pale blue bow. "I need another pair like these, but in red."

He took my hand and kissed the back of it. "For you, anything."

I kissed him on the lips again, then edged the door open, peeking out to ensure no one was in view. "Go."

CHAPTER FORTY-SIX

Leaning with my back against the door, I cradled my new shoes. My lips still tingled from the press of Etienne's lips. I wanted to run after him, run away from this house. But I took a deep breath and dashed up to my bedchamber. I had already decided I would wear these shoes to dinner that evening. Lisette could help me choose a dress to complement them. I rushed into the room only to find her standing at the window, weeping.

"Lisette? What is the matter? Are you ill?" I went to her.

She shook her head and held out a piece of worn paper. "A letter came today, from my sister, Apolline. She has decided to accept the royal recruiter's offer of a dowry."

"A dowry? I don't understand." Then it dawned on me. "To go to New France?"

Lisette nodded. "My father does not have the money for her to marry. And Apolline refuses to consider the convent. She feels she has no other choice but to accept the King's support to find a husband."

"Can't she go into service, like you?" I sat on the bed and patted the mattress next to me.

"She wants a family. Children," she said sitting down with a grateful smile.

"But New France?" That place still gave me chills. "Your sister must be a very brave woman."

"Or foolhardy. They say there is snow on the ground eleven months of the year, and it is beset by horrible savages."

"I think those rumors are exaggerations on both accounts. My friend Perrette made the voyage to New France and found a husband right away. She says the natives are quite friendly. Most of them."

"But, Madame, I will never see her again." She sobbed anew.

I pulled her close and held her, silently cursing my father for coming up with such a scheme.

At dinner that night I mentioned the plight of Lisette's sister to René.

"I think it unwise of the King to spend so much money attempting a colony over there," he mused, slicing the pork loin on his plate. "I expect the returns on his investment will prove it a poor plan."

Was that all he thought about, the economics of the situation? "I have granted Lisette some time off to visit with her sister before she leaves."

He set down his knife. "Without first consulting me? Sylvienne, I do wish you would come to me when such decisions are to be made. Who will serve you in her stead?

"I can dress myself if need be. I did so before coming to court. And Fleurance can be spared to help with my bath and other amenities."

He lifted his wine glass. "I suppose."

The footman stepped forward with a platter of braised herbed vegetables. René helped himself to a hearty serving. I scooped a single spoonful, then waited for the young man to leave the room.

"On another matter, I wish to visit my mother in Amiens."

"I think that would be an excellent idea. Once the season is over, we'll make plans."

"You wish me to wait until the end of summer?" I set my fork down, my vegetables uneaten.

"You have responsibilities here. However, when we are free of our social obligations, I would be happy to let you go." He speared a chunk of meat and forked it into his mouth.

Watching him eat took my appetite away. How could someone so handsome be so callous? I lifted a hand to signal the footman to take away my plate. "There is one last thing."

"Yes?"

"I require an allowance for shoes."

His fork stopped in midair, the piece of pork threatening to topple. "Only for shoes?"

How stupid of me! I fought to maintain a dispassionate visage. "For an entire wardrobe, of course. Dresses, outerwear. A duchesse must not appear underdressed, especially in light of the dinners we will be hosting."

"Of course. You are right. Let me know the names of the vendors you wish to utilize, and I will set up the appropriate accounts for you."

"Merci." I set my napkin on the table and folded my hands in my lap to wait until our dinner was over.

Later that week, a formal invitation arrived by royal currier: *The Crown requests the presence of the Duc and Duchesse of Narbonne at the Royal Residence at Versailles.*

René grumbled as we sat together in his library, he going over finances while I wrote to Maman. "I was looking forward to a season in Paris. I abhor hunting, and that's all the King cares to do at Versailles."

"There will be other entertainments," I offered. "Dances. Cards. Theatrical productions."

"Hmm. Well, as soon as we can politely leave and return to Paris, we will. We'll save the dinner invitations and menus until later in the season."

A soft knock sounded on the library door. Ignacio entered with the mail tray. "A letter for Madame la Duchesse."

I took the missive and thanked him.

"What is it?" René asked, setting down one ledger and picking up another.

"An invitation from Monsieur. For lunch."

René rubbed his chin in agitation. "Inconvenient, to say the least. I'll have to reschedule an important bank meeting."

"I'm sorry, but..." I shifted in my chair. "The invitation is for me alone."

A flash of anger darkened René's eyes, but he straightened his shoulders. "Good. I won't have to re-arrange my schedule after all."

Was it the banker, I wondered, or the banker's wife with whom he had such an important meeting? I held my tongue.

I stepped out of the carriage in front of the Palais-Royal, a grand domicile on rue Saint-Honoré. Now known as the House of Orléans, it had been the personal residence of Cardinal Richelieu, Chief Minister to King Louis XIII, and then the home of Princess Henriette and her mother during their exile from England. As fate would have it, after Henriette and Philippe married, King Louis invited them to live in this palace and it quickly became the social center of Paris.

Now a widower awaiting the order from his brother to remarry, Philippe still enjoyed entertaining here. But today was to be a private luncheon, just the two of us. And for that I was grateful.

The majordomo escorted me to an exquisitely intimate sunroom where Philippe sat at a table reading *La Gazette*. He rose when I entered and bussed me on both cheeks. "Ma chérie. Come sit. Are you wearing new shoes? I recognize the handiwork."

"Do you like them?" I held out one blue satin clad foot and then the other.

"So much so that you will be interested to know I have employed my brother's own shoemaker while he is here in Paris." Philippe grinned. "In fact, he is here today."

"Etienne—I mean, Monsieur Girard—is here? In the palace?" Butterflies filled my stomach.

"I've granted him one of the apartments to use as a temporary workshop. He has been taking measurements all morning and is now creating designs for me to peruse." His eyebrows arched conspiratorially. "Perhaps you would like to stop by his workshop for a fitting after lunch?"

"I wouldn't want to disturb him," I said, though my heart wished the opposite. "He must be incredibly busy."

"Ah, but you need shoes. Lots of shoes. I am sure he won't mind. Sit. Let us eat first."

Liveried servers set out dishes of blanched artichoke hearts in a crème sauce, a pigeon tart, and candied fruit. Delicious as it looked, anticipation prevented me from tasting any of it.

When the fruit plate had been taken away, Philippe's valet appeared in the doorway of the sunroom.

"I trust Matthieu with every nuance of my life," Philippe said, a mischievous glint in his eyes. "He will take you to the shoemaker's workshop."

"Merci, mon Oncle. I am indebted to you for inviting me today." I kissed him on both cheeks.

Matthieu led me through a maze of corridors to a little-used wing of the palace. He stopped in front of an unmarked door. "Should I wait?" he asked.

"Merci, but I can find my way out."

"As you wish, Madame." He bowed before turning on his heel.

I lingered until he disappeared around the corner. Taking a deep breath, I knocked, then turned the knob. Stepping into the room, I willed my heart to quiet itself.

Etienne looked up from the large oak table where he had been drawing sketches in a notebook. Swatches of fabric, measuring implements, and shoe forms were scattered about. A puzzled expression creased his brow, then he stood, clearly elated. "Sylvienne."

My voice breathy, I said, "Monsieur suggested I stop by for a fitting." I closed the door and, reaching behind me, turned the large brass key with a soft *thunk*.

Etienne stepped toward me, embraced me, his lips finding mine. Before either of us could register what was happening, I began unbuttoning his blousy, ruffled shirt. I kissed his chest, nuzzled his neck. He tugged at the bows on the back of my bodice but growled in frustration.

"No," I moaned. "It's designed to be impossible."

He pulled me over to the velveteen divan fronting the fireplace. Kneeling, he lifted my skirts and removed my shoes, my garters, my stockings. His hands and lips caressed me in places I had never been caressed before. Athénaïs's words thrummed in my head—*If it's love you want, take a lover.* I moaned under his loving touch. When I could wait no longer, I begged him to come inside me. Never had I felt so desired, or so desirous of another.

Our bodies united, we moved in a rhythm that left me breathless. When, finally, our ardor was spent, we lay entwined, our hearts slowly calming. It seemed the firmament had shifted. I would never be as happy or fulfilled as I was in that very moment.

After a long silence, Etienne spoke, his voice husky. "You shouldn't have come."

"Do you wish I hadn't?" I brushed a damp tendril of hair from his eyes.

"No. I am happy you did." He kissed me again, slowly, tenderly.

"I must go." As much as I wanted to stay, it would be reckless to linger much longer.

He put a finger over my lips, then covered my mouth with his. I could feel his heat rising. To my elation, he entered me again, and we made love again, slowly, tenderly.

At home, I hurried up to my room to wash and change clothes. Lisette had already left to visit her sister, and I was grateful for the time alone. Sponging the area between my legs, I smiled at the delight Etienne had taken in my body, and of the unexpected ways in which I had responded to his lips, the gentle teasing of his fingers, the fullness of him inside me. I had never known such pleasure could be had in another's touch. I understood now why Athénaïs was so eager to receive the King whenever he commanded, her devotion driven by more than the promise of jewels and power.

After dressing, I wandered down to the library, thinking to settle in with a book or perhaps write some letters. To my surprise, René was there, hunched over ledgers on his writing table, a glass of brandy near empty.

"You are home early," I said, masking my disappointment.

He tossed his quill onto the table and rubbed his temples. "My meeting was cancelled."

"Postponed for a later date?"

He grunted. "We'll see. You were gone a long time."

"One cannot choose to just up and leave when lunching with the King's brother." I ran my fingers along the spines of the books on one of the shelves, hoping he couldn't see my face.

"You must have had a lot to talk about. It's already..." He pulled the timepiece I had given him as a wedding gift from his waistcoat pocket and opened the hinged silver lid. "Well past four."

"We had much to talk about, family history to share."

He stood and gathered the ledgers. "Perhaps you should spend more time learning the particulars of running this household."

"Perhaps you need to spend more time in residence to teach me."

He froze. "I have ongoing business at the bank to attend to."

"Business with Monsieur le Banquier? Or with Madame la Banquière?"

In two strides he crossed the space between us and, grabbing me by the arm, spun me around and slapped my face. "You will not speak that way again in this house or anywhere. Do you understand?" His breath was hot in my face, the reek of brandy overwhelming.

Reeling, I forced myself not to put a hand to the spot on my face that stung so badly. I looked him in the eye. "I understand perfectly."

He strode out of the room. Only then did I set my fingers against the warm, tender flesh of my cheek to feel the swelling that had already begun.

I spent the rest of the afternoon in my bedchamber, curled up on my bed, staring at nothing, clutching the pearl necklace my mother had given me. I had no memory of having opened the jewelry box in which it was kept—the jewelry box René had given me as a wedding gift—nor of retrieving the necklace. But I needed a reminder, a talisman of love. My thoughts were a desolate jumble. Etienne's caresses. René's open hand. If anything, I should have been punished for my lapse into fornication that day, however pleasurable it had been. Instead, I was struck for daring to acknowledge that my husband had a mistress.

Later, in the mirror, I could see a black-and-blue smudge forming under my right eye. I made excuses for not attending dinner that night and requested a bowl of broth be delivered to my bedchamber. When Fleurance came to help me prepare for bed, I could tell by the concern in her eyes that she noticed the bruise. To her credit, she said nothing.

CHAPTER FORTY-SEVEN

René's slap still rankled as I sat in front of the mirror the next morning. My cheek looked puffy and the bruise under my eye more evident. I dipped a cloth into the washbowl and held it to my face. It was then I noticed the small ceramic pot Fleurance must have left on my table when she opened the curtains for me that morning. In the pot was a thick ointment, not white like the powders so many women favored these days, but a creamy bisque that closely matched my skin. I lifted the pot to my nose. The soothing aroma of aloe and chamomile brought the comforting feel of home and Maman. Scooping a small amount of the ointment, I rubbed it over the bruise. The cooling sensation was reassuring, and as I peered into the mirror, it seemed the discoloration was less noticeable. I smoothed on more of the lotion until the bruise had all but disappeared.

I wondered if Fleurance had a salve to heal my bruised heart.

In the breakfast salon, René greeted me as if nothing had happened the night before. The footman set a plate of poached eggs in bearnaise sauce in front of me.

"I'll be out for most of the day," René said. "You might go through the larder with Christophe to see what supplies need to be ordered. If you have any special requests for meals, he'll need to know."

"I'll seek him out later this morning." I stared at the eggs with little appetite.

He sipped at his tea. "I have approved the list of clothing vendors you gave me." He set the delicate porcelain cup aside. "You'll want to get fitted for some new gowns before we leave for Versailles."

"I will do that."

He forked the last bit of egg into his mouth, then wiped his lips with the linen napkin. He stood. "I will see you at dinner."

Once he was gone, I pushed my plate aside. "Joseph," I said to the footman. "Can the cook brew coffee?"

"I am quite sure he can, Madame. I will ask." He removed my plate. A short while later he returned bearing a cup of the dark, heavenly scented brew I had learned to enjoy at Versailles.

I poured cream from a porcelain carafe until the coffee was milky, then added sugar. The first sip was all it took. I closed my eyes, my mood lifting.

When the cup was empty, I made my way down to the kitchen to meet with Christophe. We toured the pantries, then reviewed the menus for the next week. When we finished, I thanked him and went back to my favorite salon with Rene's copy of *Letters of a Portuguese Nun* in hand.

Ignacio found me an hour later, bearing a parcel. "A delivery for you, Madame."

He bowed and left me alone to unwrap a pair of red shoes that made me smile. I pushed off my house slippers to try them on. Tucked into the toe of one shoe was a folded note. My pulse quickened.

> *Please light a candle for me if you happen to attend Mass tomorrow. When you hear the Angelus bells, say a prayer to my patron saint for me.*

I studied the familiar handwriting, puzzled at the meaning of the message. Why did Etienne want me to light a candle? And why mention his patron saint? Then it hit me.

Saint-Étienne. The Church of Saint-Étienne. The Angelus. He wanted me to meet him at the church tomorrow at noon. I refolded the note and tucked it into my bodice right next to my wildly beating heart.

I waited until René had left the house the next day before asking Ignacio to order the carriage and driver. The air was clear but still cool, so I threw a hooded wool cloak, a deep plum color, over my shoulders. Once settled onto the leather seat, I instructed the driver to take me to the Palais-Royal. To my relief, Monsieur was in residence.

"Sylvienne! How lovely of you to stop by." Philippe bussed me on both cheeks.

"I have a favor to ask." I glanced up to see the Chevalier de Lorraine hovering on the staircase of the grand foyer. "It's private."

Philippe waved a hand over his shoulder. "Lorraine, take yourself back to the bedchamber. I'll be up shortly." When Lorraine vacillated, Philippe said, "Do as I say, or I'll boot you out on your ass."

Rolling his eyes, Lorraine stomped up the stairs and disappeared.

"Now, how can I be of service, ma chère nièce?"

"Will you lend me your carriage and a driver?"

He glanced out the foyer window to see mine still waiting in the morning sun.

"I need to send my husband's home," I said.

"Ah, yes. Of course." He rang a bell and Matthieu appeared. "Tell Madame's driver he can leave. I will see her home. Then call up Henri with the cabriolet."

Matthieu bowed and strode out the door. Moments later René's carriage rolled away and a cabriolet with a single horse pulled up in its place.

"Merci, Monsieur. How can I ever repay you?"

"Ah, ma chérie, the drama of it all is payment enough."

I stood on tiptoes and kissed him on both cheeks.

Outside, the driver handed me up into the carriage and we left the palace at a swift clip, crossing the river on the Pont Neuf. Before long we passed the famed Sorbonne University, pulling up in front of the church of Saint-Étienne du Mont. The driver helped me down and stood at attention until I reached the church entrance.

I was almost an hour early, but I went inside anyway. The lingering tang of incense, day old flowers, and burning candles brought me back to Saint-Michel's in Amiens. On the altar, the priest intoned the final prayers of the daily Mass. The swell of the organ playing a familiar recessional anthem washed over me. The priest and his acolytes marched down the aisle between double spiral staircases and the thick pillars lining the nave.

When the music stopped, the congregants stepped into the aisle, genuflected, and hurried out. An acolyte snuffed out the altar candles, spirals of smoke rising from the deadened wicks. Only one lone parishioner sat in silent prayer on a bench near the shrine encasing the remains of Sainte Geneviève, patron saint of Paris.

Something about the shrine drew me to it, flames in a stand of votive candles flickering in the hazy light from the stained-glass window high overhead. I dropped some coins into the alms box and, picking up a long wooden taper, held it to the flame of one candle then to the unlit wick of another. After dousing the taper in the small leaded box of sand, I gazed up at the statue of the saint on her pedestal above. Crossing myself, I said a quick prayer of thanks for all the blessings that had been given to me, despite the disappointment of my marriage.

Dismayed to see the hooded penitent had not yet left, I tapped my foot impatiently. He must have heard me, for he turned in my direction. Slowly he pushed back his hood. I covered my mouth to quiet my laugh of relief.

Etienne stood and came to me, taking my hands, kissing me on the forehead. "I'm glad you could come."

I resisted the impulse to throw my arms around him.

"Hungry?" he asked. "I know the perfect place for a secluded picnic. There is a market nearby. We can buy food."

"I would love that."

We hurried out into the sunshine and walked toward the avenue where Philippe's cabriolet was parked in the shade of a tree. The driver had made himself comfortable, slouching in his seat, his hat pulled over his face to shield it from passersby. A soft snoring drifted from under the hat as we walked past.

The market was busy with vendors hawking their wares and Parisians from all walks of life haggling over prices. The smells of spices, baked goods, and fresh meat offered another reminder of the life I had lived before coming to court. Keeping our hoods low over our faces, we dashed from stall to stall. Etienne purchased cheese, a baguette, and a carafe of wine.

We walked back past my driver still snoring under his hat, and around to the back of the church. Etienne led me along a maze-like path to a small grotto created in honor of the Blessed Virgin and hidden by tall hedges. Judging by the condition of the statue — her blue mantle was faded and the lips of her sad smile chipped — I suspected no one had been to visit the area in some time.

Etienne spread his cloak in the shade of a mulberry tree, and we sank upon it to enjoy our repast, the bells of the Angelus ringing out. He reached over to stroke my cheek but paused, then ran his finger under my eye. "What happened?"

"I was clumsy. I walked into an open door."

His brow furrowed. "I doubt that." He leaned in, kissing the bruised spot. "Does that make it feel better?"

"Very much so."

"Are you injured anywhere else?"

"My cheek, right here, is a bit sore."

His lips brushed my skin.

"And perhaps my lips..."

His lips met mine with an eagerness I couldn't resist. As we fell back upon his cloak, his fingers reached for the ribbons on the front of the bodice I had chosen with purpose that morning, his lips, his tongue, exploring, teasing, finding new ways to delight me. Moments later, he was inside me and we made love there in the grotto. The Blessed Virgin gazed down upon us, the expression on her lovely face one of bruised rapture.

"You went to the Palais-Royal again?" René asked that evening at dinner.

Of course he knew about my use of the carriage. "I did." I lifted my glass of Chablis and took a sip, my eyes never wavering from his.

He regarded me as if pondering which way to go with the conversation. "Well, I suppose there is an advantage to be had in currying the favor of the king's brother."

Indeed, there was, I thought.

"You may direct the staff to begin packing in the morning," he said. "We are expected at Versailles in five days time."

My heart soared as our carriage rolled up to the golden gate fronting the courtyard of the palace. June, with its clear blue skies that extended into the early evenings, was my favorite time to be there. How I had missed court life! The balls and ballets, concerts, plays, walks in the garden, dinner with the royal family, even afternoons at the gaming tables. And of course, riding in the woods.

Etienne, too, had been called back to court. He had been on loan only temporarily to Monsieur. His craftsman would make the shoes Etienne had designed for the King's brother. Our opportunities to meet would be limited, however. Even rides in the forest together might be difficult to arrange. I vowed to find a way.

At the door to the royal audience chamber, René handed his card to the Master of Ceremonies who announced, "Le Duc et la Duchesse de Narbonne."

Had it only been just over a year since my first audience with the King and Queen, walking through this same crowd of now familiar faces?

"Daughter." King Louis stood and embraced me, kissing me on both cheeks.

Queen Marie-Thérèse offered me a tepid smile. When Louis sat again, I fell into a deep curtsy before the Queen and lifted the hem of her skirt to kiss it. There was a moment of awkward silence. Finally, she put her hand on my head. "Welcome back to court, Madame la Duchesse."

When I looked up, relieved, her smile was one of triumph.

"Well done," René whispered as we took our places among the crowd in the audience chamber to watch the presentation of other new arrivals.

Later, when the ceremony concluded, my old friend Carufel appeared, offering to escort us to our assigned chambers.

"There is a definite advantage to being married to the daughter of the King," René said surveying our suite—a bedchamber, a fully furnished salon, two closets each large enough to house Lisette and Ignacio, and a receiving room. Indeed, it was a generous and spacious accommodation, far more than that granted to most of the nobility. I hid my dismay, however, at the single bedchamber with its one large bed.

René hurried out to the gaming tables, leaving me to supervise Lisette and Ignacio as they unpacked our wardrobes. A short while later, Ignacio answered a knock on the door and announced, "Madame de Montespan."

Athénaïs swooped in looking sumptuous as ever. I noted that she wore a new robe battante. We both dropped into curtsies and rose in tandem. At my questioning look, her rouged lips curved into a wry smile. "My dear, I do believe you outrank me now."

"I think I will never stop deferring to you," I said leaning into her hug. "And how is Louise-Françoise?" I had not seen Athénaïs's baby since before my wedding.

"She is a sprite. Chubby and full of mischief. We are fortunate to have Madame Scarron in charge of her."

"Perhaps we can visit her while I am here?"

"Of course. Right now, though, I want to hear about you."

I invited her into the salon. "I missed you at the audience with the King and Queen today."

"Hmm, well, mornings are a bit challenging at the moment." She grimaced, then planted a smile on her face, easing herself onto the settee. "So, tell me about married life. Are you enjoying your role as a duchesse?"

I grunted.

"That bad?"

"What can I say? In some ways, René is a commendable husband. All my needs are taken care of."

"Is it too soon to have found a lover worthy of your attention?"

My eyes widened, then I turned away, biting my lip.

"Sylvienne, look at me." Her voice held a note of alarm. "Tell me you have not kept up an assignation with that shoemaker."

I looked down at my hands but could not keep the corners of my lips from curving up.

"Oh, Sylvienne, no. No good can come of it. You must end it. There are numerous young bucks among the courtiers who would give their right hands for the opportunity to make you happy." When I remained silent, she reached out and touched the back of my hand. "Promise me you will not see him while you are at Versailles. The walls here have eyes, and everything gets reported back to Louis."

When I did not respond, she rose with a sigh of dismay. "Please, just please, do not be reckless."

René was jovial at dinner that night. He complimented Queen Marie-Thérèse on her necklace and earrings, a comment in which she took obvious delight. And he joked with the King about his losses at cards.

After we returned to our chamber, the mix of brandy and rum on his breath and his awkward attempts to fondle me told me he missed his Madame la Banquière. For three nights in a row, he tried to be amorous. Finally, on the fourth night, he staggered to bed too drunk to do anything but snore. I relished my freedom to fall asleep without being bothered.

We had been at Versailles most of a week before I caught sight of Etienne hurrying, head down, across the courtyard on his way to the palace, a leather satchel slung over one shoulder, several notebooks in hand. He didn't see me.

Several more days went by. Restless, I composed a note:

Please make yourself available for an appointment the hour before noon tomorrow to measure myself and my friend Phoebe for shoes.

I gathered up some swatches left over from the dressmaker's visit, tucked the note into the fabric, wrapped the bundle with ribbon, and handed it off to my trusted Lisette for delivery. The next morning, I hurried to the stables and requested that Phoebe be saddled. As I approached her stall, the potent tang of freshly mucked hay added to my excitement. Her soft nicker welcomed me.

"Bonjour, Phoebe." I stroked her nose, her lips seeking the apple slices I always brought along. "Shall we see whether an old friend awaits?"

We headed past the gardens toward the forest lane. Under dappled leaves, I breathed air so fresh it almost hurt after the constant fetid odors of Paris. We hadn't gone far when I spotted a horse and rider half-hidden on the side of the lane. I tugged ever so lightly on Phoebe's reins to turn her off the path and through the trees, pulling her alongside Jolie.

"There is a woodland pond not far from here," I said. "Not many know of it."

Etienne followed me through a stand of oak until we came to the pond hidden by the draping branches of an ancient weeping willow tree. I slid off Phoebe and threw myself into Etienne's arms, seeking his lips with a ferocity that took him by surprise. When, finally, he pulled back, he took my chin in his fingers. "Any more encounters with doors?"

I shook my head. "My clumsiness was short-lived. I think it shall not happen again."

He kissed me under one eye. "If it does, you let me know. I want you never to feel a bruise anywhere on your precious body again."

He spread his cloak among the jonquils scattered under the willow at the edge of the pond — an invitation I readily accepted.

CHAPTER FORTY-EIGHT

"Where were you? I've been looking for you everywhere." René looked up from buttoning his waistcoat.

I tugged off my riding gloves. "Taking in the air."

"We have been invited to a salon hosted by Madame de La Fayette." He was clearly irritated with me. "It's a last-minute affair and begins in less than an hour."

"Wonderful! It won't take me long to dress."

In my chemise, I washed, careful to leave no evidence of my tryst with Etienne. Lisette, a sly smile playing upon her lips, combed bits of leaves and grass out of my hair, then helped me step into an elegant dove grey skirt, before lacing the contrasting lavender and black bodice. A tingling warmth overcame me as I slid my feet into one of the many pairs of shoes Etienne had made for me. René called out impatiently, and I hurried to catch up with him.

We were among the last to arrive at Madame de La Fayette's small apartment, but Athénaïs had saved a seat for me. René was content to stand behind us. La Grande Mademoiselle and Madame de Sévigné were among the dozen or so in attendance, as was Philippe. I suppressed a groan when the Chevalier de Lorraine burst in at the last minute, taking his place behind the Prince's chair.

Madame de La Fayette—unlike Mademoiselle de Scudéry who conducted her salons from her nest of divan pillows—sat on an upholstered wingback chair with her feet crossed demurely in front of her. The discussion of the day centered around Molière's intent in writing the play *L'École des femmes*.

René declared *The School for Wives* to be a ridiculous conceit. "The playwright mocks a husband who fears his wife's potential for infidelity, but what do you expect, considering the bloated education women receive today?"

"René, you can't be serious!" Mademoiselle de Scudéry protested.

"I am quite serious. Gratuitous education gives women ideas beyond their station and encourages wanton lewdness."

"Then I say, society could do with more lewdness," Athénaïs countered.

As the discussion devolved into a quarrel, it was all I could do to ignore my husband's comments. I appreciated Etienne more than ever for always championing my desire to learn as much as I could.

When the salon concluded, I took a moment to exchange pleasantries with la Grande Mademoiselle. I was determined to make her an ally rather than a competitor. As we chatted, Lorraine approached with a disarming smile and asked, "Did you enjoy your ride this afternoon, Madame la Duchesse?"

A chill coursed through me. Had he seen Etienne as well? My eyes darted to René, deep in conversation with Madame de Sévigné. He appeared not to have heard.

"The fresh air was quite welcome," I said, returning Lorraine's smile.

"I would imagine that someone as well educated as yourself would find it to be..." He lifted a hand, languidly placing his finger on his lower lip. "Quite a glorious afternoon." He flashed a sly smile before strutting off.

"Ugh! That man!" La Grande rolled her eyes.

"What was that all about?" René appeared at my side and took me by the elbow to escort me toward the door.

"I haven't the least idea." I fanned myself to reduce the heat in my face.

"Stay away from him. He makes my skin crawl."

"I will not argue with you on that point."

René suggested we make an appearance at the gaming tables, and I readily agreed. The chatter and laughter made me feel at home as we entered the room. Friends greeted us. A table of men hailed René.

"Darling," he said, "I see there's an empty chair at Madame de Polignac's table. Why don't you join them?"

The men he wished to join were all high stakes players. I raised an eyebrow but knew better than to say anything in front of them. I made my way to Madame de Polignac's table.

"Madame la Duchesse!" she said. "You have perfect timing. We were looking for someone to complete our foursome."

Grateful for their welcome, I sat down to join the play and to eavesdrop on the gossip of the day.

Mademoiselle de Baude, next to me, arched her eyebrows. "Did you see? Madame de Montespan is wearing her robe battante again."

Madame de Polignac chimed in. "They say her breakfast ends up in the chamber pot on a daily basis."

"And Monsieur!" De Baude's eyes lit up. "Did you hear the King has chosen his next wife?"

"When?" I asked. "Who?"

"A princess from the Palantine," de Polignac said.

"Poor Madame." De Baude sighed. "I miss her so much."

"There shall be a new Madame soon," de Polignac said. "Whether Monsieur likes it or not. Would you care for one card or two, Madame La Duchesse?"

A new Madame. Someone to take Henriette's place. I wondered what Philippe thought about the Princess Palantine. Not that he had a choice in the matter. None of us who were in the King's orbit had free choice, as I so recently learned.

I helped myself to a glass of Bordeaux from a passing footman, noticing René had helped himself to the brandy tray more than once. Despite the delectable tidbits shared by my companions, it wasn't long before I felt a headache coming on. I excused myself. When I stopped at my husband's table, I was dismayed to see the amount of money he had managed to lose.

"Darling," I said, "Would you care to walk in the garden with me? I think some fresh air would do us both good."

He waved me off. "You go. I'll meet you later."

There was no point in arguing, so I strolled out to the garden alone where I found King Louis and Athénaïs, with their ever-present entourage of courtiers. The royal spaniels charged me, begging to have their ears rubbed.

"Will you walk with us?" King Louis asked, doffing his hat as he always did.

"I would enjoy nothing more."

Several courtiers stepped aside to allow me to walk next to the King.

"We are happy to have you back at court, *Madame*." He stressed the honorific with evident delight and held out his arm for me.

"I am happy to be back, Sire. I have missed everyone more than I can say."

He patted my hand at that. Then he turned to Athénaïs. "I would like a moment alone with our Sylvienne."

She inclined her head in assent and strolled toward a nearby pond, the entourage following her like goslings flocking after their dame. King Louis and I walked on, the dogs chasing alongside us.

"I have not had a chance to ask. How goes the Duchy of Narbonne?" he asked.

"Very well, I must suppose. My husband does not enjoy traveling there, so I have not yet visited the estate."

"Ah, well. He will go in the spring when the taxes are due. I've no doubt he will take you along. You are the best ambassador a landlord could employ."

I thrilled at the compliment, though I doubted I would like the Duchy of Narbonne any more than my husband did. It was so far away and, I expected, quite foreign. I was happy to keep my world close to Paris and the court. Close to Etienne.

We stopped at the edge of the pond, the dogs lapping up the water.

"I understand the Duc has more than a financial interest in the Banque Nationale de Paris," he said.

I stiffened.

His voice took on a fatherly tone. "You must not be dismayed. A man has many needs which he will seek to fulfill in…the usual ways."

After an awkward pause, I ventured, "And my needs?" I focused straight ahead, not daring to look at the man they called the Sun King.

"Your needs are to fulfill your role as the Duchesse de Narbonne."

I girded myself for the coming lecture as the dogs leaped into the water, chasing after a flock of ducks.

"Your first duty is to your husband, to provide him with heirs."

"My *first* duty?"

"Your second is to me, your King and father." He cupped my chin with his fingers, so I had to look at him. "You are the liaison, the ambassador, between your husband's estate and that of the Crown. And for that privilege, I have endowed you with both a title and a pension. I expect you will not disappoint me by disappointing your husband."

At King Louis's signal, the dogs scuttled out of the pond, shaking the water from their fur.

That evening, dressing for the grand couvert, I sat at my toilette looking through my jewelry box. René leaned close, brandy evident on his breath, and set a paper down in front of me. The gazette with the pen portrait of "Charlatynne."

"Why do you have that here?" I pushed it away.

"Why do you have so many shoes?" His voice low, unnerving.

"You are the one who insists a duchesse be properly dressed. I can't wear shabby shoes with new gowns."

He slammed his hand on the table, causing me to jump. "What is this gossip about the King's shoemaker?"

My heart thumped erratically. "I don't know what gossip you speak of." I looked straight ahead, not daring to meet his eyes.

He leaned close again, his breath hot against my ear. "If I find out you've been betraying our marriage —"

I caught his eye in the looking glass now. "Why should you care? You have your Madame la Banquière to take care of your...needs."

He put a hand on my neck, just tight enough to be uncomfortable as he spoke into the mirror. "What I do is my business. What *you* do is my business. I will not have you sully my reputation." He tightened his grip. I grabbed at his hands, digging in with my nails, panic rising within me. "Is that understood?"

I could barely get the word out. "Oui."

He let go all at once. I gasped for breath.

"Good." He picked up the gazette and tossed it at the mirror. "We leave for dinner in ten minutes. Wear the rubies. Rubies always look good on you."

At dinner René was pleasant and charming. Toward me, toward everyone. He lubricated his conversations with multiple glasses of wine, offering toasts to various members of the royal family. Afterward, he said, "You've had a busy day, Madame la Duchesse. I think you should retire early. You need your beauty sleep."

"Are you coming?" I asked, hoping he wasn't.

"Not right away, darling. Gramont has received a shipment of rum from the Caribbean colonies. He's invited several of us who are considering investing to sample it."

I cringed inwardly. What he didn't need right now was more alcohol. On the other hand, maybe he would drink himself into a stupor.

He leaned over and kissed me. "Have a good night."

De Baude invited me to a soirée in her chamber. I begged off, claiming a headache, which was the truth. Also, I didn't want to press my luck with René and have him come home to find me not there.

My dreams that night were a jumble of nonsensical images: Papa climbing a ladder to find Etienne on the roof. Atlas mounting Phoebe. Jolie swimming in the river. Me floating with Madame in the pond under the stars, except it wasn't Henriette, but the new Madame, the one they called Liselotte. Bees on the windows, so many the house grew dark. I awoke with a start. I looked around, disoriented. Where was I? At Fontainebleau? I loved Fontainebleau. No, Versailles. I drifted off again.

A while later, my sleep ruptured with a jolt, the covers ripped off me. I screamed, but René clasped his hand over my mouth. The brandy laced with rum on his breath nauseated me as he leaned close to my face. "*Merde!* What are these whisperings about you riding out to meet someone?"

I pushed his hand away. "You're drunk. Get out of here."

He pressed on. "If I didn't know better, I'd bet on that churl, d'Orléans, even if he is more interested in pretty men than women. I forbid you to see him again. I don't give a hornet's ass if you are related to him."

He grabbed me by the legs and pulled me to the edge of the bed. "That shoemaker everyone is agog over. The one who makes shoes for the royal family. Your shoes. He doesn't know how to ride, does he? Does he ride you?"

"Stop!" I kicked at him and raked his arms with my fingernails, but he slapped me and threw me onto my stomach.

"I'll show you what it feels like to be ridden." He came at me from behind in a way that was unnatural.

The pain was searing, and I screamed. But of course, no one would come. No one would intervene. He was my husband, and he could do with me as he wished. He shoved against me frantically, eventually gasping then going limp. Pushing me away with a grunt, he climbed onto the bed where he passed out, snoring loudly. I curled up on the floor, sobbing.

After some time, I hobbled to the chamber pot, letting my husband's seed drip out of me.

Availing myself of one of the neatly folded cloths next to the water bowl, I plunged it into the cold water, determined to erase his impurity from my body. When I wiped myself, there was blood on the cloth. I vowed I would never let him touch me again.

Shaking—from the cold or the pain I didn't know, I only knew I couldn't go back into that bed—I took the candle René had left burning on the bedside table and let myself into Lisette's closet. She didn't question when I crawled onto the pallet beside her. She simply blew out the candle and threw a protective arm over me.

Several hours later I awoke, disoriented at first, aching. The warmth of Lisette's body and her soft breathing reminded me where I was, what had happened. Fighting tears in the darkness, I longed for Maman, for her comfort, her advice, her practical words of wisdom. Her strength. After a while, I wiped my face with my sleeve and, careful not to wake Lisette, crawled off the pallet and out of the closet. The sky outside the bedchamber window had changed to a dull grey.

René still snored loudly in the bed. Nothing was going to wake him from his drunken sleep.

With a new resolve, I pulled on a simple wool dress then packed a small satchel with some personal items. Lisette appeared in the closet doorway wringing her hands, her eyes filled with concern. "Where will you go?"

"It is better you do not know." I hugged her tightly.

Wrapping a hooded cloak around me, I made sure no one was in the hallway then tiptoed out into the predawn air. The brightest of the stars still hovered as I hurried up the path toward the shoemaker's workshop and rapped softly on the door.

It was a moment before Etienne, bleary-eyed, pulled it open. "Sylvienne?"

He glanced past me to see if anyone was nearby, then quickly pulled me inside.

"What's wrong? What happened?" He wrapped his arms around me and held me. "You're hurt."

I began sobbing. My shoulders shook. "I have to leave. I can't stay here."

He peered into my eyes, alarmed. "Do you mean leave court? Where would you go?"

"Anywhere. Anywhere away from that man, this life. I will not be his wife any longer."

He was silent a moment, still holding me. The smell of him, his unwashed nightshirt, the faint essence of leather and lanolin, comforted me.

"We'll go together," he whispered into my hair.

I pulled away, suddenly frightened for him. "But you can't. You have a career here. It would be ruined."

"My career is nothing without you. My life is nothing without you. Where you go, I will go, too."

I looked up into his eyes, the blue dark and stormy. "Are you sure?"

"More than I have been about anything." He kissed me, and I knew then that I wanted never to be apart from him.

"I'll pack a few things, then bring Jolie around."

"And Phoebe. I can ride Phoebe."

"No. I'll be in trouble enough for running away with the wife of a duc and the daughter of the King. If I steal one of the King's horses, I'll be drawn and quartered."

I shivered. He wasn't joking. He pulled out a stool for me to sit on while he packed his own small satchel. When he picked up his sketchbook, there was no room left for it. With a sigh, he set it back on the worktable amongst the scattered tools.

"Give it to me." I held out my hand. "I'll carry it."

He kissed me again and tucked the sketchbook into my satchel. "Wait here. I'll be right back." He stepped out into the gloom of the cloudy dawn, closing the door behind him.

Exhausted, I pushed aside the tools and laid my head on the table. What seemed like moments later, the door opened again. I sat up. "Etienne?"

Framed by the timbers of the doorway stood René, the red orb of the rising sun at his back, his face a knot of fury.

CHAPTER FORTY-NINE

I stared at my husband with disbelief. He wore the same wrinkled tunic and breeches he had fallen asleep in. His hair was disheveled, his face stubbled with the bristle of overnight growth. But it was the look in his eyes that frightened me. A madman would not have eyes as livid as those.

"What are you doing here?" In my haste to stand and move farther from his reach, I knocked the stool and sent it spinning from the table. "How did you find me?"

He pushed into the room. "I have a mind to do to you what I did to that pitiful excuse for a maid of yours."

Lisette! My stomach lurched. "Stay away from me. I will never go back with you."

He strode across the room and grabbed me by the arm. "You will. And you will do so right now."

I fought him, kicking and clawing, but he twisted my arms behind me and slammed me against the wall.

"You think you can cuckold me with the likes of a common cobbler?" His reeking breath, hot in my face, nauseated me. "I'll teach you who can and cannot cockrot you."

He slapped my face hard then grabbed my hair and dragged me to one of the worktables. With a sweep of his arm, he sent the cobbling tools clattering to the floor, then bent me over as he had just hours before. Struggling to breathe, I thrashed and kicked at him, but he pulled up my skirt and spread my legs with his knee.

A growl brought him up short. "Get away from her!"

Oh, God. Etienne. I screamed for him to get away.

René only laughed. "Are you going to attack me with that hammer, shoemaker? You'd better be practiced with it." He wrenched me from the table and, yanking his dagger from his belt, held it to my throat. "Do you think you can plant your cock in my wife without consequence?"

"If you hurt her..." His voice edged with steel, Etienne clutched an iron mallet with a split claw on the opposite end.

"This girl is nothing but a whore. Maybe we should draw cards to see who gets to rut her. Or how about dice?"

"Let her go."

"No? I have a better idea. I'll dispose of you, like the vermin you are." He shoved me aside and stepped toward Etienne with the dagger.

"No!" I cried. "Stop!"

The two men circled each other, weapons in hand.

"Duel! Duel!" a voice from the doorway shouted. "Call for the guards!"

Etienne hurled the hammer at René, hitting him in the upper arm, causing him to drop the dagger with a cry of pain. Etienne dove for the dagger. René kicked it out of the way before lunging toward the fireplace to seize the fire iron.

"Etienne!" I screamed. In a panic, I snatched a pair of oversized shears from the table.

Etienne swiveled in time to see René coming at him swinging the fire iron. He ducked, stepped back, tripped over the stool I had earlier knocked over, and fell onto his back. An easy target for René.

I charged at my husband with the shears, but he batted me away, sending me to the floor, the shears skidding under the table.

Etienne tried to backcrawl away from René but found himself cornered against the wall.

Groaning in pain, I struggled to my knees. René's dagger lay inches from me. In two strides, he was upon Etienne. With a snarl, he raised the fire iron to thrust the blackened pointed end into Etienne's heart. I grabbed the dagger, scrambled to my feet and, lunging at my husband, shoved the blade into his back.

René froze, the iron inches from Etienne's chest. He half-turned toward me, eyes wide with shock. After a moment, he coughed. Blood gurgled from his mouth. Then he collapsed, nearly landing on top of Etienne, who rolled out of the way in the last moment.

Gaping at my dead husband, I shuddered. The room began to sway. Etienne scrambled to me, his arms enveloping my shaking body.

"Are you hurt?"

"I don't know." Shouts sounded from outside, people running toward the workshop.

"I'll tell them it was me," Etienne said. "That I killed him."

Everything became clear in that moment. "No!" I couldn't let him face consequences that should be mine.

"It's the only way." His voice was resolute.

"You'll be imprisoned. Most likely hanged." I glanced over at the growing pool of blood under my husband's body and shuddered. "You must go."

"I won't leave. You saved my life."

"You must. Please. What good will it do to have saved you if I must watch you be put to death?" I wrung my hands. The hands that had plunged the dagger into my husband's heart. I sensed Etienne's resolve waver. "I am a daughter of the King. No harm will come to me, I promise."

A crowd was growing outside the door. In the distance I could see royal guards striding through the throng. I reached up and kissed him then pushed against his chest. "Go."

He sucked in a ragged breath, regarded me with pained eyes. Finally, he turned and ran out the back door where Jolie awaited.

Grief, fear, relief poured over me like a deluge. I sank to my knees and sobbed.

CHAPTER FIFTY

The guards took me to a dismal little room with only a bench and a small table in the servants' wing of the palace. There to keep me under lock and key until the chief of palace security could question me. I told him I had gone to the shoemaker's abode shortly after sunrise to have a shoe repaired, but Monsieur Girard was not there, and I chose to wait.

"People in the area say they saw two men dueling."

"They are wrong. They saw me and my husband." I told him René had burst in, furious that I had gone without his permission. That he had beat me and in defending myself I had stabbed him.

"In the back?" The officer raised a skeptical eyebrow.

"I took advantage of a moment of distraction on his part. I assure you, I feared for my life in that moment."

The officer noted the fresh bruise under my eye but made no comment. He left, and I waited in anxious solitude until, hours later, a guard opened the door to say I had been summoned to appear before the King.

I was taken to Louis's private council chamber rather than the public adjudication hall. Bontemps met me at the door, escorted me to the inner chamber, then left without a word. After my curtsy, King Louis lifted my chin to peer at my face. The bruise along my cheek had darkened, and I could feel my eyelid growing puffy, much like the first time René had struck me. Louis shook his head.

"You had only one duty to me in regard to your husband." When I did not respond, he said, "I am deeply disappointed. There will not be a public trial, but I will need time to sort out the ramification of your betrayal."

Betrayal? Of whom? My husband the Duc, or of the King himself? I dared not ask.

"What of the shoemaker?" he asked. "Are the rumors true?"

I squared my shoulders. "I don't know what rumors you speak of. One of my shoes needed repair, that's why I was there."

"So I was told. There are witnesses who saw three people within his abode, who saw the men dueling. And who saw the shoemaker ride off afterward. Why would he leave you to take the blame?"

"I am the only one to be blamed. The Duc died by my hand."

He studied me for a moment before saying, "Then the rumors of your affair are true. No woman would speak as you have if she weren't under the influence of a misguided sense of love."

I wanted to scream. To argue with him. To tell him my love for Etienne was anything but misguided. That it was my life at court that was wrong. That His Majesty should never have stopped by our house that hot summer day. He should never have had an affair with Maman, whose love for him all those years ago was the love that was misguided. What did he know of love? A king who used women like baubles put on this Earth for his amusement. But again, I remained silent.

"I will allow you to reside in your chambers until I have made a determination, but you are not to go out in public."

The relief of not being imprisoned overwhelmed me. "Thank you, Sire."

He turned his back. The audience was over. A guard accompanied me to the apartment I had shared with René. I was glad to see Lisette was still there, though in much pain. The palace physician had already attended her, having set her broken arm and applied salve to her badly bruised face. He gave her laudanum to help her sleep. I moved her from the cot in her closet to my bed. I resolved that I would take care of her until Fleurance could be sent for to take care of both of us.

Ignacio had left. The King would give him a small pension and ensure his employment elsewhere. No lock was placed on the door, but a guard was positioned outside. I had a strange sense of déjà vu, recalling the guard that was assigned after I had been told of my royal parentage.

In the morning, I couldn't look at the sumptuous breakfast provided. My stomach roiled with nausea. Still, I made sure Lisette ate something. Thus we lived for the next several days while I waited for my father to decide my fate.

When I was again summoned to the royal council chamber, both Athénaïs and Philippe were there. She sat on an upholstered stool near the fireplace. Philippe stood at the window. The chagrin and displeasure in their expressions was evident. I had failed both my mentors.

King Louis, my father, sat on a large throne-like chair in the center of the room. He bade me kneel before him. "You've caused quite a storm at court, Madame."

"I am truly sorry for your inconvenience and your displeasure, Sire."

He sighed. "Sylvienne, upon reflection, it was a misjudgment on my part to give you over to Narbonne. I looked into his affairs, and I see he was neither a faithful nor a protective husband to you. He had some political and economic dealings that were misaligned as well. However, that does not excuse your actions." He waved away a servant tiptoeing in with a tray of letters. "The Narbonne family is calling for your head."

"To be executed?" I swayed, still on my knees, the room tilting. Nausea roiled my stomach again. For the first time in my life, I knew real fear.

"I have talked them out of it. No one will force me to put my own child, legitimate or not, under the blade. However, there are other factions who have spoken against you."

Athénaïs, her voice filled with disdain, said, "It seems your step-uncle, whom Louis so graciously released from the Bastille last month, would have you put to the stake."

I gasped.

"That won't happen either," King Louis said. "But you cannot stay at court."

"I understand." I would go home in disgrace, but I would go with my head and body intact.

He cleared his throat. "I have received word from Mère Abbesse at the cloister in Compiègne. She has consented to take you in."

"The convent?" My breath caught in my throat. The Carmelites in Compiègne were said to be the strictest order in all of France. "No, Sire. I beg you…"

"Or…there is a merchant ship at La Rochelle waiting my permission to leave for New France. For Quebec."

I could feel the blood drain from my face. My choice of punishment was between two kinds of hell. To be locked away with a group of women who lived lives of chastity and who rose every three hours in the middle of the night to pray. Or to travel across the vast ocean to a land filled with savages and primitive villages inhabited by hunters and trappers.

I didn't hesitate. "I'll go on the ship." As awful as the idea of New France was, at least there I stood a chance of determining my fate.

"Very well." King Louis bade me rise. "Pack what you can tonight. A carriage will take you to La Rochelle on the morrow. The ship will leave once you are aboard."

"So soon? I won't be able to say goodbye to Maman." *Nor to Etienne.*

"It can't be helped." He looked truly sorrowful. "The danger is too great if you linger."

I glanced over at Philippe, his arms tightly crossed. The look of grief in his eyes was the same as the day Henriette died. He nodded his agreement.

"I will supervise your packing," Athénaïs said. "Let us not tarry."

Fleurance, with what help Lissette could muster, packed the trunk Blondeau had so lovingly made for me, tears streaming down both their cheeks. The embroidered silk pouch Maman had given me before I left Amiens lay on the dressing table. I opened it, letting the stones tumble out.

What a shame I'd never had the gift of being able to read them. I remembered with a jolt Maman's words as she read the stones so long ago. "There will be a storm." I shuddered at the thought of the tempest I had created here at court. What kind of evil wind had driven me into the arms of René Lorgeleux, Duc de Narbonne? And why had I not realized how much Etienne loved me when there was time to act upon it? My chest tightened with grief.

Maman had not been able to see what lay beyond the storm. Now I wondered with dread what lay on the other side of that wide expanse of ocean. To add to my trepidation, the sickness I was experiencing each morning had not abated. And my courses were a week past due.

Returning the stones to their pouch, I tucked it into a small shoulder bag along with Etienne's sketchbook. I penned a farewell letter to Maman and asked her to take Lisette in. Tatie would care for her in my absence, and when she was healed, Lisette would take care of Maman. Fleurance assured me she could stay on at the house in Paris, which went to a brother of René who had assumed the title Duc de Narbonne.

I had one last mission I wished to accomplish. I threw my cloak over my shoulders. Athénaïs waited for me in the doorway. When we arrived at the house on rue de Vaugirard, Madame Scarron met us at the door. The look of pity in her eyes made me turn my head away.

Athénaïs waited in the antechamber while Madame Scarron led me into the nursery where my baby sister suckled at the breast of a wet nurse. I waited until the baby hiccupped and pulled away with sleepy eyes. She smiled with anticipation when she saw me.

The wet nurse handed her to me and removed herself to the other side of the room. I cradled little Louise-Françoise in my arms, nuzzled my lips against her soft cheek. How wonderous it was that for the first time in my life I had a sister. And how heartbreaking that we were to be torn asunder before we ever got to know each other.

I knew now I had other siblings as well. Louis, the Dauphin and little Marie-Thérèse, whom everyone called La Petite Madame, both of whom were delivered of the Queen. And Mademoiselle de La Vallière's issue—Marie Anne de Bourbon and Louis de Bourbon, already named Comte de Vermandois. There were whispers of others by other mothers, but they were only whispers. And another soon to come, for Athénaïs was already several months along. But what good was this knowledge to me now?

Louise-Françoise gurgled and poked at my lips. Did she sense my deep despair? Would she ever learn of me? Or would I be just one of the many whispers in her life? My heart ached. "*Adieu*, my sweet love." Handing my baby sister back to her wet nurse, my tears flowed freely.

The early morning sun cast fierce streaks of red over the city of La Rochelle. Out the carriage window I could see the three-masted merchant ship groaning against the dock. A parade of dock hands pulled, pushed, and dragged wagons loaded with sacks and crates of goods to be hauled onto the ship. In the harbor, a half-dozen similar ships bobbed idly, waiting for their turn at the dock, or for the tide to turn in the Bay of Biscay to take them past the two sentinel towers and out into the open waters of the cold Atlantic Ocean. I pulled my cloak tighter around me. La Rochelle would be the last bit of homeland soil I would ever tread upon.

Before leaving Versailles, I had said *adieu* to Lisette, Athénaïs, and Philippe, all sorrowful on my behalf. The last to kiss me on both cheeks was my father, Louis, the fourteenth of that name, King of France.

A pair of dockhands pulled my trunk off the back of the carriage and heaved it onto a one-wheeled handbarrow to take to the ship. When the time came, my old friend Carufel opened the carriage door, handed me down, and accompanied me as far as the wooden gangway leading onto the vessel. On the deck stood several dozen women, some looking anxious, others seeming exhilarated—all of them bound for New France and a new life.

Squaring my shoulders, I took a deep breath and walked up the wooden ramp and onto the ship to take my place among them.

THE END

AUTHOR'S NOTE AND ACKNOWLEDGMENTS

Courting the Sun is a work of fiction that arose from my overwhelming desire to discover my French ancestry, and from my own childhood dreams of experiencing a life grander than the one I lived growing up in a small town in Michigan's Upper Peninsula. The prime inspiration, however, came from my 7th-and 8th-great-grandmothers who left France in the 17th century and emigrated to Canada, a number of them as *Filles du roi* (King's Daughters). These great-grandmothers had accepted King Louis XIV's sponsorship and traveled to New France (Canada) to marry his soldiers, fur traders, and farmers and to help populate his new colony.

My driving question was: Why, even with the reward of a dowry and passage paid by the Crown, would a young woman leave France and travel for months across a cold and dangerous ocean to a raw and dangerous land simply to find a husband?

While there are many wonderful books, both fiction and nonfiction, written about the actual Filles du Roi, I chose to have fun with my question. I let my imagination run wild. I created a young woman who was unaware of her mother's past and her relationship with King Louis, and whose destiny forced her to choose between going into a convent or leaving France. Thus was born Sylvienne, a wholly fictional character who, unlike other women going to New France and referred to as "Daughters of the King," is an actual daughter of King Louis XIV, albeit a bastard one.

The real Filles du Roi had many reasons to emigrate, including poverty, being orphans, or simply having no prospects for marriage in a country where a dowry was necessary. There were women of the noble class who accepted the King's sponsorship for their own reasons, but very few, and none that I know of who descended from royal blood.

Sylvienne, Etienne, and all the characters from Amiens in my book are entirely fictional, as are minor characters at court, such as Lisette and René Lorgeleux. King Louis XIV, of course, and various members of his family—Queen Marie-Thérèse, his brother Philippe (*Monsieur*), Princess Henriette (*Madame*), the Duchesse de Montpensier (*la Grande Mademoiselle*, the King's cousin), as well as Louis's mistress Athénaïs de Montespan and her children's governess, Madame Scarron (who eventually became Madame Maintenon, Louis's secret wife)—were all actual historical figures. The reader may recognize a few others. However, I used all of them fictitiously.

The lives and experiences of the real Filles du Roi in France, most of whom were recruited from Paris or Rouen or other French towns and villages, were nothing like that of Sylvienne; except perhaps there may have been some who loved and were unrequited in that love.

I strove to be as historically accurate as possible when dealing with King Louis's court, his palaces, and the cities of Amiens and Paris. On occasion, however, I collapsed or stretched time or changed known historical characters and facts for the purpose of the story. For example, King Louis XIV's first lover is historically considered to have been Catherine Bellier ("One-eyed Kate"). I chose to make that story a myth. And Louis's first real love, again according to historians, was Marie Mancini, niece of Cardinal Jules Mazarin, a chief advisor to the young Louis. I made his first love and lover Isabelle, Sylvienne's mother.

King Louis XIV had many illegitimate children by his mistresses, most of whom he acknowledged and even legitimized, giving them titles and property. Sylvienne d'Aubert, however, was not one of them. Nor was Isabelle an illegitimate daughter of Gaston, Duc d'Orléans (Louis's uncle).

I hope you have enjoyed this story for its historical backdrop and for the lives, loves, and hard lessons learned of its fictional characters.

I wish to express my gratitude to Reagan Rothe and the team at Black Rose Writing for seeing the potential in my story and for allowing me to tap into their expertise to produce and publish a book of which I am incredibly proud.

I am ever thankful to my good friend, Christine DeSmet, an amazing writing coach, for applauding me, supporting me, and mentoring me in my journey to publication.

Merci beaucoup to my critique partners and muses Lucy Sanna, Carol Larson, and Anne Keller for joining me on this journey into the fictional past, for reading draft after draft after draft, and for challenging me to rise to their expectations when it comes to the craft of storytelling. My sincere thanks also to Mary Joy Johnson, Julia Hoffman, and Jean Joque who read my work-in-progress and provided much needed feedback and encouragement.

A special thanks to agent Deborah Ritchkin for her unwavering belief in my story and for working so hard on my behalf; and to Dr. Anais Boulard for checking all my French words and phrases. Please note, however, that any remaining errors in the French are mine and mine alone.

I am indebted to my daughter Erin and son Joshua, their spouses Jonathan and Hana, and to my grandchildren Cameron, Zen, and Lilyenne for their loving patience with my dream and my work.

And finally, I offer my undying gratitude and love to my husband, Mark, for always believing in me, supporting me, going off on grand research and writing adventures with me, and encouraging me regardless of what project I am working on, but especially in this particular endeavor. *Je t'aime, mon coeur.*

ABOUT THE AUTHOR

Peggy Joque Williams is the co-author of two mystery novels under the pen name M. J. Williams, *On the Road to Death's Door* and *On the Road to Where the Bells Toll*. She is a recently retired elementary school teacher as well as a freelance writer and editor. An avid genealogist, she has traced her family tree back through French-speaking Canada to France of the 16th and 17th centuries. *Courting the Sun* is her debut solo novel. Peggy lives with her family in Madison, Wisconsin.

Visit the author at www.peggywilliamsauthor.com.

NOTE FROM PEGGY JOQUE WILLIAMS

Word-of-mouth is crucial for any author to succeed. If you enjoyed *Courting the Sun*, please leave a review online — anywhere you are able. Even if it's just a sentence or two. It would make all the difference and would be very much appreciated.

Thanks!
Peggy Joque Williams

We hope you enjoyed reading this title from:

www.blackrosewriting.com

Subscribe to our mailing list – *The Rosevine* – and receive **FREE** books, daily deals, and stay current with news about upcoming releases and our hottest authors.
Scan the QR code below to sign up.

Already a subscriber? Please accept a sincere thank you for being a fan of Black Rose Writing authors.

View other Black Rose Writing titles at
www.blackrosewriting.com/books and use promo code
PRINT to receive a **20% discount** when purchasing.

www.ingramcontent.com/pod-product-compliance
Lightning Source LLC
Chambersburg PA
CBHW032136090325
23231CB00007B/56